The Collapse by Rusly Almaleky is published under Enigma books, sectionalized division under Di Angelo Publications INC.

ENIGMA BOOKS

an imprint of Di Angelo Publications The Collapse Copyright 2017 Rusly Almaleky in digital and print distribution in the United States of America.

Di Angelo Publications

4265 San Felipe #1100

Houston, Texas, 77027

www.diangelopublications.com

Library of congress cataloging-in-publications data

Rusly Almaleky: The Collpase

Downloadable via Kindle, iBooks and nook.

_____

Library of Congress Registration

Paperback

ISBN-13: 978-0-9850853-9-1

1. Fiction

2. Fiction ——Crime and Thriller——United States of America with int. Distribution.

THE
COLLAPSE

RUSLY ALMALEKY

Translated by

Saba Naseer Zainel

Cover and book design

Ali Hujazy

Arabic edition published in 2015

The author, Rusly Al-Maleky, thanks everyone who helped and participated in making his novel, The Collapse, come out the way it is now. He stands in gratitude for even the smallest assistance provided to him throughout his journey of eleven months to complete this work…

Thanks to:

Mustafa Bahjat, Eng. Faten Al-Rubay'ee, Junayd Aamer Hameed, Ali Hujazy, Zainab Najm, Nada Jalal, Khanzad Gharadaghi, Dr. Samer Al-Awsi, Steven Nabeel, Dr. Mohammed Jelaw, Saba Naseer Zainel, Tayseer Al-Qaysi, Dr. Nash'at Faraj Hanna, Dr. Nabil Ghazi Al-Khateeb, Dr. Hayat Al-Jebaji, Zeena Waleed Saeed, Ahmed Al-Husseini, Dani Misho, Ahmed Dhiyaaldin, Fadia Boles, Haleem Mahmoud, S'oud Al-Merani, Jumana Al-Bujari, Hanan Al-Obeidi, Ahmed Al-Saffar, Dr. Khaled Abdelkareem Khaled, Dr. Mohanned Al-Ma'mouri, Karin Schaechtele

Appreciation and gratitude to the great professor Dr. Abbas Badr Al-Ryahi, may he rest in peace, whom fate did not allow to see the finished The Collapse.

Parents ..

And to …

Sarah …

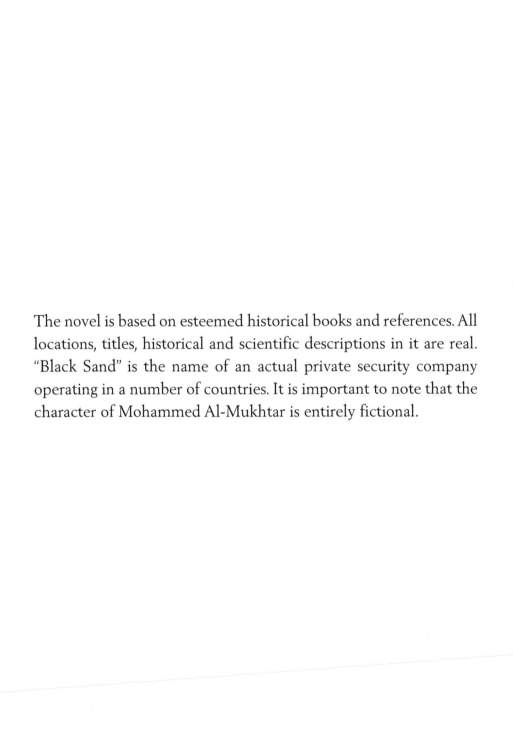

The novel is based on esteemed historical books and references. All locations, titles, historical and scientific descriptions in it are real. "Black Sand" is the name of an actual private security company operating in a number of countries. It is important to note that the character of Mohammed Al-Mukhtar is entirely fictional.

Dedication...

To those who will suffer the collapse to death...

They will beg...

Grapple...

And die...

All over the world...

While the doers will toast their new wealth...

Rusly AlMaleky

You will realize how right I was...

For doing what I did...

For us to live how we want...

At a time when everything is collapsing around us...

Relentlessly...

THE
COLLAPSE

Chapter 1

It was one after midnight on a cold January night when the cellphone rang its virtual ringtone in his small, quaint bedroom. He awoke, surprised by the sound of the phone. He was not used to it ringing at such time of night. He felt up the surface of the small bedside cabinet with his fingers and reached for his glasses. He put them on and looked his cellphone's screen, but it only confused him more.

It was a *private number.*

He hesitated for an instant, but then his curiosity coupled with remembering the case he was trying both pushed him to swipe the green button on his smartphone's screen to answer, and the line was opened…

"Hello, sir!" croaked a hoarse voice on the other end of the call.

"Hello. Yes?" he got up from his bed.

"This is Captain Salam from the Palace."

"Excuse me?" he was surprised by the source of the call. The Palace!

"There is an SUV waiting for you from Palestine St. side."

He gathered his thoughts to respond, but the speaker went on.

"As soon as possible, sir. Goodbye!"

The captain hung up, leaving the lawyer, Mahdi Al-Ali, in utter confusion.

He prepared himself to go where the car was waiting for him as described.

Chapter 2

Counselor Mahdi Al-Ali's house was in the elegant neighborhood of Zayouna in the middle of Baghdad's Rusafa, specifically, behind the Iraqi Fashion House. His house was around 300 meters from Palestine St., which he crossed in quick steps to reach the main street. As he noted to himself what a particularly cold January night it was, he saw a black Chevrolet Tahoe SUV with tinted windows. He stopped on the sidewalk and started watching the car parked on the street near him. He was trying to make sure that it was the car he was supposed to find…

And as soon as possible. he remembered.

The car plate indicated that it was a government vehicle. He took out his cigarettes from the pocket of his grey jacket while stealing glances at the vehicle whose communication antennas were swinging under the cold wind blowing once, and quieting another.

He flashed his lighter to light his cigarette, and along with it, the Chevrolet's front lights flashed. He took his first inhale and looked to it. Its front door opened and a young bald man with a thick moustache and strong build stepped out. He was dressed in a sports jacket and trousers, with side pockets that gave it the look of military attire. He put his hand in his pocket and motioned to Mahdi with the other to come closer.

Mahdi blew the smoke from his cigarette and stepped into the street getting closer to the car. He tossed the cigarette to the ground and the bald man motioned for him to get into the vehicle.

"Hello!" greeted Mahdi with steam billowing out of his mouth.

"Hello. Go ahead, sir,".

Mahdi got in the car and closed the door behind him. He felt the complete change in climate as he was hugged by the car's warmth when he got in. He tried to relax after his muscles had tensed up from the cold outside, but he was surprised by his nerves tensing up this time due to the high speed the driver started driving with. The streets were almost empty of cars, and the driver made use of the opportunity.

The driver ignored his companion and the constant calls coming from the communication device inside the vehicle as he drove—calls of security nature. He seemed relaxed talking to the officer next to him. Mahdi did not understand what they were saying because the transmitter was loud, continuous, and mixed with an intermittent beeping. The bald officer turned to Mahdi offering to raise the heat; to which Mahdi responded with thanks. The car swerved to get on the highway heading to the city center.

Chapter 3

At the 5th Division Headquarters in Baghdad, the atmosphere was quite different from the normal everyday situation—there was security mobilization around the building's perimeter, and SUVs inside the headquarters' courtyard, which was subjected to high-security measures.

The 5th Division is considered one of the most important bases of the Iraqi Military Intelligence. It transformed post-2003 to an important base for the Iraqi Intelligence. It has tens of holding cells in addition to gallow rooms that had witnessed many executions during the ousted President Saddam Hussein's time. Saddam Hussein himself was hanged in one of them.

That building incited great awe in the hearts of Iraqis. Hundreds of stories floated around—stories of those who were imprisoned, tortured, and executed there dangled in the air, just as the ropes that remain dangle.

The Chevrolet transporting Counselor Mahdi Al-Ali stopped at the gate of the 5th Division Headquarters. The bald officer lowered his window and spoke to the policeman at the building's gate. After a few seconds of short conversation and the standard protocol of the officer showing the policeman his identification as well as waiting as the policeman checked the vehicle's type and plates, the door was opened and the Chevrolet entered the building's courtyard.

The officer got out of the car after parking in the 5th Division's courtyard and he opened the door for Mahdi Al-Ali to exit the vehicle. Mahdi was shocked by the place. He was pleading his last case at a courthouse, not at the State Intelligence Headquarters.

Everything seemed confusing. Mahdi looked to the officers and the intelligence personnel who were busy making calls and moving about the building awkwardly. The officer held Mahdi's elbow directing him to move, and he lead him to the office of the build-ing manager.

Mahdi felt as if he was being detained by the authorities. The late night call, the Chevrolet with government plates, the State Intelligence Bu-reau—everything was mysterious to him. He drew his breaths with great difficulty. The adrenaline was overtaking every essence of his being. With every step he made alongside the bald officer, his heart-beats were quickening bit by bit. The cold added to his confusion, and the images of each moment seemed to move slowly before him as he walked with a body that felt the anticipation of what was coming.

I am now at the 5th Division! Mahdi thought to himself excitedly.

The two arrived to the office of the building manager after passing through several hallways and corridors. The bald officer entered first, stomping the ground with his foot in salute. He pointed out that the counselor had arrived as he had been asked to do, and then he nodded to Mahdi to enter.

Mahdi entered the building manager's office and began to internal-ly note his surroundings. The man was tall and dressed in an official security uniform – a navy blue suit with his rank insignia shining on its shoulders—three silver stars arranged in a pyramid form un-der the state emblem, an eagle. The Brigadier-General, Director of the 5th Division, had left his seat behind his desk and was roaming about his office worriedly smoking his cigarette. Mahdi looked at the man, gathered his courage, and said hello.

"Hello, sir. Come in!" the Brigadier-General responded.

Mahdi sat on the couch facing the right side of the Brigadier-Gen-eral's desk. A sense of relative relief swept through him for the way the Director spoke. The Brigadier-General sat next to Mahdi and put out his cigarette in an ashtray on a table across from the couch and turned to Mahdi.

"Sir, I'd like to inform you that we have moved your client to this building yesterday evening. Orders from the high-level authorities at the Intelligence Bureau decided to move the prisoner from his previous prison to here."

Mahdi felt both anger and relief at the same time. It was natural for the authorities to move a prisoner from one place to another, but he was angered for having gone through that chain of events by the authorities that night. It was possible to inform him over the phone of the prisoner move, or call for him without sending a security car with government plates to pick him up.

"Sir, thank you for letting me know. I can visit him at a later time if you wish," Mahdi quavered, wishing to leave the place as soon as possible.

The Brigadier-General seemed more at unease lighting another cigarette and drawing a deep breath of smoke. He looked to his office's ceiling as if to gather his strength, and looked at Mahdi.

"You can see him now," he asserted, smoke billowing from his nostrils after he spoke.

Mahdi felt a thousand questions fill his head. He looked into the officer's bewildered eyes and nodded in agreement. The Brigadier-General got up from his desk and pressed a button on it. A man armed with an AK47 rifle and a 9mm gun came in. He saluted.

The Brigadier-General directed the security man to accompany "the Professor" to cell number 12.

While resisting his ever-increasing curiosity, Mahdi got up from his seat and looked at the Brigadier-General with a faint smile. The Director nodded his head and went back to smoking his cigarette. Mahdi walked with the security man out of the Director's office. He found himself walking many corridors with the armed security man. After he was sure they had passed all the corridors that the Director's office overlooked, he asked the security man for permission to use his cellphone. After slight hesitation, the man nodded his head and took a few steps away from Mahdi but without taking his eyes off him.

Mahdi took out his cellphone and prescription glasses and started writing a text message. He finished writing and set the recipient name—Maha student—and hit send.

"I'm at the 5th Division. If anything happens, you know. Be careful."

Mahdi Al-Ali was a lawyer and a professor at the College of Law at the University of Baghdad while Maha was his fourth-year student at that college. She was one of his distinguished students. His relationship with her developed when he supervised her graduation thesis. Their long discussions in politics and law were also a motive for the intellectual closeness between them, particularly the discussions relating to the recent events in the country and a new government ruling and exposing cases of corruption that its predecessor had created. The media had been preoccupied with those cases of corruption that had been raised against the members and leaders of the former government.

The relationship between Maha and her professor developed into a special kind of relationship. He revealed to Maha some of the secrets of the recent case he was trying as he trusted her and admired what he saw in her as a promising and articulate future lawyer. He called her "Hammurabi's granddaughter", the king who set the infamous law.

After receiving the receipt confirmation report, Mahdi placed his phone in his jacket's pocket and folded his glasses back into his pocket. He motioned to the man with a gratuitous smile and they proceeded their walk to cell number 12.

Something seemed to be happening at the end of the corridor. A number of security and police personnel were talking amongst themselves, and others seemed to have already entered the cell.

Mahdi and the security man approached until they reached the men across from the cell. Some of them were wearing white gloves, while others started making calls over special communication devices.

An officer with the rank of captain dressed in his military uniform motioned to the security man and his companion –Mahdi– to stop. The security man spoke to the captain to inform him of his companion's identity. The Captain motioned to Mahdi to come closer while the security man walked back to the end of the corridor.

"Hello, Captain!" said Mahdi, looking at the officer's shining insignia on his shoulders.

"Hello, sir. Could you hand me your cellphone?"

Mahdi found the Captain's request strange. "Ah, of course," he acquiesced, "I hope to see my client so this night's nightmare at this depressing building would come to an end!"

He smiled and took his phone out of his pocket. The Captain received the phone without responding to Mahdi's remark. He held his hand and they walked towards the cell that was only a few meters from them now.

The Captain furrowed his brow and leaned in to Mahdi so as to speak intimately. "Professor Mahdi, what you will see now will remain a secret between us." Mahdi stopped in his tracks and felt a wave of anger wash over him.

What happened to my client?

"Captain, if anything has happened to my client, I cannot promise you to keep that a secret!" Mahdi blurted with an angry tone.

The Captain squeezed Mahdi's hand and calmly spoke, "Yes, you will."

Mahdi controlled his temper and walked towards the cell. The Captain let go of Mahdi's hand to go towards it and see what happened.

He was shocked to see the forensic team coming out of the cell with their white gloves and cameras. He got closer to the cell's entrance and was overwhelmed by a state of fear of the unknown and curiosity at the same time. The lighting coming from the cell's ceiling clearly showed what was inside the room. The silence engulfed his ears at that moment despite the voices of the security and investigation personnel who were talking in the midst of the sounds of the communication devices they carried.

He looked at a tan man lying on a bed by the left wall of the cell. He stepped across the sliding rail of the cell door on the ground and was inside the prison room alone with a corpse laying on its bed with its right-hand dangling from its end. The cell's smell was loaded with the dampness of the walls. It was similar to the smell of cement that has just been mixed with water.

A green blanket covered the lower half of the body while the upper half was exposed.

Mahdi felt cold sweat seeping from every pore of his body. He walked closer to the corpse's bed, whose head was towards the cell's door. He bent more to look at the deceased man's face. He did not know why he felt that this man, his client, had been assassinated rather than having died a natural death—yet nonetheless, the feeling was overwhelming.

Mahdi's head spun with the insurmountable implications.

Mohammed Al-Mukhtar...murdered at Baghdad's most secure prison!

Chapter 4

2:20 a.m.

Counselor Mahdi Al-Ali stood still in the cell before his client's body, the accused Mohammed Al-Mukhtar. He couldn't take his eyes off the body. There were no apparent stab or bullet wounds. The Captain entered the single cell that held the body and indicated that Mahdi should not touch it. Mahdi asked the Captain to move back to take away his shadow from the body, and so the light could clarify its details. He felt nauseated and dizzy.

If it was a nightmare!

He could not stomach it anymore, so he left the cell and leaned on the wall by the door. He closed his eyes and spoke to the Captain who was standing close by. "What the hell happened to him?"

"The investigation is still ongoing. We will start the procedures for sending the body for autopsy to find out the real cause of death," the officer replied.

Mahdi drew a deep breath and opened his eyes as if he was coming from underwater. He exhaled. Despite hesitating to do so, he re-entered the cell. Something inside him was insistent that he enter it again. He looked to the security personnel who were looking at him as if trying to read his thoughts through his eyes. He pulled down his jacket and entered the cell once more.

He crossed the cell's threshold and there he was, again, overlooking his client's body, which looked like it was about to raise a storm of questions. His urge to stare at the body was interrupted when he noticed writing that had been made with a green spray on the cell's wall above the client's bed. The number 39 was drawn in their original Arabic form, but soon enough he made himself forget about that number and was back to looking at his client's body. He stood by its head looking at it again, leaving the cell's door open with its iron mesh like a colorless chessboard. The door's rails rang under the soles of the Captain's khaki military boots as he re-entered the cell. He stood by Mahdi with his arms crossed, looking at the same thing. Mahdi looked back to the number 39 on the wall and asked the Captain about it.

"Was this writing here originally?"

"No. It seems like someone drew this number when he entered the cell. It could have been one of the personnel who had just drawn it. We'll follow up on it," the Captain answered.

Mahdi couldn't avoid the notion that the number conveyed a message.

"Do you have any idea what this number signifies?" Mahdi asked.

"Not yet. The investigation will reveal what it means," the Captain explained nonchalantly.

Mahdi looked at the number 39 on the wall once again.

What does it mean?

The silence was engulfing the cell and the quietness surrounding the place. The security personnel were busy speaking to one another outside the cell. The Captain stood silently watching Mahdi's movements and reaction.

Deep in thought, Mahdi did not move his eyes away from the drawing of the number 39 on his client's cell wall. His train of thought was cut by the sound coming from the transmitter on the Captain's waist. It made a loud whistling noise followed by unclear words, but it was clear that it was about the deceased Mohammed Al-Mukhtar's case.

Mahdi moved towards the door and held the Captain's hand who was lowering the volume of his transmitter. They crossed the door's rails stepping into the corridor.

"How long has it been since he passed?" Mahdi asked as he looked to the empty corridor save from a few of the forensic investigation team and the security men.

"One of the guards noticed he wasn't moving ten minutes past midnight, when his shift began. I'd like to let you know that the questioning of the guards from both shifts have begun."

"May I leave now and meet the Brigadier-General?" Madhi asked.

"Of course. He will have your cellphone. Good night."

The Captain placed his hand on Mahdi's back and pointed to the policeman that had accompanied him from the Brigadier-General's office to cell 12. He had been standing at the end of the corridor unable to hear the two's conversation. He approached them and saluted. Mahdi nodded to the Captain and walked with the policeman. He took out his cigarettes and offered the policeman one, but the policeman only thanked him without taking it.

Around the corridor's corner, Mahdi pretended to be looking for his phone in his grey jacket's pocket. He knew that the policeman accompanying him had no idea that the Captain had already confiscated his phone.

"Oh, I forgot my phone in building manager's office. I think it's on the couch. The 5th Division makes you forget everything!"

The policeman smiled to Mahdi and the two kept on walking. "May I use your phone?" Mahdi surprised the policeman with his question. The policeman felt that the Mahdi was somehow exempt from the 5th Division's regulations that prohibit the visitor's use of cellphones inside the building, as the way the security personnel treated Mahdi added an aura of respect to him. The way Mahdi was received by the building manager, the Brigadier-General, and sitting in his office comfortably also aided in the policeman's over-all perception of Mahdi. He smiled and took out his phone from his pocket. It was a regular cellphone with no camera or advanced digital technology as in the new phones. He looked behind him to make sure the corridor was clear from other personnel and surreptitiously handed over his phone.

"Please hurry up! The situation today does not give way for us to show our personal phones!" whispered the policeman through clenched teeth while adjusting the strap of his automatic machinegun on his shoulder.

Mahdi nodded to the policeman and turned towards the corridor's wall. He threw down the cigarette he had just lit and put out with his shoe. The policeman stood a few meters away, watching the empty corridor with its depressing lighting and dampness-filled walls.

Quickly, Mahdi opened the text messaging application and, with sweaty hands, he wrote a few words. He wrote the receiver's number by heart and sent the message.

After seeing the confirmation that the message had been received, he deleted it and advanced towards the policeman, handing him back his phone with a grateful smile. He walked with him to the hallway leading to the Brigadier-General's office.

In her room, Maha was in a deep sleep, unable to see the silent phone's screen light up, announcing the receipt of a second message—but from an unknown number this time. The message was very short.

"Maha, it's Prof. Mahdi. They have assassinated *the President*."

Chapter 5

A man with a heavy build and elegant suit sat alone in a wood-walled room, holding a remote control and watching a tape which contents were displayed on a television in the middle of the room. The smoke from his fine cigar was clouding the clarity of the TV's image under the low lighting of his wood-walled space. he rewound a scene more than once to a particular instant. He was not sitting behind his desk as he usually did, but instead sat in a regular chair facing the TV. He drank his coffee with eyes that did not leave what is displayed on the TV. He put his brown cigar out and sat down his coffee cup on a table beside him. The light from the TV reflected brilliant shimmers of light from his whitening, dignified salt and pepper hair.

Ten minutes passed, during which the man in the elegant suit rewound the scene more than seven times. The reflection of the rectangular TV appeared in his sharply focused eyes, and in it was the face of a man who seemed as if the camera was fixed on him. The man in the elegant suit's eyes narrowed every time the man on the TV spoke the words rewound on the tape.

«They lied about what they did not know.»

The man shook his head and put down the remote control allowing the tape to continue playing.

Chapter 6

At the door of the building manager's office stood Mahdi, a close distance from the security man who crossed through the door, saluting the Brigadier-General. He gestured for Mahdi to enter. Mahdi entered the Brigadier-General's office while the security man left. The Brigadier-General was sitting behind his desk and speaking over the intercom. He nodded his head, pointing for Mahdi to enter. He motioned for him to sit on the couch. It seemed like he was speaking with someone of a higher rank.

"Yes, sir. We will take the measures as you have ordered exactly, if God's willing...God be with you..."

The Brigadier-General hung up the phone and reached for his pack of cigarettes. He took out one, offering it to Mahdi.

"I don't change my cigarettes," Mahdi smiled as he drew his own pack from his jacket's pocket.

The Brigadier-General lit up his cigarette and looked to Mahdi. "Have you been informed of what had happened?"

"Yes, Brigadier-General. Frankly, it can only be negligence from the building's management. It was important to check his health condition," Mahdi blew his smoke gently to the side after speaking.

The Brigadier-General expelled his smoke and his eyes narrowed. Meanwhile, a security man walked in and saluted. The Brigadier-General nodded his head giving permission.

"Sir, Captain Fadhel sends you the counselor's phone as you have ordered."

"Fine. Bring it." the Brigadier-General said as he put out his cigarette in an ashtray on his desk full of the bottoms of his previous cigarettes. The security man entered and handed the phone to the

Brigadier-General before moving back. He saluted and left the office.

The Brigadier-General looked at Mahdi's phone turning it in his hand.

"I'm sorry about this. But I believe it is a necessary measure in such situation to prevent your contact with the outside world for the time being at least, Professor."

"Fine, Brigadier-General," Mahdi took a breath from his cigarette. "Assuming my phone will remain with you, how about if I talked to someone outside about what I have seen?" he said, looking to provoke him.

"We are confident that you will not talk to anyone, because you are spending the night here!"

Mahdi felt shocked hearing that from the Director of the 5th Division. Here? Where?

"These are the orders of the Major-General, Director of the General Intelligence. You will remain here until the Intelligence decides the date of disclosing this issue. Only then you will be able to leave." Continued the Brigadier-General.

Mahdi stared down the Brigadier-General angrily and unable to respond at the same time. He took a breath from his cigarette and looked to him again saying, "Brigadier-General, I cannot spend my night in such a building. I can promise you that…"

"I'm sorry, Professor," interrupted the Brigadier-General, "by the way, I will turn off your cellphone now, and believe me, as soon as the authorities tell me to let you go, I will."

Despite the fact that Mahdi's phone had a passcode, the Brigadier-General pressed its power button and selected the first option to turn off the device.

"Brigadier-General, whether you let me go or not, people will know what happened tonight in this building soon, and the negligent will be held accountable. I swear it!" Mahdi hissed, overtaken by anger.

"I hope we get the investigation results soon, Professor" The Brigadier-General finished his words calmly and rang the bell on his desk. The security man with the automatic assault rifle and 9mm gun entered and saluted. "Listen, go right away and have the officer in charge of rooms set up one next to my room; and make sure there is heating and covers."

"Yes, sir," the man responded. He saluted and went on to carry out the orders. The Brigadier-General drew his transmitter from somewhere on his desk.

"3C to 3D. How do you hear me, copy?" the Brigadier-General said adjusting the device's sound.

"3D to 3C. I hear you loud and clear. Send," a voice shouted through the device after a period of noise.

"3D, head to the Director's office immediately."

"3C, roger," answered the device.

The Brigadier-General answered with the call's last words, "3D, over," and he put the device on the desk.

Putting out his cigarette in the ashtray, Mahdi Al-Ali looked up from his wristwatch which was reading 2:45 am of the worst night of his life. He was both angry and sad at the same time. He wished that he had been accepted into the college of mass communication as he had wanted for himself, to become a journalist away from all this trouble. But his father's will had more effect on his choices as pushed him towards the college of law and told him to finish his law studies. After his father passed away, Mahdi went on to get his master's degree while he prepared for his PhD degree.

He remembered Maha and his relation to her. Maybe if he was a professor at the college of mass communication now, he would not have met her. No! The fates always make us meet the ones who will have an effect on our lives! Maha had both the beautiful looks and the vast mind. She was also a practical girl, so she built the relationship between her and him on the basis of study and law specifically. As for him, he was practical too. His conversations with her did not leave the scope of studying, her graduation research, and the political events on the country's theatre of events.

Had she read the messages now, he wondered? He felt a rush of blood rising to his head.

Will she tell anyone what I have told her? I have been forbidden by the authorities from saying anything.

He started convincing himself that he had told his student of the death of the country's former President in his prison so she would announce that if something happened to him inside the building he was in now being that President's lawyer. But a scruple inside him was telling him that Maha might expose the issue before it is time. Rumors would spread and the media would go into a frenzy. He would end up becoming the target of long investigations about the information leak, especially due to Maha being a member of the student's union in her college and everyone knowing of the closeness between her and her professor, the former President's lawyer.

He reassured himself. *She won't tell anyone. She would need to call me again to confirm the information before trusting it. Besides, she's a lawyer, she would know how to act.*

Interrupting his train of thoughts was the officer stomping the ground in salute as he entered the Director's office. He gave Mahdi a side glance. Mahdi touched his right wrist with his left hand remembering that officer squeezing it earlier. "I cannot promise to keep that a secret…"

"Yes, you will!" The words rang in his head.

The Captain was 3D whom the Brigadier-General has called for. The same one who has overseen Mahdi entering the cell and confiscated his phone. Captain Fadhel.

"Captain Fadhel, I have ordered a room be set up for Professor Mahdi. I hope you will be near him while he stays over to attend for his needs," the Brigadier-General commanded.

Mahdi felt that the Captain would be a guard watching him throughout his stay at the 5th Division. The Captain nodded his head and motioned for Mahdi to get up. Mahdi got up from his seat and looked to the Brigadier-General before turning towards the door. The Brigadier-General said goodnight to him, but Mahdi did not respond and walked towards Fadhel.

Mahdi's room was on the same corridor as the Brigadier-General's bedroom.

Thank God he did not order that I spend my night in a cell!

Mahdi walked with the Captain towards a corridor lined with rooms, in which one he would be forced to spend the night.

***

In the wood-walled room, the man in the elegant suit had just received a USB thumb drive. He looked at it in his hand, turned off the TV with the remote control, and removed himself from his chair to sit behind his desk. He moved his finger on the touchpad of his laptop and watched as the screen lit up. He inserted the thumb drive and lit another brown cigar.

Chapter 7

Captain Fadhel and Mahdi arrived to a corridor lined with rooms with wooden doors. They heard a voice behind them.

"Sir!"

They turned around to see a young lieutenant approaching them. He saluted the Captain. "Sir, the Professor's room is ready as the Brigadier-General has ordered, I am ordered to take you to it."

The Lieutenant walked in front of them and took out a ring of keys from his pocket. He stood before a grey wooden door and started picking out the correct key. Behind him stood the Captain with his hands on his waist while Mahdi's eyes were wandering around the roof and walls of the corridor of the depressing building.

The Lieutenant opened the door and reached for the light. The fluorescent light flickered before it settled. The room had a bed covered by a white sheet and a green blanket was neatly placed on it. There was an iron closet next to the bed, and on the wall hung an air-conditioning unit with its face taken out and metal slices apparent. The Lieutenant walked towards it and turned the heat on, and the air compressor made a loud noise.

The Captain motioned for Mahdi to enter. Mahdi entered the room and turned to look to the Captain.

"If you need something, go out into the corridor and you will find me or one of the protection personnel at the end of it. The bathrooms are by the next room from the direction we came." the Captain explained.

Mahdi thanked the Captain. The Lieutenant walked out of the room and the Captain closed the door as they walked out, talking together.

The corridor that contained Mahdi's room was composed of wooden doors on both sides. To the right, the rooms are adjacent, while to the left, there were the bathrooms first followed by two adjacent rooms. Mahdi was spending his night in the second room. At the end of the corridor there was a wooden door with tinted glass in its middle part. The Director's bedroom.

Despite the noise from the heating system, Mahdi was still able to hear the sounds of calls over transmitters at the end of the corridor as echo reflects easily in such concrete hallways engulfed with this much quietness. he sat on his bed and took off his jacket. The bed was next to the wall in a relatively small room clear of furniture aside from the bed and iron closet. He clasped his hands behind his head and leaned on the wall, remembering what all had passed throughout his night.

The assassination of the former President at the State Intelligence Division!

He felt he was at the center of a whirlpool of thoughts. He tried to remember the last meeting he had as a lawyer with the President in prison. It was exactly one week prior. He asked to see his client and the authorities permitted it. The President was detained in a prison inside the presidential Green Zone in Baghdad before he was moved to this place yesterday, as the Brigadier-General said. Mahdi's meeting with the President was short; not 15 minutes had passed before the security personnel asked him to end it. After that, the President met Mahdi the next day in court, and that was their final meeting. The trial was publicly aired on TV after some omissions. Mahdi did not appear in the trials, only his voice.

The noise from the building's heating system became deafening to Mahdi's ears. He became wrapped in his memories of his last solo meeting with the President. He closed his eyes and felt the warmth around him. His body relaxed on the bed while the fluorescent lights hummed its tune to his ears, accompanied by the array of all of the other sounds that surrounded him.

Meanwhile in his wood-walled room, the man in the elegant suit put on his reading glasses and the image of the green number 39 reflected on its lenses. He started flipping through the images on his laptop. Ten photos appeared on the screen, shot from different angles, of a cell with a body lying on a bed and a green number on the wall. He flipped back through the images. He closed the last image, ejected the thumb drive from the laptop, and put it in the inner pocket of his fine suit. He closed his laptop and took a puff from his brown cigar.

Chapter 8

The body of the murdered President Mohammed Al-Mukhtar was still the same. Its right arm dangling from the edge of the bed with the number 39 above it. The white lighting shining on the body from the cell's ceiling. The body's lips looked white and its eyes sunken. He slowly got closer to its face until it became closer to his eyes. Everything around the body seemed foggy. The silence was engulfing the place and an icy expression on the body's face. Everything seemed to move in slow motion. And suddenly, President Mohammed Al-Mukhtar opened his eyes from his mysterious death. He opened them as if waking up from a killer nightmare. He opened his mouth wide and drew in a deep breath back to his consciousness. He started breathing fast, his eyes protruded, his breathing sound quickened, and he stared terrified. The waking dead's terror increased bit by bit. He battled his breaths more. His brows rose and his eyes widened as if he wanted to scream. He raised his chin up a little drawing in as much air as possible. His forehead was soaked in sweat and with rapid half breaths that sound like knocks on wood, he raised his tongue to speak, and with tremendous terror, the President spoke his words.

"Everything will collapse!"

As his chest was rising and falling rapidly, he started screaming and his mouth widened, "Everything will collapse." The President raised his arms from his sides and strongly grabbed him by his clothes and violently screamed again, "Everything will collapse!" He tugged his clothes and yelled in his face.

"Mahdi!"

In a sudden strong reaction, Mahdi cowered himself and opened his eyes. He drew in a deep breath. His name was echoing in the place. He looked around him. The metal closet, the fluorescent light, the heater. He has just awoken from a terrifying nightmare, but the voice returned.

"Mahdi!"

It was coming from the room's wooden door. He realized he was in his room in the 5th Division. In his unconscious state's nightmare, he was listening to the President's knocks on wood sounding breaths. That sound was actual knocks on his room's door. The President's calling his name was coming from the knocker calling his name after he had knocked on the door several times with no response.

He looked at his watch. It was pointing to quarter past five in the morning. He rubbed his eyes as he got up to the door. He pulled the handle down. The door squeaked. Captain Fadhel was standing at the door looking somewhat angry.

"I knocked for a long-time Professor Mahdi!" the Captain growled.

"I'm sorry. I was fast asleep," he responded while trying to fully open his eyes to kick off sleepiness.

"Fine, Professor. Please bring your jacket with you. The Director has called for you." This time, the Captain spoke with more tact.

Mahdi looked at his watch again. A quarter past five in the morning. He walked back to the bed, picked up his jacket and headed back in the Captain's direction. The Captain closed the door behind Mahdi and the headed towards the corridor, towards the office of the building manager, the Brigadier-General.

As they walked the corridor, Mahdi revisited the President's words from his nightmare in his head.

Everything will collapse, Mahdi!

They made their last turn towards the Director's office and arrived to the room after a few steps. The Captain entered first. He saluted and turned to Mahdi, indicating for him to enter. Mahdi entered the Brigadier-General's office with his grey jacket folded over his right arm. The Brigadier-General was sitting behind his desk browsing what seemed to be a file. He raised his eyes to Mahdi, "Have a seat!" Mahdi sat on the couch and the Brigadier-General closed a file he had been reading quite intently and put it on his desk.

"Firstly, I apologize again for what happened to you tonight." Mahdi pursed his lips and shook his head as he looked away. The Brigadier-General continued, "I wanted to ask you about your client's health condition. As you know, he was moved here yesterday and I did not get a chance to review his medical files that were sent along with him. I have only just started looking through it moments ago," he held the file in front of Mahdi. "Tell me what you know about the accused's health."

Mahdi looked directly at him. "Sir, my client was allergic to dust and some scents. He could not bear them if there were high concentrates of them in the air. It would lead to his having an intense cough. He was also allergic to wool. Merely touching it would ignite a severe dermal allergic reaction, especially in the winter months. His skin would be irritated because of this allergy and if he experienced any nervous activity," he leaned toward him and continued, "so, sometimes when I met him in his cell in the Green Zone, he was in his underwear only due to the prison heating despite the cold weather outside."

The Brigadier-General frowned, his brows sinking. "Anything else?"

"No, why? Has anything cleared up about his death?"

"No, not yet. I just wanted to know about his health status."

Mahdi felt disappointed. He shook his head and stared at the ground. The Brigadier-General clasped his fingers and leaned on his chair.

"Anyway, I wanted to let you know that we have received a call from the Major-General, Director of the General Intelligence, ordering your release."

Mahdi looked to the Brigadier-General eagerly. *Now?*

The Brigadier-General reached to his desk's drawer and took out Mahdi's phone. "The Directorate's car will take you home now."

Mahdi looked to the Brigadier-General in disbelief. The biggest question ran through his mind. *Will the authorities reveal what happened?*

He closed his eyes for a second, then looked to the Brigadier-General. "Well, sir, I would be grateful!"

The Brigadier-General responded while extending his arm to hand over the phone. "Here's your phone. We are sorry for your client's death and I promise you we will look into the reason."

Mahdi and the Brigadier-General both stood up and the Brigadier-General leaned over to hand him the phone. Mahdi took the device and turned it on before placing it in his pants' pocket and returning to the couch. The Brigadier-General pressed a button on his desk and the man with the rifle and gun entered and saluted.

"Call for First Lieutenant Hesham," the Brigadier-General commanded from his chair. The security man turned around and went ahead to carry out the order.

Mahdi reached for his pack of cigarettes in his grey jacket's pocket which was lying next to him on the couch. The Brigadier-General went back to the medical files of the accused Mohammed Al-Mukhtar. Mahdi looked at him and lit up his cigarette. He leaned on the couch and his eyes wandered towards the ceiling.

I wish my father were alive to see what has happened!

With that thought, he remembered his beginnings and how he had become President Al-Mukhtar's lawyer. Mahdi's father was an Economic Advisor to the President. He had assumed his position as soon as President Al-Mukhtar had become the country's president ten years ago. He was one of the most faithful statemen to Al-Mukhtar and his program, but he passed away three years after assuming position, leaving the President to rule another seven years without him. The President's relationship with Mahdi's father was strong to the extent of friendship. As a result of that relationship, the President was aware of his advisor's son, Mahdi and his work as a new instructor at the time at the college of law. He also knew that Mahdi was just as patriotic as his father, the Advisor. Mahdi met the President twice during his father's work with him. It was during the first and second anniversary of the President's rule of the country. Dinner buffets were held at the Palace for the occasion where the President's closest state men and some of their family members would attend.

Mahdi would have short discussions with the President during those parties. The President always seemed impressed with Mahdi's ambition to reach the top in his legal work despite the delay in his acquiring his PhD in law at that time.

The President trusted Mahdi's father greatly. After his father passed, the relationship between the President and Mahdi continued through invitations from the Palace to attend the following annual parties, and the President regularly sending flower bouquets to Mahdi on the anniversary of his father's death alongside an obituary signed by President Al-Mukhtar.

Later on, Mahdi became a skilled lawyer, and still had—as did his father—the President's trust. The President who ruled for two terms of four years each and two years of a third term that he did not complete because the Council of Representatives withdrew confidence from him after accusing him of corruption and embezzlement. That was followed by the Supreme Federal Court issuing an order to arrest and hold the President while looking into those accusations. The President asked the court to write Counselor Mahdi Al-Ali to defend him and with patriotism no less than his father's; he complied with the President's request and defended him throughout the trials that lasted for three months— without reaching a negative or positive conclusion regarding the accusations made against the President before he was moved from his prison in the presidential Green Zone to the 5th Division.

The bald officer with the thick moustache walked into the Director's room and saluted—the officer that brought Mahdi from the Zayouna neighborhood to the 5th Division.

"First Lieutenant Hesham, you will take the counselor with you to his home," the Brigadier-General instructed.

The officer nodded, "Yes, sir."

"Make sure to get him there fast. He's tired after tonight!" The Brigadier-General continued.

First Lieutenant Hesham nodded his head.

Putting out his cigarette, Mahdi got up, put on his jacket and looked to the Brigadier-General, "Thank you, sir. We will be in touch regarding what happened."

The Brigadier-General smiled, "Goodbye, Professor."

Mahdi walked out along the bald officer to the corridor and then to the 5th Division courtyard where the Chevrolet was waiting for him.

Chapter 9

In the surveillance room where tens of cameras across the corridors and cells of the 5th Division connect to, the Hyena was sitting in front of one of the computers that connected to the surveillance system. He seemed nervous looking through the narrow opening in the door overlooking the corridor. There was no one else in the surveillance room. The other members of the room were preoccupied with an urgent call from the Brigadier-General. He looked at his watch and then got up towards the door worriedly. He opened the door slightly more and looked to the completely vacant corridor. He narrowed the opening again, went back to his computer staring at the screen, and focused his eyes on the green copying line.

Copying – Four minutes remaining

He sat on the chair facing the machine and started knocking with his fingers on the table as he watched the green copying line move…

Please hurry!

The computers and camera systems lined up on a long table where the surveillance room staff would sit in front of their machines' screens. Above those machines was a line of small rectangular shaped windows overlooking the outer corridor, and above them were the internal AC units which provided just the right temperature for the room and the electronic devices in it.

Three minutes remaining

The Hyena grew more nervous as he followed the content on the screen being copied. He hastened his knocks on the table. Suddenly, the screen turned off hiding with it the copying line. It turned into a silent black screen. The Hyena's face reflected on its glass.

He looked at his reflection. The old wound on his right cheek was clear in it while the room's lighting reflected on the heavy sweat soaking his forehead and bald head. He moved the curser with his mouse and the screen was back on after it had temporarily gone into screen saving mode.

Two minutes remaining

Meanwhile, he heard footsteps coming from the corridor in the direction of the surveillance room. Quickly, he turned his rotating chair in half a circle and looked at the main screen in the middle of the surveillance room, which was divided into eight squares, each broadcasting a live image from one of the building's cameras.

He looked at the square of the camera directed at the corridor. The sound of footsteps seemed in sync with the steps of the person on the screen. His eyes widened and he was filled with terror.

***

The Chevrolet stopped in front of Counselor Mahdi's house in Zayouna. Mahdi reached for the car door's handle to get out of it.

First Lieutenant Hesham turned to him, "There is something you're supposed to receive before you leave." Mahdi's eyes narrowed. He looked to the Lieutenant who took out a plastic bag from his sports jacket containing three discs. Hesham turned to Mahdi who was sitting in the back seat, "Here you go."

Mahdi received the batch of disks and looked through them. He opened the bag and found between the disks a folded paper. He took it out and opened it. It read:

The full recordings of the trial of the accused Mohammed Al-Mukhtar – Counselor Mahdi Al-Ali's copy

He looked to First Lieutenant Hesham, "But I have the full copy up till the last session!"

"I prefer you check this version," Hesham replied.

Mahdi was present in all the trial sessions during which he defended his client.

Have I missed a part of it?

Mahdi closed the bag and prepared to get out of the car. "Alright, thank you for driving me," he said and opened the door.

"You're welcome, Professor," Hesham replied.

Mahdi got out of the Chevrolet and closed the door. He headed towards his house door while First Lieutenant Hesham told the driver to move. The Chevrolet moved leaving the street with Mahdi's house. Mahdi looked to its governmental plate number get farther away, then turned to open his door.

***

In the wood-walled room, the man with the elegant suit's phone rang.

New message.

Chapter 10

One minute remaining

The Hyena's nervousness grew further as he watched someone coming closer to the surveillance room. He turned to the computer screen. The green line was still on its way to complete copying the content. He looked to the corridor from the door's narrow opening. The shadow reflected on the corridor's flagstones and the man's footsteps grew closer to his ears.

30 seconds remaining

He turned looking for a place he could hide in inside the room. The surveillance room did not have closets or high shelves.

No shelter for me inside!

He looked towards the corridor from the door's small opening again. The man looked like a black ghost as he passed a dark spot of the corridor which was split into dark areas and other lit areas because of the way its ceiling lights were distributed.

I'm not getting away!

No shelter inside and no chance to run out of the room through the corridor, the Hyena knew that that moment would expose what he has done and just as a man who was about to lose everything, he reached for his waist and touched his gun waiting for the person to enter the room.

***

Mahdi threw himself on the bed exhausted from his night at the 5th Division. Lying on his stomach, he looked at the bag of disks he had thrown on the table facing his bed. He started to feel an urge to know what they contained but he was unable to move. His eyelids got heavier and he fell into deep sleep.

Chapter 11

5:45 a.m.

Close to the surveillance room, in the dark part of the corridor, the man became very close to the room's door. As he passed it, he stopped for a second. He noticed the light coming from the room through the narrow opening in its door. It seemed like a shadow moving in an isolated corridor like a haunted house. And suddenly, he quickly stepped towards the room and with great speed, he held the door's handle and forcefully opened it. He was surprised to see the Hyena before him like that. His eyes widened looking at him.

The Hyena was very calmly sitting behind the computer with his fingers clasped behind his head. He looked to the man standing at the door.

"Captain Fadhel, sir! Are we still under a state of alarm?"

Captain Fadhel entered the room. He looked to him firmly. "What are you doing here?"

"There is a technical issue with this computer. It requires a system format." the Hyena replied.

"At this hour?"

The Hyena responded laughingly, "Do not postpone today's work until tomorrow. You know this is my motto. Besides, my shift is until nine in the morning."

He said it with a smile as the light was shining on the scar on his right cheek. His eyes seemed to smile slyly. Captain Fadhel looked at the computer. This one was not connected to the surveillance system. He stared at his screen. The screen was black filled with white writings in English. The last line had a percentage that was going up towards 100%. Fadhel turned to the Hyena who seemed to look at the screen in front him and move himself on his rotating chair.

"Hyena, you will postpone the maintenance of this machine until tomorrow when your shift starts again."

The Hyena looked to Fadhel and said in surprise, "But I was just about to start the format process!"

"I said leave the surveillance room immediately!"

The Hyena shrugged his shoulders disapprovingly. The text "(Y/N)?" appeared at the bottom of the screen.

The Hyena pressed N and Enter. The format process was canceled.

The Hyena shut down the machine and took the disk containing the operating system that was on the table. He got up and left the room. Fadhel followed him out and closed the door, locking it.

"Be well, sir."

Fadhel shook his head and headed in the opposite direction of the corridor from the Hyena.

Captain Fadhel knew of the Hyena's super computer skills. His comrades referred to him with that name for his genius in dealing with computers, in addition to hacking and overtaking personal accounts on the internet. The Hyena worked as an Administrative Officer in the Computing Unit at the 5th Division. This unit's job was to maintain and follow the work of all the computers in the building. He was called by the staff more than anyone else to fix their computer problems, but at the same time he was the smartest and most cunning of the Division's staff. That was known about him through his personal dealings with the staff, which is why Captain Fadhel despised him so much. He treated him roughly.

Moreover, the Hyena loved wild hunting because of his wild desire to use guns and shoot animals.

Fadhel was still walking the corridor away from the locked surveillance room but, just like a clock that suddenly stopped working, he stopped on the spot. He felt a killer heat rise in his head. His eyes widened and his shoulders rose. He turned around quickly and hysterically ran towards the surveillance room. He ran as fast as he could on the slippery tiles of the corridor while looking for the room's key among the cluster of keys in his hands. Captain Fadhel has never been seen in such a flustered state before.

Meanwhile, the Hyena finished a short visit to the building's vehicles room and headed to the main door on his way out.

Chapter 12

With great agitation, Captain Fadhel was opening the surveillance room's door again looking uneasy. Struggling with his trembling fingers, he unlocked the door, pushed it, and walked in. He headed to the camera control machine. He opened the recording of the camera installed in the surveillance room itself. The camera set to record what takes place inside the surveillance room was above the main screen in the room. He sat in front of one of the computers connected to the machine controlling the cameras and started watching the internal camera's recording from ten minutes earlier.

The surveillance room's staff appeared on the tape in front of their computers one after the other except the second computer to the right, which was switched off and had no one facing it. Some of them were watching the main screen that was placed in the facing direction of the chain of computers. Beside that screen, from both sides were a number of smaller screens. Fadhel continued to watch the recording. One of the staff in the room appeared to have received a short phone call. He turned to his companions and briefly spoke with them. Then, everybody got up and left the room. The surveillance room remained clear from staff and its door closed for about a minute, after which the door was opened and a young bald man whose skin tone leaned toward a shade of dark tan came in.

The Hyena came in and headed to the second computer on the table. He sat before it and turned it on. Then he turned to the first machine next to him and kept staring at it. He got up from his place to sit before it leaving the second machine with an almost black screen.

Captain Fadhel continued to watch the tape. The Hyena sat before the first machine for a long while. A short time after, he got up to the door, touched it with his hand, then went back to sit before the machine. After another short while, he turned to the surveillance screen behind him. His face looked clear in the recording when he turned to look at it. After that, he quickly leaned on the first machine and got up to sit before the second machine. He leaned on the chair and clasped his fingers behind his head.

Fadhel continued watching the recording. The Hyena was sitting as is when Fadhel himself walked into the surveillance room and had his conversation with him.

Fadhel stopped the recording and left camera control machine. He headed for the first computer, moved the curser and performed some quick tasks on it. Then, suddenly…

Impossible!

He strongly hit his forehead with his hand as he felt a tremendous shock. He ran towards the surveillance room's door, exited, and locked it hurriedly. He turned around running in the corridor looking hysterical. Struggling with his fat body, he let his legs run as the wind in the corridor. Two of the security personnel were walking through the corridor when Fadhel passed them and yelled "Have you seen the Hyena?"

He was yelling at the top of his lungs. One of the security personnel shook his head. Fadhel seemed angrier as he pushed through the corridor. His shoulder banged against the security guard's shoulder violently and he continued to run towards the night guards' room. He reached the room and pushed the door open. His face was red and he was sweating profusely. There was a young lieutenant in the room sitting behind his desk doing paperwork. He was surprised to see Captain Fadhel push into his room.

"Have you seen the Hyena?" Fadhel gasped breathlessly.

Confused, the officer replied while looking at a schedule on the table in front of him.

"Sir, as far as I know, he should have left the building by now since his shift ended at six o'clock sharp."

Fadhel's eyes widened.

Six in the morning!!

He remembered what the Hyena said about his shift end time, "My shift is until nine in the morning."

Fadhel went closer to the officer's desk and picked up the phone's handset. He dialed three digits to make an internal call. The phone rang in the building's security room at the main gate of the 5th Division. One of the personnel answered and an all tense Fadhel said to him, "Listen, have you seen the Hyena leave the building?"

"A few minutes ago, sir. He got into a cab." the security man answered.

Fadhel went into a frenzy. He smacked the handset on the table violently and turned to leave the room and the officer in a state of complete astonishment. He headed towards the main corridor and ran until he reached the last turn leading to the building manager's room. He stood at the door, drew in a deep breath, then walked in and saluted the Brigadier-General with apparent nervousness. The Brigadier-General was sitting behind his desk which was just left by the surveillance room staff after a short meeting with them a short while earlier. He looked to Fadhel and noticed the nervousness and sweat on his face.

"Captain Fadhel? What is the matter with you?" he asked in surprise.

Fadhel grimaced, taking in quick breaths, "Sir, the Hyena has done it...The camera recording of cell 12 is gone."

Chapter 13

The surveillance room staff returned from the Brigadier-General's office to their spots behind the computers after they had a short meeting with him. The Brigadier-General called for them after Fadhel had convinced him it was necessary to speak with them about keeping the confidentiality of what the surveillance cameras recorded during the incident of Mohammed Al-Mukhtar's assassination. During the meeting, the Brigadier-General was waving about the strict punishments to the surveillance team if any tape the cameras recorded that night was to be leaked.

"How did you know that?" asked the Brigadier-General to Fadhel, who looked broken.

"Sir, I have just gotten back from the surveillance room. I rewound the tape from the camera inside the room. The Hyena was maintaining one of the computers but he used the chance when the room was vacant from its staff and deleted the recording from the camera in cell 12. Then he disappeared from the building."

The Brigadier-General closed his eyes and grinded his teeth, "Do you know what this means?"

"Yes, sir. We are in trouble before the authorities."

The Brigadier-General looked to Fadhel, "What will our position be in front of the Major-General? Fadhel, I want a full report regarding the Hyena's movements tonight since we found out about Al-Mukhtar's death."

"Sir, based on the schedule, he should have had just entered the building. His entrance and the death notice took place at the same time, at exactly midnight according to the recording he has deleted."

"And if he entered the building before his shift?" The Brigadier-

General asked and pushed a button on his desk. The armed man entered. "Call for the internal security officer."

"Sir, no need for that. I will handle it. I will try to understand the purpose of deleting the cell's recording by the Hyena in my own way. What matters now is we capture him alive."

The Brigadier-General and a few officers, including Captain Fadhel, had entered the surveillance room and watched the recording from the camera in cell 12 immediately after the notice of Al-Mukhtar's death. A male custodian entering the cell coincided with Al-Mukhtar appearing to have been asphyxiating. A few minutes after the custodian left the cell, the President was reported to not have been moving, which later lead to confirmation of his death. While playing the tape, it was discovered that there were two seconds missing, hiding with them the most important part on the tape, the custodian's face. Furthermore, during the incident, all the surveillance room staff had been called in to fix a major break in the surveillance cameras system in the adjacent building. They returned to their location after the alarm was sounded after the incident.

"Sir," said Fadhel, "It was a mistake for us to keep the tape in the control machine only. We should have made a second copy for the investigation just in case."

The Brigadier-General lit up his cigarette. "Fadhel, what could explain the break in the surveillance system in the second building and the President's asphyxiation incident during the same time, and the important cut in the recording from the camera in cell 12, and then deleting it entirely later?"

"The one who deleted the tape that way…"

"He did it!" Interrupted the Brigadier-General. He took a breath from his cigarette. "Captain Fadhel, you will, confidentially and internally, take a security force and get me the Hyena," he banged his desk with his fist, "today!"

The Hyena has just entered the place he had been residing in for weeks. He opened the door of the apartment on the first floor of the building and went in. The apartment's balcony overlooked the street leading to Furdous Square coming from Karrada. He could look from its balcony to where Saddam Hussein's statue used to be; the one that the US tanks brought down in 2003.

He turned on the lights and locked the door. He sat on a leather couch in the living room, drew in a deep breath, and then took out a memory unit from his coat's pocket. He looked at it in his hand and said to himself, "You will see what I've done!"

Chapter 14

The first light shone on the capital, Baghdad.

At exactly seven in the morning, three Chevrolets with tinted windows were fully prepared to implement a quick operation to carry out the Brigadier-General's orders to capture the Hyena. Captain Fadhel put his black helmet on the front of the first vehicle parked next to the other two vehicles in the 5th Division courtyard. He wore his desert color-spotted bulletproof vest. He yelled for the persons participating in the mission ordering them to gather. Twelve persons formed three sides of a square before the Captain. They were all dressed in desert pants and shirts with bulletproof vests and ammunition pockets, and black sports jackets on top of it all. They were armed with US-made M16 and M14 machine guns and had black helmets with no spotted cloth covering on, and on their thighs were the Austrian-made black gun holsters.

With the sound from the Chevrolets' engines that were running to heat up and prepare to raid on the Hyena's den, Captain Fadhel's voice was sonorous before the convoy members. He took out a map from his pants' side pocket and started explaining to the team the details of the tasks of each of them from the get go till they complete the mission in Karrada and go back to the 5th Division headquarters again. He explained that while reserving the name of target and replacing it with a code name: The Lamb.

He set the presumed time for the mission to be 40 minutes.

In the wood-walled room, the man in the elegant suit had just closed the door leaving for his residence that lay close to his office room. As he was walking towards the building's exit, his cellphone rang. He did not want to answer until he left to his base's garden. He opened the line and brought the phone to his ear.

A short call.

He seemed angry by the contents of that call. He switched off the device and put it in his pocket. Someone opened the back door of his tinted car. He got in, leaving the office.

***

On the embroidered carpet laid on the room's warm floor and by a single sized wooden bed, two beautiful female feet with red painted toenails landed.

She put her fingers through her blond hair and pushed it back. She yawned and looked at her cell phone on the bedside cabinet. The blue light on the phone was flashing intermittently. She reached for the phone and opened the screen lock with a zigzag movement from her thumb.

2 new messages.

Chapter 15

The golden rays of sun shone on the eastern side of The Furdous Mosque's dome and minaret with their spectacular Islamic ornamentation. They overlooked the square of the same name.

The Hyena went down the stairs from his apartment to the ground floor. He exited the building's door and entered a small stationery store in the same building overlooking the street. An old man had just opened that humble store of his for the day. The Hyena greeted the old man and asked him for a small envelope. The old man smiled and took one out of one of the shelves that covered the store's walls. The Hyena took the envelope and returned to his apartment. He closed the apartment's door and sat on the couch, and then he took out a pen and started writing a few words on a piece of paper. He put the paper in the envelope and stuffed it in his coat's pocket.

He remembered the address he had read on the vehicle's room board.

That board was used to set the information for any of the 5th Division's vehicles movements towards their targets, the direction of their missions, the addresses of the targets, the names of the officers using them, and their time of departure. The information remained on the board until the vehicle returns from its mission when the information would be erased and the vehicle's key would be hung waiting for a new mission and a new user. The direction was clear; no room for error.

He looked at his watch: 7:30 a.m.

He got up to the apartment's kitchen and made himself a cup of tea.

Mahdi opened his heavy eyes at the sound of his ringtone. He sat on the bed and took out his phone from his pocket.

Maha student.

He answered the phone.

"Hello, Maha, and good morning…Ah…Yes, no, we cannot talk about that over the phone. We have to meet soon…Yes, I'm at home…Fine…I will be waiting for you."

He hung up and looked at his watch. He got up, took off his jacket, and headed to get a hot shower.

Meanwhile, the Chevrolets had crossed the Aema Bridge towards Furdous Square, downtown where the Hyena resided.

The Intelligence had sufficient information on all of its staff. That information was used to reach anyone at any time. Besides, the cell phone networks provided a tracking service on the calls from the phones of the staff of the Intelligence.

Captain Fadhel was silent in the front seat of the first vehicle of the convoy. He looked out through the tinted glass thinking of the possibility of completing the mission successfully. Fadhel was one of the Intelligence's most loyal men to the Intelligence institution. He gained with his intelligence and success track record the approbation of his superiors, especially the Brigadier-General. He got used to having all the sensitive missions assigned to him.

Excited for the mission, he checked the Taser gun he had put on the seat between his thighs.

This kind of gun shot out two electrical wires in super speed wherein the two wires embed in the victim's body due to their sharp metals ends. As soon as the two wires are embedded, an electric current goes through the wires from the gun in the shooter's hand to the victim's bodies causing severe muscle contractions and paralysis for a short while to enable law enforcement men to capture him without severely injuring him or killing him if they used live ammunition guns. He was hoping to capture the Hyena alive to find out what he had done during his presence at the Directorate last night.

The Hyena sat on the couch after he inserted the thumb drive into the laptop on the table before him. He opened the drive's contents and leaned as he drank his tea. A recording from a fixed security camera appeared on the computer's screen. The Hyena smiled as he watched. Excellent resolution.

What was shown in the recording was cell number 12. The Hyena had copied the camera recording of that cell from the surveillance room at the 5th Division before leaving it this morning. In the recording of the cell, there was a twin sized bed by the wall and the accused, Mohammed Al-Mukhtar, was sitting on it in his underwear only. The cell's door opened and a cleaning man in a yellow suit wearing a work hat of the same color entered. The door was closed behind him and he started to clean the cell. The cleaning went on for five minutes. The man finished and sprayed what appeared to be an air freshener. As soon as he started to spray it in the cell, Al-Mukhtar seemed upset. There was a quarrel with the cleaning man. The Hyena continued to watch the tape.

Mahdi finished his shower and started preparing coffee while Maha's car entered the street he lived on. Maha lived with her mother in their house at Palestine Street near Zayouna neighborhood. She had visited her professor's house before when he lent her a legal reference from his library to use in her research. She had accompanied him in her car from the university to his house then.

Mahdi watched the coffee on its way to be ready as the events from last night started playing before him in every detail. Suddenly, the house bell rang. Mahdi moved to his room's window in the upper floor and looked towards the street. The 20-something girl had her sunglasses on top of her head, pushing back her blond hair. She was wearing a brown leather jacket, jeans, and long brown leather boots. Mahdi went back to the kitchen and put out the fire under the now ready coffee pot. He went down to towards the door where Maha was waiting for him.

The Chevrolets touched the beginning of Sa'doon Street coming from the Tahrir Square, which holds the Iraqi Freedom Monument, on their way towards Furdous Square where the Hyena resided. The force's leader, Captain Fadhel, was continuously making calls with his superior, the Brigadier-General, to personally let him know of the force's movement.

There were no more than minutes separating them from the Hyena's den.

Chapter 16

The cleaning man started apologizing to President Al-Mukhtar for spraying the air freshener. He turned towards the table by the President's bed presenting his back to the camera. The President appeared to be coughing from the particles of the air freshener spreading in the cell.

The Hyena continued to watch the tape.

At the building's door where the Hyena resided in one of its apartments, three tinted Chevrolet vehicles stopped and six armed men headed by Captain Fadhel, who prepared his electric Taser gun while the others prepared their lethal machine guns, got out of them. Fadhel's orders to the personnel were clear:

Capture the Hyena alive.

The six men led by Fadhel went up the building's stairs quietly. One could not hear a sound in the building's corridors other than the taps of military boots trying to not make a sound. Like robots, the security personnel, with Fadhel at the forefront, went up the stairs leading to the Hyena's wooden apartment door on the first floor one step at a time, while the others remained in the street around their vehicles watching the situation from outside. Fadhel and his men got closer to the Hyena's apartment door until they were right in front of it. He indicated with his fist for the men to stop. They assumed fighting postures in the building's hallways, stairs, and the apartment's door. They checked everything around them with hawk eyes.

The Hyena reached the last seconds of the tape. The cleaning man finished a small task by Al-Mukhtar's bed, which he was lying on, and turned facing the camera. His face was clearly apparent to it.

The Hyena stopped the tape and smiled.

This is what will confirm it for him!

Suddenly, there were three soft knocks on the apartment's door. The Hyena was surprised.

Who would it be at this time?

He closed his laptop's screen on the table and pulled his gun's safety trigger and held it behind his back as he headed for the door. Captain Fadhel was on high alert putting his finger on the electric gun's trigger and pointing it towards the Hyena's apartment door.

The Hyena stepped forward to the door and put his hand on its round handle. He felt the cold sweat between his fingers making his hold on the gun slippery. His heart's drums were beating before the wooden door. He clenched his gun, drew in a deep breath, and tightened his grip over the door's handle. Outside, a drop of sweat snuck from under the helmet Captain Fadhel was wearing to his forehead. He too tightened his grip on his gun's handle. His forefinger teased the electric gun's trigger waiting to press it. He felt the gun become a part of him. He clenched his teeth. His breathing became quicker, waiting for the crucial moment.

Quickly, in a sudden move, the Hyena moved the door's handle and pulled it towards himself. Forcefully, Captain Fadhel kicked the door and pushed through like an arrow into the Hyena's apartment, followed by two of his men. The Hyena was surprised by his guest. His grip on the gun softened before what he saw. The old man from the stationery store was standing smiling in front of him.

"Sorry, sir. I forgot to give you back the change."

The Hyena smiled and took the money while thanking the man. The old man went back down the stairs and the Hyena closed the door.

Fadhel and his men searched the Hyena's apartment that was registered in their records as his permanent residence. No one!

The Hyena had been moving for weeks between his apartment and his friend's apartment who had traveled out of the country for his mother's treatment. He would go to his friend's apartment sometimes. It was three buildings away from his original residence on the same street.

Fadhel hit the wall strongly. He got away!

He ordered his men to leave the apartment after they searched every inch of it. He closed the door and withdrew his men from the building. He got in the Chevrolet and held the communication device to let the Brigadier-General know exactly what happened.

A few minutes later, the man in the elegant suit became furious speaking over the phone.

"I want him *alive*!"

Chapter 17

Signs of surprise and shock appeared on Maha whose hand with which she held the coffee cup trembled at what Mahdi told her of last night's events, the death of the President, and the number on the cell's wall.

She put down the cup from her hand and asked, "Professor, do you think you are in danger now that you have told of what had happened?"

"That depends on one thing. If the authorities announced it to the media, I would be safe. They have nothing to fear. But if they kept quiet about it for more than 24 hours, I would really be in danger."

Maha put her hand over her mouth and fearfully looked to her professor. "Professor, you have to disappear for a while!"

"You cannot run away from the State Intelligence," Mahdi said, "I will stay here and see what happens."

Maha seemed confused and scared of the consequences of what happened, especially that the general situation in the country was still tense after the removal of the President.

Mahdi got up and brought the disks bag that Lieutenant Hesham had given him—the ones that specifically said Counselor *Mahdi Al-Ali's copy.*

"This is what they gave me." Mahdi said as he took out the first disk and headed to the disk player in the room. He inserted it and took back his seat. He put the two remaining disks on the table in front of him.

Maha pushed her hair behind her ear with her fingers and reached for the bag. "What is this?"

Mahdi turned on the TV with the remote control, "We'll see now."

The Chevrolet vehicles withdrew from Karrada area back to the 5th Division Headquarters in Kadhumiya. Fadhel had received a call from the Brigadier-General telling him to find an alternative plan to capture the Hyena. He seemed anxious waiting to reach the Directorate and discuss the matter with the Brigadier-General.

Meanwhile, the Hyena received a call from his neighbor who owned the apartment next to his original apartment asking if he was alright after what appeared to be a special force had raided the apartment. The Hyena assured his neighbor that it was only a prank from a coworker before hanging up.

Quickly, he got up and changed his clothes. He wore a sports outfit and a baseball hat with rounded modern sunglasses. Ready to leave the apartment, he grabbed the envelope and reread the text he had written on the enclosed paper. He smiled and took out something like a 7.62 mm machine gun's bullet from his pocket and put it in the envelope next to the paper. He hid the envelope in his pocket and then took some IDs and passport and stuffed them in his clothes. After that, he took out his phone's sim card on which he had received his last call and broke it.

He went down to the street with his hand in his pocket clenching the envelope. He motioned for a cab with his other hand. The cab stopped in front of him, he spoke with the driver, and got in the car.

The image of a scale appeared on the screen…

"And if you judge among people, judge with fairness."

The image remained for a few seconds. Mahdi and Maha were extremely curious to know what the disks' contents were despite what was written on the paper enclosed with them of simply being recordings of President Al-Mukhtar's trial sessions. A strong feeling took over Mahdi…

There was something else other than the trial sessions.

The disk player started showing the contents of the first disk among the three disks Mahdi had received. A white text on a black background appeared after the scale image had disappeared: The 20th Trial Session. Mahdi was surprised and looked to Maha, who seemed just as astonished too. The first disk started with a very late session.

"This should be the first session!" Mahdi exclaimed.

Maha replied while confirming the numbers on the back of the remaining disks, "We did not make a mistake. This has to be the first disk!"

The tape started playing the 20th trial session. Mahdi and Maha were very attentive to what was being played back.

***

From the vehicle's board in his head, the Hyena retrieved the memories he received.

The destination could not have been mistaken. With his hand in his pocket and as he looked through the car's window to the street, he felt the envelope and touched the bullet's head with his fingers. He smiled. This is what will confirm it for him!

Chapter 18

Fifteen minutes into the 20th trial session playback. Mahdi was completely detached from the outside world. He clasped his hands behind his head and watched the session that he had attended at the time, while Maha was also attentively watching the tape as she gathered her hair round her right shoulder with her fingers.

"Have you noticed anything that you may have possibly missed during that session, Professor?"

Mahdi shook his head to say no. All what he was seeing now had happened in his presence and before his eyes.

Meanwhile, a cab entered from Palestine Street to the Zayouna area carrying a young tan man in a baseball hat and sports outfit with an old scar on his right cheek.

The destination could not be mistaken!

The Hyena asked the driver to drive slowly as he looked to the houses' number plates that were fixed next to their doors.

On the trial's tape, the judge was directing another question to Mohammed Al-Mukhtar.

"How do you explain your involvement in implicating the State Intelligence Bureau in supporting and assisting the African pirates takeover of oil ships and commercial shipments passing through Bab Al-Mandeb Strait to the Red Sea, and from it to the Suez Canal and the Mediterranean, then Europe, and asking for a ransom in exchange for letting them go? You secretly provided them with arms and information. We have received written orders by you through the public prosecution directing the Intelligence regarding that."

Mahdi and Maha were still watching.

The President answered smiling. "But they denied what they could not encompass the knowledge of…"

That was a quotation from the Quran.

The scene repeated twice. It replayed after it ended. It seemed like a technical problem to Mahdi and Maha. Then the same ten second scene repeated for the third time. Mahdi looked to Maha. He grabbed the remote control and stopped the playback, then let it continue in an attempt to overcome the technical problem on the disk.

The scene ended with the Quranic verse the President recited and then repeated for the fourth time.

Mahdi got up and ejected the disk from the player. He looked at it sideways and the light reflected on it.

The disk was undamaged with no scratches.

He put it back into the player and looked to Maha on the couch. She reached for the remote control and played the disk. She fast-forwarded it to the same point.

"But they denied what they could not encompass the knowledge of…" The President finished the Quranic verse, and it repeated again.

The disk seemed to have no technical issues. The scene was re-peated on purpose by using a montage software to appear so. The footage's resolution and the lack of visual or auditory issues along the tape proved it.

"Let it go on." Mahdi said and Maha put down the remote control and crossed her arms.

The scene repeated its ten seconds for seven consecutive times before continuing to display the remainder of the trial session.

The Hyena got out of the cab and closed the door. The street was clear from passersbyers as the residents of Zayouna were used to their neighborhood being one of the quietest and least populated neighborhoods in the capital.

He looked at the small feminine car by the door of the target's house. He matched in his mind the information of the residence with the information he obtained from the vehicles room board. The Hyena had obtained Counselor Mahdi's address from that board when that address was listed on it while Mahdi was being returned to his residence by a vehicle affiliated to the 5th Division the previous night. The officer assigned to taking the lawyer back home set the address on the board before returning to the Directorate's base and erasing that information.

The target's home.

He took a few steps away from the house and entered a nearby shop about 20 meters from Mahdi's house. He bought a pack of cigarettes and left back towards his target.

With confident steps, the Hyena approached Mahdi's house. He went up the gardens to the side of the street adjacent to the front fences of the houses. Mahdi's house was a few steps to his right. He pressed the envelope in his pocket in his fist. He took out the envelope. Mahdi's house was right to his right. He threw the envelope containing the paper and bullet over the outer fence into Mahdi's house inner garden. He stepped down to the street, passing Maha's car and continued on his way.

Meanwhile, the scene where Al-Mukhtar recited the Quranic verse repeated itself seven times. Then the disk went on to show the remainder of its contents. Five minutes after the remainder of the contents were played, the disk stopped announcing the end of its contents.

"It's over," Maha said.

"Let's play the next disk," a confused Mahdi responded.

Maha took out the second disk according to the order written on its back from the bag of disks. She got up to replace it with the first disk in the player while Mahdi grabbed the remote control waiting to see its contents.

Maha went back to her seat. Mahdi pressed the play button and it started.

The scale appeared once more.

"And if you judge among people, judge with fairness," the image stayed on for a few seconds and then a white text on a black background: The 20th Trial Session.

Mahdi and Maha were surprised. He looked to her, "The 20th again?"

Maha seemed as if she was trying to find an explanation for it as the playback started repeating the same contents of the first disk. She looked to Mahdi, "Let's watch it!"

Mahdi nodded his head in agreement.

***

At the 5th Division, Captain Fadhel had entered the Brigadier-General's room after his return from the failed raid on the Hyena's den. Holding his helmet in his hand and wearing his full fighting uniform, the Brigadier-General motioned for him to enter.

"Sir, the Hyena getting away from us like this confirms our suspicions about him," he said as he entered the room.

"Relax," said the Brigaider-General. Fadhel sat on the couch after he took off his armor and put it on the ground but kept his helmet in his lap. "Here's the alternative plan."

Meanwhile, the Hyena decided to play cat and mouse with the authorities. He got into a cab and headed to the capital's western outskirts.

The second disk appeared to exactly match the first in its contents. The 20th trial session with a repeated scene of the President speaking for seven consecutive times.

"And so it is so," Maha said feeling as shocked as Mahdi. "Do we try the third disk?" Mahdi nodded his head in agreement while she got up to replace the disk with the next one.

The 20th Trial Session. The last disk appeared to contain the same content too.

As soon as Mahdi saw the contents of the last disk, he got a strange idea.

"Maha, the secret is in the recording!" He said that to her while she stood with her arms crossed. She pushed back her hair from her eyes with a move of her head and sat before Mahdi.

"How?"

He looked to her, "The repetition is intentional. The Intelligence cannot make a mistake like that by making three disks with the same contents. Moreover, why would they hand me a recording for something I had already attended in the first place?"

Maha thought then said, "And if we assume the person assigned to making these disks for you made a mistake in collecting three disks with the same contents in one bag, why were there three copies of these disks' contents made anyway?"

Mahdi smiled, "See?"

He pressed the remote control fast-forwarding it to the scene with the seven repetitions.

At the 5th Division, an ambulance with no number plates had just left accompanied by two armored SUVs affiliated to the Directorate heading to the Forensic Medicine Department in Bab Al-Mu'adham in central Baghdad, carrying the murdered President's body.

Chapter 19

Mahdi pressed the play button on the remote control. The seven times repeated scene started playing. The President was smiling as he answered the judge's question. He quoted a verse from the Quran in his response, "But they denied what they could not encompass the knowledge of and its explanation did not come to them and so denied the ones before them, so look what was the outcome of the wrongdoers."

Mahdi remembered that event well. The President said those words at the time and sat back in the accusation cage without answering the judge's question regarding supporting the African pirates.

Maha turned to Mahdi to hunt for his face language, but nothing appeared on it except that he was deep in thoughts.

"Professor?" she asked.

He looked to hair raising an eyebrow, "Hmm?"

He took out a cigarette from the pack on the table. "I don't know if that was the President's message or the Intelligence's message to us."

"If there was a message from the President, he would have told me about it during my solo visits to him. He talked to me about many issues relating to the case but I did not ask him why he recited that verse in court," Mahdi said.

Maha pushed her hair back behind her hair with her fingers. "Why didn't you ask him?"

"I thought it was just an answer he was using to evade responding to the court. I did not know what would happen and that the Intelligence would pay special attention to this verse. Moreover, the President used to quite often quote Quranic verses and poetry lines during the trial sessions."

"I suggest we read the whole text in the Quran. Perhaps what the President mentioned was part of a larger text that carries some message." Maha said.

Mahdi looked to hear seeming eager, "Let's do it!"

He got up to the small bookshelves by the TV and brought out a Quran the size of a palm. He returned to sit and held the book. He knit his eyebrows and looked to Maha with confusion. "We have to know the location of the verse in the book first!"

Maha pursed her lips and then said, "I'll look it up on the internet."

Mahdi nodded and pointed to his laptop on a nearby dinner table. He put the book on the table.

168 cm tall, Maha got up and headed for the table. Her heels made tapping sounds when she left the carpet and started walking on the tiles. She returned with the laptop, sat before Mahdi, and opened the machine.

***

At the 5th Division, Fadhel felt a kind of relief that the start of implementing the alternative plan was approaching. The Brigadier-General had told him that the Major-General's orders, the Director of the General Intelligence, were to close all border crossing points and airports before the Hyena by informing them of his details and an arrest order in addition to the Intelligence setting up a plan to implement checkpoints in coordination with Internal Security to capture him.

The call to those authorities is waiting to be implemented.

The man in the elegant suit returned to his wood-walled room. He seemed somewhat tired from the previous night. He ordered a cup of coffee for himself and then made a phone call with a high authority figure in the government. He hung up…

Everything will be alright.

Maha's eyes went over the Quranic verse on the laptop's screen as she read it in her feminine voice, from the beginning of the page until its end, passing through the verse Al-Mukhtar had mentioned; while Mahdi was listening and trying to decipher the mystery of the verse the President had answered the judge's question with on the 20th session. She finished reading and looked to Mahdi. He drew a deep breath and leaned on the couch closing his eyes.

The text did not carry any solution to the questions.

Maha looked back to the screen focusing on the verse the President had mentioned. Suddenly, her eyes narrowed and she pushed her hair back behind her ear.

"Professor?" Mahdi opened his eyes and took a last draw from his cigarette.

He looked to her, "What?"

"Come and look."

A thousand questions went through Mahdi's mind during that instant. He put out his cigarette and got up to grab his prescription glassed from the table in front of him. Maha slid away on the couch to make room for him to sit. He put on his glasses and sat next to her looking at the screen.

Maha moved her fingers on the mouse and with it the curser on the screen moved pointing to the verse's number.

Mahdi was shocked seeing that the number on the President's cell wall is the same number of the verse Al-Mukhtar recited in the recorded trial.

He looked to Maha, "Verse 39!"

She nodded, "From the Chapter of Jonah!"

Mahdi took off his glasses and threw them on the table. He got up, put his hands on his hips and drew in a deep breath.

What does that mean?

Chapter 20

The Hyena had just gotten out of the cab and closed the door. He looked back and saw from afar the winged statue of the legend, Abbas Bin Fernas.

Bin Fernas was known as an Arab man who was the first to attempt to fly using wings around one thousand years ago. He succeeded in flying for a few minutes before crashing down and dying because, as it was said, he had not made a tail for his primitive plane. The Iraqi authorities put a statue of him at the gate of Baghdad International Airport as a symbol for an early Arab attempt at reaching the skies.

The ends of the statue's wings flashed in the Hyena's eyes with the reflection from the sun's light on it. He adjusted his hat and entered Baghdad International Airport's gate.

He headed towards the passenger shuttle vehicles available at the airport gate and got into one of them. The vehicle moved, leaving behind the airport gate heading east on a wide road to reach the center of the airport where the airline companies were within the airport building itself.

Looking from the window, the Hyena remembered the way Baghdad Airport used to be a few years earlier and the complicated security procedures the passengers had to go through before reaching the center of the airport: police dogs and checkpoints along the road between the gate and the center of the airport, but those procedures were reduced with the introduction of alternative methods to keeping the security of the country's most important airport.

The vehicle passed a large sign with "Iraq bids you farewell" written on it. The Hyena was hoping to finish his travel stamp at the airport as fast as possible. Another ten minutes in that vehicle and he would be at the heart of Baghdad International Airport.

Meanwhile, the Intelligence had just begun conducting preliminary measures via a vast communication network to inform the borders crossing points and airports of information relating to the Hyena as a wanted suspect in order to close the way before any anticipated attempt by him to escape Iraq.

Ten minutes passed and the vehicle transporting the Hyena arrived to the center of the airport. The Hyena got out and headed to the airport building's entrance. He adjusted his baseball hat and pushed the oval frame of his oval glasses to his eyes with his forefinger. Crossing the first door, he picked up his speed to the airline companies desks to start booking his ticket out of Iraq.

The Iraqi Airways sign reflected on his sunglasses that he had not moved from his eyes even inside the building. The sign was above the ticketing desk of the national airline company. He approached the desk and greeted the ticketing officer. He asked her about the nearest available trip to his destination and got his answer.

Destination: Ataturk International Airport – Turkey

Estimated time till the trip: two hours from now.

He paid the price for a one way ticket to Turkey and got it. His name was now available for the airport authorities as a traveler waiting for his trip on the Iraqi Airways flight to Ataturk International Airport. He smiled to the ticketing officer, leaving her to finish her work with another client. He took the plane ticket and left the desk.

At the time, he was supposed to get his visa and boarding pass. Instead, the Hyena headed back to the airport's exit gate. He passed it in quick steps towards the building's courtyard to get into another vehicle to take him back to the main gate by the statue of Bin Ferans again.

He will not travel.

The Hyena wanted to preoccupy the authorities with his name registered with one of the airline companies as leaving the country while he headed to another destination. A game to gain time!

In those moments, the order to close the airports and border crossing points before the Hyena's face had become effective. The authorities at Baghdad International Airport received a clear order from security authorities to capture the suspect. The security authorities provided the airport authorities with his full name and picture describing him as a dangerous wanted person. Within minutes, the airport system discovered the Hyena's real name as a passenger who had shortly prior purchased a ticket to Ataturk International Airport on the Iraqi Airways. The authorities determined the desk the ticket was purchased at and the time of purchase. Urgently, the security men in the airport's security control room rewound the surveillance camera recording on the Iraqi Airways ticketing desk to the same time the ticket was purchased. They watched the suspect clearly purchase that ticket. The security men followed the recordings of other surveillance cameras to know the point the wanted man went to. They were surprised to see him exit the airport building.

Meanwhile, the Hyena had gotten into the passengers' shuttle vehicle back to the airport's outer gate. He passed a sign on the road with "Iraq welcomes you" written on it. Another 12 minutes and he would reach the gate overlooking the airport highway that had Bin Ferans' statue in the middle of it.

Due to its great importance, the Baghdad International Airport authorities had a large number of surveillance cameras dispersed in and around the airport in addition to tens of carefully elected security men. Baghdad Airport represented one of the most important spots in the Iraqi capital in addition to the presidential Green Zone which was only a few kilometers from the airport via a highway leading to that area.

The security men followed the live broadcast of the surveillance cameras watching the road leading to the outer gate. The suspect has no option but to leave through the main gate overlooking the highway. The security men watched the footage from the camera fixed on the outer gate waiting for the Hyena to appear on it while the security authorities were informed of the airport authorities locating the suspect and the continuance to look for him.

Meanwhile, Captain Fadhel was getting into a Chevrolet vehicle coming towards the airport with two of his comrades, hoping to capture the Hyena himself. He gave the order to the department that was communicating with the airport authorities to not capture the suspect until a force from the State Intelligence arrived, but to keep watching the target's movements and provide the Intelligence with information of those movements. The Chevrolet was cruising through the streets of Baghdad at an insane speed aiming to reach the Hyena at the right moment.

After around ten minutes, the Hyena got out of the passenger shuttle vehicle and headed towards the pavement where cabs wait. He adjusted his hat and walked towards the street. On the edge of the pavement, an old man had parked his yellow cab and stood next to it, waiting for one of the returning travelers so that he might drive them to their destination for a fee. He looked to the Hyena who appeared to have the signs of a returning traveler; the baseball hat, the designer sports uniform, the also seemingly expensive designer shades, and a not a copy brand sports shoes. The man approached the Hyena who seemed in a hurry.

"A cab, sir?"

The Hyena looked at him, "Where is your car?"

The man pointed with his car keys in the direction of his parked car on the nearby street.

The Hyena moved closer to him. "Alawi bus stop, please."

The old man smiled and went with the Hyena to get into the car.

The Alawi bus stop was across from the Iraqi National Museum in a crowded area of Baghdad's Karkh, where Muthanna Airport borders it from the northwestern side and the Zawraa Park from the western side, in addition to its proximity from the Grand Festivities Square, which holds the Iraqi Military parades. That bus stop was used for ground travel to any other Iraqi governorate via hundreds of vehicles waiting in lines for the travelers.

Captain Fadhel felt the Hyena was his prey that he could not give up. He did not want to see the Hyena fall into the hands of another security agency as he might tell them information the Intelligence do not wish to expose, even to another national security agency.

***

Mahdi felt his nerves about to explode. "What do they want to say with those disks?" He said hysterically.

Maha closed the laptop's screen and put it on the table. "Professor, we have to understand the reason behind their sending this signal to you."

Mahdi lit up another cigarette as he walked the room back and forth. "That's the question!"

Maha asked again, "Do you think the President's death was planned by the Intelligence? We have to consider that as a possibility. The number you saw in the cell matches the number of the repeated verse on the disk. Isn't the Intelligence worried you would tell the media what happened with you and of you exposing that suspicious match between the two numbers?"

Mahdi stopped and looked to her, "Maha, there is no evidence.

How would I prove to the media that I have obtained these disks through the Intelligence? And how would I make the connection between the repetitions and the number on the President's cell that no one but me has seen? If we assume someone leaked the information about the state of the President's cell and the number on its wall, how would I make the connection between that symbol and the repetitions on a recording? The media would call it insufficient evidence and the repetitions are a result of an unintentional technical error."

Maha drew in a deep breath and put her head between her hands. She looked to Mahdi, "Professor, you need to rest. I will leave you alone and try to find an explanation for what's happening."

Mahdi sat on the couch, pushed his head back, and sighed, "Maha, this puzzle has to be solved!"

Maha responded with a confused expression, "Please Professor, do not exhaust yourself with thinking. Everything will become clear later, I'm sure."

Mahdi nodded his head and got up with her going down to the house's courtyard heading for the door. The garage that fit one car was the path leading from Mahdi's house inner yard towards its outer door. Parallel to the garage from the left side was a small garden filled with grass and weed that extend to the side of the path leading to the door. Rose and jasmine plants surrounded the grass garden from three sides without their flowers due to the chilly winter. Maha and her professor walked the way leading to the outer door while discussing what happened. Suddenly, Mahdi stopped looking to the house's small garden. He coldly threw away his cigarette. Maha turned to him and noticed his looks fixed on a point in the garden. She looked to it and saw what he saw.

An envelope.

Without talking, he leaned down onto the garden's grass and Maha followed him. He picked up the envelope from the ground. The envelope's paper was folded irregularly due to pressing it.

"More trouble!"

With eyes full of confusion and wishing it to not be so, Maha said, "Let's open it."

While opening the envelope from its side, a 7.62 mm rifle bullet fell from it onto Maha's brown shoes before settling between her feet on the grass. The two froze in their spots.

During the Iraqi civil war in 2006 and 2007, an envelope containing a bullet meant the residents of the targeted house should leave the house or die. The armed groups used this method to send that message to the residents, and that terrified Mahdi and Maha.

Maha leaned to pick up the bullet from between her feet while pushing her hair back. She looked to Mahdi who seemed to swallow and breathe fast. She felt the bullet's head with her fingers.

"They want to kill me!" Mahdi said feeling pure fear running through his blood.

Maha felt the severity of her professor's psychological state but she noticed the lightness of the bullet in her hand. Mahdi took the bullet from her and started to feel it up while trying to understand his predicament.

"Professor, have you felt how light weight it is?"

Mahdi held up the bullet to his eyes. "Yes, it resembles a bullet but it does the same purpose of sending the threat message to me."

Maha took the bullet from his hand. She felt the separating line between the bullet's cartridge and its head. It looked like a child's toy. She held the bullet's head with the fingers of her right hand

and the cartridge with her left fingers and pulled them into opposite directions.

"What are you doin…," Mahdi asked.

The two parts separated from each other exposing what lay between them. A thumb drive in the shape of a bullet. The two looked to each other feeling shocked.

Due to his fondness for hunting trips and animal shooting, guns and everything that had to do with guns, the Hyena had a set of objects resembling those guns and what affiliates with them, including thumb drives in the shapes of bullets and small grenades, lighters in the shape of guns, metal boxes for cigarettes carrying military slogans and drawings of rifles and machine guns. His comrades envied his collection but never tried to ask him for them because they knew how much he treasured those kinds of objects.

Curiosity peaked for Mahdi and Maha to find out what the drive held.

"We open its contents now?" Maha asked while returning the bullet's cover.

"Of course, I'm afraid it may be the beginning of new trouble," Mahdi responded.

"Relax, Professor We'll find out its contents and know what's on it."

Mahdi and Maha returned to the house and the room on the upper floor to identify the contents of the thumb drive.

***

The cab transporting the Hyena crossed over the bridge, which passed in front of Um Al-Tuboul Mosque. The architecture of the mosque appeared like an architectural art piece overlooking main streets, as the mosque was situated in an open area like a wonderful monument, especially under the night lighting and the overlook of its minarets on the surrounding area.

The old driver was humming with a song by Fairouz that one of the Iraqi radio stations was playing. "Morning Bulbul" as the Arabs called her, was one of the voices people in the Arab world wanted to listen to in the morning. The driver felt he found a way out of his attempts to open conversation with the Hyena who was characterized by quietness and who did not display any interest in exchanging conversation with him.

After crossing the bridge, the Hyena noticed a small traffic jam on the road. Three short lines of vehicles waiting their line to cross a checkpoint that was suddenly set up.

***

Maha sat on the couch with the laptop on her lap waiting to display the contents of the memory drive while a very nervous Mahdi sat next to her. The contents window appeared:

One icon with a virtual title.

She moved her hair from her eyes with a move of her head and double clicked the icon. A program window opened and started to play a video. Mahdi felt that something in what was appearing in the video was not new to him.

Cell number 12.

Chapter 21

The cab carrying the Hyena reached the first of the line of vehicles before the checkpoint. Two military SUVs were stopped nearby and there were men in military uniform and others in civilian clothing with metal ID badges on their chests and communication devices in their hands. The Hyena felt the severity of the situation.

I cannot back down. I have to cross the checkpoint peacefully.

One of the security personnel, an officer, stopped the cab. He approached the driver's window and peaked in to see the passengers. His eyes radiated confidence and iciness. The Hyena avoided looking at him and kept looking ahead from behind his sunglasses.

"Where did you come from and where are you going?" The officer asked the driver in a confident voice.

The Hyena felt his heart drop like an elevator whose wires were cut.

"Sir, I came from the airport and heading to Alawi bus stop."

"May I have your IDs, please?"

"Certainly, sir."

The driver presented his ID while the Hyena did not want to show his ID as a man who works for the State Intelligence Bureau, so he only presented his personal civil ID. The security man checked both IDs. He glanced over the driver's ID but carefully looked at the Hyena's. He raised his eyes from it. "Your glasses, sir."

Hesitantly, the Hyena removed his glasses and looked straight into the officer's eyes. His face was tanned and an old scar while his eyes appeared like two icy shiny stones. The officer looked at the Hyena's ID again and asked him. "You're coming from the airport, sir?"

The Hyena nodded his head affirmatively.

"Where did you return from?" The officer asked again.

The Hyena wanted to find any country's name to lie about returning from a trip to it, but he considered the possibility that the security man may ask for his passport to see the entry stamp.

"Frankly, I couldn't travel. My mother is in a bad health condition and she called me due to the further deterioration in her health this morning."

The officer did not remove his eyes from the Hyena although he gave him and the driver back their IDs. He tapped on the edge of the driver's door and said and waved them along.

The cab moved and the Hyena felt like a heavy rock was moved from over his chest. As soon as the car started to get farther, the officer at the checkpoint held his communication device and called to another, "The target is in sight, sir!"

After what the Hyena felt from the looks of the security man at the checkpoint, and in a step that indicated wits, he wanted to leave the cab before reaching the bus stop but was afraid the driver might get more suspicious. He pretended to make a short phone call after which he asked the driver to change the destination to Bab Al-Mu'adham instead of Alawi for an emergency.

Neither the Hyena nor the driver noticed that a military Ford pickup was following them since there was nothing more to see in Baghdad than the huge numbers of vehicles mixed in with the Internal Security vehicles. The vehicle following the Hyena was tasked with providing the Hyena's exact coordinates to Captain Fadhel directly. The vehicle started following them after the call the checkpoint officer had made.

Retired soldier Sarem had received a phone call from Captain Fadhel detailing to him the destination he needed to head towards meeting his target, the Hyena. He provided him with his exact location and the plate number of the cab transporting him. Sarem had been a soldier in the former Iraqi Special Forces. He participated in the Gulf War in Kuwait in 1991 against the Coalition forced. He was injured during those battles. The forty-something former soldier had high combat and gun use skills. He became a hitman for a number of political parties after 2003, and due to his relation to him, Captain Fadhel wanted to use him for his personal gain outside the scope of the intelligence work to eliminate the Hyena.

Sarem moved from his position in the Utaifiya area in central Baghdad in his Nissan sedan to meet the Hyena's cab based on the information he was receiving from Captain Fadhel, who in turn was getting it from the security vehicle following the Hyena. Armed with a silencer pistol and a wild desire to eliminate the target, he quickly headed to the point where he anticipated meeting the Hyena's cab.

A few minutes later, the cab carrying the Hyena was on Haifa Street in Baghdad's Karkh, heading to cross Bab Al-Mu'adham Bridge towards The City of Medicine at the heart of the capital. There was light traffic in the area at that time and no traffic jams on the street.

As soon as the cab carrying the Hyena entered the street, the security Ford vehicle disappeared to be replaced by a cab carrying an intelligence agent overtaking the task of following the Hyena.

Before the commence of the operation to follow the Hyena, the Major-General and Director of the General Intelligence had sternly informed the Director of the 5th Division that he would punish him and Captain Fadhel if the Hyena was proven innocent in the investigation from the 5th Division's accusations as the alert that was declared at the border crossing points and airports was in response to the Brigadier-General and Captain Fadhel's accusation that the Hyena had done something suspicious in the surveillance room the night Al-Mukhtar was murdered and the possibility of his causing a disaster to the national Intelligence, such as exposing what had happened at the 5th Division that night. Therefore, after the threat the Director of Intelligence had made to the 5th Division, Captain Fadhel preferred to eliminate the Hyena than to capture him alive. He could claim that the Hyena had resisted the security men during the case which lead to putting him down. That, in addition to the personal animosity between him and the Hyena, made the Captain seek the opportunity to eliminate his adversary.

Fadhel knew well the seriousness of the threat by the General Director of Intelligence despite his excellent relation with him. Major-General Maher Abdelfattah was one of the Iraqi Government's hawks and had a long reach to his enemies. Major-General Maher was 56 years old with a piercing look and a vision, which made him a director to one of the state's most critical and sensitive agencies.

The cab affiliated with the Intelligence kept on following the cab the Hyena was taking, giving details of the Hyena's cab directions to Fadhel. A little while after, suddenly, the old man's car started to experience some problem. It started to shake as if something had broken.

The old man turned to the Hyena and said smiling, "I'm sorry about that. I will try to fix it!"

The old man swerved from the road leading to Bab Al-Mu'adham Bridge going down the road leading to the riverbank. The Hyena felt something fishy was going on. A little ahead, in the direction of the old houses located to the back of Haifa St. to the right of the Tigris. The old man's car came to a full stop.

He parked it to the side of the road. He opened the door to get out and fix the problem, but because of the Hyena's feeling of uneasiness, he grabbed the old man's wrist. "Sir, I'm in a hurry. I would like to pay your fare and get another cab."

"There is no need for that. It would only take a few minutes and we'll be back on the road," The old man responded.

But the Hyena insisted on getting out of the car, having a feeling of the danger lurking.

Nearby, Sarem got out of a car he parked far from the Hyena's eyes. He carried his gun with the silencer in his clothes and kept watching from afar.

The Hyena got out of the car after he paid the old man his fare. He adjusted his sunglasses and headed for one of the narrow bystreets with worn-out houses on both their sides. Sarem followed him. The area was almost clear from passers at that time, Sarem made use of the situation. After the Hyena took a few steps on one of those old bystreets, where at first he could only hear his footsteps due to the quietness of that area, but then he heard other fast approaching footsteps behind him. He picked up speed only to hear footsteps behind him quickening too. He decided to assure himself by seeing the person hoping to see that it was not a danger threatening him, but as he turned, the last thing he saw was a 40-something-year old man raising a gun with a silencer to his face—a rusty flash accompanied by a momentary hissing sound.

With one bullet, and a red hole in his forehead.

The Hyena was killed.

Chapter 22

"It's the President's cell!" Mahdi said.

In the recording appeared a cleaning man in a yellow uniform suit and a hat of the same color entering. Mahdi and Maha thought it strange that the man should enter without a security man to accompany him. The man put a cleaning kit in a corner in the cell and started to sweep the ground. President Al-Mukhtar was sitting on his bed in his underwear only despite the cold. Five minutes passed during which the cleaning man finished his work sweeping the cell's floor with his back to the camera. He then took an air freshener from his things in the cell's corner and started to spray it in its atmosphere. The President appeared annoyed and it seemed like an argument took place between them.

It looked as if the man was apologizing to the President. Mahdi and Maha continued to watch the recording.

After that, the man headed to the small bedside cabinet at the head of the President's bed. On the bedside cabinet were a few of Al-Mukhtar's things; his watch, his notebook, his pen, and some medication for his respiratory illness which the prison administration allowed into his cell due to Al-Mukhtar's health condition and his need for them. The man stopped in front of the cabinet giving his back to the camera. He seemed to clean the bedside cabinet's surface while the President was sitting and starting to cough because of what appeared to be the effect of the air freshener on his respiratory system. The two went on watching.

The cleaning man finished his work on the bedside cabinet and headed to the corner of the room to collect the dust he had gathered somewhere on the ground. He grabbed his broom and plastic dustpan and started gathering the dust. The President, coughing, turned to the metal bedside cabinet and took his inhaler from on top of it, which he was used to using whenever he felt difficulty breathing. He stretched his legs on the bed and put the inhaler in his mouth, pressing it twice.

Mahdi knit his brows as he followed on. More severe signs of asphyxiation appeared on the President after he took the inhaler. He struggled with his breaths for a few seconds, and as if his heart was pumping pain to his whole body, he cowered on himself like he had just taken a bullet in his stomach. He stretched his right leg hitting the bed with the sole of his foot over and over while he bent the other leg. He stretched his right arm and the inhaler dropped from his hand to the ground. He held his neck with both hands as if trying to remove hands that were choking him. He strongly closed his eyes taking in pain like the pain of a knife penetrating his side. He forcefully grabbed on to the bed sheet. He clenched his teeth and turned his head to the right and his fists on the bed sheet loosened. He lifted his right hand a little and it fell to his side. He stretched his legs and their movements started to decrease. With a few weak kicks that lasted for seconds, President Mohammed Al-Mukhtar turned into a lifeless body. Mahdi's eyes widened as he watched while Maha gasped at the horror she saw.

The cleaning man got up and looked to the motionless president. He calmly put his hand in his yellow suit's pocket and approached the body. He got close and took something out of his pocket and what was in his pocket became clear, a metal cylinder.

He stopped next to the bed and started spraying the contents of the cylinder, which appeared to be a spray paint, on the cell wall by Al-Mukhtar's bed in a non-arbitrary way. He finished drawing the number 39 on the wall, and then put the cylinder back in his pocket and covered the lower half of the President's body with a blanket. In an intentional move, he turned to face the camera.

Mahdi was shocked by what he saw. The face was familiar…

Captain Fadhel.

Chapter 23

"The Lamb was eliminated."

With those words, Sarem finished his phone call with Captain Fadhel who was hastily heading to Haifa Street with two of his Intelligence comrades. Fadhel felt great relief but he did not want the Hyena's body to remain lying in place nor for Sarem to run into the other Intelligence agents. He made a direct call to the Brigadier-General, Director of the 5th Division, informing him of the Hyena's ending and requesting him to send the closest security patrol accompanied with an ambulance to the Hyena's killing location while he reached him.

The Brigadier-General sighed in relief and promised Captain Fadhel to send the patrol and ambulance immediately.

Sarem was thinking of the four thousand Dollars promised to him in exchange for accomplishing the task. He roamed the area under the bridge close to the place where the body remained to make sure no one notices what happened.

It was not the first mission Sarem had done for Fadhel. Two years ago, he assassinated a new officer in the 5th Division. That officer was committed and sure of himself which pushed Fadhel to believe him a competitor at the Directorate who was starting to steal his light before the Brigadier-General and Director of the Division. Therefore, Fadhel got rid of him through Sarem two months after he was hired. Fadhel's relation with the Major-General, Director of the Intelligence, helped close the investigation and regard the new officer's assassination an act of terrorism by an unknown assailant.

After less than ten minutes, Sarem heard the ambulance and police car sirens closing in. He walked quickly under the bridge leaving the Hyena's body in its place in one of the narrow bystreets. The orders of the police patrol were to surround the scene of a crime whose victim was a security man and to not lift the body until a force from the Intelligence arrived. Sarem continued his steps under the bridge turning back to Haifa Street. He reached the other street facing the bridge. He looked to the right and left and crossed the street while the police car and ambulance arrived to the blood stain the authorities described for them. The two cars stopped and the security men got out, approaching the scene of the incident as it was described to them.

They reached the Hyena's body.

Sarem continued to move towards the low part under the bridge again. He glanced over at the security car and ambulance surrounding the place. The Hyena's death has become confirmed for Fadhel.

He kept moving towards his parked car, got in, and drove away.

Ten minutes passed before a Chevrolet carrying Captain Fadhel arrived to the scene of the crime. The car parked close to the Hyena's murder location and the Captain and one of his companions got out. Fadhel stepped towards the security men surrounding the place while hiding a smile behind a fake mask of shock for losing a colleague from the Intelligence at the hands of someone.

The Intelligence did not wish to inform other security agencies that it was them who executed an operation against one of its men.

Chapter 24

At Mahdi's the recording stopped playing after the end of its contents. He was at a total loss of what was going on and could not find an explanation for the President's murder by the Intelligence and the way the tape was delivered to him. Maha looked to him, worried that agitation might affect his health condition. Mahdi was quiet despite the volcanic emotions that were stirring inside him.

"Replay the recording," he said to Maha.

Maha played the silent recording again. The cleaning man entered, closed the door, and put his things on the ground near the corner. Mahdi noticed that the man's body was exactly the same built as Captain Fadhel's. The playback continued for five minutes during which the murderer cleaned the cell, then he collected the dust in the room's corner, took out an air freshener, and started spraying it, which angered the President.

"He knows exactly of the President's allergy to air fresheners and dust," Mahdi said.

"I agree with you. That's why he is using the spray," Maha responded, "that's what I understood."

The argument between the President and the killer unfolded. The killer apologized to the President and headed to the bedside cabinet. He finished his cleaning while the President kept coughing, wearing his underwear only.

"Is the cell that hot? Despite that it's January?" Maha asked.

"The cell is warm due to the air-conditioning system in it. Al-Mukhtar had a skin allergy in winter of too much heating and nervous conditions. That caused him a painful itch, which made him prefer to stay away from clothes and fabrics, especially wool."

The killer finished cleaning the bedside cabinet's surface and started to walk away.

"Stop the film!" Mahdi suddenly burst.

Maha stopped the playback. Mahdi focused on the President's inhaler on the bedside cabinet.

"Did you notice?" He asked Maha.

"Notice what?"

"Rewind and pay attention to the inhaler," Mahdi instructed with his eyes glued to the screen.

Maha rewound the scene to when the man started cleaning the bedside cabinet's surface.

The F shaped inhaler mouth piece was pointing towards the cell's closest wall before the killer cleaned the table, and appeared pointing to the opposite direction after the killer finished cleaning the table.

"Do you mean the inhaler's direction?"

"Exactly. He switched it while working on the cabinet's surface when his back was to the camera."

The killer walked away from the cabinet and started collecting the dust on the room's floor. The President stretched his legs on the bed and reached for the inhaler, two presses, and he started to suffocate. He lay on his bed and his nerves seemed to stiffen. He started bending and stretching his legs like a drowning man trying to catch his last breath. The inhaler dropped to the cell's floor and soon he became a lifeless body.

"What the hell is in the inhaler?" Maha asked exasperated, feeling her heart throbbing faster at the seeing the President dying, although it was her second time watching the recording.

"I don't know, but it appears to be a fatal substance. It killed him quickly," Mahdi responded as he passed a hand through his hair.

The killer got off the ground and took out a bottle of spray paint after he was sure the President was dead. He sprayed its contents on the wall, drawing the number 39. The symbol he drew seemed very clear on the wall. He finished drawing the symbol and turned towards the camera in what appeared to be an unintentional move. Maha stopped the playback.

Mahdi stared at Captain Fadhel's face who disguised himself in a cleaning man's uniform to commit his act. Mahdi was sure of the Intelligence captain's features. A thousand questions went through his brain. My client's murder is implemented inside the 5th Division's jail, and someone brings him the recording, and the killer's picture appears on that recording! It is extremely complicated.

After a few seconds from Maha resuming the playback, it ended.

"Give me the memory drive," Mahdi said calmly.

Maha ejected the "bullet" drive and gave it to him. He closed it with its cover and took the envelope from the table to put it back in it and hide it until its right time comes. He opened the envelope to put the "bullet". His eyes became riveted like he was looking at something.

Maha put the laptop on the table and looked to her professor, "Something wrong?"

Mahdi reached his fingers into the envelope and took out a paper from it that was attached with the memory drive. He opened the paper. Maha drew her head near him to see its contents alongside him. Mahdi grabbed his reading glasses from the table and put them on. The handwriting was not neat as if it was written by a hand that pressed the ink pen too much:

The Intelligence killed him, this will confirm it for you.

In the paper's left lower corner, the signature was:

"Al-Mukhtar's admirer".

Chapter 25

12:00 p.m. Baghdad time.

On Baghdad International Airport's runway, the Iraqi Airways' Boing 777 landed like a white monster with green stripes coming from Berlin. On it was forensic professor, Dr. Salem Jerjis, whom the authorities in Baghdad had asked to cut short his attendance of a forensic medicine conference there and have one of his assistants replace him. Berlin was hosting that conference which the International Academy of Legal Medicine (IALM) organized and was attended by many experts in forensic medicine and forensic sciences from all over the world to discuss developing that particular type of science according to the modern laws.

Professor Jerjis was not aware of the reason for his urgent recall, or that what was waiting for him was the former country's President's body that required an autopsy; even though he was welcomed by a high-level Intelligence officer at the airport, who accompanied him in civilian vehicles to a destination that remained unknown to him.

Professor Salem Jerjis was known as the most-senior Iraqi forensic doctor. He was a 62 year old Christian noted for his height and the grey hairs on the sides of his head. The state put its confidence in him during the criminal crises due to his long history of serving it and providing the reports the authorities wanted to the public in accordance with the country's higher benefit.

The Intelligence vehicles went on transporting the Professor to its destination in Baghdad, while Mohammed Al-Mukhtar's body was put in one of the morgues under constant security protection by the Intelligence to prevent anyone working onsite from identifying the victim.

Chapter 26

Fadhel stood with his hands on his waist looking at his nemeses' body lying on an old bystreet in that river-adjacent neighborhood. Sarem's bullet had caused a large hole in the Hyena's forehead. The blood that ran from it formed a puddle under the body's head. He looked into the Hyena's sharp eyes. Their light had turned off and their sharpness cooled down, while a thin line of blood ran like a slow train running between the grains of dust on the ground towards the street by the low part of the wide river.

Fadhel's eyes did not leave the Hyena's face on the ground. He turned and asked one of his men to search the body after he ordered the other security men to step away from it and widen their perimeter around the scene of the crime. One of the Intelligence men accompanying Fadhel searched the Hyena's clothes. He took out his passport and a plane ticket to Turkey from his clothes, in addition to his ID as an Intelligence staffer, some Iraqi cash, and around 300 US Dollars.

Nothing suspicious was found.

Fadhel turned and ordered the ambulance driver to transport the body to the morgue. He felt that the Hyena's death ended a tiresome chapter of his day.

No one will know what I have done.

He smiled watching the Hyena's body enter the ambulance's back, folding with it a page of tiresome chase.

***

Mahdi was not sure that the sender of the recording was really a "supporter", or if it was just another game by the Intelligence. Maha was sitting before her professor looking at the paper attached with the envelope in her hands. She folded the paper and put and the memory drive with it in the envelope.

"Professor?"

Mahdi looked to her. He was playing with the pack of cigarettes on the table in front of him.

"Are you sure the person who appeared in the cell is the Intelligence officer whom you met yesterday?"

"Perfectly, Maha! Perfectly!"

"I don't want to be curious, and my question may be related to one of your secrets as the President's lawyer. But I'm wondering whether there was any conversation between you and the President before about the number 39; bank accounts, an estate number, a secret weapon, something of the sorts."

Mahdi stared at her and drowned in the memory of his solo meetings with him. All he remembered about this number is…

Absolute vacuum.

He shook his head in negation. His eyes were rigid in the room's space.

"Professor, two messages in one day. The number on the cell's wall and the Quranic verse's number. Try to tie in the secrets the President had disclosed to you and find the relation between them and the number."

"Maha, the President did not mention anything to me about this number before. I'm certain."

Maha's eyes wandered around the room, pursing her lips and thinking of her next question.

"And what do you know of the President's relation to the African pirates the court asked him about?"

Mahdi fixed his sitting posture and looked to her. He lit the last of his cigarettes and breathed in the smoke.

"Yes, the court accused the President of supplying information and weapons in secrecy to African—specifically Somalian—pirate gangs to takeover international oil tankers and ships transporting oil and commercial shipments between the Far East and the Middle East from one side, and Europe from another across the Red Sea and the Suez Canal. The President was supporting the overtaking of those ships by those pirates who would demand that the companies and companies that own them to pay a ransom reaching at times millions of dollars in exchange for releasing them. The President was using the commercial information and intelligence he got on the movement of those ships and providing those pirates with them through a chain of people and agencies that delivered the information until the origin of the information appeared unknown. Additionally, he would buy weapons through persons and networks, and provide the pirates with them indirectly. Despite that, I denied those charges against him in court, but he had told me he had really done it."

Maha put her fingers through her hair and pushed it back, "Do you mean the President was supporting piracy and terrorism!"

"I asked him about the reason. He said, 'Mahdi, a successful leader is one who wins the battle before entering it.' He explained to me that he had not done it for piracy and sharing the profits with the pirates at all, but the pirates themselves had not known who was delivering the intelligence assistance and weapons to them due to the large number of mediators Al-Mukhtar had used to support them. Maha, Al-Mukhtar was smarter than using piracy for financial gain."

"How?"

He exhaled his cigarette's smoke and flicked its ash on the ashtray on the table, continuing. "He told me the reason. He had done it to make the Strait of Bab Al-Mandeb insecure in the eyes of international navigation to push the ships using that strait to reroute to Strait of Hormuz, then the Arabian Gulf and Basra ports, where they would unload in Faw Port and move through the dry channels across Iraq towards Europe via the Basra—Berlin Line. That would yield billions of dollars to Iraq annually. This was the reward Al-Mukhtar had wanted. He had not meant any of it for personal gain, but the national profits."

Maha was surprised by Al-Mukhtar's cunningness. "Hmm, and what does that have to do with the battle he had told you he should win before entering?"

"He always felt the ghost of global economic crises, and at the same time was obsessed with establishing a strong national economy relying on Iraq acquiring yields from various sources, even the illegal ones, which pushed him to commit some major violations to support that idea of his. After international bodies revealed the circumstances behind that, the new Council of Representatives' politicians did not understand the real reason behind what he had done. They moved a case against him in court and accused him of doing that to increase his personal fortune. They made accusations against him of supporting global terrorism and sharing with the terrorists their looting."

Maha smiled a half smile. "But, the principle of the end justifying the means is not always right!"

"Everything is permissible in politics, Maha. The only sure thing for me is that Al-Mukhtar did not embezzle anything for himself, but he did those illegal acts to secure the country's future and diversify the income sources."

"Was this the biggest violation the President had done?"

"I don't know which of them I could consider a violation, or call it work for the country's benefit. Al-Mukhtar was smart and had an unbelievable cunningness."

"Hmm, a diplomatic answer!" Maha said laughingly.

"You can consider it so. Believe me, my father and I know President Mohammed Al-Mukhtar more than any other Iraqi. He was crazy about making Iraq go back to its natural state economically, politically, and martially. The first step to accomplish that in his eyes was accomplishing economic stability and yielding large revenues that rely on other sources aside from the oil revenues. Don't you remember his many speeches where he would refer to Iraq with the phrase 'the land of the Sun'? He loved calling it that in appreciation for the Sumerian who had called their country with that name."

"Yes, I remember that!"

"He was looking at Iraq like Noah, who should reconstruct the country after the flood."

"The flood?" she said in surprise.

"Yes, I asked him once if he considered what happened after 2003 was the flood, he shook his head and said, "Mahdi, that flood that took place in Iraq and then the whole area will be minute compared to what's to come!"

Maha's eyes widened looking to her professor, "Did he mean that the war in 2003 and what followed from internal conflicts and wars in Iraq and some other countries would be minute compared to the coming unknown?"

"Exactly, on a global level!"

Thoughts scrambled in Maha's head like bubbles, each struggling to be the first she should ask her professor. For a second, she felt the future was hopeless and at some loss of her professor's words which he conveyed from her country's former President, who had left the world leaving behind countless unanswered questions.

The phone rang in her purse cutting her chain of thoughts. She took it out and answered the call. It was her mother calling to check in on her and ask her to come home soon because she needed her. She was suffering from a severe narcosis in her right shoulder joint and was preparing to travel to Turkey to get treatment there.

"I have to go back home. I'm really late for my mother."

"Very well, Maha. Try to think with me about the number 39. Two brains thinking is better than one."

"I promise."

Maha left her professor's house, returning to her home on Palestine Street. Mahdi walked her to his door and nodded goodbye.

In his living room, the bullet remained in its envelope with the paper signed by "Al-Mukhtar's admirer". Next to the envelope were the three disks with the seven repetitions—all waiting for the puzzle to be solved.

Chapter 27

Captain Fadhel was riding in a Chevrolet SUV accompanying the ambulance that carried the Hyena's body to the forensic medical facility followed by a police car.

His mind wandered off as he looked through the window remembering the previous night's events at the 5th Division. He remembered his last meeting with Major-General Maher Abdelfattah, Director of the General Intelligence. It had been three days earlier when the Major-General assigned him the task of killing President Al-Mukhtar in his jail cell secretly and without any other member of the Intelligence knowing about it, except for one officer whom the Major-General trusted well in addition to Fadhel. Otherwise, it was kept confidential to all members of the 5th Division, including the Brigadier-General, Director of the Division.

Captain Fadhel was briefed on the details of the operation and the hour of execution. He had ordered his comrade, the Shadow Officer, to secretly cause a problem in the surveillance camera system in the second building. The Shadow Officer carried out the order and most of the adjacent building's cameras went out of order. Fadhel headed to the Brigadier-General, Director of the Division, and advised him to call for all the officers working the surveillance room in the main building to fix the problem in the adjacent building's surveillance system, but keep his assistant, the Shadow Officer, in the surveillance room alone to watch the cameras dispersed through the main building.

As a result of that, the Brigadier-General ordered the surveillance room's staff to head immediately to fix the defect in the second building's surveillance system. The Shadow Officer remained alone in front of the screens, displaying the footage from the camera in cell number 12. Fadhel moved quickly to change his clothes that disguised him as a cleaning man. He assassinated President Al-Mukhtar with a lethal gas, then he turned towards the camera and his face showed. He finished the assassination and took with him the President's inhaler from the ground and returned his original inhaler on the bedside table and left the cell. He changed into his regular clothes. The Shadow Officer's mission was to keep the recording that Fadhel's face appeared on in a confidential location on the computer for a later time when Fadhel would come back to take it. He left the recording file with that part cut out of it in its obvious location on the machine. Fadhel's turn to the camera was intentional. He wanted to deliver the complete recording to Major-General Maher to let him know he had accomplished the mission himself professionally. As for the cut-out recording, it would remain for the 5th Division, hiding with it the killer Captain's face.

While Captain Fadhel was undertaking the mission and entering the cell, the Shadow Officer left the surveillance room, pretending to enter the restroom. He timed his exit with Fadhel leaving the cell. That was what the camera in the surveillance room itself recorded.

After a few minutes, the surveillance room staff returned to their duty station after fixing the defect in the adjacent building's camera system without noticing Al-Mukhtar's death as he appeared through the cameras to be fast asleep on his bed—until someone realized that the President had not been moving for a long time. At the same time, one of the guards near the cell noticed the President's unnatural situation and his immobility, and he notified the Directorate's authorities. When the news reached the Brigadier-General, he called Fadhel and went with him to the surveillance room to watch the recording from the camera in cell 12. The Brigadier-General and Fadhel watched the recording with two seconds cut out, hiding the cleaning man's face. The Brigadier-General left the surveillance room. He called for the Forensic Evidence Police and informed the Major-General, Director of the Intelligence, of what had happened over the phone.

Meanwhile, Fadhel convinced the Brigadier-General that it was necessary to take measures by surrounding the crime scene and warning the surveillance officers and other personnel from saying any word about what happened. The Brigadier-General felt the necessity of that, so he called the surveillance room staff to his room to warn them from disclosing what had happened to the outside until further notice, and to emphasize the necessity to keep the camera recording of cell 12 to help the Forensic Evidence Team see the last seconds of Al-Mukhtar prior to his death.

Meanwhile, taking advantage of the surveillance room being vacant again, Fadhel was heading towards that room to copy the original file and deliver it to Major-General Maher to confirm Fadhel had accomplished the task before completely erasing it, but he was surprised by the Hyena being there. So, he had him leave and closed the door, intending to return after he was sure the Hyena had left the corridor in order to not raise suspicions. He would copy the original recording, then erase it and leave behind the cut recording. However, he suddenly felt the possibility that the Hyena had seen the contents of the computer with the footage of the camera from cell 12 and the original recording; ultimately knowing the real perpetrator, especially that the Hyena had dangerous computer skills and was able to seek out the secrets on a computer, including the original recording showing Fadhel's face as the perpetrator. He hurried back to the surveillance room and quickly erased the cut recording, copied the original one, and then erased it too. Later, he accused the Hyena of erasing it to keep suspicion away from him and to destroy the recording that could incriminate him.

Fadhel felt that the Hyena entering the room was a great coincidence for him. Personal vendetta and keeping away suspicion were the two main reasons for accusing the Hyena of the crime and convincing the Director of the Intelligence of the Hyena's involvement in it. Therefore, he endured the trouble of chasing the Hyena and eliminating him using someone from outside the Intelligence without even Major-General Maher knowing about it. Two birds with one stone. Finishing the task perfectly and eliminating an adversary. And a third bird—keeping out suspicions.

But despite his cunningness in undertaking the mission, Fadhel did not know what the Hyena had done of thoroughly searching the computer, finding the original recording, copying it, and delivering it to the lawyer. Despite that, he felt he had gotten rid of the possibility of finding concrete evidence against him in the President's assassination case.

As for the Hyena, he too had his motives for behaving that way. He copied the recording and delivered it to the lawyer due to his likeness of Al-Mukhtar and feeling that the President had been unfairly removed from power. And then he was killed at the hands of Captain Fadhel, the officer with whom he has a long history of hostility. The Hyena saw Fadhel as a wild boar, wallowing in the mud to please his masters at the Intelligence Bureau no matter what they ask of him.

The Chevrolet and ambulance reaching their destination cut the train of the previous night's memories in Captain Fadhel's head. The two vehicles entered the Department while the police car stopped outside.

Chapter 28

The Intelligence's vehicles had just entered the Green Zone, bringing with them Professor Salem Jerjis. The vehicle carrying Jerjis entered alone into the presidential area and headed to one of the small bases where an important figure in the government waiting for the Professor.

The presidential Green Zone covered a wide area in Baghdad's Karkh, stretching from the Tigris River's west bank to Zawra Park to the north and the Suspended Bridge connecting to the Jadriya area in the south. It held the Iraqi Presidential Palace which was considered one of the most important and largest palaces in the Green Zone. It could be seen from the east bank of the Tigris with its bluish green dome. The US forces used it as their headquarters after invading Iraq in 2003. Next to it, a group of other palaces, including Sujood Palace, Sinbad Palace, Adnan Palace, and Conferences Palace were dispersed in the area, in addition to other important governmental buildings such as the base of the Chief of Staff and the Ministry of Defense.

The Green Zone was surrounded by an impenetrable wall of concrete blocks, explosive detection devices, surveillance systems, and elite forces to protect it. Some of the Iraqi landmarks had been enclosed within its walls, such as the Unknown Soldier Monument and the Grand Festivities Square, in addition to the Baghdad Clock that has become a base for the Supreme Federal Court of Iraq.

The Green Zone's buildings reflected the Abbasid architecture in their designs, as well as implicated the megalomania that had overtaken President Saddam Hussein, who built many palaces and monuments in that area. The Green Zone only had the Republican Palace and the Conferences Palace before Saddam came into power in 1979, but he built those large landmarks. One of the most significant landmarks President Hussein built that reflected his passion for wars was the Victory Arch on the Grand Festivities Square, which was composed of two crossed swords being held by huge bronze hands that looked like his hands with an Iraqi flag in the middle of their intersection. Below the hands of that arch, there were around 5,000 helmets from a similar number of Iranian dead dispersed for all to see. President Hussein had them brought in from the battlefronts during the Iraq-Iran war to be put under his giant hands so the Iraqi Military would parade over them on the 6th of January of every year. The Iraqi governments of post-2003 tried to remove that monument but Iraq and American organizations strongly objected; therefore, it was restored and the military went back to parading below it after the Iranian dead's helmets were removed.

Jerjis was entered into the base accompanied by the Intelligence officer. He was hosted while waiting for the person that called for him.

***

Meanwhile, strange preparations were happening in one of the Republican Palace's conference halls in the presidential area. That hall was being used for that particular purpose for the first time.

Everyone was waiting for six o'clock.

Chapter 29

The small base that Jerjis was in was not familiar to him, and it did not carry any official status or a sign indicating what it was, which made predicting who the person coming quite difficult for him.

Half an hour passed since the Professor arrived to that base in the Green Zone. He was offered two consecutive cups of tea during that time. He was watching the clock hung on the wall in front of him, waiting for the person he would be meeting. His mind wandered, trying to guess the reason the authorities would ask him to return to Baghdad so hastily and cut his participation in the Berlin conference. After he drowned in his thoughts, he returned to reality when two men in black suits entered. They opened the door leading to the small salon Jerjis was waiting in and stood, flanking both sides.

The Professor focused his gaze to the door in front of him, waiting for the authority man whose protection staff got in before him to enter the small base. A full-figured mid height man in sunglasses loomed towards the door. He buttoned his suit after he got out of the sedan that carried him. He arrived to the door and took off his glasses as soon as the roof dropped its shadow on him. The man appeared familiar to Jerjis. Major-General Maher Abdelfattah, Director of the General Intelligence.

As the Major-General reached the center of the hall in the small base, a courtesy smile to Professor Jerjis appeared on his face. The Professor got up, welcoming the absolute fiercest statesman. The Major-General launched cold words to accompany a quick handshake of Jerjis' hand. He sat close to the Professor after he unbuttoned his suit. He drew in a breath and exhaled.

"How was the trip to Baghdad, Professor?" Asked the Major-General while looking to his reflection on his shades in his hand.

"Fine. I'm used to the length of the way, Major-General."

The Major-General gave the two men at the door a look and they disappeared out of the small base, closing the door behind them. The Major-General put his shades on the table before him and looked to Professir Jerjis.

"Professor, you must be anxious to know why we've called for you."

The Professor nodded his head and the Major-General continued.

"A murder took place last night of a person whom the global political lights shine on currently. We need your usual patriotism to spare your country problems with other countries."

The Professor looked to the Major-General with eyes that wanted to draw out more words. The Major-General drew in a deep breath and continued.

"President Al-Mukhtar was assassinated last night!"

Professor Salem Jerjis felt the Major-General's words fall like knives penetrating his ears. The man's image before him slowed down and he sensed the sound of his heartbeat in his temples.

"Excuse me, sir?"

"Yes, Professor. You know many countries await the result of Al-Mukhtar's trial after they too, filed lawsuits against him at the Federal Court of Iraq regarding supporting terrorism and other illegal activities. We have to show the world that Al-Mukhtar died suddenly without having been assassinated; otherwise, those countries would accuse us of killing him to hide his crimes, and ultimately make us accomplices in their legal suits, which would put us in endless political crises."

"Have you identified the killer?"

"It doesn't matter. What's important now is that you perform an autopsy as a routine procedure, even before the government, and come out with a medical report that reflects our transparency in dealing with the case and confirm that Al-Mukhtar's death was of natural causes. Your international reputation will make it easier for the international community to accept the report you will issue."

Silence engulfed Professor Jerjis, who suddenly found himself in the middle of a complicated whirlpool of events. He wiped his hair with his palm, looking to the Major-General.

"Major-General, where is the body now?"

"Under strict surveillance at the Forensic Medical Facility. Professor, regardless of what the cause of death is, Al-Mukhtar died from a sudden heart attack."

Professor Jerjis nodded his head, feeling the ground spinning underneath him. The Major-General got up, buttoned his suit, and shook hands with the Professor who got up alongside him.

"Good luck in your task, Professor. You will be resting a little in a room in one of the nearby buildings before you head to work."

"Thank you, Major-General."

The Major-General turned his back to the Professor walking towards the door. The two men opened the door wide open and the Major-General disappeared under the winter sunlight outside.

An hour later, Professor Jerjis was staying in a small apartment at a nearby building inside the presidential area to get the rest that the Major-General promised him before heading to the Forensic Medical Department where an extremely complicated case awaited him.

Chapter 30

4:00 p.m. Baghdad time.

Exhaustion from thinking wore out Mahdi Al-Ali making him give in to a shallow nap on his couch in front of a table that had on it the mystery's threads alongside an ashtray with cigarette butts sticking out of them like random tombstones on grey soil.

The sound of his phone's ringtone snuck into his ears, bringing him back to consciousness from his nap. He opened his eyes and looked to the stage of depressing items before him. He reached for his prescription glasses, put them on, and looked to his phone's screen—it was Maha. He answered the call.

"Hello! Yes, Maha. Hi…"

On the other end of the line, Maha explained to her professor what she saw on TV.

The official TV channel announced that it would call the viewers' attention to the Ministry of Interior, which would shortly have an important press conference live in the presence of journalists and correspondents from news agencies and TV channels, but it did not disclose what the conference would be about. Maha asked him to follow the official channel to know what would be talked about in that conference. Mahdi finished the call with her and turned on the TV to the official channel, waiting for the events of that "important" conference.

The authorities will definitely disclose what happened.

Meanwhile, a large number of correspondents from TV channels, and local and international newspapers arrived to the location where the events of that conference would take place. However, all of them had never attended a press conference for the Ministry of Interior at that specific location. The correspondents were used to attending press conferences at the Ministry of Interior's Media Office Hall at the Ministry's building in the middle of Rusafa, but this time it was being exceptionally held at one of the Republican Palace's halls. Thus, the location of the conference to be held in two hours raised a lot of questions of what it would be about, in addition to the anticipation the media and viewers felt regarding it.

In his wood-walled room, the man in the elegant suit had just hung up his phone, leaning on his chair behind his desk. He reached for the remote control and switched the channel to the official one. He looked to his watch waiting for six o'clock.

Chapter 31

Baghdad, the large city that was the 3rd largest among the Arab capitals in terms of population, had not yet calmed down after the recent events that had stormed the country post the removal of President Al-Mukhtar and members of his government based on charges they were accused of. Some of Al-Mukhtar's supporters were still roaming the main streets and quarters demanding freeing their former President.

At the same time, often many countries that had accused Al-Mukhtar of supporting global terrorism, embezzling money and acquiring them illegally, considered themselves concerned with what the court would decide regarding those accusations, especially the United States, some European countries, and countries from the Far East, in addition to a number of international countries and other organizations. The Somalian pirates were but one of the cases those countries set against Al-Mukhtar. But all those parties would be disappointed whenever the Iraqi President's trial would go on longer without convicting him despite those countries and many entities providing evidence to the Iraqi court proving Al-Mukhtar's actual involvement in his illegal acts. Some countries and companies waived filing a suit in the International Court too, in case the Iraqi Judiciary was not transparent and conclusive enough during the trial.

As for inside Iraq, Iraqis were preoccupied with the polished recordings the official television was broadcasting of the ousted President's trial sessions. On many occasions, the streets were not clear from clashes between Al-Mukhtar's supporters and his adversaries. The Anti-Riot Police would end those clashes forcefully, which made the authorities impose a curfew at night at times in the cities that witnessed such events.

That evening, the television channels and local and international news agencies sent their best people from their offices in Baghdad to the Republican Palace, where the upcoming conference was to be held in a few minutes, and which the authorities called important.

At the same time, on satellite TV channels, millions of eyes in Iraq and the world gazed at the TV and the analytic studios of those satellite channels started preparing and setting up satellite calls waiting for the event. Among those expectant eyes were those of Mahdi Al-Ali, Maha the student, Professor Jerjis, and of course, the man in the elegant suit.

Chapter 32

5:58 p.m. Baghdad time.

While the world was watching, two adjacent squares appeared on the official channel. A young newscaster occupied the left one while on the right, there was a wooden podium with dozens of colorful microphones carrying the logos of local and international TV stations waiting for the speaker. To the back of the podium on the left was the Iraqi flag in its four colors, while in the back of the scene was a large oil painting that had been carefully painted.

"Dear viewers, we move to the Republican Palace to convey the press conference proceedings held by the Media Office of the Iraqi Ministry of Interior…" The announcer said that phrase in haste and disappeared with his left square giving way for the wooden podium to take up the whole screen.

Mahdi was sitting with his arms crossed looking to the screen. The oil painting behind the wooden podium carrying the Republican emblem caught his attention. He had seen that painting before with its large dimensions, curved from the top and squared from the bottom. The painting was not strange to him. Mahdi had seen what is known as the "Missile Painting" at the Republican Palace when he had attended the second anniversary of President Al-Mukhtar coming into the Presidency.

The Missile Painting carried a drawing of seven missiles launched into the sky, leaving around them heavy smoke. In the middle of the painting there was a large launched missile that had the Iraqi flag on it, the one from before 2003, while six others were to its sides, appearing farther from the large middle missile. In the sky, the sun rays snuck through a wall of clouds toward the destination of the missile heads.

By exactly 6 p.m. Baghdad time, 3 p.m. GMT, a man in a security uniform and a rank of brigadier-general took the stand. He adjusted his prescription glasses and greeted around 35 correspondents from various news agencies sitting before him. The world followed the first moments of the important Ministry of Interior's press conference while Mahdi's lips received a cigarette with its first breaths.

The Brigadier-General cleared his throat as he prepared to talk from the podium in front of the Missile Painting. He pursed his lips and adjusted his glasses again before starting to speak. A stinging silence engulfed the hall and the journalists' eyes and cameras gazed waiting for his words.

"I would like to announce to our people and those concerned with the Iraqi affairs in the world that the removed President, Mohammed Al-Mukhtar, has died last night in his cell under mysterious circumstances…"

A loud noise arose in in various languages in the hall. The Brigadier-General raised his voice and continued.

"We, as the Ministry of Interior in the country in cooperation with the Ministry of Justice, have opened a thorough investigation to discover how the accused died, but the preliminary evidence points to a natural death at this moment."

Mahdi was still watching. He felt President Al-Mukhtar had been subjected to injustice in his prison. The truth as he had seen it on the bullet film totally contradicted the Ministry of Interior's spokesperson's words.

He was like someone who wants to scream on a remote island where there were no ears to hear his screams no matter how loud they got. He felt like his soul had become like salty damp walls burdened by sadness and feeling of injustice. He was confident now that regardless of what he would do now to expose what happened, the world would not hear the truth's voice over the voice of the confident and facts falsifying governmental media. President Al-Mukhtar's sacrifice had been for nothing.

The spokesperson went on, "Therefore, I urge the citizens to have self-control regarding what happened and to not overreact until the final results of the investigation are released."

The Brigadier-General finished what he had to say. Hands were raised raucously to ask questions. He started answering some of them. Mahdi smiled half a smile noticing the Brigadier-General's unintentional body language like a mirror reflecting the amount of falsehood he was speaking of. He was evading looking into the correspondents' eyes directly, drinking water from the plastic bottle next to him at times or adjusting the papers in front of him at other times, and looking to the upper right corner, pretending to remember, while that corner meant turning to imagination to find an answer contrary to the left corner that indicated using memory. Moreover, the Brigadier-General went around the answer when responding to many questions without giving a satisfying answer.

Minutes later, the press conference ended with the Brigadier-General leaving the podium. The camera moved back, showing the back of the journalists' heads. It remained that way for a few seconds, busy with the journalists leaving the hall while the Missile Painting remained clear in the middle of the screen before broadcast ended with the young announcer coming on again, reiterating what the Ministry of Interior's spokesperson said in the conference to the viewers.

The man in the elegant suit switched off his TV with the remote control while still thinking of what Mahdi could find after this conference.

Chapter 33

Mahdi was at home following the reactions of the news agencies on TV and switching from one station to another. He noticed that most agencies had found it strange that the conference was held at the Republican Palace instead of the Ministry of Interior itself, while some stations replayed scenes from the press conference to comment on it.

Suddenly, a light sparked in Mahdi's head from what he had seen on the conference. He felt the sky had given him an idea that may be right to a great degree. He looked at his watch which was pointing to 6:30 p.m. where the sun's scale was leaning to setting.

He got up quickly and reached for his laptop. He opened his Facebook page and the messaging tab with Maha. He did not want to use the cellphone in case the call would be monitored. He sent his first message, hoping she would receive it as soon as possible.

- "Hello Maha!"

A few seconds passed without the text being delivered. The screen with its blue frame was reflected on his prescription glasses as he watched the chat square. Suddenly, a short grey text appeared below his message text: Seen.

He felt Maha's answer coming soon. He needed her to think and share what he felt after what he had been through in such a busy day. Seconds, and three grey dots appeared (...).

- "Hello, Professor!"

Mahdi smiled as he punched the keyboard's letters responding to her.

- "How is your mother now?" he wrote to her.

- "Fine. I gave her some painkillers and I'm finished packing her suitcase to travel to Turkey tomorrow for treatment. How are you after the conference?"

- "Thank God for her wellbeing. The conference, hmm, that's what I've contacted you for now."

- "Why? Has something cleared up?"

- "I don't know if what I noticed was intentional or by coincidence."

- "What is it?"

- "The location where the conference was held…"

- "The Republican Palace?"

- "Yes."

- "What could be strange about it?"

- "Maha, the painting behind the podium."

- "???"

- "Yes, did you notice it?"

- "I didn't pay attention well, but I remember the background was a large colored painting."

- "Maha, the point isn't in the Republican Palace as a location, but in choosing this hall in particular."

- "I don't get it."

Maha wrote that and waited for Mahdi to respond more thoroughly. He was late in writing his next message.

- "Look. The painting was drawn during Saddam Hussein's reign. It represents the Iraqi missiles the Iraqi forces launched on Israel in 1991 during the Gulf War."

- "Aha!"

- "The Iraqi forces launched 43 missiles then in bursts throughout the 43 days of war."

- "Yes?"

- "The Israeli – American made – Patriot missiles destroyed four of them before they reached their targets. That's what the global media said then."

Maha received the last message. She felt her professor's words strange. She was a little late in responding, then she tapped two digits on the keyboard and two exclamation marks:

- "39!!"

Mahdi smiled and responded.

- "Yes." he continued, "The number of missiles that hit their targets were 39 missiles!"

Maha sent a surprised sticker. Mahdi received it with a smile.

- "So, that was a new sign, Professor!"

- "Exactly, Maha. Think tonight of what that means. I will also try to find the link between these signs."

- "Okay. You have shocked me, Professor."

- "I'm also shocked. Try to find the solution."

- "Okay, I promise."

- "Good night."

- "You too."

The last message from Mahdi was seen by Maha. He closed his laptop's screen and clasped his fingers behind his head as he leaned back deep in his intertwined thoughts.

The Missile Painting hung in a square hall of 30x30 m2 and 7 meters high. The oil painting, with its square dimensions at the bottom and curved at the top, occupied the middle of one of the hall's walls. The painting was around four and a half meters high and two and a half meters wide. Facing it on the adjacent wall was another painting with the same geometric design and dimensions of the Dome of the Rock of Jerusalem in Palestine.

The marble floor stretched in the hall with geometric designs and a large flower with eight petals in the middle, and more complex embroidery. The hall had five wooden doors with golden embroidery spread as two doors to the sides of each painting, and a single door in the third side of the hall. Eight chandeliers hung from the hall's ceiling that had an octagonal shaped fold higher than the primary ceiling carrying meticulous brown and golden color embroidery. In turn, that fold had another higher fold in its center with a blue belt and Quranic verses inscribed in Arabic calligraphy in white. All those verses pointed to the punishment and history of the Children of Israel as mentioned in the Quran. Above all those levels of magnificent ceilings was a dome; inside it is a panoramic painting of the Rock of the Dome Mosque, again surrounded by rebellious horses on a background of sky.

Post-2003, the missile hall was a stage for important conferences, such as the Counter-Terrorism Conference in 2014, but it was not once used to hold a press conference for the Iraqi Ministry of Interior.

That evening, after the press conference on President Al-Mukhtar's death, Professor Jerjis had just gotten into a private vehicle that the Intelligence sent for him with a designated driver to transport him from the Green Zone to the Forensic Medicine Department in Bab Al-Mu'adham. The vehicle moved towards the gate of the presidential area leaving for its destination.

At the same time, Captain Fadhel had just finished handing the Hyena's body over to the Forensic Medical Department and headed back to the 5th Division in Kadhumiya where he would get some rest after a tiring day.

The man in the elegant suit left his wood-walled room and headed to his nearby residence.

Chapter 34

8:00 p.m. Baghdad time.

Wearing his special outfit for the autopsy room, Professor Salem Jerjis entered the autopsy hall accompanied by two dissectors sent by the Intelligence to help him perform an autopsy on Al-Mukhtar's body and keep the task confidential. The body was entered into the autopsy hall completely covered and tagged with the number 3297, with no indication on it of its true identity—just a number.

With him and the forensic team entering the hall, the door was closed behind Professor Jerjis and his companions who would help him remove the organs he decided to remove and perform lab tests on them. The Professor and the team were alone in front of a fully covered body except for the feet; the right one carrying the number 3297 tied to its toe.

The Iraqi Government had no knowledge of Al-Mukhtar's cause of death and was not involved in it. Therefore, the government was facing a hard test before the public eye to prove the real cause of the President's death. While Major-General Maher Abdelfattah, the only man who knew the minute details of what happened to him, wanted to perform an autopsy as a sound procedure before his country's government in addition to convincing the concerned countries and organizations that Iraq had performed a transparent and convincing autopsy with the help of world renowned Professor Jerjis, despite that Abdelfattah had already prepared a final report for the cause of death.

That night, the Forensic Medicine Department was possibly the most protected it had ever been. The building was surrounded by a number of checkpoints with heavy security presence. On the inside, the halls, entrances, and exits were planted with security and

Intelligence men with their various uniforms in that building that was already watched over by thorough surveillance cameras.

In slow steps, Professor Jerjis stood before the body of his biggest case. He looked to the team on his right and reached his hand to the cover over the body. He grabbed it from its end and removed it from its face.

President Mohammed Al-Mukhtar.

The body's eyes were still open looking ahead, while the glow of the lighting prism facing the body from above was shining its bright light on the details of its face. Jerjis looked closely into the body's eyes. Its pupils were clearly dilated. From the look of them, the puzzle of the President's death was forming its first pieces in the Professor's head. Jerjis, who was extremely experienced in his job, was able to identify the primary cause of the death from the general outlook of the body he was dissecting. He removed the cover from the body's chest with a pull of his hand. He started roaming with his eyes over its pores.

The professor reached his hand to the body and grabbed its hand. He started moving it carefully and felt it lignifying. He moved it harder and felt its resistance to his moving it. It was quite lignified.

The body was affected by rigor mortis, its lignifying was by the effect of ingesting toxic gases. This kind of body showed resistance to movement and if its limbs are moved more violently, the limbs could break and the joints shatter.

While he returned the arm to its place, the puzzle of Al-Mukhtar's death was still gathering its parts in the Professor's head. Jerjis put the primary cause of death as a secret between him and himself, and he finished the procedure to be perfectly sure that that was the cause.

He pulled his medical glove around his wrist and indicated to the forensic team to start opening the body.

"I want a blood sample. Then, remove the stomach, liver, kidney, heart, brain, and lungs."

None of the staff working at the Forensic Medical Department or the lab analysts could identify the owner of the body whose organs would be sent to them from the morgue. They would be dealing with number 3297 in total anonymity. They would run tests and send the results to the Professor without knowing that they are testing the organs of their former Republican President. Additionally, the Forensic Medicine Department issued various numbers on the organs of the bodies being dissected at the Department that night and whose samples would be tested to disguise the number the President's body holds.

As soon as the two dissectors finished their preparations, they opened the body's chest. Blood drops from the scalpel's route on its chest leaked. Professor Jerjis touched the blood drops. He smudged one of them and brought it to his nose. He felt the puzzle soon to complete forming in his head as a smell similar to the smell of bitter almonds seeped into his nose very clearly. He shook his head announcing to himself knowing the cause of death conclusively, but he did not say a word to the team, one of whom was busy opening the body.

***

Meanwhile, in his nearby residence, the man in the elegant suit was turning the pages of a book he held dear, because he knew that President Al-Mukhtar considered it his favorite book. He opened it to one of its pages that he had previously folded its corner and looked to the text in the middle of it. It contained four short lines stacked above each other like poetry in the middle of the page.

That text was surrounded by a circle of red ink like a marking. The man in the elegant suit read it for the hundredth time since he marked it with that red circle. He finished reading it, put a pen in the page, folded the book, and put it on the table that was before him. He grabbed his cellphone and started making a call to someone.

***

One hour after it started, the removal of organs of the autopsy of President Mohammed Al-Mukhtar was over. Professor Jerjis ordered the removal of those organs in addition to some other samples to send them to the lab for tests tagged with the number 3297. The lab analysts would work for hours to find out the cause of death, where those results will be sent back to Professor Jerjis to put a final report on the causes that lead to the death of the owner of body number 3297, while the Professor would come up with a report on President Al-Mukhtar's death that would completely not match with the results of the organs of the body carrying that number, but with the will of Major-General Maher Abdelfattah.

Meanwhile, Major-General Maher was in constant communication with the Director-General of the Forensic Medical Department to inform him of Professor Jerjis' status and the level of confidentiality of what he was doing. The Director informed him that the dissection stage and removal of organs and required samples was over and those outputs would be sent to the lab discretely, while Profssor Jerjis would spend his night at the Department's building under heavy surveillance.

Chapter 35

7:00 a.m. Baghdad time.

That day was one of the Spring break days in the Iraqi academic year which allowed Mahdi and his students to remain, just as other professors and students across the country, with no attachments to a work schedule. Additionally, Baghdad was witnessing a slow traffic day since there was no movement of students who were numbered in the hundreds of thousands in the capital.

Mahdi opened his eyes on his bed quietly. He did not move a muscle. He was lying on his back looking at the ceiling. He did not want to get up from bed. He felt the bitterness in his mouth after all the cigarettes he smoked the day before. Engulfed in a sticky silence, he started recalling the nightmare he saw of the President opening his eyes from his death.

Everything will collapse.

Despite that, he had deep clarity of mind and his ability to think was better than ever. He recollected his scattered thoughts around number 39. He floated above his sporadic thoughts like scattered clouds in the middle of an Iraqi spring blue sky. He was listening to the bird chirps on his shaded window that reflected the outside like mirrors. He was used to waking up to those birds every morning, those naïve birds pecking the window as they see their images reflecting on it. The recording that he received in the form of a bullet in an envelope went before his eyes. He remembered everything.

Captain Fadhel, the inhaler, Al-Mukhtar's admirer, the 5th Division…

He cleared his head again and those images faded like dust on wood the wind has suddenly swept away. He turned to his left breathing the air out. The flashing blue light from his cellphone caught his attention. He immediately got up from his bed and took his phone and glasses, putting them on and unlocking the phone.

A new message.

Mahdi was wishing that it was from Maha telling him she found the link connecting the pieces of the puzzle so he would call her and hear it. He truly wished that.

Struggling with his fear on the one hand and his curiosity on the other, he opened the messaging app.

His phone had received a message from an unknown sender. No number.

He touched the message while his heart went on throbbing rapidly again. He opened it…

It was four short lines stacked above each other like poetry in the middle of the screen. Mahdi's irises jumped over the words, then the lines.

At night the last one will be strangled in his bed

For he became too involved with the blond heir elect.

The Empire is enslaved and three men substituted.

He is put to death with neither letter nor packet read.

Mahdi stood still. He felt his thoughts exploding in a conic shape with that message as its launching point like the big bang.

At night… the last one will be strangled in his bed…

In a flash, the image of Al-Mukhtar dead on his bed and the number 39 on the cell's wall appeared before him. He caught the sound of one of the communication devices the security men and forensic team carried at the cell's door that night. He recalled the sound of his shoes tapping on the deaf concrete floor of the corridor in the 5th Division.

Strangled…the last one…everything will collapse…Mahdi!

He is put to death…with neither letter…nor packet read!

The world got distorted in his eyes. His earlier clarity of mind shattered into flying fragments. That message blew up his thoughts like a reckless shell would blow up a wall of cork.

The blond heir elect…

Three men substituted…

He closed his eyes and collapsed onto his bed.

Meanwhile, the man in the elegant suit entered his wood-walled room starting his new day.

What would Counselor Mahdi Al-Ali be thinking now?

***

That morning, the organs of body 3297 were spread on the test labs at the Forensic Medical Department while Professor Salem Jerjis was forced to finish the task without leaving the Department's building.

Chapter 36

At night the last one will be strangled in his bed...

Mahdi reread that text ten times. A text from an unknown sender approaching with its words what had happened to President Al-Mukhtar.

Attempting to decipher its code, Mahdi read the words to the end.

The blond heir elect...

The Empire is enslaved...

Three men substituted...

The alleys of his thoughts were all dark, ending in a deaf wall of questions.

That morning, Maha was on her way to meet with an Iraqi Airways plane. Her mother was ready to go to Turkey to have a shoulder joint replacement operation for her narcosis affected joint, paid for by a grant from the Ministry of Health. Maha's cousin would remain with her mother on her treatment trip while she stayed in Baghdad working on her graduation paper.

In an hour and a half, her mother would be on a plane headed to Ataturk International Airport while she would be headed back home in her small car.

The strange text that Mahdi received added to the mystery in his head. Its language was strange and mysterious like the castles from the middle ages. It did not seem like rhymed poetry or a previously heard prose.

He is put to death neither letter nor packet read...

As was in that text, as the deceased President's lawyer, Mahdi had not received from the Intelligence any messages or belongings from his inheritance after his death. He was not informed of anything about him. His curiosity peaked wondering what Al-Mukhtar may have left for his lawyer that the Intelligence denied its deliverance to him. He thought of appearing in the media as the President's lawyer to tell them what he had, but he knew the Intelligence was closing in on him from all sides. Any uncalculated move could cause him a disaster. He did not even answer his friends and colleagues' calls since he found out about the President's death. Their curiosity pushed them to talk to Mahdi about Al-Mukhtar's death to ask him personally about what had happened to him, but they did not get an answer to their calls.

At the same time, Mahdi heard his conscious calling him every time he remembered President Al-Mukhtar in his dream yelling:

Everything will collapse...

Like he was asking him to move to save something that would collapse and no one else can stop its collapse although he had no idea what that something might be. In addition to not understanding Al-Mukhtar's mysterious phrase in that dream, the text message from the morning added to the mystery of everything that had happened to him and left him fighting in the middle of a whirlwind of surging thoughts.

He considered contacting a colleague from the university to include him in the whirlpool of thoughts that he had fallen into and dragged Maha into as well, but his fear of making things worse stopped him from contacting anyone, even those close to him. All he was left with was to call Maha again. She was the person who would keep his secrets deeply hidden. He grabbed his phone and made the call. Her phone rang while she was on her way home.

"Hello!"

"Good morning, Maha! I hope you're alright."

"Good morning, Professor Yes, I have just dropped my mother off at the airport. She's waiting for her flight to Turkey now."

"Ah, good," he did not want to open the subject on the phone, "can we meet?"

"Sure. Where do you prefer?"

"We'll meet at Palestine Street, Beirut Square, and then we'll decide where we'll sit."

"Alright. I'll be there in 15 minutes."

"Perfect, thanks. Bye."

Mahdi hung up the phone and prepared to meet Maha to discuss the latest message.

In the wood-walled room, the man in the elegant suit was browsing the internet checking the reactions of the news agencies to the Ministry of Interior's press conference that the Iraqi television aired last night. The death of President Al-Mukhtar was on the front pages of many local and international newspapers, while internet sites were also busy discussing the case and reporting on it.

He felt bored following the electronic news. They were all the same. He closed his laptop screen and took a sip of his coffee.

***

In Beirut Square, Mahdi Al-Ali was standing on the pavement across the bridge passing over the square. A few minutes later, right on time, Maha parked her car in front of him and asked him to get in. He got in and felt the warmth inside the car. Maha's attractive Nina Ricci perfume seeped into the depth of his lungs.

"Good morning," Mahdi exhaled.

"Good morning, Professor! Where shall we sit?"

"Just drive."

Mahdi asked Maha to stop her car at a parking lot near the square itself. They got out of the car, heading towards a nearby recently opened coffee shop. They sat at an isolated table. The coffee shop was designed similar to old Baghdadi coffee shops: the wooden seats, fifties songs, and black and white photos covering the walls were iconic of that place that was almost empty from customers at such an early time. They sat across from each other at that table.

"Maha, have you thought about the symbol?"

"Yes, hard and long. Unfortunately, I got nothing to connect all those symbols."

"Hmm, okay...I asked you to meet up because I have received a strange message this morning from an unknown sender with no number."

Maha looked to him with surprise and curiosity at once.

He took out his phone from his pocket and opened the message he recently received. He handed her the phone and her eyes jumped over the words, then the lines.

> *At night the last one will be strangled in his bed*
>
> *For he became too involved with the blond heir elect.*
>
> *The Empire is enslaved and three men substituted.*
>
> *He is put to death with neither letter nor packet read.*

She knit her brows as she read it twice.

"Professor, does this look familiar?"

"What do you mean?"

"I don't know, but I've read something similar before. I mean something with this kind of writing."

"Like what?"

"Hold on a second, please."

She took out her smartphone and connected to the coffee shop's Wi-Fi. She entered the first words of the text in the search engine's bar.

At night the last one will be strangled in his bed.

The search circle appeared requesting to wait, then the search results…

"What's there?" Mahdi asked.

"As expected!" Maha turned her phone's screen and pushed it forward to her professor.

Search results: The book of centuries…Nostradamus…New York… Nostradamus' prophecies…Two great rocks…Smoke at the center of the world…

Mahdi was shocked at what he was reading. He scrolled down and kept reading.

"Professor, when I read the text, its style reminded me of something I read a while back. Indeed, I've read some of Nostradamus' prophecies not so long ago on the internet and remembered them as soon as I read this message," Maha said.

Mahdi focused his gaze on the phone. He chose the first output in the search engine's results where words of the text Maha searched for were in grey. He opened the webpage. It was a page of an Arabic website that had the book of centuries' quadruplets with an explanation of the prophecies. He looked through hundreds of texts for the text he wanted.

Maha got up and sat to his side following his search with him.

The quadruplets had the same numbering as the book of centuries written by Nostradamus predicting the coming world events. Under each quadruplet was an explanation of the prophecy it carried or confirmation of that prophecy having come true and the event that is believed the prophecy had meant despite having been written hundreds of years before their happening.

Mahdi scrolled down, passing over the hundreds of earlier prophecies. The Prophecies book that was printed in 1569 had 400 prophecies divided into four hundreds. The first hundred quadruplets started with the number 1 and ended with 100, then the second hundred followed the same sequence, and so on. It was said that around 80% of those prophecies had come true, while 20% remained a mystery.

Mahdi finished the page of the first hundred quadruplets without finding the required text. He started going through the second hundred looking for an explanation of the prophecy he received its text this morning from an unknown sender.

The tenth prophecy…

> *A coffin is put into the vault of iron,*
>
> *Where seven children of the king are held…*

Mahdi scrolled to the following texts.

The 22nd prophecy…

> *A thing existing without any senses*
>
> *Will cause its own end to happen through artifice…*

He scrolled more looking for the text of the message he received… it might solve the puzzle.

The 37th prophecy…

Shortly before sun set, battle is engaged.

A great nation is uncertain.

Overcome, the sea port makes no answer,

The bridge and the grave both in foreign places.

This was not what he was looking for either. He passed on to the next prophecy, and it too was not what he wanted, so he passed on again and the text appeared...

At night the last one will be strangled in his bed

Because he became too involved with the blond heir elect.

The Empire is enslaved and three men substituted.

He is put to death with neither letter nor packet read.

Mahdi and Maha were shocked to see the prophecy's sequence number...

Number 39 appears again...

this time from the book of *centuries.*

Chapter 37

That morning, Professor Salem Jerjis was still at the Forensic Medical Department under heavy surveillance. He felt as if he was under house-arrest. He would not be able to move until the lab results were back. The testing of President Al-Mukhtar's organs would take approximately 72 hours after their removal to say the least. That, if the labs worked all their efforts to come up with the results and deliver them to him. Major-General Maher Abdelfattah's calls to the Director of the Department had not stopped since last night. He continued to follow up the Forensic Medicine's course of action in terms of the autopsy of President Al-Mukhtar, and, of course, to check up on the Professor's course of action.

Mahdi was extremely shocked to find out that the prophecy he received on his phone this morning was prophecy number 39 of the second hundred of Nostradamus' book.

"Let's read the explanation of the prophecy. It may lead us to something," Maha suggested.

Mahdi agreed with her and started reading the prophecy's explanation of what has come true of a historical event believed to be what Nostradamus had meant by his 39th prophecy.

The 39th prophecy – Explanation:

"The death of Louis Bourbon of Condé 1830:

The last Condé, Louis, was found dead, strangled one night in 1830, but not in his bed. He was hung from the ceiling of his bedroom. It is possible that he was murdered for his support of the case of Duke of Bordeaux, Count of Chambord, whom Nostradamus described as truly elected because he was Charles X's grandson and heir to the French throne. As for the three who usurped power, they can be explained as the three systems that followed Charles

X, Louis Philippe, the Republic, and then the Bonapartes. Or the quatrain may more accurately refer to the three men who plotted against the Condé family, Charles X, Duke of Angoulême, and Duke of Bourgogne. Le Peletier said that Condé was blond and he had written a will in favor of Duke of Bordeaux. It is said that that will was replaced with a former one written in favor of Duke of Aumale, son of Louis Philippe who became king in 1830."

Mahdi finished reading the text aloud. He could not find a link between it and the current events, and so could not Maha's eyes as she intently.

"I didn't reach anything that has any connection to what's going on," Mahdi sighed.

"Me neither. I think the puzzle isn't in the explanation, but in the number."

"Damn it! It's a sick game!"

"Go back to the prophecy. Maybe something in it explains why it was chosen by the sender."

"OK, let's think about it one hemistich at a time."

Mahdi read the first hemistich of the text.

At night the last one will be strangled in his bed...

He looked to Maha who said, "It's clear. The President was killed by suffocation as we saw in the bullet recording."

"Precisely." Mahdi replied.

He continued reading.

Because he became too involved with the blond heir elect...

"Hmm, did the President ever talk to you about an heir to rule after him, for instance?"

"Never. The republican system in the country does not pass on as you know. Besides, Al-Mukhtar hadn't married until he died. This is not about inheriting power but something else I'm not sure what it is."

"Maybe someone close to him whom Al-Mukhtar prepared to rule after him?"

"No, I don't think so."

"OK, let's move on to the next part and see," Mahdi said and continued, "the blond heir elect."

"Hmm, the blond," Maha replied deep in thought.

"Yes, I don't know if that indicated something or the text was sent to me because the key lies in another phrase of it," Mahdi pondered.

"Is there something else that the word blond may refer to?"

Mahdi delved into the depth of his thoughts looking through its alleys before floating back to their surface again. All he found in his mind again was...absolute vacuum.

"I haven't the slightest idea." He said while rubbing his eyes from under his glasses.

"Fine, what's the next phrase?" Maha asked.

"The Empire is enslaved and three men substituted," Mahdi went on.

Maha was at loss as well listening to those words. Was the message sent only to reference the number 39 again or did it have another meaning? It had to mean something. The first hemistich carried the details of the President's death by suffocation which confirmed that the remaining hemistiches of the prophecy must have some meaning.

"Which empire could be enslaved? Didn't you tell me that the President used to call Iraq 'the Land of the Sun'? Iraq had consecutive empires in the past, from Assyrian to Babylonian reaching to Abbasid when Baghdad was the capital of the largest empires at the time. What do you think?"

"I don't know, Maha. Besides, who would enslave it?" Mahdi answered with exasperation.

"That's the question."

Mahdi went on, "And who are the three men? The new system in Iraq does not allow individuals to rule the country as before. The system has become parliamentary since 2003."

Maha leaned on her wooden chair. "Stop thinking like this! Let's get something to drink now."

Mahdi switched off the phone's screen and took off his glasses. "I'll have coffee. What about you?"

"I'll have the same."

Mahdi called the waiter while thinking of the confusing puzzles that had confounded his mind for two nights.

***

On the other side of the world, a strange movement was taking place in the stock and currency exchange markets. The economic media was buzzing with reports of the rapid decrease in most of the stock markets, a growing number of clients withdrawing their money and trusts from banks, and talks of economic problems, while some American banks were suffering from insolvency, which is what happens when the clients' liabilities are more than the assets.

That was the first step for those banks towards *bankruptcy*.

Chapter 38

After meeting with Maha, Mahdi took a cab back to his home in the Zayouna neighborhood. She also went back to her home when the sky started pouring rain down on Baghdad.

Mahdi felt the situation becoming more serious with every sign he received. He had to find a real connection among all those signs that would help him reach what he needed to know exactly. He recollected the signs in his mind: the number on the cell wall, the number of the repeated Quranic verse on the trial tape, the Missile Painting and the number of missiles it contained, and Nostradamus' 39th prophecy.

He lit up a cigarette and opened his phone's messaging inbox again to read the prophecy message.

What made it stranger for him was that some of the prophecy's text was quite similar to the events that faced him and it carried that number at the same time. The puzzle had to be solved. He put aside his phone to get some rest and escape what he was in. He grabbed the remote control, switching the TV on.

His cigarette's smoke filled the place.

While flipping the channels, a red ticker at the bottom of one of the channels caught his attention. It was a breaking news regarding the financial crises that had begun to take place in a number of countries. He did not care for that news as his legal specialty did not oblige him to follow the stock and exchange markets. He was not interested in that anyway despite the fact that his father had been an economic expert and an advisor of economic affairs to the President; but he did not care much for economics.

He pressed the remote control's buttons again flipping through several channels. Another flash news stopped him.

A rapid increase in the global prices of gold due to an increase in demand.

That breaking news was at the bottom of a screen displaying images of printing US 100 dollar bills to accompany the aural economic report. Despite not caring for economic affairs, Mahdi felt that the financial news was taking up more space than usual on the various channels today. His curiosity had him turn the volume up and listen to some of those reports.

At that time, the economic problem had started to exacerbate in most of the capitalist countries and was sure to cast its shadow on the economy in other countries because, for instance, the US Dollar was greatly tied to the economy of most countries. Therefore, any problem facing it would also inevitably affect the economy of those countries, especially business within the countries and gigantic companies that made transactions in US Dollars and European Euro primarily, followed by other currencies such as the British Pound and Japanese Yen consecutively.

In turn, the man in the elegant suit was in his wood-walled room following the news with great interest. He flipped through the TV stations, listening to their updates. His laptop was also displaying on its browser several windows of economic websites with interests in currency exchange and the status of the market.

He wondered again, *what would Mahdi be thinking now?*

Meanwhile, Mahdi spent an hour following economic news with interest for the first time in his life. He noticed the successive news on the rapid increase in the prices of gold and platinum in the global markets despite the slight differences between the former and current readings of those prices, while the indicators on the screen were indicating clear fluctuation in the exchange rates of main currencies.

Mahdi did not understand what all the media fuss was about. Out of curiosity, he reached for his phone and called a colleague from the university, Dr. Husam Mohammed Saleh, Professor in Economic Sciences at the Faculty of Administration and Economy at the University of Baghdad. He and Mahdi had been tied by the bonds of colleaguesmanship and friendship for some time now. Mahdi wanted to understand what was happening on TV with the aid of his colleague.

Dr. Husam's phone rang showing Mahdi as the caller.

"Hello, Doctor!" Mahdi exclaimed, happy to speak to an old friend.

"Ah, hello, Professor Mahdi. How are you?"

"I'm well. It's been a while since we last met."

"Indeed. Say, Professor Mahdi, where are you now after the news of the President's death?"

Mahdi felt at unease by Dr. Husam's question. He did not want to talk about that over the phone.

"I'm around and fine. How about yourself?"

"I'm fine. Professor Mahdi, I want to understand more about Al-Mukhtar's death. Tell me about it."

"Yes, Doctor, the President is dead and the investigation is ongoing. This would be a long conversation; leave it for another time."

"As you like, but I'll discuss it with you for long when we meet. I don't buy what the Ministry of Interior said about his dying of natural causes according to the preliminary investigation, but..."

"Doctor, please!" Mahdi interrupted, letting a tone of anger seep through his voice, "I will explain that later." he went on, "I wanted to ask you about something new in light of your expertise in economy."

"Ah, of course. You'll surely ask about the recent economic news." Dr. Husam said jokingly.

"Yes, how did you know?"

"Because you're the third colleague so far who has called me to ask about this."

"Of course, it's a curious thing, Doctor! Tell me, what's going on the economic scene? I'm a lawyer; my specialization and knowledge do not equip me to understand what's going on."

"Don't worry, Professor Mahdi. This is the beginning of a financial crisis that may happen soon. This happened a few years ago and the world overcame it, but be certain that it's a passing thing. Besides, we're so far from all of it. Our economy won't be affected."

"Would you clarify it more for me, Doctor."

"Professor Mahdi, when some countries and companies get affected by a financial crisis, it is often made up. Bank clients rush to withdraw their trusts and safeguard them somewhere else, other than banks. Those banks suffer a cash flow insolvency and start taking loans from other entities. Currency fluctuates between going up due to the high demand, and going down due to the lack of trust in it. To ensure the value of what they have, people turn to buying gold since it's the only thing able to preserve its value, but the high demand on it raises its price."

Things started clearing for Mahdi. "Ah, the picture is clear now, although I don't know how this crisis started."

Dr. Husam replied laughingly, "Oh, Professor Mahdi, all I could advise you now if you lived in those countries is to turn your money into gold immediately."

"Alright, I'd do that when I'm there."

"Yes, gold. Mother Nature, my friend."

"Alright, Doctor. I'm grateful for your valuable information and promise to meet soon."

"Certainly, but it won't be an economic meeting. This time I'll grill you about what happened to the President."

"If God's willing, Doctor. I promise."

"Well, Professor Mahdi, rest assured of the country's economic situation."

"Thank you, Doctor. Goodbye."

Mahdi hung up the phone and thought about what Dr. Husam said about the recent crisis. The phrase 'mother nature' stuck in his head.

He remembered President Al-Mukhtar's long conversations about his obsession with the economy. He was often doubtful of the global economy which was how he justified his actions of acquiring revenues from various sources, including the illegal ones, in order to face any possible financial crisis with a huge reserve of foreign currency and gold.

Suddenly, he remembered the letter Al-Mukhtar had given him in one of their meetings in his cell during the trial. At the time he told him, "You'll understand what I wrote here in the right time."

Mahdi felt he had to read the letter again. The President's economic obsession may have had something to do with the current crisis.

He moved towards his wardrobe and took out the envelope containing the letter Al-Mukhtar had given him and made him promise he would not show it to the public until the right time. At that time, Mahdi did not understand what 'the right time' meant. He still did not understand it. He took the letter out and started reading its first part.

Just as before...

It's going to happen once more...

Bellies will be inflated...

And many necks will be hanged...

What Babylon had minted will be minted again...

And cotton will turn into ashes...

People will displace...

And the rich will flee the despotism of the hungry...

Life will turn on the doer not knowing what he has done...

My love...

You will realize how right I was...

For doing what I did...

To live how we want...

At a time when everything is collapsing around us...

Relentlessly...

Look within yourself for salvation...

I have thrown you the buoy...

So hold on to it tightly...

Don't reach your hand for it before it's time...

That it would turn into a gallows noose...

Nor too late...

That everything would be over.

Mahdi read the text admitting to himself the difficulty in deciphering its code, but something about it reminded him of what the President had once told him. A spark in his head brought him back to one of his meetings with Al-Mukhtar in his cell. The President told Mahdi that day that he had done what he had to in order to protect the country's future from an imminent economic danger. The President told Mahdi exactly what he had done...exactly what he had hid...

What Babylon had minted will be minted again...

And cotton will turn into ashes...

Inspired by that memory, Mahdi quickly moved to his phone and opened Nostradamus' prophecy message that he received this morning. He read it again.

At night the last one will be strangled in his bed

Because he became too involved with the blond heir elect.

He freaked out as it all became clear before him. The senders of the message were looking for what the President had hid to save the country—the reason they suffocated the president in his bed.

They are looking for the blond heir elect...

They are looking for...

Gold!

Chapter 39

9:00 p.m. Baghdad time.

She finished a hot wintery shower and came out from among the steam particles pushing through the shower room's door, wrapping her hair and body in pink towels. Maha stepped towards her room with her youthful body to get dressed. She hummed her way into the room and carelessly glanced over her research papers scattered on the bed. She was stopped by the scene of her laptop that she left on the bed with its black screen after going into screen saving mode. She took off her slippers, sat on the bed, and stretched out her legs on it. She grabbed her laptop and moved the curser. The browser window appeared on Facebook as she had left it. She looked to the messages icon that was indicating a new message received.

She crossed her stretched out legs on the bed putting her laptop on her thighs and opened the messages.

Mahdi Al-Ali (1)

She clicked on the inbox messages box and opened it.

- "Maha, I've solved the puzzle."

Mahdi had sent her that message after he had reached a theoretical solution to the puzzles that had kept him up for nights. Maha smiled feeling a push of relief by her professor's new message. She started typing on the keyboard.

- "Really? Tell me."

The message was not seen for a little while. Mahdi was busy re-reading the President's letter, much of which was still completely mysterious. He was trying to decipher the meaning of the words Al-Mukhtar had written in his cell while the ashtray in front of him filled up with the cigarette butts he had been burying in it one after the other. Ten minutes passed since Maha sent her message without a response from Mahdi who was busy away from his computer.

Suddenly, Mahdi's phone rang. He turned to the table facing the couch and to his phone. It was Maha.

He reached his hand to his phone but the call ended. He knew Maha was nudging him to let him know she was on Facebook. He had told her earlier to limit the use of phone with him except when necessary since he believed his line was tapped, or to call without talking about Al-Mukhtar's case and the developments that followed.

He got up to his laptop which he had left on the facing couch. He opened his hibernated laptop and received Maha's message on Facebook's chat box.

- "Hello, Maha!"

Maha, who was anxiously and curiously waiting for him, responded.

- "Hello, Professor! Tell me what you were able to understand."

- "OK, Maha. Have I told you before about the President's letter that he had left with me?"

- "No, you haven't."

- "Well, Al-Mukhtar had left with me a letter in his handwriting and told me that the time would come and I would understand what he had written in it."

- "Yes?"

- "He had made me promise not to show it to the public until it was time."

- "What's in the letter?"

- "A mysterious letter that I read and remembered what the President had done during his reign and what he was persecuted for."

- "Okay?"

- "Al-Mukhtar had told me what he had hid to guarantee the country's future. It's the thing they're looking for."

Maha responded curiously.

- "Have you solved the prophecy or what?"

- "Yes. The blond heir elect is what the entities playing the game of symbols want. I understand what that means."

- "I don't understand anything. What does the number 39 has to do with all of this?"

- "Okay, I'll tell you what I understood."

Mahdi started explaining to Maha what he was able to understand from all those confusing puzzles.

- "Look, Maha. The entities that killed Al-Mukhtar, painted the number 39 on the cell wall, sent the disks with the repetitions, set the press conference in front of the Missile Painting, and sent the prophecy message, they used all of that drawing attention to the number 39 to indicate something."

- "What is it?"

- "What I understand is that they wanted to point to the global entities that would raise the global economic problem which Al-Mukhtar was preparing to face."

- "Aha."

- "And as you know, supporters of the conspiracy theory always blame the global crises on the global Freemasonry."

- "Right." Maha wrote as things started to clear up for her.

- "And in the minds of many, Israel is one of the hands of Freemasonry. Whether that's true or not, conspiracy theory always ties Israel to Freemasonry, especially in the minds of Arabs, despite the fact that the movement gathers many nationalities and religions around the world."

- "Exactly."

Mahdi went on.

- "They placed the number 39 on those puzzles to point to Israel. Despite the Arab wars with Israel which Iraq has participated in all, the most prominent historical connection between Iraq and Israel was Iraq hitting it with 39 missiles. Then, they emphasized the idea by showing the Missile Painting."

- "Hmm."

- "They wanted to tell me that 'the Freemasonry' represented by Israel and the entities controlling the world would make up a global crisis. Then they sent Nostradamus' message to point to what the President had hid to save Iraq from that crisis."

Maha was shocked by the explanation Mahdi has come up with.

- "Right on, Professor! Excellent explanation."

He continued.

- "They purposefully sent the prophecy that points to the blond heir elect, which is what the President had hidden. They think I know where it is."

- "What is it?"

- "Gold."

- "Gold?!"

- "Yes, Maha. President Al-Mukhtar had hidden tons of gold. He told me about it but never where. Instead, he gave me a mysterious letter."

- "You mean the letter you have?"

- "Exactly." He went on. "The code has to be deciphered to know where the gold is, but I don't know whose hands will get it if we found it."

- "Why haven't the entities chasing you with their puzzles asked you about the gold's location directly instead of going around sending those puzzles?"

- "That's what I couldn't get. Not to mention that the governmental media has never spoken about the gold Al-Mukhtar had hid although they've been looking for anything to indict the President."

Maha felt that a piece was still missing.

- "Hmm, I don't get that. They could interrogate you and tell the truth. And how can tons of gold reserve as you said disappear from the eyes of the country's government?"

- "Maha, Al-Mukhtar was certain the gold would turn up in the right time. I don't know how he felt that."

- "When's the right time?"

- "I don't know." Mahdi responded, "He told me to show it to the public in its right time, and from what I understand, the global financial crisis is the right time for the gold to turn up. That's what I understood from one of my economist colleagues. Although he assured me our economy will not be affected, gold is the savior, but is this the crisis, or not? I don't know."

- "We were unfair to Al-Mukhtar when we accused him of embezzlement and money laundering." Maha replied, "He did it to save us."

- "Exactly, Maha. Look, we'll meet tomorrow. It's necessary."

- "Sure. I'm quite curious to read that letter."

- "Fine. Sorry to bother you."

- "Not at all, Professor! I'll call you tomorrow."

- "OK, goodbye."

- "Goodbye."

Mahdi closed his laptop and went back to following the economy news again while Maha reread the chat with her professor to better understand what he said.

Chapter 40

At midnight of that night, Mahdi opened the President's letter again and reread it. He finished its second and last part.

Three men save the empire...

A first did...

A second carries the first's secret...

And a third unveils the curtain...

Follow the souls of the living dead...

In a blue tomb...

Standing on pillars of souls...

In the first marble pillar...

In the forty-fourth brick...

The second stands carrying a homing pigeon.

What ended the letter on its lower left corner was Al-Mukhtar's handwritten signature.

Mahdi felt that the second part was too complicated and difficult to analyze and decipher. He read it over and over without reaching the shore of realization of the President's meaning of that part, but his main focus was on the first line of that text.

Three men save the empire.

As soon as Mahdi read that phrase, the prophecy message he had received on his phone resurfaced on his mind.

The Empire is enslaved and three men substituted.

A big resemblance.

Al-Mukhtar left an almost impossible puzzle to solve. His doubts over a question that was stuck in his head increased…Is this really the crisis Al-Mukhtar had anticipated? Mahdi remembered the words of his colleague, Dr. Husam, about the crisis…

Our economy won't be affected.

He wondered if he had to wait more before searching for the missing, or the moment of quest has come.

He looked at the letter again.

A first did…

A second carries the first's secret…

And a third unveils the curtain…

He felt that that chain would not be easily found. He wondered if the President had meant by those men real men, or it was just metaphor for something else?

In the midst of that mental mess, other questions circled his thoughts.

If the gold was found after the code was deciphered, who will put their hands on it?

Why did Al-Mukhtar not admit to the court what he had done and hid?

Why did he not explain what he had done before the court?

Why did he not tell anyone of the gold's location?

He felt his head grow like a balloon about to explode from all those questions.

He wanted to recall everything that had happened to him since his phone rang that night with a call from the Palace when a man, who introduced himself as Captain Salam, asked him to go out into the street and get into the SUV. He roamed in his thoughts of his meetings with the President at the inauguration anniversary and the President's relationship with his father, the advisor. He passed through the alleys of those memories like an archeologist excavating for antiquities that extended for the ten years of President Mohammed Al-Mukhtar's reign. His thoughts steered him towards his conversations with his father regarding the governance and his position as Advisor to the President.

Mahdi's father was loyal to Al-Mukhtar and a skilled economist, but in the last three years of his life, he suffered from a suffocating isolation after his wife, Mahdi's mother, passed away in a car accident. He focused his all on his work as Advisor to the President during the day and looked for a companion to spend his evenings in warm conversations with. Mahdi sensed his father's loneliness, so he would set a quiet sitting area in the house's garden sipping tea with his father and talking about his most favorite topic: the economy. Although Mahdi felt his ideas and inclinations far from his father's economic inclinations, but he would talk with his father about it because he knew how much he loved talking about such topics.

Remembering those nostalgic nights with his father brought Mahdi back to his conversation with him one night when his father told him about the first Minister of Finance in the first Iraqi government, and what he had done for the country of establishing an independent and durable economic system. Mahdi still remembers that conversation in detail. His father told him about the Iraqi economy's shrewd first Minister of Finance, Hasqil Sason.

Sason was an Iraqi Jew. On 13 August 1923, during the monarchial rule, he was assigned to be a negotiator with the British on the concession of the Iraqi – Turkish oil company, which was a British company. What Sason had firmly decided then was that Iraq's payments of that company's revenues of the sold oil should be in golden shilling. Despite the British's objections to that, Sason insisted on adding the phrase "of gold" in the contract and made the British submit to his demand. Thus, Iraq's share was paid in golden shilling instead of the British paper currency, which supported the country's economy greatly due to the gold's consistent value after the British currency's value fluctuated during what followed that era of events.

Gold. Mother Nature, my friend.

That phrase Dr. Husam Mohammed Saleh came back to Mahdi's mind again after he remembered his conversation with his father about Hasqil Sason. President Al-Mukhtar was right in all he had done.

Mahdi recalled some of the cases made against Al-Mukhtar during trial. In addition to the case of supporting the African pirates, there were many other cases. One of which was the seizure of quantities of gold from the country's Central Bank treasury. Al-Mukhtar implemented that operation in cooperation with his Intelligence masterfully. After that, it was announced that an investigation had been opened into the matter to silence the public. Then, Al-Mukhtar declared that Iraq had to cover the shortage of gold in the bank treasury as a result of that robbery by buying enough gold with Iraq's foreign currency. He wanted to exchange the foreign paper currency into gold bought from abroad in a way that would not raise the global organizations' suspicions about what Iraq was doing. He used that as an excuse. If Al-Mukhtar bought the gold directly from the global market, some organizations and countries would have noticed Al-Mukhtar's suspicious move and his questionable collection of gold. Therefore, he seized some of the bank's gold and hid it, then he publicly bought more gold with the excuse that the country's treasury was robbed of its gold, which made what he did beyond reproach.

That insane operation Al-Mukhtar pulled off, and which talk of later faded away with his government's promises of capturing the perpetrators, was one of the actions that translated his worry of the upcoming global crisis, and it was what the Public Prosecution raised against him in court.

The President wanted the gold and the money he would later replace with gold as soon as possible and in any way, as there was another nightmare chasing him. The nightmare that some major countries in the world were seeking alternative energy sources instead of oil, and since oil was the main source of Iraq's yields, those countries finding other energy sources, such as the Cold Fusion technique and shale oil, would allow them to dispense of the global oil, which Iraq's oil constituted a large portion of, bringing the country huge amounts of money. Hence, Iraq's yields would decline causing its revenues to decrease. Therefore, Al-Mukhtar wanted to do the impossible to make use of the world's need for Iraq's oil currently and secure the country's future with a reserve of gold that could be invested into establishing non-oil revenues in the future before the day came when the need for Iraq's oil diminished or ended.

He was extremely masterful—not just in how he collected the gold, but also in how he hid it to the point where no entity had declared knowing what he had done until now. All Al-Mukhtar had left was a code of cryptic symbols and phrases that had to lead to finding that treasure that no one seemed to know much about except those who were trying to point Mahdi's attention to what the President had hidden, and who seemed to believe he knew the secret to finding it.

That is what Mahdi understood from his monologues that night. He was wallowing in prickly thoughts. Those thoughts were cut when the 80's Baghdadi clock in his salon rang declaring the time to be one o'clock after midnight.

Chapter 41

9:00 a.m. Baghdad time.

A black Jeep Cherokee had started to trace lines in the street where Counselor Mahdi Al-Ali lived, going back and forth ever so slowly with two unknown individuals riding it. It seemed like a patrol car with a black antenna sticking out of its surface and bending with the SUV's movement.

That morning, as per usual, Mahdi made himself a cup of morning coffee and placed the President's letter on the kitchen table glancing it at thoughtfully as he moved about his kitchen.

Follow the souls of the living dead...

In a blue tomb...

Standing on pillars of souls...

As he was sipping his hot coffee he has just made, his cellphone rang. He sighed a breath of relief as it was Maha.

Mahdi's focus on the second part of the President's letter made him forget his plans with Maha whom he agreed with to come to his house today. He put on his glasses to better see her name on the screen and answered.

"Hello! Good morning, Professor! I hope I didn't wake you."

"Hi Maha! No, I'm awake."

"Well, may I come over now?"

"Ah, of course. I'll be waiting."

"OK, I'll be there in 20 minutes."

Mahdi hung up and put back the first part of the letter with the other placing it in his pocket and waiting for Maha to come so he could tell her what he was able to interpret from the cryptic letter and what was still difficult for him to crack so far.

That morning, the first reports of the lab tests of the organs of body 3297 started reaching Professor Salem Jerjis. Their results matched what he had deduced in his mind as the cause of President Al-Mukhtar's death as soon as he had seen the body that night. Nevertheless, it did not matter. The report had already been prepared in advance under orders of Major-General Maher Abdelfattah.

In his wood-walled room, the man in the elegant suit was still following the fallout of the global financial crisis. What was expected started happening; the U.S Dollar's value rapidly decreased as a result of that crisis while the gold kept on rising insanely to reach figures that seemed would soon be...a record.

When Maha's feminine car reached the street where Mahdi's house was at in Zayouna, the black Jeep Cherokee was watching her car stopping in front of Mahdi's house. Meanwhile, the air around the Cherokee bore communication signals the black SUV has sent to some entity letting it know of the details of what was happening on the street of Mahdi's house.

Maha got out of her small car and rang the doorbell. The Cherokee was still watching as it continuously passed through the street. Mahdi came out and welcomed her, and the two went inside.

"Keep watching and observing."

That was the last phrase the two men in the Cherokee received... in English.

Maha sat on the couch facing Mahdi who took out of his pocket the first paper of the letter.

"I think I was right in my analysis this time."

"I'm so eager to see the letter," Maha responded.

Mahdi put on the low table a piece of white unlined paper with writing in blue ink. Maha looked at it and took it.

She was curious looking at the murdered President Mohammed Al-Mukhtar's handwriting, who had left a treasure for his country and kept it to save it, or rather was murdered to keep it until its right time.

She drew in a deep breath and said after she finished reading the first paper: "OK, tell me what you have figured out."

"Read me the letter and I'll tell you what I understood of it," Mahdi said.

Maha started reading:

"Just as before, it's going to happen once more," she looked to her professor.

"Yes, Maha." Mahdi said, "He means the financial crisis. A similar crisis, the Great Depression, took place in the 30's. That crisis caused major global economic disasters. It happened again in 2008 but to a lesser degree. Here, he noted that it would happen again. That's what I understood from these words."

"I believe you got that right, Professor," Mahi continued. Mahdi nodded in agreement.

"Bellies will be inflated, and many necks will be hanged."

Mahdi lit a cigarette. "Maha, there are causes behind every financial crisis. Don't think that those crisis happen without hidden hands manipulating them. My father had told me some information about that. The goal of creating a crises is to benefit very powerful global organizations and control the global economy. As for how powerful those entities are, well, they can even control the decisions of superpowers. Of course, as soon as they accomplish the crises they wanted, their fortunes would multiply, and that's what Al-Mukhtar meant by 'bellies will be inflated'. As for the broke small bank owners, as a result of such crises, they would pay their clients all they have and go bankrupt, which would leave them with one of two options: either borrow from those powerful entities, or go bankrupt. Some of those bank owners commit suicide, or have lawsuits brought up against them and they'd receive judgements. This is what Al-Mukhtar referred to with 'hanged'."

Maha was looking in astonishment to her professor who told her all that information with the aid of what has clarified of the President's letter and his conversations with his father during those nights. She absorbed Mahdi's words and went back to the letter:

"What Babylon had minted will be minted again and cotton will turn into ashes."

Mahdi smiled remembering a conversation with the President once when he told him exactly what he had done. "The President trusted gold more than paper currency, Maha, no matter the source of that currency or the power it holds. He means the return of gold as a source of power. What Babylon had minted was the metallic currency…gold, silver, and copper. He is referring to the return of dealing in metals such as gold and silver because the ancient Iraqi civilization was the first in history to use the metallic currency instead of barter to buy and sell products. Here he is hinting to the return of dealing in metal when the paper currency turns to ashes."

"But why did he call the paper currency cotton specifically?" Maha asked.

"Simply because it's not made out of paper, but cotton." Mahdi responded.

Maha gaped as she tried to gather what her professor was saying. Her curiosity made her continue reading the letter:

"People will displace and the rich will flee the despotism of the hungry."

Mahdi blew out the smoke from his cigarette. "In short, Maha, chaos will take over the world if this crisis is what Al-Mukhtar had meant. People will look for something to assuage their hunger after the value of their money hits rock bottom. The Arabs once said 'I am astonished by he who does not find a loaf of bread in his home and does not go to the public wielding his sword,'"

Maha felt the seriousness of what is happening. If it is true that the current crisis is the beginning of the collapse of the global economy, that would be a distinguished disaster.

She returned to the letter and continued.

"Life will turn on the doer not knowing what he has done."

She looked to Mahdi. She felt the lump in his throat when he heard that phrase.

Mahdi exhaled, "The President wanted to keep the secret deep. He did not want to save himself from the trial and the new government by telling them exactly what he had done. He knew he was going to be the victim."

Maha pursed her lips sorry for his words about Al-Mukhtar, and got back to reading.

"My love…

You will realize how right I was…

For doing what I did…"

"To live how we want…"

"*...at a time when everything is collapsing around us...*" Mahdi interrupted.

And together they said, *"relentlessly!"*

Mahdi leaned and said, "He's talking to *Baghdad!*"

***

The driver of the Jeep Cherokee was looking at his watch while watching Mahdi's house. He was bored of his task, on which a more patient colleague of his was accompanying him. He raised the car's stereo and they started listening to American country music while Baghdad's sky seemed to resume yesterday's downpour.

The two men did not notice that a security camera fixed on the wall of a nearby house was recording their car's movement and its constant stationing in the street. In Zayouna, and some other neighborhoods in the capital, it was natural to see security cameras above houses pointing their lenses towards their outer fences and gates as a precaution against robbery, but that specific camera was doing an entirely different task.

Chapter 42

"Look within yourself for salvation...

I have thrown you the buoy...

So hold on to it tightly..."

Maha was still reading the President's letter passionately and waiting for her professor's interpretation of the text Al-Mukhtar chose.

"The President is hinting here," Mahdi said, "that the gold he is hiding is in Baghdad itself. Look within yourself, Maha. Baghdad is not a small city. The quest will be difficult."

"Professor, the President didn't give you any hints when he told you about the gold? Any places? Any persons?" Maha wondered.

Mahdi replied confidently, "Never. The letter in your hand is all I have received from him about the gold."

Maha looked back to the letter and resumed reading.

"Don't reach your hand for it before it's time that it would turn into a gallows noose, nor too late that everything would be over."

Mahdi put out his cigarette and said angrily, "How can we tell when is the right time?"

He drew in a deep breath and continued, "He wants to find it at the time when gold would be a savior, not too early and not too late. He described finding it before it's time with a gallows noose, and finding it late is clear. The collapse would have totally destroyed the country's economy. But what collapse? When? The current one or another? I don't know!"

Maha nodded her head imagining the sizeable responsibility the President had laid on his lawyer. Thoughts and questions crowded her head.

How did Al-Mukhtar hide the treasure from the state's eyes?

Where did anyone who had been helping him hide it go?

"Professor, there has to be others who know where it is because one person alone cannot do all of that."

Mahdi took out the second paper of the letter from his pocket and presented it to Maha. "This might answer your questions."

Maha looked at the second part of the letter. The President's handwriting was still talking on the paper before her. She looked at the text aligned on the paper like poetry and read.

"A first did...

A second carries the first's secret...

And a third unveils the curtain..."

"Who are those three?" she wondered.

"Whoever they are, they need to be identified. I assume the first is the President himself as he did the whole thing. As for the second, there are some cryptic details about him in the remaining text. Go on."

She looked at the paper and went on.

"Follow the souls of the living dead...

In a blue tomb...

Standing on pillars of souls..."

"Did you get anything from that?" Mahdi said.

Maha did not respond and continued in her voice.

"In the first marble pillar...

In the forty-fourth brick...

The second stands carrying a homing pigeon."

She looked to Mahdi, feeling completely fused with the President's words. "How could a tomb be made out of marble pillars and that many bricks?" She asked.

Mahdi got up and he, too delved deep in those words.

Maha resumed, "Professor, you said Al-Mukhtar had hinted that the buoy, which you have interpreted as gold, is here in Baghdad."

"Exactly. Look within yourself for salvation!"

She asked again, "Do you know anything about a blue tomb in the capital?"

Mahdi roamed his thoughts. "Maha, the cemeteries in Baghdad are few. As you know, the major Iraqi cemetery is in the Peace Valley in Najaf Governorate. Rather it is one of the largest cemeteries on the face of the earth."

"And if you would think of those few cemeteries in the capital," said Maha, "Al-Mukhtar may have buried his treasure in one of those or nearby one of them."

Mahdi stood still in place, having an epiphany. He sat before Maha, "Do you think Al-Mukhtar, by blaming it on conspiracy theory, wanted to tie the treasure and English Cemetery in Baghdad?"

Maha was shocked by that thought. It could be right, that the President tied his treasure to the English Cemetery! But there was no blue tomb in that place.

The cemetery of the bodies of the British Forces' dead was in Waziriya area in the middle of Baghdad on Rusafa side. It held the remains of more than 2,000 English, Polish, Indian, Sikh, and Muslim soldiers who passed during the British operation in Iraq during

World War I. Among them also were a few Turkish soldiers who had fought alongside the British Empire against the Ottoman State that Britain was in war against. All those soldiers of different nationalities represent the Commonwealth Forces that fought against the Ottomans and took Iraq from under their occupation that had lasted for four centuries. The British Forces were able to enter Baghdad in March 1917. In the middle of the cemetery, rises a three meters high landmark in the form of a grey dome. Under its shadow stretches the tomb of Lt. Gen. Frederick Stanley Maude, the leader of the British campaign in Iraq who was killed by the cholera on 18 November 1917. That disease was not kind to him and his forces, as not the Iraqis were during the British occupation of their country.

Among all those thoughts about the English Cemetery, Mahdi and Maha were thinking of the possibility that Al-Mukhtar meant that cemetery by burying a secret in it, but that would not be gold probably. One could not mess with that cemetery easily, it being an exposed location with nothing separating it from the passersby except a metal fence. Moreover, the British Embassy watched the cemetery very closely and took care of its upkeep. Therefore, anything like that the Embassy would consider an act of sabotage and it would cause a media raucous, which is the last thing Al-Mukhtar would want to happen while keeping his treasure. Additionally, the Turkish Embassy was just across the street from the place, which made the area special and surveilled. It seems the Turks chose that place for their embassy to raise their flag on its building so it is facing the cemetery of yesterday's enemies, the British, as a form of proof of existence despite that a near distance, in Bab Al-Mu'adham area, is the Turkish dead cemetery which held the remains of about 32 soldiers. Turkey surrounded their cemetery with an elegant iron fence, and white alabaster pathways stretched between their tombs starting from a gate with a sign carrying the phrase "The Turkish Martyrs Cemetery" next to the Turkish flag.

"That cannot be the English Cemetery," Maha proclaimed, "Al-Mukhtar is clear in his words. A blue tomb. The English Cemetery does not have any colors other than the grey landmarks and white tombs."

"I don't know why I feel he meant it, Maha," Mahdi murmured.

Maha looked back to the letter.

Follow the souls of the living dead…

"*The living,*" that word stuck in her mind. In Islam and its Holy Quran, the verses asserted that "who is killed on the path of God is alive and well."

"It's an Islamic martyrs' cemetery, Professor," she asserted.

"How?" Mahdi asked anxiously.

"The dead can't be living unless they are martyrs as in the Quran. Al-Mukhtar referred to the dead as the living, and he often quotes Quranic verses as we saw in the trial. He is a strong believer in the Quran," Maha replied.

Mahdi knit his eyebrows, "Possibly, but there are no outstanding martyrs' cemetery in Baghdad. The wars' martyrs have been buried in various cemeteries in the country."

Maha looked closely to the letter again.

In a blue tomb standing on pillars of souls…

She remembered one of her school trips when she was a kid. She revisited those memories that had not been erased from her mind to date. She closed her eyes and shook her head thinking of the surprise she had seen.

"Professor, Al-Mukhtar was masterful in painting words…"

"How?" asked Mahdi, still bemused.

"He means the *Martyr's Memorial!*"

Chapter 43

On the other side of the world, the banking panic has spread widely in the United States. People started rushing to the banks like crazy to withdraw their money after one bank declared bankruptcy and news followed of the stock market crashing.

Television channels did not stop following the decline of the US Dollar value in the US and some other countries that are directly tied to it. One of the biggest news was the announcement by the US Federal Reserve System a.k.a. "the Fed" of its intention to reduce the interest on its loans drastically to avoid the disaster that may happen as in 2008 when the Fed tried to raise the interest a little and it erupted a financial crisis that made it reduce it again to almost zero.

"I'm sorry, my friend. I was wrong. Our economy will be affected if things kept going like this."

Mahdi received the message from his colleague Dr. Husam Mohammed Saleh who had assured him yesterday that the national economy would be fine and here he was apologizing for his wrong assessment.

Mahdi felt his nerves tense up after reading that message and he told Maha about his call with Dr. Husam regarding the current economic crisis and what the message meant now. Maha felt herself lucky to witness such a battle that would define the country's fate. A tinge of excitement to look for Al-Mukhtar's treasure ran through her blood.

"Professor, it's time to move."

Mahdi shook his head, "Who guarantees that this is the right moment to start looking?"

"Professor, Dr. Husam seems certain now of the seriousness of the situation. I think we should go to the Martyr's Memorial immediately and look for what the President wants us to look for." Maha responded.

"Not before I meet with Dr. Husam first, Maha." Mahdi replied.

Maha felt disappointed by what he said but she also needed to know precisely what was going on around the world.

"Will you tell him about the secret?"

"No way, Maha," Mahdi gasped, "but he will notice my interest in the economic aspect this much. I have to convince him that it is just curiosity."

"Fine, I'll help you out of this problem."

"How?" Mahdi inquired with surprise.

"Professor," Replied Maha, "Dr. Husam works at the Administration and Economy Faculty, which is a separate building from our university. He won't know I'm your student. Tell him I'm a student at the Faculty of Administration and Economy at the University of Mustanseriya and need the expertise of a professor at the Faculty of Administration and Economy of another university to prepare a research on the global economic collapse."

Mahdi laughed from the heart at her words, "And if he asks you about your economic information, counselor? I will not defend a lazy student such as yourself."

Maha laughed and said, "Leave it to me, Professor. Let's call him."

A few minutes later, Mahdi finished his call with Dr. Husam asking to visit with him, to which he received an agreeable response mixed in with his usual humor.

In his wood-walled room, the man in the elegant suit was pacing the room back and forth after hearing the morning economic news.

The nightmare is about to happen.

He moved to his hard pine-wood made desk. He picked up the phone and made a short call before hanging up. "Mahdi has started moving."

***

After the January rain calmed down, Maha's car left behind Mahdi's home street, transporting Maha and Mahdi out of Zayouna and into the main Palestine Street. The two did not notice the black Jeep Cherokee with an antenna on its roof following them.

A few seconds after he hung up the phone, the man in the elegant suit received a phone call. He nodded, listening, and then hung up. He grabbed his cellphone and made a call feeling extremely nervous.

Chapter 44

Dr. Husam Mohammed Saleh's house was in the Jadriya neighborhood in central Baghdad. It was one of the neighborhoods close to the Tigris in the capital's Rusafa. The icon of this neighborhood was the main compound of the University of Baghdad, the country's largest university with its famous arc that does not meet at the top designed by German architect Walter Gropius in 1957 to symbolize that science and knowledge are unlimited.

As soon as Maha's tires hit Palestine Street heading toward Jadriya, the Cherokee disappeared into another route while something small under Maha's car's rear tire cover was flashing red intermittently.

After Maha's car got closer to the University of Technology intersection in Karada towards Jadriya, a yellow cab started following them closely. The two in the car did not notice that the cab was after them.

In Major-General Maher Abdelfattah's room, the phone on his desk rang with a call from the Director of the Department of Forensic Medicine. He answered the call and felt relieved that the sham procedures of the autopsy of President Al-Mukhtar's body were almost over.

He would soon announce to the world that the President died as a result of a sudden heart-attack and close the curtain on this case, especially that the world would be preoccupied now with the mess of the banks and some of the superpowers falling one after the other due to the current financial crisis.

Somewhere in Baghdad, a heavily-built blond man received a call over a special device telling him that the target was heading west in a small feminine vehicle. He was ordered to continue watching the signal coming from the tracker with the red flash stuck underneath that car.

That man was Scott Oziling, the head of one of the private security companies in Baghdad. He was a forty-something American with a muscular build and a blond goatee. He has a tattoo of a tiger face on his left arm that seemed as if it was protruding out of his arm due to its high 3D drawing quality.

Waiting for an update on the information he received regarding Mahdi's direction, Oziling got up from his desk to make himself a protein shake. Behind his desk was a black sign, with an image at its center that appeared to be a copy of the tiger tattoo on his arm, and below it was the phrase "Black Sand" in English.

Black Sand was considered one of the most horrific private security companies in the world. It had thousands of mercenaries dispersed all over the world having strong bodies, highly trained, and armed with light to medium weapons, in addition to their armored vehicles and small Bell Huey helicopters. That company provided its services to governments and persons all over the world in exchange for hefty amounts of money. Black Sand's mercenaries carried various nationalities, but it was an American made private company.

In Iraq, the new Iraqi Government that came into power after ousting President Al-Mukhtar used Black Sand to protect powerful persons in the country. It was done under an agreement between some persons in the Iraqi Government and the Council of Representatives with that company to pass a law to use Black Sand in exchange for getting a commission of the money paid to the company by the Iraqi Government.

It was a pure financial corruption, in addition to pressure by American entities on the Iraqi Government to allow that company to provide its services in Iraq after President Al-Mukhtar was removed from the country's helm.

Maha rang the bell to Dr. Husam Mohammed Saleh's house waiting with Mahdi and carrying some papers and a pen in hand to pretend that she was a student seeking information for her graduation research. Dr. Husam received them at the door with his wide smile and let them in while the cab passed in front of Dr. Husam's house conveying what was happening to the entity that had sent it on its mission.

Meanwhile, the security camera fixed on the house across from Mahdi's house was still watching the street and, in particular, Mahdi's house. It noted the Cherokee's return to the street again and its low speed.

Chapter 45

Mahdi and Maha immediately felt the warmth as soon as they walked into the guests' reception room at Dr. Husam Mohammed Saleh's house. Mahdi looked to the classic furniture in the room that had not changed in the years he has known Dr. Husam. It looked like a retired English general's house with its fireplace and a mummified deer head hung on the wall. His white spotted with black cat, Tara, was sleeping by the fireplace close to a rocking chair Dr. Husam used.

The two sat on a couch facing Dr. Husam's rocking chair where he left them by themselves and entered the kitchen. Husam lived alone in his large home after his two sons immigrated to a European country while his wife traveled to see her sons at their invitation to visit.

As soon as Dr. Husam returned to the room, Mahdi and Maha smelled the Arabian coffee he made for them. His calm smile assured Maha, who was feeling strange in the unfamiliar place.

"Well, Professor, you said your student needed assistance," said Dr. Husam as he presented the coffee to them.

"That's what I called you about, Dr. Husam," Mahdi reassured, as he started to prepare his answers for his pretense.

"What's your name?" Dr. Husam directed his question to Maha. She answered him shyly. He then said to Mahdi, "Where do we start now, Professor?"

"Um, Dr. Husam, think of it as I am the student and want to understand the economic collapse well," Mahdi mumbled.

Dr. Hussam laughed from the heart. "Fine, my friend. I will explain it to you."

He drew in a deep breath and went on. "We have to understand that what's going on is not a coincidence. Those who own the money industry can destroy it for their own reasons, of course. What we are on the verge of the end of the currency era, and the rule of farms and metals."

"Farms!" Mahdi exclaimed.

"Yes," answered Husam explaining, "if you have a small farm, it may keep you alive when the paper currency turns into ashes."

Mahdi remembered the words from Al-Mukhtar's letter:

What Babylon had minted will be minted again…

And cotton will turn into ashes…

"Go on, Doctor," said Maha, pretending to write what Husam was saying in her papers.

Dr. Husam spoke again, "Let's start from the beginning. Since the human race used the barter system, some ancient civilizations, like the Iraqi civilization, used gold, silver, and copper as coins to buy goods and services. Because people feared their gold may be stolen, one of them invented an impenetrable safe to keep the gold of those people. In return, he gave them contracts and bonds to guarantee their right to the gold they entrusted him with. From there the idea of paper currency came to be and it became an easy and successful alternative to using gold. As such, the idea of banks and depositing valuables in exchange for bonds and currency spread. Up to this point everything is fine until the hands of those aspiring to enslave people extended to the money. It started in Middle Ages Europe, and specifically, Frankfurt, Germany."

Mahdi and Maha looked to each other and Dr. Husam went on.

"That was the beginning of the conspiracy when 13 of the largest gold and silver tradesmen started working for Mayer Amschel Rothschild's bank, the Jewish family, and they decided to impose their control on the natural and human resources of the whole world by uniting their fortunes as a singular financial power. They schemed and set up the liquidation for anyone who stood in the face of their devilish project, aiming to enslave people through economy. It happened after the Jewish moneylenders found themselves facing the historical discontent of the European governments. As stretching from the 13th century, those governments forcibly deported them for their moneylending activities, which they had been practicing on others and on the poor Jews themselves, too."

He took a sip of his coffee and resumed.

"Let's go back to Rothschild and his family. The Jew, Amschel Moses Rothschild, had a son named Mayer Amschel whom he trained on money exchange and finance. He died when his son was 11 years old. The son started his career as a clerk at the banking firm of Simon Wolf Oppenheimer, proving his merit in everything money exchange related, which made the owner of the bank make him a partner in his bank. He soon returned to Frankfurt to run the financial institution his father had left him. As for the name Rothschild, he gleaned from the red shield that was hung above the institution during the father's time, so he decided to use that shield as a name for the family as Rothschild in German means the red shield. Thus, it became the Rothschild family."

Husam went on explaining when Tara jumped onto his lap.

"Mayer Amschel had five sons who, with their father's training, became geniuses in finance and economy. One of them was 21 years old when his father sent him to England to take charge of its economy. That was Nathan Rothschild. As for his father, he met in Frankfurt with 12 of the richest to join their wealth and establish a single economic group that would have the effect of causing economic problems for the benefits of those hands."

"Only 12 men?" Maha asked.

"Yes, Maha. You will find out what those men did."

Husam continued.

"Rothschild's control was imposed over France after he and the 12 men agreed on a plan that would end up giving them control over France economically by maneuvering their combined wealth, which would cause disturbing and critical economic circumstances where unemployment would spread widely in France. Thus, the blame would fall on the King, the Royal Court, the Noblemen, and the factory men, in addition to the bought fifth column who would work on spreading fear and chaos and then come out demanding rights and revolting against the authorities. Then suddenly after the revolution, people would find themselves with total freedom, which would allow for the class tendencies within society.

That atmosphere would allow the conspirators to put their hands on the economy. As for the new rulers, they would have no choice but to borrow from those rich to revive the rickety economy. This, of course, would be through money sharking which would be applied by those conspirators with their wealth against those young governments, which in turn would make them under the mercy of those rich, with Rothschild at their forefront."

Mahdi was taken by Husam's explanation. "But Doctor, didn't that government feel that messing hand despite all it had done?"

He laughed. "It did, my friend. Queen of France, Marie Antoinette, received a letter from her sister warning her of a conspiracy being planned by the larger bankers but Marie did not believe that. She was not convinced that Freemasonry in France could deliver her head to the guillotine."

"Freemasonry?!" said Mahdi in surprise.

"Freemasonry was closely tied to the Rothschild family and those with them. Some of the most important weapons of that movement throughout its history were economy, media, and military power. Therefore, Marie Antoinette's mistake in estimating the power of Freemasonry in France did, in fact, deliver her to the guillotine after the Freemasons vilified her on the one hand, and starved the French on the other by maneuvering their huge wealth, so the French people revolted on Luis XVI and his wife, Marie Antoinette, and destroyed them in their French revolution."

"But the French," Maha broke in, "were free after that revolution and they respect it greatly."

"That's right, but that freedom also served the conspirators, too. In fact, it was their freedom to control peoples' fates as the governments that formed after the revolution found themselves enslaved to the rich bankers who provided their services as saviors of the new economy while they clenched their fists on it." Dr. Husam replied.

"So," Mahdi mused, "France was their first victim."

"And Britain followed." Dr. Husam said, "After Napoléon Bonaparte swarmed Europe and declared himself an emperor, Nathan Rothschild divided his four brothers over Europe to control the economy of the European nations. They made Switzerland their base; hence, Switzerland remains neutral to this day. Have you never wondered why Switzerland never took part in any war to day? And why the most important banks in the world set their headquarters in it?"

Mahdi and Maha exchanged surprised looks while Husam continued.

"The biggest gain for Rothschild and those with him was the trade of wars. They incite it between any two powers with a similar level power for financial gain and to drown the nations with debts and then take hold of them through their money. They controlled the weapon factories, ship making industry, mines, steel ovens, and others of which are used in making weapons. Do you believe that what destroyed Napoléon's army was not Russia's coldness? It was cutting supplies on his army by the invisible system. They were able to force him to leave the throne in the end. They destroyed Napoléon's army with a network of their agents, whom they used to spread disorder and chaos in his army, which is something that not even the strongest armies would survive. They worked on both fighting sides at the same time as they create wars and extend them to the level that would fulfil their greedy whims and then stop them whenever they wanted and however they wanted."

Mahdi writhed uncomfortably in his seat, "And what happened with Britain?"

Husam answered him, "Nathan Rothschild, who was in Paris, used two networks of agents. The first was working on finding out the results of the battles Napoléon was having against the English Army. That was the Battle of Waterloo. The second was in the UK broadcasting the news that Nathan Rothschild would send to there. When Nathan was certain of the English Forces' victory, he sent the inverted news to England and spread the rumor that their forces had been defeated. Terror overtook the English and the financial markets crashed hard. The Great Britain Pound's value declined to a single shilling. Then, Nathan moved to England in a small ship and bought everything that could be bought: bonds, lands, stocks, and property. He and his partners. When the real news of England's victory reached it, the prices went back to normal and Rothschild and his partners made unbelievable profits. Within three years of conspiring against France and Britain, the Rothschild Family fortune reached around six billion USD in various currencies. In fact, it was rising at an annual rate of 7%, which is an unbelievable record figure compared to the dollar's value at the time."

Mahdi and Maha were shocked by what Dr. Husam was saying. He went on.

"To celebrate that victory, the Rothschild Family lent the English Government 18 million GBP to restore the havoc the war with France had wreaked. When Nathan Rothschild died, he had total control of the English banks."

"Professor," Maha exclaimed, "you are a strong believer of the conspiracy theory!"

Dr. Husam laughed and got up carrying his cat towards his glorious library. He passed his fingers over a number of books lined on the shelves. He turned to Mahdi and Maha.

"It is possible to falsify history for two, three years, but it cannot be falsified forever. In front of you is a book, half of which was written by Americans, English, and Chinese—all of whom agreed that it was one conspiracy, and it is as I explained to you."

He let go of Tara and went back to sitting before Mahdi and Maha. Mahdi lit up a cigarette and his eyes narrowed as he asked, "What happened after the UK's economy fell into their hands?"

Husam sighed. "Their next destination was America when Rothschild's partners met with Benjamin Franklin, the scientist and American politician. At that time, Franklin attributed the American Colonies' thrive to the Americans issuing their own currency themselves commensurate with keeping their economy. That information caught the attention of the Rothschilds, and the aim was to draft a law that would prevent the American Colonies from issuing their own currency. That was possible because America was still a dispersed state under the British colonization, which Nathan Rothschild had just seized control of yesterday. At the same time, Mayer Amschel Rothschild was still in Germany providing Britain with German mercenaries for 8 GBP per soldier. His influence was enough to issue the required law to control the American economy. Thus, the American paper money became practically worthless, so the American Colonies had to deposit money and guarantees in the Bank of England that was already controlled by Rothschild to obtain the currency it needed. Discontent in America started exacerbating among Americans due to the new system, but few of them realized that the expensive taxes and economic sanctions placed upon them were by invisible greedy hands that had taken control over the British Treasury."

Mahdi felt Husam's words like water quenching the thirst of the land of his curiosity.

"After the independence of America and the declaration of George Washington as its president, the armed clashed between the British and the colonies' men started. The struggle that lasted for seven years, the money sharks had pledged to fund it. They made tremendous profits by supplying the British Government with German mercenaries until the British Army surrendered and America officially declared its independence in 1783. The only loser was the British people. The national debt grew huge, which paved the way for the British Empire to be dismantled at the hands of the money sharks.

As for young America, the money sharks established what they called the Federal Reserve System as a private bank and a supporter of keeping the issuance of currency in the hands of the elected government, but in reality, it was doing the exact opposite. The Fed's capital was 12 million dollars; 10 million dollars borrowed from the Bank of England while the American rich contributed the remaining two million; and here America went back into the hands of the money sharks already in control of the Bank of England." Dr. Husam continued his explanation.

"But that was not enough for them. A few years in and they clenched their hands on what was left of the American Treasury. They bought what is worth 250 thousand dollars to go back into their property, too, making the whole American Treasury in their hands. Later using their influence in the Congress, they banned the Bank of America from issuing its own currency on the excuse that the cash the Congress would issue would be useless outside whereas the cash based on loans and guarantees would have a legal guarantee. Thus, they controlled the money in America, and at this stage, the media played its part by promoting the ideas of luxury and construction, so the Americans invested their money. Then, the Rothschild Group issued confidential instructions to stop making offers and guarantees, and to press the currency in the market, which caused a serious financial crisis that lead to a horrible economic collapse. The prices went down just like in England; so, the money sharks bought real estate and guarantees in millions of dollars, gaining more control over America's young economy. When the Americans noticed the invisible powers' actions, the money sharks caused a new war to impoverish the American Treasury until it kneels down begging for more loans. And it happened. The loan sharks agreed to give more loans in exchange for renewing the Bank of America's privilege to continue its game."

Mahdi felt the weight of Dr. Husam's words on his mind due to its rich historical economic information that he has suddenly pumped on him.

"Doctor, would you tell us about our current crisis?"

Husam looked at him seriously. "Professor Mahdi, you have to know that time that has been moving since that date to date has been decreasing the value of the US dollar bit by bit. That's the point of origin if you wanted to talk about our current time."

"How?" asked Mahdi.

Dr. Husam glanced at his cat that suddenly crouched by the fireplace.

"The Rothschild family had seized control over the American economy when they established the US Federal Reserve System or 'Fed' that specialized in printing currency. In fact, they and other major families, like the Rockefeller and Morgan families, had overthrown six US Presidents who had dared to stand in the face of their economic ambitions by attempting to limit the control of the Fed over the dollar."

He sighed and said, "The last of those presidents was John F. Kennedy who was publicly assassinated in front of TV cameras. Today, neither the Congress, nor the CIA, nor even the US President are allowed to tell the Fed what to do or not do. Simply put, they print the dollar in the amount that suits their needs and at the right time."

"Even the US President?" Maha gasped in surprise.

"Yes, Maha." answered Husam. "By the way, paper can never be trusted as currency. The only trust is for gold. Let's take an example of that. The US dollar's value has stabilized for more than a hundred years because it was not being printed unless the US Treasury had an equivalent amount of gold; until the US got involved in the Vietnam War that greatly exhausted it economically, which made President Nixon end the convertibility of the dollar into gold to provide freedom to print the dollar without limiting it to the size of its gold stock. Since then, the Fed started printing the currency in proportion to the demand on the market without limitation. Whenever the banks exhausted their treasury in loans, the Fed would print them dollars in the requested figures and provide them with it for interest, of course. What's the reason behind the increase in the dollar quantity opposite the decline in its procurement value? Let me ask you something, Maha. What could you do now if I gave you 400 USD and sent you to the market?"

Maha thought for a bit and said smiling, "I'll buy fancy dresses with bags and high-heeled shoes."

Dr. Husam laughed deeply, "How women think! How spendthrift they are!"

Maha lowered her head in embarrassment. Husam looked to her sharply.

"Do you know that in 1920, these 400 USD would have gotten you a brand new same year model car from an American manufacturer?"

Maha swallowed in surprise. Husam went on. "Have you noticed the decline in the value of the dollar over the years? That car could be bought for 20 ounces of gold, but now, the same car in this year's model would cost you tens of thousands of dollars…But also 20 ounces of gold!"

Maha spoke hesitantly, "You mean the gold's value has not changed like the money?"

"Exactly." said Husam, "Mother Nature, dear. This is what explains the decline in the value of the dollar. The constant printing of it causes currency inflation, i.e. a decline in its value."

"Doctor," Mahdi interrupted, scratching his ear, "you haven't told us about our current crisis."

"What's the hurry, my friend?" asked Husam. "There is an origin for each event. If I wanted to get ahead of your haste, I'd tell you what is happening today. As I said, the huge amount of dollar available in the US and the world now will be hit by an intentional quake incited by the descendants of the men who controlled the economies of France, Britain, and the US in the past, and whom I have just explained what they did. All they are doing is inciting terror and panic among people about an economic crisis. That doesn't come out of nothing. The money masters are withdrawing their money all at once from the stock market which makes it collapse, and a state of economic panic arises from that. People would clench to the money they own without wasting it while others try to withdraw their deposits from the banks that start to bankrupt, in effect falling down one after the other like dominos due to insolvency caused by the increase in payments for the clients opposite little input. The collapse of the banks would exacerbate the state of economic panic. To assure people and push them to spend their money in buying goods and services and restore the economic activity, the state would print more currency via the Fed and pump it into the market, as holding the money would cause unemployment and recession. The government would try to restore the economic activity to the market by pumping more dollars, but the economic panic is still there, so the government prints more and more money. Then, by one economic media move, the market is assured of stability. People would start spending the now huge amounts of money they have due to the constant printing of the currency and its availability. When they start buying goods and services assured of the achieved stability, the market would drown in the many dollars and its value would decline, which means the beginning of the economic collapse for the dollar; and that's what we are currently living."

"What's the end game for who is playing at all of this?" Maha asked.

"And if we assume," said Mahdi, "That we replace the foreign currency, the dollar, that we have in our country to euro, would that save us from the damage that would affect the dollar?"

"Euro, Yen, Yuan, all of them, when the dollar collapses, the US would rely on putting out the foreign currency it has to suck back its excess dollars from the market to restore its value. Hence, the value of those currencies would decline due to being pumped in excess by the US, and for those countries to avoid the collapse of their currencies, they would put out the dollars they have for sale.

Imagine that China alone has around four trillion USD and would sell it in the market to restore its currency's value. That would cause the dollar to totally collapse. So would Europe and Japan. Trillions of dollars in their hands would be sold to save their currencies, which would cause the end of the dollar. Thus, each country seeks to save its currency by selling the other currency. In the end, money in all its currencies collapses around the world and the era of gold would have begun. As for the end game of those who manipulate money in all this, during centuries of the finance and currency barons controlling the world economy, they have gained huge amounts of gold. When the paper currency and stocks collapse, the world will go back to gold, i.e. will go back to them. That would be the stage where countries rebuild their economy according to the new system; which means borrowing and giving concessions to them to get gold. That is to say that the whole would kneel before them and their gold. That's the ultimate goal."

Mahdi thought about getting an answer for what was on his mind about the right timing to start looking for Al-Mukhtar's treasure.

"Well, Doctor, is the gold we have in the country's treasury enough to survive this disaster?"

"Absolutely not. The tons of gold we have will not be enough. Don't forget that Iraq still owes many countries and companies in the world due to its repeated and continuous wars. We need tons more gold to survive. At least for those quantities to be the nucleus of the new economic system structure in Iraq according to the new economic system in the world." Husam answered.

"If Iraq had, for instance, a gold mine, would it have to start extracting the gold immediately or it has to wait until the gold price reaches its prime?" Mahdi asked again.

Husam thought for a bit. "If that mine needs months to extract the gold it contains, then it would be too late. We need the gold now and that's impossible. The collapse is coming inevitably!"

Mahdi leaned back feeling the weight of the responsibility that was laid upon him.

He must look for Al-Mukhtar's treasure...now!

"Well, Doctor, we're sorry to occupy you with our questions. We must go now," Mahdi said indicating for Maha to get up.

"Where to? You haven't told me what happened to President Al-Mukhtar," Husam replied.

Mahdi responded, "I'll tell you all the details once I confirm what happened, Doctor, but now we have to go."

Husam did not like Mahdi's response much, but he gave in. "Okay, I hope your student has benefited from our talk; rather I hope she finishes her research before it's too late and becomes a part of history."

Mahdi smiled putting out his cigarette. He and Maha got up, readying to leave, and Husam got up to bid them goodbye.

***

A quarter of an hour after Mahdi and Maha left Dr. Husam's home street in Maha's small car, Husam was surprised by four men in civilian clothing storming his home pointing their guns. They blindfolded him and lead him and his cat, Tara, which he insisted on taking along, in an SUV to an unknown destination.

Chapter 46

Maha's car was making its way in Baghdad's streets that were still wet from the intermittent downpours.

"To the Martyr's Memorial, Maha," Mahdi said that feeling apprehensive of what he has heard from Dr. Husam about the oncoming collapse. "The gold must be found at soon as possible."

Maha pressed on the gas pedal maneuvering between cars and hurrying to reach their destination. The Martyr's Memorial was around 15 minutes from Jadriya by car. Maha tried to reach it fast, curious of what the President had hid there.

The Iraqi Martyr's Memorial sat in the middle of Baghdad's Rusafa side, between Palestine Street and the Army Canal Highway. It was established in 1986 and is primarily composed of an Abbasid style dome split in half, 40 meters tall, with weather-conditions-resistant turquoise ceramic tile cladding. Between the huge two halves of the dome rose a 3-meter-tall Iraqi flag sticking up from the ground with another flag wrapped around it to indicate that the martyr's tomb had split while his soul represented by the flag remained connected to the sky. Near the wrapped flag was a circular water spring with water fountains in the middle flooding the ground of the lower floor of the monument to symbolize the replenishment of blood defending the country. Surrounding that water spring was a black frame inscribed with Arabic poetry lines by Arab poets who wrote them about martyrs. The split dome with the flag between it and the water spring lay on a circular platform made from white alabaster with a diameter of 195 meters. It sat upon an underground museum stretching along the area of the circular platform, while this whole crew sat upon a wide artificial lake. The use of optical illusion in that monument was apparent. Passing through the surrounding streets, the two dome halves would seem closed on each other, then start to split gradually as the watcher continues to move, showing the Iraqi flag between them wrapped up towards the sky before going back to close again.

The cab was still watching closely Maha's car cross the highway towards Palestine Street and giving real time information of its directions to the entity that sent it.

In his office, Oziling was still following the news he was receiving from the tracker attached under Maha's car.

Chapter 47

That evening, Professor Salem Jerjis received the final report of the cause of death of body 3297. The cause was as he concluded from the state of the body when he first laid eyes on it.

Assassination by hydrogen cyanide.

Hydrogen cyanide is considered one of the most used gases in silent assassinations as it is lethal and highly toxic and does not take time to kill the victim if administered in a sufficient dose. A mere 0.2 gram is enough to kill an adult victim. Cyanide is used as a liquefied pressurized gas that turns back into a lethal gas once in the air. It has no color and smells like bitter almonds.

Physiologically, the cyanide entering the blood stream turns the hemoglobin into hemoglobin cyanide which is an ineffective form of transporting the oxygen in breathing to the tissues. The gas causes the victim to breathe faster and feel suffocated before losing consciousness. Then, the heart stops and sudden death occurs.

Professor Jerjis folded the tests results papers that he received and walked back to his room at the Department of Forensic Medicine building.

Meanwhile, Major-General Maher Abdelfattah had just finished a call with the Director of Forensic Medicine Department. He hung up and ordered one of his assistants to send an Intelligence vehicle to bring Professor Salem Jerjis to the Green Zone to start preparing for a press conference where Jerjis, as head of the autopsy committee, would explain the cause of the President's death as agreed upon.

Heart attack.

***

The Iraqi authorities had closed the Iraqi Martyr's Memorial before the public and tourists after 2003 when the US Forces that had used it as a base for it for a while handed it over to them. Those authorities later allowed some school field trips to it only as a monument this huge and important could not be fully opened under the circumstances when it may be targeted by extremists.

Maha's car reached the main entrance of the Martyr's Memorial on Palestine Street. One of the policemen indicated for the car to stop. When it did, the security man came closer to Maha's window that she rolled down and received the policeman with a charming smile.

"Where to, ma'am?" the policeman asked.

"Excuse me," said Maha, "But I thought we could visit the monument and enter it," she continued, "my name is Maha and I'm a new journalist at a private newspaper. I wanted to roam around the monument with Mr. Mahdi to prepare an article about it after the events of 2003. We hope you could help us."

The security man knit his eyebrows while his eyes looked at Maha's beauty and her overflowing feminism.

"Well," He looked to Mahdi, "What does Mr. Mahdi do?"

Maha got flustered a little, but Mahdi saved the day. "Actually, I'm a friend of her father's. This is her first visit to the monument. I came with her as a touristic guide since I have visited it before. We won't be more than half an hour here."

The policeman went back a little and took out his communication device making a call to his supervisor clarifying what is going on. He ended the call and approached them. "Ms. Maha, do you have an ID proving your work as a journalist?"

Maha smiled, "I told you, I'm still new in this profession. This report may get me the ID as an acceptable journalist in that newspaper."

"Well," said the policeman, "you can park your car by the entrance and go into the monument on foot."

"Thank you!" Maha smiled. "I'll get you a copy of the paper issue with the article."

The policeman smiled while Maha moved her car and parked by the entrance.

"You crafty liar!" said Mahdi within Maha's laughs who felt her ability to deceive.

Close to the monument on Palestine Street, a yellow cab stopped and a forty-something-year old man got out of it. He opened the engine cover and pretended to fix something in the car while watching Mahdi and Maha go inside the "Martyr's Memorial".

Chapter 48

Mahdi and Maha crossed the entrance of the Martyr's Memorial on foot and were on the path leading to the turquoise dome halves. They had to walk 500 meters on the white alabaster stretching from the entrance to the center of the monument. Mahdi looked to Maha who was pushing her steps next to him. "Maha, what makes you so sure Al-Mukhtar meant this place in his letter?"

"Simply put, Professor, the blue tomb is the monument. As for the phrase standing on pillars of souls, the main part of the monument sits on a museum below it, and according to my information, the walls of that museum were inscribed with the names of the fallen soldiers in the form of pillars. We have to find the first pillar and look for the forty-fourth name on it as that is what Al-Mukhtar pointed to with the forty-fourth brick," Maha replied.

Mahdi was listening to her and he liked her explanation which seemed very logical.

Follow the souls of the living dead...

In a blue tomb...

Standing on pillars of souls...

In the first marble pillar...

In the forty-fourth brick...

The second stands carrying a homing pigeon.

Mahdi had visited the monument during the reign of Saddam Hussein. He knew well that the inside walls of the museum and the outside walls of the trench surrounding it were filled with the names of the hundreds of thousands of soldiers.

He started recalling. What he remembered were walls inscribed with names in alphabetical order with letters indicating the fighters' rank. "I don't remember where they start and end. We'll ask someone, Maha."

The two reached stairs leading down below the courtyard that dome halves sit upon. They went down the stairs and were now in the trench surrounding the ground museum from the outside. The gardens surrounding the trench were behind them as they faced the wall of names in front of them. In the middle of it was a glass door that appeared to be the main entrance of the ground museum. The door was locked. They looked at the marble wall engulfing the museum from the outside while the roof above them was a part of the wide disk upon which the dome in its two halves stand.

Maha looked to a cleaning man passing close by. "Let's ask him, Professor."

Mahdi nodded and Maha called the cleaning man who approached and said hello.

"I wanted to ask about the entrance to the monument's museum, please."

The man pointed to a nearby door to the right. Maha thanked him and walked with Mahdi to the door.

When they entered through the door, Mahdi and Maha found themselves overlooking a small conference hall with dark red seats in the form of a theater. They kept on forward and were greeted by a young man in his twenties.

"Come in!"

Maha smiled to him. "I'm Maha, a journalist…"

"The newspaper article. I have been waiting for you. The commander told me you were coming. Come this way," the young man interrupted.

Maha looked to Mahdi and he understood her look…This guy cannot accompany us! The two did not want anyone to know what they were looking for.

"I wanted to…" Maha said to the young man, "thank you for your kindness. Mr. Mahdi knows the monument well. We'll be fine on our own. If we need anything, we'll let you know."

The young man knit his eyebrows. "Okay, go from the conference hall down to the beginning of the museum and roam around from there. My room is here if you need any assistance," he pointed to a room above the conference hall.

Mahdi thanked the young man and they went down the hall. There was a small door in that hall leading to the museum entrance. Mahdi and Maha crossed it and found themselves in a spacious place. To the left, their attention was caught by a circular light colored ground with a cubic piece in the middle that seemed like a small seat. The two looked up to the ceiling over the circle. The Iraqi flag sticking between the two halves appeared from below with the rays of light entering from its glass endings to light up the circular ground. It was breathtaking.

The two turned to the right where the beginning of the museum was. To their left was a glass barrier behind which appeared the water falling from the spring up. They kept going towards the beginning of the wide museum. The museum was circular with a diameter of 190 meters where the one walking in it could finish a full circle passing by the walls with the names and the glass displays of the belongings of the Baath regime victims as the belongings of the soldiers fallen during the Iraqi-Iranian War were replaced with the belongings of citizens, politicians, and clergymen executed by Saddam Hussein's regime. After walking through the vast circular museum, one finds himself back at the place he started from after finishing a 360° turn.

Mahdi and Maha traced the letters the soldiers' inscribed names started with. They noticed those names started with later letters in the Arabic alphabet. They kept on looking for the letter 'A' as the first letter in the alphabet hoping to find the first pillar.

Maha was astonished by the vast museum below the monument. That was her first time there since she visited as a child in elementary school on a field trip once. It was wonderful. Below a high ceiling and breathtaking lighting, the shining alabaster ground reflected the circular ceiling lighting across the spacious circular museum. The two followed the names on the walls. It was getting farther from the first Arabic alphabet letters.

Meanwhile, the cab was still stopped close by the monument and the forty-something year old man was still pretending to fix it when the sky started another of its downpours, which forced him to close the engine cover and get back in his car, turning on his car's yellow lights and watching from inside.

As for Scott Oziling, he was comfortable in his office watching through his surveillance team Maha's car movement. He knew now that it was parked by the gate of the Martyr's Memorial in Palestine St.

After spending around quarter of an hour looking for the names of the soldiers beginning with an 'A', they found themselves back under the flag hanging in the monument's ceiling again. They were back to the same spot without finding what they were looking for.

"I'm afraid we have to ask the young man that met us when we entered." Mahdi sighed.

Maha replied jokingly, "Don't worry, Professor. You have seen my abilities in deception. Let's go and ask him."

Mahdi smiled half a smile and walked with Maha to the conference hall again on the way to the young man's room. When they arrived, he was sitting behind his computer. They greeted him.

"We enjoyed the tour in the museum but I wanted to ask about the place where the names start. We did not find it inside." Maha cajoled.

The young man smiled, "If you had asked me, you would not have needed to look for it in the museum. The beginning of the names start on the outside wall of the monument museum not the inside one."

The two were surprised.

The young man got up and walked towards the room's door. "Follow me."

The two moved behind him as he walked back to the door leading to the outer trench facing the gardens. Mahdi and Maha felt the pure cold air as the sky was spraying rain which they were protected from by the circular ceiling of the split dome's courtyard. After a few steps towards the stairs they used to enter the trench, the young man looked to them and pointed to the marble wall.

"From here the names start," the young man said pointing to a piece of the wall. Mahdi and Maha looked to the wall inscribed with the fighters' names. Indeed, all the names inscribed on it start with an 'A'. Mahdi approached the wall with Maha alongside him. The soldiers' ranks were written in shortened letters before their names. Meanwhile, one of the people working in the monument called the young man who has accompanied Mahdi and Maha. He excused himself and left them in front of the first pillar of the soldiers' names.

Mahdi looked at the designated wall and started reading the names starting with the first name:

PV2 Aba Algha'eb Ali Hussein

"We made it, Professor. We have to count now to the forty-fourth name," Maha said as she examined the wall.

The two started counting:

PVT Aba Ther Ibrahim Saleh Sa'eed

PFC Aba Ther Jaber Adawa Mnofi

They counted until they reached the forty-fourth name as the President's letter indicated and read the name together:

PV2 Ibrahim Ahmed Mahmoud

Maha looked to Mahdi and said surprised, "Hmm, what does that mean?"

Mahdi was silent with his arms crossed and his hand on his mouth.

He broke his silence with few words...

"Maha...it's my *father's* name!"

Chapter 49

3:00 p.m. Baghdad time.

Mahdi and Maha were standing in front of the forty-fourth name of the first pillar of the soldiers' names inscribed on the outer wall of the trench of the Martyr's Memorial while the sky's downpour increased on the magnificent monument above them.

Maha remembered her professor's father's name when she recalled Mahdi's full name which she had written on the cover of her graduation research that she was preparing. She wrote her professor's full name as supervisor over the research.

Mahdi was still staring at his father's name before him. That was the name of one of those soldiers whose names were inscribed on the walls of the monument, and it was an exact match to his father's name. Al-Mukhtar used that match to point to Mahdi's father as the second man…stands carrying a homing pigeon.

"Professor," Maha whispered. Mahdi turned to her and she felt the bitterness he was feeling being faced with this shock. "I'm so sorry, but it seems Al-Mukhtar trusted your father greatly to the point he made him one of the three men he entrusted with that secret."

"Exactly, Maha," he drew in a deep breath. "now what?"

Maha pursed her lips. "In the first marble pillar, in the forty-fourth brick, the second stands carrying a homing pigeon."

Mahdi realized he had to trust Maha's analysis as her analysis of the phrase a blue tomb standing on pillars of souls was bull's eye.

"A homing pigeon, I think," Mahdi said, "my father has left a letter too. Homing pigeons symbolize letters that were being sent by those birds in the past."

"That's exactly what I thought, Professor," Maha nodded, "let's go back to the house now and think about what your father could have left as a letter."

Mahdi nodded in agreement and the two headed for the stairs leading to the path reaching the entrance of the monument where Maha's car was. Suddenly, they heard a voice behind them.

"Mr." They turned to him.

The young man had returned apologizing for being busy.

Mahdi gestured with his hand. "Thank you. It will be a detailed report." The young man gestured with his hand and returned back to his office inside the monument's building.

Mahdi and Maha faced the rain on their way to the entrance where they left the car. Maha turned to cast a final look at the magnificent split dome behind her. It looked huge standing under the rain that washed it and turned its color to dark blue.

Chapter 50

Mahdi and Maha got into the car and headed for Zayouna. The rain had dampened some of their clothes. They thanked the policemen and Maha moved her car towards the main street.

Meanwhile, the cab driver followed Maha and started his calls to the entity that sent him. He kept on watching her car as it went back to Zayouna.

From his office, Scott Oziling had given his ordered for the Cherokee to prepare for the arrival of the car transporting the lawyer to his home street in the neighborhood. The two operatives in the SUV received the instructions and remained alert.

"What do you think your father's letter contains, Professor?" Maha questioned while carefully crossing the intersection back to Zayouna in her car.

"I'm afraid the letter is somewhere I don't know, Maha," Mahdi answered.

"I'm not going to lie to you, Professor. Despite the danger of what we're doing, I feel I'm doing something important for the country. What about you?"

Mahdi laughed, "When you chose to be a lawyer, you're on the right track for trouble."

Maha smiled and pressed on the gas pedal. A few minutes later and they arrived at Mahdi's house…followed by a cab and with a tracking device attached under their car.

Chapter 51

3:30 p.m. Baghdad time.

Professor Salem Jerjis arrived to the small residence inside the Green Zone. He took a small opportunity for a restless nap, preparing for what he needed for the press conference he had to hold under orders of Major-General Maher Abdelfattah.

The Director of the Forensic Medical Department would have to finish legalizing the required report on the death of President Al-Mukhtar so that in case any entity asked to see the forensic report of the President, it would be ready and official. The Ministry of Justice was formally notified of the cause of death of President Al-Mukhtar via the Director of Forensic Medicine confirming the story that the President had passed…by a heart attack.

The Professor's apartment door rattled with a knock. Jerjis knew who his guests would be. He received a call earlier from an Intelligence agency informing him that they were sending two agents to arrange for holding the press conference by the Professor. The press conference would be held…that evening.

A few minutes later, the two Intelligence agents were discussing with Jerjis what should and should not be said in front of the media in that conference. In addition to that, they informed him that it was possible to convince the media with an electronic version of the forensic report later.

Meanwhile, the man in the elegant suit had just hung up after being informed of the latest on what the Ministry of Justice would do of a press conference for the forensic doctor who has overseen the autopsy of the President's body. He was assured now. He lit up another cigar and went on watching the latest global economic news.

The global stock markets at that hour were starting to face a disastrous fall. The US dollar had been admitted into the ICU room after its value has declined to an unprecedented level while the gold kept rising in the midst of the whirlpool of economic collapses.

The man in the elegant suit looked to the gold price indicator at the bottom of the TV screen as reported by the Standard & Poor's, the largest company in publishing global financial research and analyses.

An ounce of 24K gold – Price 2,144.20 USD

The price for gold per dollar has doubled. He nodded his head knowing that that's just...

The beginning...

Chapter 52

Maha's car reached Mahdi's house, bypassing a black Jeep Cherokee on the street. She parked her car in front of his house and the two quickly got out of it and into the house as the rain had started to fall heavily.

The security camera on the house facing the lawyer's house was still sending its images to the entity that had put it there. Of what it sent:

The lawyer and his companion reaching his house; and the Jeep continuing to move about the street. As for the yellow cab, it changed its direction to an unknown destination when Maha's car turned onto her Professor's street.

Inside Mahdi's house, Maha took off her shoes and entered into the warmth of the living room. She sat on the couch while he went on to light the fireplace in the room.

Suddenly, like lightening had hit his head, an idea sparked about the place where he could look for what his father had left.

"Maha, if there is a place to look for what my father left for us, it would be his private wing behind the house." Mahdi confirmed while getting up from in front of the fireplace that was searing now.

Maha got up to get closer seeking the warmth.

"Professor..." she did not finish as Mahdi grabbed her hand and looked into her eyes.

"Maha, now we are two citizens who got involved in a mission to save the country. We are no longer a professor and a student. You don't need to call me professor anymore."

The blood rose in her cheeks. "But...I don't know...I can't..."

"Maha!" He said firmly, "I am Mahdi, and only Mahdi. At least outside the university."

Maha smiled, looking into his eyes, "Okay, Mahdi. Deal."

His eyes did not leave hers while her perfume was overtaking his nostrils. Her eyes were sparking the color of the fire that she was looking at shyly running from his eyes.

She broke the silence by saying, "Okay, Mahdi. What were you saying about your father's private wing?"

He returned to the world of crisis in which he was living. "Aha, listen. My father had his own wing to spend his free time at. It's composed of a large hall behind the house and has his private belongings and his precious bookshelves. He asked me to promise him to not sell the house when he left this world. He also told me not to open that hall unless necessary, and if I do, I am not to move any of its things. It was the place he rested at, planned his work as an Advisor to the President, and later proposed his ideas to Al-Mukhtar regarding economy. Do you believe that I have not opened that wing since his passing seven years ago?"

Maha was surprised to hear about the private world of one of the closest state men to Al-Mukhtar. "Seven years?"

"Yes," Mahdi nodded, "I don't know what happened in that place, although I have its keys. I guess the time to open it is right now."

Maha nodded her head and felt a wave of curiosity of what the President's Advisor's private wing would be like. Mahdi smiled, "Now that we are soaked like this, how would you like a cup of coffee?"

Maha smiled and shook her head, "I'll make it for you today."

He nodded in agreement and sat on the couch next to the fireplace while she went into the kitchen.

He grabbed the remote and turned on the TV while waiting for Maha's coffee. As he flipped by the official channel, the breaking news ticker at the bottom of the screen was indicating that the Ministry of Justice would be having an important press conference at exactly 6:30 p.m. regarding Al-Mukhtar's death. He called Maha and read her the ticker aloud. She returned to the living room to follow with him what was happening on the screen. The two looked together to the clock on the wall…four o'clock.

Two and a half hours separated them from one of the most important press conferences in the life of the new government.

***

Meanwhile, Jerjis met with a delegation from the Ministry of Justice at his residence location after the two Intelligence agents left him. He started preparing with the delegation how the press conference would go while the staff of the conference hall at the Ministry went on setting it up before the various agencies' reporters started arriving to it.

Chapter 53

Mahdi and Maha had just finished their coffee while watching TV. Mahdi sheathed his cigarette in the ashtray in front of him, turned off the TV, and directed to Maha. "Let's move to my father's wing now before the press conference, Maha."

She nodded. Mahdi got up to the display in the room, opened one of its glass doors, and took out a small box. He opened it and calm music started playing. He reached his fingers and took out of it keys that were tied to a chain from which hung a keychain in the form of the Iraqi Republican Emblem. He closed the box and put it back in the display closing its door. He pointed for Maha to get up and the two headed for the door.

Mahdi's father's wing lay isolated to the back of the house. A narrow, open from above pathway surrounded from both sides by plant pots carrying various plants, lead to the wing. Maha had to put her shoes back on since the pathway was already wet from the downpours that seemed to lessen in those moments. Mahdi stood in front of a metal door to the right. He took out the keys and put one in the door lock, unlocking it. He pushed it and it made a gloomy squeak.

The two walked into a dark place—a room where nothing could be seen yet, but it carried the smell of old dampness that seemed to originate from a forgotten carpet. Mahdi reached his hands to the wall and pressed on the light switch, filling that long hall with low lights; that hall that had not been opened in seven years.

The scene was both shocking and amazing to Maha at the same time. She gaped, looking at a place that seemed ancient in its furniture and design pattern. Her amazement was no less than Mahdi's who had forgotten many details about that place over the past seven years.

The hall was rectangular. On its walls hung photos of Mahdi's father with President Al-Mukhtar from different occasions, in addition to monochrome photos from the Advisor's childhood and school years. The first Republican Emblem represented by the Sumerian sun was hung on one of the walls while the second Emblem represented by the Arabian eagle was on the opposite wall. A plastic statue in military uniform from the Islamic Empire era stood with his sword in one of the hall's corners, and a two-meter high figure of the Obelisk of Hammurabi stood in another corner. To the back of the hall stretched from one end to the other large wooden bookshelves filled with hundreds of books. Close by was a table with an hourglass on it whose sand has long sunk in its lower half. The dampness had eaten up some of the walls and ceiling, making the place stinging cold.

Dust covered all of the room's furniture, even the couches set in an isolated corner of it. Spider webs gathered moving with the light air like ghost movement. Being in a place like that was like standing on a mountain of forgotten memories for Mahdi, who stood in place with his arms crossed remembering what remained in his mind of memories of that hall; while Maha stepped forward taken by an overwhelming amazement. She moved forward casing the place with slow movements from her eyes.

Mahdi smiled to her, "Okay, Maha. You've seen the place. Where do you think we should start our search from?"

Maha did not answer. The thrill of being in such place controlled her mind. She took a few more steps towards the strange belongings spread across the room and on its walls like a raid by an army of red ants. She felt she had to lessen the pressure of her feet fearing she might damage the velvet carpet laid on the floor. Everything was from a past time.

Mahdi followed her as she approached the bookshelves at the back of the hall. She passed her fingers over the plastic knight's face and looked at her fingers that dirtied up from the dust. She touched its sword and looked into its eyes that were sparkling proudly. "How lucky I am, Mahdi!"

Mahdi scratched his head smiling and looking at her. She finished her steps towards the bookshelves. The hourglass on the metallic table to the side caught her attention. The face of the table covered the bottom of the hourglass with a piece of white sheet.

Mahdi was watching her walking about the room. She put her hand on the hourglass that ran out of time seven years ago. She turned to Mahdi waiting for his approval since he told her his father had not wished anything in the room to be moved. He closed his eyes and nodded his head in agreement. She held the hourglass and was about to turn it upside down to start counting again, but she felt some resistance pulling the hourglass downwards. Mahdi felt something was up. He approached her.

"It seems like it does not want to count again!" she said.

"Turn it. I have memories with this hourglass," he replied, looking at her.

Maha pulled the hourglass up with more force. It seemed like it was connected to something from the bottom. The two looked underneath it. It was a wool thread tied to the base of the hourglass from below. Maha pulled it up higher. On the table below it was a small hole through which the thread connected to the hourglass's base passed. As Maha picked up the hourglass with greater force, the piece of sheet covering metallic table started rising as the sheet's bottom ending was connected to the wool thread at the base of the hourglass. Maha turned the hourglass and the sand started falling while what was behind the sheet that partially rose was exposed.

Mahdi reached his hand and pushed away the white curtain from the table, and, with Maha, looked to what was hiding behind it.

A metallic safe with a circular dial.

***

The man in the elegant suit was still following the global economic news. He looked at his watch waiting for 6:30 p.m. to switch to the official channel that would broadcast the events of the Ministry of Justice's press conference.

There is still a lot of time.

Meanwhile, the price of gold in USD was still showing at the bottom of the screen. The USD had lost a lot of its value until now.

The disaster will move to Iraq…soon.

***

Mahdi did not recall his father having a bulletproof metallic safe. Maha turned to him, "Do you think…?"

He interrupted, "Yes, we should open it fast."

The low lighting in the hall's ceiling did not clearly show the safe's grey face, which made Mahdi take out his cellphone and use its light. He pointed it at the metallic safe's face…and the two were surprised by what it had on its face.

The Advisor left in his handwriting using a black marker the numeric phrase 1000 & 1. Mahdi and Maha exchanged surprised looks of what they had just read. Calmly Mahdi said:

"Maha…The secret lies in this room."

Chapter 54

The darkness started to approach the longitude on which Baghdad falls. A rainy storm blew on the capital that was preparing for a new storm that would be entirely different this time…economic.

Mahdi and Maha were trying to understand the phrase the Advisor had left on the safe. It seemed to have been written in a clear handwriting and a firm hand… *1000 & 1.*

Maha sunk into her thoughts while Mahdi walked about the room nervously like a train breathing out cigarette smoke towards the ceiling.

"One thousand and one." He said. "It cannot be a number to open the safe, Maha, and the owner of a safe would not leave its code on its door."

"How many digits do we need to open it?" Maha asked.

"Three pairs of digits. I have one like it in my room upstairs, but slightly smaller. Three numbers to be turned in a specific form before it is ready to be opened." Mahdi responded.

Maha thought while looking at the number, sitting on her knees facing the safe. "One thousand and one." She said. "What do you say we partition the number into three pairs?"

Mahdi smiled and breathed out the smoke from his cigarette. "Do you think my father would leave it this easily? Write the key to the safe on its door?"

She ignored what he said and isolated in her mind what could be the key… 1001…can be partitioned into…three pairs.

"Let's try what's on my mind."

He looked to her. "What's on your mind?"

She took out a pen from her jacket and wrote on her palm:

10

00

01

She turned her hand to Mahdi. He looked at it, "I don't think it's that easy, but nonetheless, let's try."

Mahdi sat in front of the safe while she held his phone to shed light over the dial. He turned the dial to the left three times and back to the right three other times, and finally settled on the number zero to prepare the safe to try the numbers Maha suggested. He started turning the dial to the heart passing by number 10 and continuing on until he turned it again passing over it once more. On the third time, he settled on 10 and stopped.

The first number was entered.

Maha was watching what he was doing. He looked at her. "The second number."

"Zero."

Mahdi turned the dial to the left twice, passing the number zero and then settling on it on the third. He looked it her asking for the third number, and she said, "one."

He turned the dial to the right, passed the number one once. In the second time, he settled on it.

The third and last number was entered.

He had to return the dial to zero so it would automatically lock and could not be turned anymore, which meant the safe would be ready to open. But if it snapped without locking, that meant the code was wrong.

He put the dial on the number zero…

But it did not lock.

He looked to Maha and pursed his lips. "Maha, the code is wrong."

She sighed, feeling disappointed and pushed her hair back looking at the writing on the face.

1000 & 1. She felt that that writing did not mean a specific number, but something else…

Something…

Mahdi got up putting his hands on his hips. He looked to the walls filled with memoirs and photos feeling despondent. His eyes looked for any hint or sign. He turned his gaze to the large bookshelves to his left and his eyes crossed over the stickers his father had left on the shelves:

The scientific section

The economic section

The literature section

He sat back before the case… 1000 & 1. He thought of making use of the books to search for something that would point to the number 1000 and one. He looked to the bookshelves again closely…

"What are you thinking?" Maha asked.

He got up checking the bookshelves sections with his eyes that widened…

"I'm thinking of…" and he found what he was looking for in the depth of his mind…

"One thousand and one nights!"

Chapter 55

«The decrease in oil demand reduces the prices to 40 USD/barrel."

Those breaking news tickers did not disappear from the bottom of the screen that the man in the elegant suit was watching. The chain of economic collapses created a recession in the global markets, which decreased the demand for oil; and due to the short demand, the price went down.

Because this issue stormed suddenly and unexpectedly, it was not discussed when Iraq set its annual budget. Hence, the continuous decline in oil prices would lead to an unaccounted for financial deficit, which would cause a huge economic problem for the country.

Gold is the savior.

***

In front of his father's glorious bookshelves, Mahdi Al-Ali stood alongside Maha to start looking for "One Thousand and One Nights" book among that huge amounts of books. They started from the literature section.

Mahdi remembered his father keeping that book. He had advised him to read it since he was a young boy; and it was one of the first books Mahdi had read in his youth from his father's collection of books. If his father had not cherished that book, he would not have advised his son to read it.

"What do you expect we'd find in it?" Maha asked.

"It may be one of the book's stories since 'One Thousand and One Nights" is a collection of old Arabian stories." Mahdi said while reading the titles in front of him:

Al-Mustatref fi Kul Fen Mustadhref

Mutanabbi's Divan

Mukhtar Al-Sehah

From among the adjacent books, he pulled out a book with the title 'One Thousand and One Nights'.

The book's cover was worn out. When he pulled it out, the smell of old dust that accumulated on its ends reeked. Its yellowing pages could not bear to be moved except carefully. Mahdi turned back towards the table in the middle of the hall and Maha followed him, looking at what is in his hand.

"What an old copy, Mahdi!"

"Yes, I haven't touched it since I was little," he responded.

Maha approached the table that Mahdi put the book on and he started to open its cover with difficulty. The two were stunned by finding themselves having to chase symbols and texts that relate to a big secret.

Mahdi started flipping the pages of the book with a look of puzzlement as the book told stories hundreds of years old told by Scheherazade to Schehryar over the period of one thousand and one nights as the legend goes.

This would not be easy.

Mahdi left the book on the table and turned to light another cigarette that might quell his confusion. Maha used his turning and held the book in both her hands putting its spine that carried its title on the table. Mahdi turned around and looked at her while blowing out his first breath of smoke.

He said laughing, "Will you read my fortune in it?" She gave him a serious look and pulled her palms farther from each other for the book to open from the middle. The aging yellow paper reeked of the smell of ancient heritage. The two looked to what appeared between the pages.

Among the book's yellow pages there was a white folded paper that was put there, which made it easy to open without the book being affected, and it showed what was hidden in it. Mahdi looked to Maha in surprise and took the paper. She closed the book and got closer to take a look with him. He carefully opened it and they started reading what was written on that paper.

The text was perfectly cryptic.

Chapter 56

What Sumer made...Remember it...

The story of creation, its Warka Vase tells...

For the Bull of Assyria, legs were fixed ...

From the north, and by the east walks...

....

The king of directions built a palace and vitrified it...

And turned bricks from clod to blue...

Shubad, the moon in the darkness, increased in beauty...

What she wears, and like lightening flares...

....

Strings of the Bull's Lyre stripped off...

The head from abuse and theft replaced...

5:20 p.m. Baghdad time.

Mahdi and Maha looked at the strange poem on the paper before them. Mahdi recognized his father's handwriting.

He drew in a deep breath from his cigarette and looked to Maha who shrugged her shoulders, feeling the strangeness. The Advisor was telling information on Iraqi artifacts that went back to the Mesopotamian civilizations.

"What's the connection between this and the safe's key?" Maha said looking at the paper again. Mahdi carefully examined the text. "There is a connection...A certain connection."

"How?"

Mahdi took the paper from her and said pointing to its verses, "Pay attention to the arrangement of verses: Two verses, another two verses, and then one verse. This could mean two pairs digits. Then one verse…I don't know why it was left alone."

Maha found his analysis strange. "How could numbers be deduced from poetic verses?"

Mahdi responded just as confused. "It may mean the times those artifacts belong to in their consecutive civilizations, or from the number of years we could derive the digits to unlock the safe."

Maha was not convinced. She took the paper from his hand and looked at it. "It's not like that, Mahdi."

She said, "It's obvious!"

"How?" he inquired.

"What I could understand from the text regarding numbers is the second verse:

For the Bull of Assyria, legs were fixed …

From the north, and by the east walks…"

"You mean the Lamassu?"

Maha felt a gleam of a solution for the puzzle. "Yes, the Lamassu's legs from the front are lined next to each other calmly, which is what the verse said, but from the side, it looks like they're walking. If we add the legs from both sides, they'd be five legs, not four. It's an optical illusion the people of Mesopotamia used when making Lamassus. I should know! I have visited the museum for my graduation research quite often."

Mahdi understood what she meant. The method to extract numbers from the text became almost clear…if it was correct.

He took out a pen from his pocket and drew to horizontal lines on his palm. "Maha, we will solve each verse on its own to find the numbers."

Maha looked back at the paper and read the first verse:

What Sumer made…Remember it…

The story of creation, its Warka Vase tells…

"Warka Vase?" she wondered.

Mahdi looked to her, "Aha… I visited the National Museum during college, and as I recall, it was a vertical vessel with some carvings on it that I don't remember specifically. It was placed in the Sumerian artifacts hall. I read on the sign on its side that it was looted and broken during the events of 2003, but the museum was able to retrieve it and renovate it. As for the number in it, I don't remember anything."

Maha put the paper on the table while Mahdi went out to throw the cigarette butt out of the hall. She took out her cellphone and connected to the internet, searching for the Warka Vase.

Mahdi came back and was approaching her when he suddenly froze.

"What's wrong?" she asked.

He smiled, "I thought it was a private moment with your holding your phone."

She laughed, "A private moment with those who lived 5,000 years ago!" Mahdi walked closer smiling.

Maha did not press the web results pages for explanation, but switched to the images tab to take a look at the Vase. She was overtaken by curiosity but her memory betrayed her and she could not remember the details of that vessel she had seen at the museum during her visits. The images popped up and the two looked at them. She picked one and it enlarged to the cellphone's screen size. As soon as Mahdi saw the vase and the carvings on it, he remembered the details of how it looked. The circular protruding carvings on it brought back some details to his mind. He took the paper from over the table and looked at it once more:

The story of creation, its Warka Vase tells.

He remembered what that meant. The words the museum guide, who had accompanied him and his companions on their visit to the museum that day had uttered, stormed his brain.

"I found the number, Maha!" he said confidently.

"How?" she said passionately, pushing her hair behind her ear.

"The story of creation, its Warka Vase tells," he took her phone from her hand and zoomed in on the image. "When my college mates and I visited the museum years ago, the museum guide explained to us what this artifact means. It talks about the stages of creation from the dust to the gods."

He started pointing to parts of the Vase in the image and continued.

"Its base here points to the ground that was created first. Then comes the second tier that points to the creation of water. Followed by the third pointing to the creation of plants. As for the fourth, it's the stage of the creation of animals."

He pointed to an empty tier of the Vase's layers. "This space indicates the gods' resting period after creating those four stages to resume the creation of humans in the sixth stage."

"You mean the fifth!" Maha said.

"No, the sixth," Mahdi said and continued, "the resting stage is on its own one of the stages of creation making the stage of the creation of humans the sixth. Then it left a space between it and the gods as a sort of uniqueness and superiority of the gods to the humans. The gods come in the seventh, highest, and last stage of creation. It's referred to as a votive vase because, as you can see, the human is carved to be bringing offerings to the gods in the top tier."

"You mean hc's pointing to the number seven?"

"I hope our thinking is right."

He gave Maha her phone back and took his pen writing above the horizontal line that he drew on the palm of his hand:

57

He turned his hand to Maha who said, "Yes, the Warka Vase: seven, and the Lamassu: five."

Mahdi nodded and they went back to the paper.

The king of directions built a palace and vitrified it...

And turned bricks from clod to blue...

"Ur-Nammu, the king of the four directions!" Maha said. Mahdi smiled and wrote the number 4 in the second space on his hand. They went on reading:

Shubad, the moon in the darkness, increased in beauty...

What she wears, and like lightening flares...

"Three," Mahdi said.

Maha did not understand why because she did not remember how that Shubad looked. Mahdi understood from her look that she did not understand him. He grabbed her phone from the table, searched for Shubad in the search engine, and chose a picture from the results. He turned the screen towards Maha. She smiled and nodded, understanding what he meant.

Shubad, or Puabi, is the name of a woman said to be a Sumerian queen. A colored half body statue of her was made and accessorized with feminine accessories and necklaces. On the top of her head three golden flowers were tied to her hair from behind, which were what Mahdi believed the verse refers to. The three flowers.

34.

Ur-Nammu… and Shubad…

"I hope we won't need another verse," Mahdi said. "the safe does not open unless with three pairs of digits and there is one single verse remaining that would not form a pair of them."

Strings of the Bull's Lyre stripped off…

The head from abuse and theft replaced…

"The Sumerian Lyre," said Maha. Mahdi nodded. The Sumerian Lyre is world renowned. In Iraq, it became a logo for many institutions and a trademark for the Iraqi cigarettes company. Some stamps also carried it as an artifact that Iraqis cherished.

The verse was clear to Mahdi in referring to the Sumerian Lyre as he remembered the museum guide telling him that the lyre's golden strings were stripped off it in fear it might get stolen; and the pure gold bull's head that was on it was replaced with a fake head while the museum kept the original head with the golden strings in one of its secret chambers.

"How will we know the number of this one?" Maha asked.

Mahdi read the verse again and knit his brows.

Strings stripped off…

"The strings!" Mahdi exclaimed with clear signs of excitement. "How many strings does it have, Maha? Remember!"

Maha put her fingers on her head and closed her eyes. "Hmm, I don't know, Mahdi…I don't know."

Mahdi tried to remember his visit to the museum again. He missed to ask the guide about the number of strings of the lyre.

"Your phone again."

Maha grabbed her phone and typed in the search bar: The Sumerian Lyre.

Mahdi wanted to check the results with her but she turned her phone away from him preventing him from looking and smiled.

"Selfish!" he said with a mischievous look although he was thinking of the sixth missing verse that should complete the three pairs of digits.

Maha read some lines in her phone then her eyes widened in surprise. She looked to Mahdi.

"Al-Mukhtar was right in choosing his advisor. The number of strings is 11. The digits are *complete!*"

Chapter 57

5:40 p.m. Baghdad time.

Two government SUVs were making their way through the intermittent downpours in the capital. They had just left the Presidential Green Zone towards Al-Salhiya area in Baghdad's Karkh where the Ministry of Justice lies. Professor Salem Jerjis was in one of them accompanied by security personnel with high training and armament.

6:30 p.m.…The time for the press conference.

With great worry, Major-General Maher Abdelfattah was making his calls with various entities to coordinate with the Ministry of Justice regarding the conference. He did not want Jerjis to make a mistake in any detail in front of the cameras of the international news agencies and the media. He also did not want anyone in the government talking to the Professor regarding Al-Mukhtar's death as any exposure of the truth of what had happened would take the head of the most powerful Intelligence men…Its General Director.

***

In front of his father's safe, Mahdi was sitting on his knees beside Maha, who was filled with hope that the numbers derived from the father's letter carried the key to that mysterious safe. The hall was swept in a concrete silence that was only disturbed by the quiet hissing sound of the sand passing through the hourglass towards its lower half.

Mahdi Drew in a deep breath and started moving the number dial. He turned it in both directions several times as required and then started turning it towards the first number:

57

He fixed the key on the first number, then turned it again to ready it to stop on the second number:

34

Finally, the moment of truth has become so close. One number; either it would open the secret safe, or Mahdi and Maha would spend hours in that abandoned place looking for a new key.

Maha's eyes were fixed on the number dial that Mahdi started to turn backwards counterclockwise.

He passed over the number 11 once and turned it in the same direction; he passed over it again, and in the third time...he stopped on it...

The numbers were fully entered:

57

34

11

With a heart throbbing like a war drum, Mahdi looked to Maha. "The dial has to be returned to zero now and then locks on it. If it lets go again...the numbers are wrong."

Maha closed her eyes and prayed the numbers to be correct. Mahdi put his fingers on the number dial and started turning it to the left...

Towards zero.

With high concentration, Maha looked at Mahdi's anxious fingers. The ticking sounds of the steps raided the room's heavy silence.

5...4...3...2...1...

***

"Where are you now?" Scott Oziling asked the Cherokee driver over the communication device.

"At the same street that I have memorized everything at!" the driver responded.

"Alright. If there is any movement, I want you inform me immediately."

"As you wish, cowboy!" the driver said while biting on a green apple and raising the volume of the radio that was playing loud American music. The darkness and quietness were overwhelming the street save for the rain knocks on the windows and roof of the black car. The other passenger was breaking his boredom by pressing on his gun's trigger and pulling back the safety after he had taken the magazine out of it.

***

Towards zero…

Mahdi stopped turning the numbers dial when he reached the number 1. One more step would reveal if the numbers were correct or not…

One step…And he let go of the numbers dial…

"Why did you stop?" Maha wondered in surprise.

He looked to her, "I consider you a good omen. You will put it on the zero. I'm sure it would lock and be ready to be opened then."

Maha agreed with shyness. Mahdi moved with his knees one step to the right and she got closer to the safe. He took the phone from her and directed the light on the dial.

Maha put her fingers on the numbers dial to move it to the left… one step…towards zero…

She pressed the dial with the tips of her fingers and turned it to the left one step…

After a short feeling of a minor resistance by the dial, it made a low ticking sound and was set in place.

It locked in…

The numbers were correct.

Chapter 58

Mahdi and Maha could not hide their happiness after the number dial on the safe locked announcing the correctness of the entered numbers. The safe was now ready to be opened.

He looked to his blond companion and had an overwhelming desire to kiss her fingers. He felt that for the first time since he knew her as a student sitting in the first row in his class. Now, she has become a being whom he did not know how he felt about exactly.

Hiding those feelings, he said to her, "I told you, you're a good omen." He said it without looking into her eyes while she started cracking her fingers in shyness and embarrassment. He gave her a strange look. A smile in his eyes and silence that vaporized with the silence engulfing the place.

He went back to looking at the metallic handle on the door of the safe trying to run from those strange feelings he was having for the first time in his life towards a woman. He held the handle with both hands and turned it to the right.

The handle made a noise of pulling the metallic tongues that lock the safe and the door was ready to be opened. He pulled the heavy metallic door towards himself while Maha held his phone and directed the light from it to the inside of the safe that was beginning to reveal itself bit by bit.

Mahdi opened the door fully and, with Maha, looked inside the safe that was lit by the light from the cellphone. It had a horizontal shelf in the middle...

But it was completely *empty*.

Chapter 59

Extremely anxious, the man in the elegant suit had just ordered his second cup of coffee and filled the room's atmosphere with the smoke from his cigar. The TV did not stop broadcasting reports and special analyses on the currency market. He has never felt this critical situation before. The counsellor had to move quickly.

He looked at his watch. He did not want to miss the press conference that the Ministry of Justice announced. Only about 45 minutes until that conference would be held. There was still enough time to follow the economic news.

***

Hitting one palm with the other, Mahdi stood up feeling tremendous anger due to the painstaking quest that ended in opening his father's empty safe. He sat on the dust covered couch in one of the hall's antique corners. Maha looked to him feeling sorry for how the quest ended. She was going to have to calm down what he was going through so he would regain hope to continue searching.

"Mahdi!" she sat next to him, "we have crossed an important stage in our quest. We have to not give up."

"Maha, I haven't known the meaning of relief since I received that ominous call that night. I don't know why my father left the quest thread cut at this stage."

She answered, "I don't know if my intuition is right, but such tight code cannot lead to an empty safe. It has to lead to some meaning, then..." she stopped, having a slight feeling of doubt.

"Could it be that the safe was looted?"

Mahdi was shocked at the possibility. "No way! That would drive me insane if true. But as you can see, the hall hasn't been had a foot stepped into it in years. There is nothing disturbing the layer of dust that covers its floor and the carpet other than the footprints that we have left since we entered a little while ago. Also, the safe is securely locked and there are no signs of mischief on it."

Maha received his words in absolute acceptance as she looked to the dust on the floor and carpet that were only disturbed by their footsteps. It was not like that before they entered.

She got up thinking of a solution to the problem. She stepped to a dust filled curtain in front of one of the hall's windows and pulled it aside. She looked through the window to the sky that was almost completely dark. She looked at her watch that was approaching 6 p.m., and felt she had to go home although she did not want to leave Mahdi like this.

She turned around to look at him and was surprised to see herself alone in the depressing place! She stepped forward towards the hall's metallic exit door. She crossed its threshold only for her nostrils to be knocked by the smell of Mahdi's cigarette. He lit another one outside. She moved closer to him trying to comfort him. He turned to her and said in a cohesive tone, "It's almost night. You need to go back home now."

"Mahdi, don't worry. I'll keep thinking about it until I find a solution to this problem."

He nodded and went back to lock the hall's door. He walked her to the house's door where she had left her car.

"Try to reach there before the press conference. It's only half an hour away." He said to her.

"Of course. I'll keep in touch but not on the phone."

He looked to her like he did not want her to leave but said, "Maha, Drive carefully, please!"

She smiled and nodded a confident nod. She moved towards the door to get into her car and leave Palestine Street.

Meanwhile, the tracker under her car was continuing to flash giving its current location to Black Sand in real time; in addition to the two members in the Cherokee watching the girl leave and telling Scott Oziling about it—all while the camera fixed on the house across the street was watching what was going on in silence.

Chapter 60

Everything will collapse...

With sadness surrounding him from every side, Mahdi buried his cigarette in the ash graveyard in front of him. He was sitting in his living room almost reaching despair from the end of the chain of quest for what Al-Mukhtar had left after reaching a dead end.

He was thinking of what could happen to the country if the intensity of the economic collapses in the world increased. The country would declare austerity, increase the taxes to gain revenue, lift the subsidizing of fuel, electricity, and water, and let unnecessary employees go. Unemployment would become rampant; recession will fall and goods will be left unsold. Then, an army of the hungry would come out pouring their indignation on everything in their way. People could not understand what the state meant when it was about bread. People would realize that they always have to hold their rulers accountable to guarantee their rights from getting lost, and that the human waves all over the world believe that bulls will not plow the fields if not followed by their whips. Such are the men of power. They are followed by people with their demonstrations and strikes to make sure they continue to work on the right track; otherwise, they would divert from it, leading their countries into the abyss.

Mahdi realized the seriousness of what would happen if he did not find Al-Mukhtar's treasure when there was still time for it to save the country. If it was too late, it would be found one way or another and get looted. Mahdi realized that it would be too late when the country's government would cease to exist at the hands of the revolting hungry. Then, no one would be able to save anything. The economy would have totally collapsed.

One man can change everything.

He thought he could prolong it more to find the country's buoy. He needed focus and calmness more than any time before to understand what the secret makers wanted to get at from a quest journey that ended with an empty metal safe. He felt that one of the most difficult situations for a human being was fighting to save his homeland, but he could not while the men in power did nothing despite having the keys to making the impossible possible. Will was what created miracles, but without true power, it was like a rifle without an ammo; good for nothing other than being a golf club, which makes it a cheap tool forgoing its goal to fight for the homeland in exchange for stripping it off its power that if found, would make the impossible possible.

With three beats, the living room's quietness was blasted by the eighties clock filling Mahdi's ears with its ringing noise announcing exactly half past six o'clock—the time for the Ministry of Justice's press conference.

Chapter 61

Scott Oziling was just informed that the small car had stopped in front of its young owner's house on Palestine Street. While Maha stayed home alone, she had just arrived to her house and entered it. She did not get to change her clothes as she headed directly to watch TV to follow the press conference on the investigation results of President Al-Mukhtar's death.

Meanwhile, Major-General Maher Abdelfattah was passionately following the announcer's words on TV announcing moving to the Ministry of Justice's press conference hall to convey the events of that conference. Mahdi was anxiously waiting for it, although the electrical current was starting to fluctuate in his home because of the storm that suddenly hit and started to affect the electrical power, going between weak and strong over and over.

The important thing is the TV still worked.

On the official channel, a tall man with grey hairs on the sides wearing a grey suit stood on a podium carrying the Ministry of Justice's logo. The Iraqi flag was placed behind him to the right. On the podium in front of him was a rainbow of logos from various news agencies and satellite channels placed on colorful microphones.

With a voice full of confidence, the man on the podium introduced himself as Professor Salem Jerjis, a medical examiner and head of the committee overseeing the autopsy of the ousted president, Mohammed Al-Mukhtar. He clarified that he was about to announce the results his committee reached regarding the death of the former president.

The Professor was standing before dozens of reporters' eyes from news agencies and local and international satellite channels, but he could not see the reporters' faces clearly. The lights from the cameras and flashes set on him obscured his vision of them. He used his voice to state what he wanted to state before them.

"As the medical examiner assigned to the case of personally overseeing the autopsy of President Al-Mukhtar's body, I hereby announce the results the committee has reached. Most importantly, and what I confirm is that President Mohammed Al-Mukhtar has passed affected by..."

Jerjis hemmed and gulped some water from the plastic bottle on the podium in front of him. Major-General Maher's eyes widened and he was beset by a wave of worry. The Professor went on.

"President Al-Mukhtar has passed affected by a sudden heart-attack..." Major-General Maher breathed a sigh of relief and Jerjis continued, "I confirm from my thorough observation of Al-Mukhtar's body that the authorities seem to have kept the ousted President's safe in his holding location, but the sudden stop of the heart is something that cannot be prevented in anyway..."

With half a smile and a hand on his cheek, Mahdi was following Jerjis' words in the press conference, which did not last for more than ten minutes followed by a Q&A with the press for another ten minutes.

The authorities are still lying!

Mahdi did not know whether the medical examiner before him was threatened to say what he said, or if he was an Intelligence agent himself. The man was saying the opposite of what he received on the "bullet" memory unit and the video that showed how the President was murdered by swapping his inhaler with another one carrying a lethal matter.

The Professor finished the press conference and promised the reporters an electronic copy of the forensic report of Al-Mukhtar's and he left the conference hall.

Starting that night, Professor Salem Jerjis would be strictly pro-
hibited from speaking to the media and would be put completely
under house arrest. Two nights later, a civilian car whose passengers would claim to be from the government would take him to
what they would claim to be an important meeting. It would take
him to an unknown destination and the Professor would forever
disappear.

As for Al-Mukhtar's case, the relevant international entities would
close it due to their occupancy with the global economic collapse.
But it would be raised and discussed internationally later, and an
international committee would be formed to dig up President Mohammed Al-Mukhtar's grave and reexamine samples of his remains
identifying the real cause of death...

Assassination by hydrogen cyanide.

Chapter 62

12:00 a.m. Baghdad time.

The man in the elegant suit turned off the TV after he was full of what he watched of the reactions of the agencies on the press conference that the Ministry of Justice held, in addition to watching many international channels to follow the economic developments in the world.

He looked at his watch that was counting past twelve. He glanced over his phone's screen and got up to leave the wood-walled room.

***

At his home, Mahdi had just finished a short conversation with Maha over Facebook. He chatted with her about what they saw on the press conference. He closed his laptop's screen and got up to make himself a cup of coffee after he was able to grab a simple bite to satisfy his hunger. But as he was entering the kitchen, he was surprised by even more disturbance in the electrical current. The light in the living room fluctuated before the electricity went out completely.

He went to the display in the room with the aid of his cellphone's light and took out a rechargeable electric flashlight from one of its drawers. He abandoned the idea of making coffee. Exhaustion overtook him drawing him towards his bedroom. He put the flashlight by his head and threw himself on his bed.

At that time, the black Cherokee left while another similar car replaced it on Mahdi's street. They swapped roles as the operatives as the first car's crew needed to rest. They withdrew in their car back to Black Sand's base in the middle of Baghdad.

In the private wing at Mahdi's house that belonged to his father, the antique hall was still locked and as was except for Mahdi and

Maha's footprints that disturbed the layer of dust stretched over the floor and carpet, in addition to the metal safe that was left open announcing its emptiness, while the One Thousand and One Nights book remained on the table in the middle of the hall.

Chapter 63

Everything will collapse...

.

.

The Empire is enslaved and three men substituted...

.

.

Look within yourself for salvation...

I have thrown you the buoy...

.

.

In a blue tomb standing on pillars of souls...

.

.

Strings of the Bull's Lyre stripped off...

Despite his severe exhaustion, Mahdi was on his bed struggling with flashes of those phrases that passed before him like a tape of events lightning in his head like the flash of lightening that was hitting the capital and sneaking its light through his bedroom's curtains. The darkness and the sound of thunder surrounded his house but his mind did not answer to sleep.

He crossed a big portion of resolving those puzzles with Maha's help.

Maha!

That patient girl that had tolerated his temper and repeated agitations. Why would she tolerate what she had seen of him like that? Rather she feared for him even from himself. Instead of devoting her time to finishing her graduation research, here she was spending time with him to help him find what he was looking for.

He remembered her Nina Ricci perfume that did not leave him… the way she looked pushing her hair behind her ear tickled his imagination. Such a move! He liked it so much when she did it as she would try to think deeply with him. She did it without realizing he liked her fingers as they passed through her blond hair, pushing it back behind her ear that was accessorized with a tiny earring. He smiled reviewing his thoughts that left the big problem and diverted to the details of one of his students. But Maha was not just a student to him. Not anymore. He felt he had to admit to himself he was attracted to her, or at least that he liked her, just like his eyelids were attracted to each other now from the drowsiness. He started to give into the first wave of sleep but something did not want him to fall asleep. The quest journey was not over yet. His mind was overtaken by the idea that the safe cannot be that hard to open only to be left empty. He had to think, but not now; he needed to rest…but his hand slowly stretched to the small wood table next to his bed. He felt it up in the dark to hold the electric flashlight and felt its side to find the power button. He pushed it with his thumb and the room was filled with light.

He got up from his bed, put on a winter robe and headed towards his room's door. Ever so slowly and quietly, he took the path leading to the outside courtyard. It was so cold his bones were trembling. He headed to his father's wing behind the house, took out the key from his pocket, and opened the metal door entering the antique room.

The smell of dampness seared again in addition to a relative warmth that surrounded his body. He passed the flashlight on the items in the room. Every now and again, the lightening was sending flashes into the antique hall from the window that Maha had partially removed the curtain from, hitting with its light some of the furniture and lighting the faces of people left as pictures on the room's walls.

He headed to the safe that was left empty and passed his eyes over the phrase 1,000 and 1 written on its door. He sat in front of it and looked at its single empty shelf. Even dust could not enter it all those years except in a small amount. He looked at the upper part of the shelf and then the lower one. He noticed a difference in the distance from the threshold of the safe to the end of its depth. The back of the safe in the upper half seemed closer to the hand than in the lower half. He reached his hand and felt up the lower half trying to measure the distance. He took it out, out it on the middle shelf, and pushed it forward...

The distance is shorter!

He felt with his fingers the face of the back of the upper safe starting with the corners and then passing on its face.

Suddenly, a strange circular bump teased his finger.

He took his hand out of the safe and pointed the flashlight inside. He looked at the spot where he felt a small bump that one could barely feel, but the bump did not have a different color from the rest of the safe on the inside. However, the flashlight helped him see the bump exactly and exposed to him the shape of that structure...

A place to enter a key!

Chapter 64

He became sure that the safe contained inside it a smaller safe as a part of it. The upper half of the safe seemed to be a tightly closed metal door with a keyhole that was cleverly disguised. Mahdi's thoughts diverted towards finding the key that would open this part of the safe.

Feeling a glimmer of hope after his former night of despair, he got up and directed the light to the room's furniture. Like a drowning man holding on to anything at the bottom of the sea, even if a straw, he pointed his flashlight towards everything around him; the Republican Emblems on the wall, his father's photos, Al-Mukhtar's photos. He shed the light on the plastic knight. He went closer to it and started checking its clothes. He searched its neck in case it was wearing a necklace with the key for that part of the safe. But he found nothing. He moved to the bookshelves. Lightning struck again and the books' titles were visible for a brief second. He wanted to find a space among the books might he find something there. He turned back looking towards the safe. Suddenly, bright light raided his eyes. It seemed so for the first moment, but after his pupils settled on it, it was not that bright. The electricity was back on. As things before him cleared up, he found himself looking at the safe itself, but what caught his attention more, what shocked him like a thunderbolt piercing his brain, was that as he looked to the safe, his eyes climbed to the table and the hourglass on it. The hourglass had finished its sand again from its upper half to the lower one leaving its top empty…

Except for a small sparkling thing in the shape of a key.

***

"You've got the words to change a nation, but you're biting your tongue

You've spent a lifetime stuck in silence, afraid you'll say something wrong

If no one ever hears it, how we gonna learn your song?

So come on, come on..."

Focused on her red nail polish that she was applying on her toe-nails, Maha was humming the words to Emeli Sande's song that she found to be representative of President Al-Mukhtar and what he had done for his country. She looked at the clock that was approaching one after midnight. She did not know why she was feeling relieved after a tiring day she spend with Mahdi. She tried to busy herself before withdrawing to sleep in order to regain her energy for tomorrow to think of what Mahdi's father left of an empty safe.

She was more relieved after the call she made with her mother two hours earlier. It was a short call. Her mother explained that she had completed her preliminary tests to have her surgical procedure done in one of Istanbul's hospitals the next day. She knew her mother's bravery and tolerance of pain. She had the same strength in that call, which assured Maha regarding her condition.

She sealed the nail polish bottle and waited for it to dry on her nails while continuing to hum to that song...

"You've got a heart as loud as lions, so why let your voice be tamed?

Maybe we're a little different, there's no need to be ashamed

You've got the light to fight the shadows, so stop hiding it away

Come on, come on..."

***

Mahdi put the flashlight on the table next to the One Thousand and One Nights book and went to grab the hourglass to break it and get the key, but what obstructed raising it from the table was the wool thread connected to its upper base after Maha had turned it upside down. He reached for his lighter in his pocket, lit it, and brought it closer to the thread.

Who said smoking had no benefits?

He easily cut the thread, took the hourglass outside the hall where the ground was solid. He let it fall from his hand to its end turning into scattered shreds, stray sand grains, and a key.

He grabbed the key and hurried back into the antique room. He took the flashlight and turned it back on, sat in front of the safe pointing the light at the keyhole, and put the key in. He turned to the right once, and again, then the key settled vertically. He pulled it towards himself and the small door was open.

With the light from the flashlight passing on it, what was behind the door was revealed. Mahdi saw something sparkling that was placed on a piece of white paper.

He reached his hand and took them out. He put the paper on the ground and held the metal item. It was a necklace with a short chain carrying one small ring. He looked at the ring that showed nothing, but its edge was carved with a fraction number:

1/40.000

Mahdi knit his brows. He put the necklace and flashlight on the ground and took the paper that he thought had something to do with the necklace. The paper carried a strange text. He started reading it overlaid with utter mysteriousness.

Chapter 65

1:00 a.m. Baghdad time.

Mahdi started reading the text on the letter he found in the safe.

A Sumerian seal...

In the middle of the Round City...

Look in it for the eleventh woman of it...

And collect from her waist the three divine jewels...

Above an altar of grapes and pomegranate cross...

And behind a cross and a banner...

And at the feet of a green crescent...

Plant the necklace where the lost knight's spear was planted...

It will turn like the sun disk...

When some of eleven arrows pierce it...

At the eleventh hour...

The light of the mirror shines...

To show a buoy opening by the meeting of the four elements of existence...

Or you will find it asleep at the cover of...

The last words of the letter was erased by drops of water that had fallen on the blue ink making the word difficult to read.

Mahdi closed his eyes and put his head between his hands sitting on the dusty ground before the safe. He felt it was getting harder. A strange feeling squeezed and twisted his heart in sadness and pain. He would not understand the meaning of the letter in time. The country would collapse before he reached the treasure to save it. He threw another glance towards the paper.

Understanding it would be impossible.

He tried hard to focus on the words in front of him, but the difficulty of what he was reading allied with his eyelids that have started to fail him and long for sleep after a trying day. He folded the paper and put it in his pocket with the metal necklace. He got up, switched off the hall's lights, and locked its door before heading to his room to sleep hoping morning would help him understand what he found.

***

On the other side of the world, the collapses were continuing to happen. Decreasing the interest to zero that the US banks declared was not enough to avoid the crisis. The dollar continued to rapidly decline in the face of gold. The disaster would reach the rest of the world more severely soon and the countries that had large quantities of dollar would lose the value of what they own…

Gold is the savior.

Chapter 66

9:00 a.m. Baghdad time.

Holding his father's letter, Mahdi started his day with a cigarette, a cup of coffee, and a distracted mind reading what was left for him of text in a blue ink on paper where the last word of it was sunken in drops of water that obscured it and deleted its letters.

There was nothing connecting the phrases other than the number 11 that he noticed it being repeated three times in that letter.

Look in it for the eleventh woman of it…

When some of the eleven spears pierce it…

At the eleventh hour…

He squeezed his brain trying to find the connection between the phrases carrying that number. As soon as he was able to solve the puzzle of the number 39 and the puzzle of the safe numbers with Maha, problem of solving the number 11 appeared in an entangled circle of puzzling codes.

Al-Mukhtar's treasure…A savior for the country…

He read the text once again.

A Sumerian seal…

In the middle of the Round City…

All he could understand was the phrase "in the middle of the Round City" as that referred to Baghdad that had been built in the Abbasid era in the form of a city with a circular wall, and the circle remained a symbol of it. But how would he find the Sumerian seal in it?

He roamed his thoughts looking for the starting point of solving the puzzle. Suddenly he found himself in his weakest states. He has endured many troubles although he did not want to give up. His carrying that responsibility was the line separating saving the country's economy and getting taken up in the raging storm of global economic collapse.

He grabbed his phone and sent Maha a text.

"We have to meet."

He put the paper aside and sipped his coffee while turning the metal necklace in his hand.

At the same time, Maha woke up to the vibrating sound of her phone on the table near her bed. She looked with half open eyes at Mahdi's message. Curiosity pulled her out of bed to prepare herself to meeting him again. She wondered if he found something else as the last thing that happened with them was an empty safe that they opened with great difficulty. She took a hot shower to prepare herself to go to Zayouna.

***

In his wood-walled room, the man in the elegant suit started his day following the economic news. The oil barrel prices reached a record low...

35 USD/barrel.

The news of strikes in some US banks and companies rolled and protests started in some cities there. At the same time, the fear of the collapses infection was covering the whole world same as the fear of that infection moving to Iraq soon took over the man in the elegant suit. The simplest thing that could happen was for the government to announce a sudden austerity for the remainder of the year, which meant increasing taxes, reducing wages, and dismissing governmental employees. Protests would erupt and chaos would prevail. That would be the prelude to a security breakdown of dire consequences.

A Sumerian seal...

In the middle of the Round City...

Mahdi repeated it to himself while looking at the bottom of his cup from which he drank the coffee without sugar. He looked at the shapes inside the cup as though he might he find something that would inspire a certain shape for him to look for. Sumerian seals were only found at the Iraqi Museum. The Museum keeps hundreds of Iraqi artifacts divided on halls based on the era of Iraq's ancient civilizations.

He looked at the eighties clock that was approaching 10 a.m. He had not received a call or text from Maha yet. He grabbed the remote control and switched on the TV.

The Iraqi television was also following the news of the global economic collapse in addition to airing scenes from inside the national Council of Representative's building where fierce arguments erupted among its members. All that was being discussed was finding ways to save the country's economic situation in light of the recent developments. The Council of Representatives was divided between those pushing for a rapid austerity measure and those refusing it to appear in the media as supporters of the public at the expense of the national economy.

Mahdi watched those scenes while feeling he had the solution to cool all those problems and conflicts, but...

He had to crack the letter's code first.

His phone flashed briefly and then stopped. He held it and looked at the screen. Maha had called and quickly hung up. Mahdi understood that she has woken up and received the last message.

He only had to wait for her to discuss what he found in his father's safe.

The Black Sand operative ended the communication with Scott Oziling who told him and his companion to not move on the lawyer no matter what until they receive direct orders from him. Despite those instructions, Oziling's orders were to stay alert and firmly and clearly observe. Any minute, the two operatives might receive orders to implement a quality mission in Zayouna in the middle of Baghdad as Black Sand operatives, in coordination with powerful parties in the country, with IDs that did not allow the Iraqi Security Forces to obstruct them. They had gained the freedom to move in the capital under a legal cover in exchange for secret deals.

Chapter 67

10:30 a.m. Baghdad time.

"Okay, same place…Deal…Eleven…I'll meet you there with some new details…Fine, bye."

Mahdi ended a phone call with no details with Maha. He conveyed to her to meet at the same café on Palestine Street at exactly eleven o'clock. He started preparing himself to go there.

Maha also prepared herself to meet him. While checking the water status in her car's radiator before leaving on time, she heard sirens of official cars that sounded like police or ambulance sirens roaming the nearby main streets. She felt something odd going on today that did not feel normal at all.

A quarter of an hour before the agreed upon time, Mahdi walked out in long strides towards the main street of Zayouna. He passed by a Jeep Cherokee that was parked in one of the bystreets. The Black Sand operative in it nodded his head and reached for the communication device while the other one adjusted his sunglasses and chewing gum waiting for Scott Oziling's orders, which came telling them not to move and continue to watch what the lawyer would do upon reaching the main street.

The Cherokee watched Mahdi's steps closely. He reached the main street and got into a cab. The black Jeep stopped and started going back to its stationing location near his house. The camera fixed on the house facing Mahdi's picked up the car's recent movements.

A few minutes later, in the old Baghdadi café in Beirut Square on Palestine Street, Maha arrived and waited for Mahdi as she listened to classic Iraqi songs that flowed from that café's corners into her ears. She glanced her eyes over the old photos on the walls of the café; Al-Sarrafiya Bridge during last century's sixties, cream sellers,

King Faisal II, and The Leader Abdelkarim Qasem. "How could the killer and the killed be on the same wall?!" she wondered.

She ignored that wondering and moved her eyes on the remainder of the pictures until she noticed a thirtyish man entering the café. It was Mahdi.

His eyes roamed the wood chairs and tables to find her sitting on the same table they met at last time. He pulled a chair and sat in front of her.

"Good morning."

"Hi Mahdi!" she looked at his unshaven beard, "you look tired."

"Kind of, but it doesn't matter," he looked at her with intensity, "Maha, I found what's inside the safe!"

She ecstasized at hearing this shocking news. She pushed her hair behind her ear.

"How? Explain to me?"

He smiled, "The safe we opened had inside it another smaller one as part of the main safe's structure. It opens with s mall key that was placed in the lower half of the hour glass immersed in sand."

"You mean you found the key in the hourglass?"

"Exactly. I broke it and took the key and opened the secret part of the safe."

"And what did you find there?" she asked passionately.

He did not move his eyes from her and reached in his jacket's inner pocket. He took the paper out with his fingertips, looked around him and was assured by the place's tranquility and no one observing them, he put the paper on the table keeping it folded. Maha reached her hand to it, but he placed his hand on the paper preventing her. "Not before we get something to drink."

Scott Oziling hung up the intercom placed on his wooden desk. He has just been informed of the place the girl's—the lawyer's companion—car was parked through the signals from the tracker attached to the bottom of her car. That was not the only information he received, but he knew the place the lawyer and his companion were sitting in: which café, which table, what they ordered to drink, and how the girl seemed nervous constantly stomping the floor.

"They look like lovers when you look at them," Oziling was told in a low volume voice…

from inside the café.

Chapter 68

"Have you noticed the strange movement on the streets today?" asked Maha, drinking her chocolate milk she ordered.

"Yes," Mahdi answered, "there is a suspicious security movement. Police cars and ambulances are heavily spread today." He gulped his black coffee. "I hope it's not a part of a precautionary measure prior to decisions that could cause disturbances in light of the global economic deterioration."

Maha closed her eyes and nodded her head, imagining the chaos that could take place if the government announced austerity precautionary measures on its citizens. She looked at him.

"Okay, let's read what's on the paper."

Mahdi reached his hand and opened the paper turning it in her direction. He pushed it towards her and she started reading what was written on it.

A Sumerian seal...

In the middle of the Round City...

Her eyes narrowed on the words.

Plant the necklace where the lost knight's spear was planted...

It will turn like the sun disk...

She followed the words to the last word soaked into a few drops that mixed in with the blue ink. She looked to Mahdi with eyes that are lost in a strange text.

"Okay," she said, "let's reread it and crack what we can of it."

Mahdi nodded in agreement and started reading:

"A Sumerian seal in the middle of the Round City." She looked to Mahdi who wiped his eyes.

"It seems that he is confirming that what he has hidden is in Baghdad, the Round City. Remember the President's letter when he said 'Look within yourself for salvation'." He said.

Maha liked that connection and said, "But the Sumerian seal, how would we infer it, and how do we find it?" Mahdi pursed his lips and indicated for her to continue.

She read, "Look in it for the eleventh woman of it."

Mahdi's memories took him back to the Iraqi Museum that he visited with his friends in college. He squeezed his thoughts to remember what he saw there for Sumerian seals.

"Maha, there are Sumerian seals inside the museum placed in the Sumerian Civilization Hall itself. The letter can't mean anything else. Al-Mukhtar does not want to refer to things that can be changed or its appearance altered. Artifacts have been at the museum for decades and will remain so."

"Do you remember there being a seal with a woman that has something to do with the number 11?" she asked in response.

He smiled. "Seals are small cylindrical items. You can't thoroughly examine the shapes carved on them easily. Besides, I did not look closely at them during that visit. I don't know. Maybe we have to visit the museum and see them."

Maha nodded liking the idea and she resumed reading, "And collect from her waist the three divine jewels."

"The problem is…." said Mahdi, "the lines are connected to each other in a strange way. You cannot move on to the next step without understanding what he means by the first. We have to find the seal first, then the woman, then identify what he referred to as the three divine jewels."

«You mean the grapes and pomegranate cross, and the cross and banner..."

He interrupted her, "And the green crescent."

She took a sip of her hot drink and continued, "Plant the necklace where the lost knight's spear was planted. Necklace?"

Mahdi reached into his pocket and took out the metal necklace. He placed it on the table making a ringing sound that caught the attention of a young tanned guy sitting on a table a few meters away.

"This is what I found with the letter, Maha,"

She took the necklace and started turning it in her hands. She looked at the number engraved on the ring hanging from the chain: 1/40.000

The ring did not show any more than that.

"The lost knight's spear," she said and looked at the letter again. "it will turn like the sun disk when some of eleven arrows pierce it."

"At the eleventh hour, the mirror's light shines. The number 100 appears three times in the letter." Mahdi said.

The length of the letter raised its difficulty. Maha pushed her hair behind her ear feeling a total loss.

"Mahdi, I suggest we start searching one step after the other. We won't understand anything like this, especially since the letter is missing its last word as a result of what has fallen on it and we won't be able to read that word," she said.

Mahdi drew a cigarette from his cigarette pack and lit it. "I hope we find what we're looking for at the right time. The quest can get lengthy and it would be too late."

"So, let's make use of every possible minute. We have to go to the museum and find the Sumerian seal," she responded.

Mahdi blew out his cigarette's smoke unsure of that step, but he had no other light. A Sumerian seal... Inside the Round City....

He called for the waiter and paid the check. He put out his cigarette and the two got up leaving the place. They headed to the car outside while the young tan man too paid his check.

Outside, a yellow cab started moving following Maha's car while the young tan man disappeared. The tracker's light under Maha's car continued to flash intermittently informing Scott Oziling of his target's next destination.

Chapter 69

En route to the museum in Alawi area on Karkh side, Mahdi was more aware of the strange state of the streets. Security checkpoints spread in an unprecedented manner. In addition to the water pumping vehicles going down the streets to disperse demonstrations with Anti-Riot Police. Helicopters of security forces and the Military were flying over the capital. Something had happened, or was about to happen.

Mahdi reached his hand to the radio in the car. He turned it on and looked for the official radio station. The announcer's voice sounded through the radio completely serious while reading an announcement.

"…Shortly we will convey to you a group of the Council of Ministers' decisions that have been approved in its emergency session this morning. We call your attention to that…"

The announcer repeated that text once more.

"Our dear listeners, we call on your attention that shortly we will convey…"

Mahdi looked at Maha who heard the announcer too as she drove towards Waziriya, intending to cross over the metal Sarafiya Bridge.

"Something is about to happen, Maha!" Mahdi was taken by a torrent of worry.

"It seems obvious. I hope we get to the museum before something happens."

A few minutes later, Maha's car was crossing Sarafiya Bridge towards Karkh. The announcer's voice sounded again through the radio's speakers. He read the number of the emergency Council of Ministers session and started to recite the most significant decisions of it. Mahdi and Maha pushed all their focus towards what he was saying. All of the decisions of the Council of Ministers were regarding the global financial crisis. The Council had made critical decisions to face the crisis.

Of the decisions issued by the supreme executive council in the country were raising the fuel prices locally by 25%; imposing taxes on importing vegetables and fruit by 10%, on tobacco by 350%, and a long list of taxes imposed on devices; vehicles; plane tickets; and communication, internet, and post companies. In addition to dismissing 15% of public sector employees according to certain criteria. All in an attempt to gain more revenues and decrease expenditures after the oil barrel price went down to below 35 dollars, while the US dollar continued collapsing by the hour in the face of a global economic collapse disaster.

The announcer finished reciting the decisions and moved to a quick newscast on the latest updates regarding the global financial crisis.

The ball of fire of had reached Baghdad.

Mahdi felt a twist in his stomach and a quickening in his breathing. He felt cold all over his body and his fingertips. His forehead was in cold sweat, and his brain was clouded by a killer fogginess.

"People will revolt, Maha!" Mahdi said breathing faster than usual. "That's why the government has spread its forces."

"I'm worried, Mahdi," Maha confessed, "worried we may not find the gold in time."

"And suppose we do find it, whose hands will it fall in? We have to think about that. Even if we find it, we have to keep it a secret until we let the people know that there is a stock that would save the country so corrupt parties in the state won't steal it or confiscate it for their benefit."

Maha felt the situation get more complicated. Her face gained a layer of worry mixed in with fear. She felt her leg shaking as she pressed the fuel pedal, but she kept on driving. The passed Utaifiya area and were not close to the Muthana Airport Highway. Mahdi noticed military units coming out of the airport in armored vehicles.

It seemed that the military will participate in keeping order too.

The yellow cab was still following Maha's small car and informing the entity that sent it of the lawyer and his companion's destination. While Scott Oziling made himself his daily milk and protein shake, he listened to the information he received from his assistants as acquired from the tracker attached to the bottom of Maha's car.

With great difficulty, among the military convoys, Maha made her way towards the Alawi area headed for the museum. She crossed over the tunnel leading to it. She and Mahdi looked at the gate placed in its doorway that was built in the traditional ancient Babylonian and Assyrian form with two fake lamassus.

She turned right towards the second door of the museum approaching a small parking lot where she could park and go with Mahdi towards the entrance of the Iraqi Museum.

A few minutes later, the cab stopped nearby while the lawyer and his companion walked towards the entrance of the museum. The security and military mobilization at the end of the street caught their attention as there lay the Iraqi Ministry of Foreign Affairs, and the very end of the street, the main gate to the presidential Green Zone leading to the Republican Palace.

Chapter 70

An armored military vehicle was stopped at the door of the National Museum. The museum appeared to be closed in the face of its visitors, which was a normal procedure during any security crisis in the capital. The authorities feared the reoccurrence of the 2003 events when the theft and vandalism gangs used the collapse of the Iraqi security system by effect of the US Forces entering to mess about the museum, looting and destroying the treasures and artifacts inside it.

Mahdi and Maha did not get closer to the soldiers standing at the gate by their armored vehicle. The answer was obvious—the museum was closed for security reasons.

"We won't get to the Sumerian Hall, Maha," Mahdi placed his hands in his jacket's pockets and looked in the direction of the military vehicles' movements on the street leading to the Green Zone. But Maha did not answer when she got a clever idea. She reached her hand into her brown jacket's pocket and took out her phone. She touched the screen with her thumb and pressed the phone to her ear. Mahdi watched what she was doing while she gave him a confident look. She turned around and started speaking on the phone.

"Yes…By the door…I know that, but it's important, Osama…I wish you could help…We won't be there long, believe me…I left the car far…Of course we won't need a camera…I'll give you the cellphones…Okay…" she turned to Mahdi and winked, "I'm grateful…we're waiting for you."

She hung up the call, put her hands behind her back, and moved closer to him. "What do you think now?"

Mahdi raised an eyebrow in exclamation. "Who did you talk with?" she pretended to use her phone's screen.

"With Osama, the museum guide. He helped me when I was looking for information regarding retrieving stolen artifacts in coordination with the Interpol in my research project that you supervise…Professor."

Mahdi closed his eyes and recalled the topic of her graduation research that he was supervising. Her research project was concerned with the efforts made by the Iraqi lawyers to retrieve stolen Iraqi artifacts from outside of Iraq. He looked to her and said, "You have made great connections thanks to that research."

She smiled, "You'll meet Osama. He's a great guy. He helped me a lot and explained to me what the museum has gone through since it was looted in 2003. I bet you will give me a high grade on that research. You have seen my efforts yourself."

Mahdi laughed full of admiration for her wits. She was looking into his eyes, but she looked behind him suddenly and her expression changed. He turned to look behind him and saw a young man of medium height wearing prescription glasses with a black frame behind the museum's metal fence. The young man approached the door and spoke briefly to one of the soldiers. The soldier looked towards Mahdi and Maha and pointed to them to come closer.

The man in the yellow cab stopped at the other side of the street ended a call he made on his cellphone during which informed the person on the other line that the lawyer and his companion have entered the museum and handed their cellphones to a young man who appeared to be employed by the museum and were out of sight.

In his wood-walled room, the man in the elegant suit was walking the room back and forth smoking his cigar. He attentively followed the news that morning regarding the heavy security spread in the capital. He thought that the lawyer would not solve the puzzle in time. He was getting more worried by the second.

People would not keep quiet about the government's recent decisions. The economy would collapse, followed by the government, and the country would drown an endless chaos.

***

Mahdi, Maha, and the guide Osama, who was very nice to them, crossed the door set for the museum staff. The main door was closed due to the recent security situation. Mahdi and Maha found themselves under a high ceiling with drawings inspired by the ancient Iraqi civilizations. Osama indicated for them to follow him. He took a left towards a long corridor with doors on both sides. That corridor contained the staff rooms and leads to a huge metal door, which the three passed by to find themselves in a closed space from all sides except the one from which they entered. Osama excused himself and entered a room whose door overlooked that space. After about seven minutes, he came back out and told them that the procedures were complete. He acquired the Museum Manager's approval to allow them to enter the antique halls. After some minutes, a middle-aged woman came out from the room with a key in her hand. The three followed her towards another metal door to the left. She unlocked the huge door and indicated for them to enter.

The three crossed the door and its sound rang behind them. The woman closed and locked it, then turned back to the room.

She locked them all there…

Behind fortified doors!

Chapter 71

12:30 p.m. Baghdad time.

Mahdi did not notice the antique statues that predated Islam and which stood on the right of the corridor that he was left in with Maha and Osama. A suffocating feeling had overtaken him after the woman locked the door and left them there. Maha was conversing with Osama near one of those statues while he remained looking towards the space they had come in from through the metal openings in the locked door.

"Mr. Mahdi!" exclaimed a smiling Osama.

Mahdi turned, "Yes, Mr....Osama?"

"This way, please," the guide instructed.

Mahdi hesitated over asking why the woman locked the door, but Osama noticed his worry of the situation, "Are you alright?"

Mahdi answered with signs of hesitation on his face, "Fine, yes."

The guide smiled and turned walking in the corridor by the statues standing there. Maha followed, and then Mahdi, whose eyes were examining those artifacts, slowly forgot the locked door. Some of those statues were two meters tall with no head. Most of them raised their left palm in a salute they used to do in those eras. After walking for a few meters in that corridor, they crossed its end and Mahdi and Maha found themselves in a spacious place with a high ceiling.

The two remember this place well. Mahdi has visited the museum once with his friends, while Maha often visited to work on her research project concerning the retrieval of artifacts. To the left of that space was a wide stairwell leading to the second floor. On the wall of the stairwell hung a gypsum mural several meters in height and width. It was carved with meticulous Islamic ornamentation.

It was an introduction to the Islamic artifacts that a door to the right led to its hall. In front of the stairwell is the entrance to a hall that contained a mixture of ancient artifacts and Islamic heritage.

The guide turned followed by Mahdi and Maha to climb the wide stairwell. After passing its stairs, the stairwell took them to the left leaving them facing a bronze sign with the writing. "Sumerian Civilization Hall".

The three stepped inside the hall that had a high ceiling, big area, and vast space. The first thing their fell upon was the Warka Vase.

"Ok, what do you want to see?" Osama asked. Mahdi and Maha exchanged looks. They did not want to tell him what they were looking for.

"Actually," said Maha, "I have spoken with Professor Mahdi about my visits to the museum for my research project and he came with me for two reasons: First, to check what I mentioned in the museum himself, and second, to satisfy his curiosity to see these artifacts after I have spoken to him about them. As I told you, Professor Mahdi is supervising my research on the role of lawyers in retrieving the artifacts that were stolen from here and smuggled out of the country."

Osama nodded his head with his arms crossed. "Okay, I have explained to you in your previous visits what is in this hall, and I have told you what was stolen of it, and what was retrieved and restored. In addition to explaining about the artifacts that were stolen but are yet to be retrieved. So, you can explain these things to Mr. Mahdi yourself and I'll be nearby."

"Walk around the hall freely with the company of the security cameras only!" he added with a hint of warning.

Maha smiled understanding the message. She indicated to Mahdi to move while Osama remained by the hall's entrance watching their movements closely. The two went to the glass display placed to the right of the entrance, which had displayed in it a collection of Sumerian seals.

Chapter 72

24K gold oz. – 2,615.20 USD.

Everything will collapse.

The wood-walled room was now filled with a foggy atmosphere due to the smoke from the third cigar that the man in the elegant suit has smoked that morning while watching the breaking news ticker on TV.

The dollar reserve will not benefit the country.

After a few minutes, he received a phone call informing him of putting the capital under heavy security presence by the Ministry of Interior in cooperation with units of the military. The nightmare of the overwhelming popular movement against the government was seriously dominating him. The government's recent measures were a play with fire in the face of millions whose power were trapped by those decisions by the Council of Ministers. He knew that the security spread would only make the situation more complicated as that on its own was a provocative act to the people who had now become furious with the government. The government would not be able to justify its decisions no matter how hard its media machine worked. And all of that was just fear on one side, but the harder side was the economic collapse that no one had a weapon to fight except Al-Mukhtar's treasure.

The man in the elegant suit sheathed his cigarette in the full ashtray in front of him. He closed his eyes leaning back and wishing the lawyer would move faster.

Through the display's glass, Mahdi and Maha were looking at the Sumerian seals it contained. Cylindrical and flat seals were placed in it, and in various sizes, in addition to rectangular shaped pieces of colored clay the stamps had passed on to reflect what had been carved on them. Tens of seals with meticulous carving, most of which captured scenes of animals and various ornamentation.

There is no sign of a woman in the seals.

Mahdi looked to Maha who read his look. They could not return empty handed. They were tied by a secret that could not be exposed, so they could not ask Osama, who was standing nearby near a seal pointing to a woman connected to the number 11 one way or another. They looked at the seals again. Hope was starting to wither with every move their eyes made from one seal to the other.

Nothing here of what the Advisor meant!

Osama noticed they were spending a long time by the seals display. He cleared his throat and Maha understood that. The guide could not allow them to stay at the museum for long due to the odd security reasons the capital was living that day. Maha looked to Mahdi, urging him to pretend to look at the hall's other artifacts. They turned passing the artifacts there. Displays with various artifacts on the right wall, and other artifacts on platforms in glass cages dispersed across the hall. Among them were the Sumerian woman mask and small statues reaching to the end of the hall where in a glass cage was placed—the original Sumerian Lyre.

Osama walked to the middle of the hall to keep them in sight although they were being watched by the security cameras in the corners and ceiling. Maha wanted to know if Mahdi has found an idea among the seals or not, but there was not opportunity to speak with Osama there.

Mahdi turned, looked to Osama while he walked towards him and pretending to look at his watch.

"Okay, the place is great, but I'm concerned of the security situation today. Maha and I live on Rusafa side and I fear they may close the bridges leading there because of these strange procedures by the security forces. We must leave now."

Osama was surprised by Mahdi's sudden decision. "You haven't spent more than ten minutes here!" He wondered.

Mahdi raised his eyebrows. "If the situation wasn't as is, I would have spent the whole night among these treasures."

Osama smiled shrugging and giving in to his peculiar visitor's decision. Maha approached them. "Okay, Professor. I too fear they may close the roads."

"If that's what you want, suit yourselves." Osama answered.

Mahdi faked a smile and walked behind the guide towards the hall leading to the stairwell. He glanced at the seals display one last time.

No hope of finding the woman there.

They were all outside the Sumerian Hall. A feeling of the mission failing boiled in Mahdi's chest, the mission of finding the Sumerian seal that the Advisor's letter pointed to, and which he said it was in the middle of the Round City. He went down the stairs following Osama's steps while Maha followed them with a heart squeezed by a feeling of failure as well. A few minutes later, Mahdi and Maha received their phones from Osama who bid them farewell at the museum's door.

Mahdi breathed deeply after the feeling of being locked up behind the museum's fortified doors has subsided. They were searched at the door when exiting by the museum security. The crossed the street heading to the parking lot where Maha parked her car.

On the other side of the street, the man in the cab informed the entity that sent him what was going on: The lawyer and his companion exiting the museum and getting into their car, while the tracker under the car continued to inform the head of Black Sand, Scott Oziling, of the lawyer and his companion's movement in real time.

Major-General Maher Abdelfattah was extremely busy making calls with his men in the Intelligence Bureau to gather any information regarding an anticipated popular movement against the government as his bureau's duty was to sense danger before it happened. Among his calls were special calls with the leaders of the security forces to coordinate to prevent any possible danger in the capital through the Intelligence and the Peace Keeping Forces. The Ministry of Interior and the National Security Services were living a dynamic day awaiting an imminent popular movement.

Chapter 73

Maha had to use Salhiya Bridge to cross to Rusafa side as the security forces had closed the road leading to Jumhouriya Bridge before vehicles due to its proximity to the main entrance of the presidential Green Zone. The streets were disturbed by the police vehicles that some of them were even driving on the wrong side of the road on the bridge blasting their sirens. It was a very confusing situation.

"We did not find anything there…right?" Maha confirmed as she drove her car down the bridge towards Khalani Square.

"Not at all, Maha. All the seals carried scenes of animals and some other inexplicable and very meticulous images, while others carried intertwined ornamentation."

"A Sumerian seal. Mahdi, let's think outside the box. Most of the secret's puzzles did not mean exactly what was written in them. It means something related. We have to think like that," she said turning in the direction of Tahrir Square in the middle of the capital.

"I agree with you. They would not leave it that simple. Besides, if we assume the seal is one of the museum's seals, how would we use it? That on its own would be a problem. A woman in the eleventh of it…God!"

Maha shook her head apologetic. Silence prevailed between them until the car entered Tahrir Square intending to head for Palestine Street via the street adjacent to the Freedom Monument overlooking the square that was buzzing with police and security forces' vehicles. It has been the main place to hold demonstrations after 2003, and since then, the security forces have been encircling it from every side during demonstrations to prevent any riots the demonstrators may do.

"Maha," said Mahdi, "I hope we don't lose hope. The country is on the line. We must…"

Like a submarine that floated to the surface of the sea cracking ice, a strange idea cracked its way into his mind as soon as he found himself in Tahrir Square at the center of Baghdad.

"I found the seal!" he exclaimed, recalling in his mind the phrase In the middle of the Round City. "It's *the Freedom Monument!*"

Chapter 74

A Sumerian seal...

In the middle of the Round City...

Like blood spread through his veins, the shock of the thought that stormed Mahdi's mind spread in it placing him before the most important monuments of Baghdad. He passed over its every detail with lustful eyes.

Maha stopped her car by the side of the road. "The Freedom Monument?"

Mahdi nodded with a half confident smile, "Yes, Maha. The Freedom Monument. It is at the exact center of the capital and is inspired by the ancient cylindrical Sumerian seals which were turned over a rectangular patch of clay to reflect the shapes carved on the seal."

Maha tried to look at the monument but she needed to stop in front of it directly to thoroughly check its details. She held the gear shifter and placed it on reverse. She drove backwards a little to be able to take the round route again so the monument would be to her right. Then she moved to the front and turned to left starting to go slowly.

Mahdi looked at the monument on his right checking the bronze pieces placed on a raised rectangular mural of white stones. He started looking at the first bronze piece from the right.

The Freedom Monument sat at the exact center of the capital. It was designed by sculptor Jawad Salim in the fifties of the last century. He died before he saw the pieces he made hung fully on its glorious monument. The monument told the story of the 14th of July Revolution in Iraq in 1958, which was implemented by the army to overthrow the monarchy in Iraq and establish the first

Iraqi Republic. The monument represented a Sumerian seal that had passed on a patch of stone so what was carved on it could be read from right to left, passing through every detail of the Iraqi reality before, during, and after the revolution as the sculptor saw it.

Maha was driving slowly, allowing Mahdi to recall the shapes on the monument by looking at them. She turned around the turnabout for the first time and tried to make another round despite the major confusion that was prevailing in the square that hour due to the increase in security forces vehicles and personnel.

"Look in for the eleventh woman of it." Mahdi muttered with his eyes not leaving the monument; his eyes that were eating up the bronze pieces one after the other from right to left. He did not know what the phrase "the eleventh woman of it" meant as there were many figures personifying women placed in the chain of shapes the monument was composed of.

Maha did not say a word as she drove slowly. She wanted to leave him and the Freedom Monument alone. She noticed his eyes gaze at the protruding shapes on the stone mural. He would need time to decipher the code of the eleventh woman of it. He repeated in a low voice, "The eleventh woman in it…" while Maha was about to finish the second circle around the roundabout.

"To the house, Maha!" Mahdi burst, surprising her with his decision.

She looked to him, "Have you cracked the code?"

"No, but this way we'll raise the security personnel's suspicion. We'll go back the house and try to decipher it there."

Maha nodded in agreement. She left the roundabout behind her and took the route to the highway, but as soon she approached hit, she noticed the gas station to the right. She glanced at the car's fuel gauge.

Her car needed fuel.

"Mahdi, since we're close to the gas station, I'll go in and fill up. We need it." He nodded and wandered off in his mind to the Freedom Monument code and the eleventh woman of it.

In front of a short line of cars entering the station, Mahdi was inside the car trying to recall the shapes of the bronze pieces on the monument with his eyes closed. He started telling himself the story of the revolution that the monument's elements carry starting with its first to the right, while Maha was listening to his hallucination as she entered the station slowly behind a line of cars.

He mumbled with his eyes closed, "...The rebelling horse, the demonstration and raised signs...Then the martyr and the women crying over him...There is a lost child...A woman holding a child...And another raising her cloak crying...Then the political prisoner behind bars... The people holding the soldier's rifle...Then the soldier setting off the revolution holding his rifle...The woman carrying the freedom torch...Then the woman representing peace...And a woman with a palm tree behind her..."

He stopped counting and opened his eyes.

He found that the car has reached the fuel pump. He looked to Maha who turned off the engine and was about to get out, "I'll fill the tank," he said and she nodded.

Mahdi got out of the car and held the pump starting to fill the tank. He reviewed the elements of the monument once again after his memory was refreshed seeing it earlier.

The horse with demonstration...The martyr...The child...The woman holding a child...The crying woman...The political prisoner...The people...The soldier...The woman with the torch... Peace...Palm tree woman...

He stopped counting again although there were more shapes on the monument. He was drawing lines with his fingers on the car's roof that was dusty because of the downpours mixed in with dust, while holding the pump with the other hand.

He looked at the lines. There were 11 lines. The eleventh shape was the woman standing in front of fronds of a palm tree.

Indeed, the eleventh shape of the monument was of a woman!

The tank was full. Mahdi paid and got into the car. Maha moved to leave the station. Mahdi looked at her without speaking.

"What were you mumbling before we entered?" she asked.

He answered, "I checked with my memory the shapes of the monument up till the eleventh shape of it. Indeed, there was a woman."

She looked at him in surprise, "Which of the women on the monument is it?"

"The woman standing in front of a palm tree. The one after it is a pregnant woman carrying the harvest." he answered.

"Do you know its significance?" she asked, exiting toward the main road.

"Yes," he drew in a deep breath and continued. "the two women symbolize the Tigris and the Euphrates. The woman with the palm tree is the *Tigris.*"

Chapter 75

The word for Tigris in Arabic Dijla means palm trees while the word for Euphrates Furat means fertility[1]. Those meanings were what sculptor Jawad Salim drew upon the idea of designing those women connected in one form on his magnificent monument. He designed the monument with clever indications to tell the story of the revolution. He divided the monument into two halves. The right one told the state of sufferings, demonstrations, martyrs falling, fear of the unknown, and loss in conflicts. Then the monument was halved by what represented the eruption of the revolution enacted by the military and represented there by the soldier in the middle of it. The people were supporting him, holding the same rifle he held while the sun of freedom shone on the soldier's head. Then the state of freedom, the sculptor expressed it by the woman carrying the torch and he left her with no feet to give a sense that she is flying without constraints.

It followed that a state of peace after the revolution—from the sculptor's point of view—which he expressed by a woman calmly closing her eyes while the olive branches rose behind her with pigeons stopping on them. After that, there were the Tigris and Euphrates women who began the age of prosperity and development. Then the Arab and Kurd farmers with their shovels, and he put a face that resembles that faces of the ancient Assyrian statues for one of them. The monument ends at the far left with the Sumerian bull, the symbol of fertility, and agricultural wealth, in addition to the worker holding a hammer as a symbol for industry.

Maha smiled uttering the first two phrases from the Advisor's letter.

"A Sumerian seal…In the middle of the Round City." She continued, "Look in it for the eleventh woman of it. You're so clev-

---

1- "Jawad Salim wa Nasb Al-Hurriya" – By Jebra Ibrahim Jebra, p.157

er, Mahdi!" she said making her way toward Palestine Street, but Mahdi felt he had to continue solving the puzzle. He looked at his watch that was referring to 2:15 pm. He reached for his father's letter in his pocket.

"Look in it for the eleventh woman of it…

And collect from her waist the three divine jewels…" He read those words aloud for Maha to hear, and went on:

"Above an altar of grapes and pomegranate cross…

And behind a cross and a banner…

And at the feet of a green crescent…"

He folded the paper and put it back in his pocket. He took out his pack of cigarettes.

"Let's get to your house first," she said. "we'll be able to think clearly there. You have just solved a very mysterious part of it; we can solve the rest of the letter's code."

Mahdi was not that sure of it as he lit his cigarette.

"Do you expect we would be able to solve the remainder of the letter in time to save the economy?"

She laughed as she crossed the intersection leading to Zayouna, "You can, you genius!"

He smiled and blew out his cigarette's smoke towards the partially rolled down window. They were close to the house.

***

"Alright, noted."

The Black Sand operative said that from inside the Cherokee by Mahdi's house. Oziling has informed him of the near arrival of the car carrying the lawyer and his companion to his home street, and asked him and the other operative to be ready for it. Scott knew of their direction via the information coming to his office from the tracker under the car.

Chapter 76

2:30 p.m. Baghdad time.

Major-General Maher Abdelfattah was raging in fury as he was listening to the news on satellite channels announcing an anticipated popular movement tomorrow morning. The news agencies picked up the news after leaders of popular, religious, and youth movements decided to make the next day a day to protest against the government's decisions of increasing taxes and announcing a harsh austerity plan.

What worried the Major-General more was the fact that there were some complaints amongst the internal security forces and the armed forces themselves, as the austerity includes their salaries too. Losing control over them, in addition to wide popular demonstrations under a major economic collapse meant the government would be in real danger and chaos would hit the country from all directions at once. But on the other hand, the government had no other solution because with the decline in the global oil prices on the one side, and Iraq's need to import in billions of dollars annually on the other, it would bankrupt the country's treasury. The insufficient gold reserve and the already globally collapsed foreign currency would not save it from the global danger that started to get at the economic stability at an accelerated pace.

Iraq was in danger.

The demonstrations were set to start at 8:00 in the morning.

Getting out of the car, Mahdi and Maha entered the house in Zayouna while Black Sand operatives were observing. That scene was also watched by the camera fixed on the house across the street.

A few minutes later, the two were in the living room watching the country's latest news on TV. Some news agencies seemed to enjoy discussing the news of the oncoming chaos in Iraq as the media always looks for any abnormal movements to send its army of correspondents to the quarters of events. There were only 17 hours separating that moment from the time of the anticipated demonstration the next morning at eight o'clock.

That put more pressure on Mahdi. Solving the puzzle of a few lines of his father, the Advisor's, letter did not mean that the treasure would be in his reach. He wished if that were possible. If it happened, and Al-Mukhtar's treasure was found, the government would be able to reconsider its decision on austerity, which would prevent tomorrow's demonstrations that could last weeks or months, taking down the country's security and stability. Finding it might give the government the economic freedom for a few years that would enable it to build a new economic policy sparing its economy from collapsing. Without that, it would have to face an overwhelming tide of popular anger and the possibility of insurgency of some security forces and military units.

Maha was attentively watching the news with Mahdi. The correspondent on the screen met one of the organizers of the anticipated demonstrations. He promised the government that the protests would go on endlessly until they changed their latest decisions, or it would take up the country like fire in the chaff.

Eight o'clock tomorrow morning…and a new crisis fuse will ignite.

"Mahdi," said Maha, "we don't have a lot of time left to find the treasure. We have to hurry and solve the remainder of the letter's code."

Mahdi lowered the TV volume and put the remote control on the table. He took out the letter and started reading it again.

Look in it for the eleventh woman of it…

And collect from her waist...

His eyes narrowed as he read those words, collect from her waist. Maha moved closer to his side and looked with him at the paper. A feeling of relief has dominated her after she understood what the first lines of the letter mean, which Mahdi explained to her...The Sumerian seal in the middle of the Round City, and the eleventh woman of it.

"You said the woman represents the Tigris?"

"Yes, they are two women referring to the two rivers, but the Tigris runs through Iraq vertically along the map. One thousand km until it reaches the gulf water." Mahdi answered.

"No," Maha responded, "remember the President's letter when he said look within yourself for salvation? You said he means Baghdad by that. We don't need to think about all of the Tigris."

"But how?" Mahdi wondered. "It cannot be put in the river! There are constant dredging works by special machinery. Al-Mukhtar isn't that naïve to throw the gold in the river that is dredged every day and silt taken out of it. Even if a whit of gold is found and the media caught wind of it, people would rise to the Tigris to find more."

"That's right," she said, confused. "it cannot be in the river, but why did he refer to it?"

"Okay," Mahdi said putting his prescription glasses on and looking at the paper again, "let's finish and see."

He went on to read what was written in the Advisor's letter:

And collect from her waist the three divine jewels...

Above an altar of grapes and pomegranate cross...

And behind a cross and a banner...

And at the feet of a green crescent...

"Her waist!" said Maha. "have you noticed anything on the woman's waist on the monument?"

"No, it's impossible that there would be anything there. Hundreds of people passing by look at the monument every day. They would notice something strange. Besides, it's not possible that Al-Mukhtar would leave something there. Not to mention that the entities concerned with monuments and statues do not allow anybody to touch them. He surely means something else."

"Her waist," Maha repeated, thinking, "the woman is the Tigris and her waist is…Don't you think he means by that the riverside?"

Mahdi turned to her, liking the idea, "Rather it is exactly what is meant!"

"Yes…the riverside," she said happily, "divine jewels by the riverside. We are solving the puzzle."

Passionately, the two looked at the letter again.

Above an altar of grapes and pomegranate cross…

"That cannot be anything but a church," Mahdi said and continued, "but churches in Baghdad are numerous. There is a strange reference to…" he focused on the letter then said, "grapes and pomegranate!"

"Grapes and pomegranate," said Maha thinking, "I don't want to shallowly think and ask about a church in the middle of grapes and pomegranate trees. We're used to this puzzle's ways which talks about symbolic things."

"Okay," said Mahdi taking out his phone. "I'll call a friend of mine I went to college with. He's Christian. He may be able to tell us what we need to know."

Maha nodded waiting what he would do. He touched the phone's buttons and started making a call to a friend of his named Danny

Na'eem. The ringing sound came through the phone's speaker and a voice answered on the other end of the line.

"Hello."

"Hello, Danny!"

"Ah, Hi Mahdi. It's good you still have my number, you selfish!"

It had been a long time since they had talked to each other.

"Well, my friend, I know, but I promise soon to meet up and remember the college days."

Danny laughed as he chatted with Mahdi and the latter asked the question on his mind.

"Right," said Mahdi, "I wanted to ask you—my religious Christian friend—about what grapes and pomegranate mean in your religion, and what it has to do with the crucifixion of Christ?"

"Why? Are you converting to Christianity?" asked Danny, jokingly.

Mahdi laughed, "Maybe, my friend!"

"Well, you are asking about my sect specifically. Grapes and pomegranate decorate our churches as Armenians. The Armenian sect uses these two symbols as its logo. Therefore, you find them at the altars in our churches in drawings, carvings, or decorations. We are unique in using them as our logo."

Mahdi nodded looking to Maha who smiled happily. This would make finding the next link of the puzzle's chain easier.

"You mean if I look in an Armenian church, I'd find grapes and pomegranate there?"

"Exactly. You can look in the Major Armenian Church in Baghdad. It's in Bab Al-Sharqi. A white building with two cone heads. And for your information, most of the Armenian churches around the world use this design."

That was new information for Mahdi, who started thinking seriously of the Chruch is in Bab Al-Sharqi.

"Well, Danny, great information. I'm grateful."

"You haven't told me..." Danny asked, "Why you are asking about this now after all this time?"

That was the part that Mahdi hated about calling for the information he needed...friends' curiosity.

"No, nothing. Just curious," he said maliciously, "and missing an old friend!"

Danny laughed unconvinced by the answer but he pretended to accept it. After a short conversation, the call ended and Mahdi hung up the line.

"Maha, we have to find an Armenian church close to the riverside."

"You mean on its waist."

He smiled, "Yes, and I believe the Armenian Church in Bab Al-Sharqi is the closest. The river is only a few kilometers from it."

"You mean the three divine jewels are places of worship?"

That answer surprised Mahdi. He looked at the letter again:

And collect from her waist the three divine jewels...

Above an altar of grapes and pomegranate cross...

And behind a cross and a banner...

And at the feet of a green crescent...

Maha was right.

"That's right!" he said, surprised, "He is referring to outspread places of worship. Church is one of them, but all of them have to be…"

"By the riverside," she interrupted, "we have to look for them all taking under consideration their proximity to it, and then we'll see what we find."

"A cross and a banner," Mahdi said, "if he means what I think, I understand what he means."

Maha pushed her hair behind her ear and asked, "What are you thinking?"

"If he means the cross that a white banner wraps around it, that's the logo of Mandaeism," Mahdi answered.

Maha looked at the letter. "Possible. If he wanted to refer to a banner tied to a pole for instance, he would have said a cross and a flag, but a banner alone is a piece of fabric."

The two felt a wave of relief for what they were able to deduce one of the letter's puzzles. They believed they were thinking clearly.

"Well, Maha. Let's start the search in order. First the church, then we have to find a Mandaeic temple, then…"

"At the feet of a green crescent." finished Maha.

Mahdi thought for a little bit and said, "Here lies the problem. The crescent symbolizes Islamic mosques, which are in the capital in the dozens."

"Remember, by the riverside," Maha said pointedly.

Mahdi pursed his lips knowing that finding the intended one would be complicated since Baghdad's mosques' domes and minarets were countless.

"Maha, let's eat something now and then we'll go to the Armenian Church to find the first divine jewel there."

Chapter 77

3:30 p.m. Baghdad time.

16 hours until the demonstrations.

Baghdad was living an extremely tense situation. People continued following the news of the downfall of the global economy and the fall of major global banks, in addition to their displeasure with the government's decisions and their fear of what was to come as they saw the armored vehicles and helicopters in the capital with its atmosphere anticipating what was to come.

The US dollar declined even more in the last few hours, especially after China declared its intention to sell billions of dollars to preserve the value of its currency, while Japan started experiencing a splitting collapse in its economic system. Several banks around the world declared bankruptcy. US banks requested support from Fed whose decision to decrease the interest on loans to zero did not have a positive effect on the situation.

The dollar was then in a state that no one envied.

On the other hand, OPEC decided to decrease the oil production and imposed that decision on the producing countries, including Iraq, so the barrel price would rise at least a little bit as the decline in oil prices like that would cause a disaster for the producing countries. But that would not help those countries anyway as the oil barrel price was still too low. That would not provide enough revenue for the OPEC members.

Mahdi and Maha finished a light lunch they made from what they found in the fridge, then prepared to head to the Armenian Church in Bab al-Sharqi in the middle of Baghdad.

Shortly after, they got into Maha's car. She turned on the engine and Mahdi looked at his watch, afraid the fast passing of time until hour zero and Baghdad would be filled with angry protestors.

Nothing would save the situation except finding the treasure… right then!

Maha moved the car into the main street. The security camera on the house across the street and the two Black Sand operatives who stayed put were watching them. For the first time, Mahdi noticed the black Jeep Cherokee when Maha passed a bystreet. He has seen this car more than once at that spot without caring much for it. He was really worried but he did not want to show to Maha what he was thinking as that would scare her. But his fear for her was larger than his desire for her to stay with him.

He pulled down the sun shield from the car's inner roof and looked in the mirror fixed on it to see the street behind Maha's car and check if the Jeep was following.

Maha was surprised by what he did as the sky was still cloudy and there was no need for a shield to protect from the sun rays. Mahdi felt her surprise and pretended to check he how looked in the mirror.

"I told you, you look tired," she said as she arrived in Palestine Street, leaving behind Zayouna.

"Hmm, that's right. I haven't shaved in days and I haven't gotten a good night's rest," then he looked at her, "Maha, the mission is filled with danger and difficulties. Please, let the church be the last place we go to together. I don't want to place you in an unknown danger. I know we were not alone. The government must be watching what we are doing, and that's never a good thing."

Maha laughed, "Don't deny me the fun of adventure, Mahdi. I realize what we are doing is dangerous, but I haven't noticed anyone noticeable following of us. The government is busy with tomorrow's demonstrations now."

"No, remember the disks with the repetitions, the bullet memory unit, the Nostradamus message, and the Missile Painting. They did not send us all of that to leave us be. I'm sure they are somewhere and we are under their surveillance," Mahdi said that believing the Cherokee was affiliated with an Iraqi governmental entity.

Maha shrugged her shoulders with indifference and looked at him with childlike eyes, "Please!"

Mahdi stopped looking at her eyes and looked in the mirror of the shield without answering her. He did not see the black Cherokee behind them. It remained on the bystreet. He shook his head giving in to Maha's stubbornness. There was no way to change her mind.

Maha's car rushed through Palestine Street, aiming to reach the Armenian Church in Bab al-Sharqi.

Chapter 78

The Armenian Church sat in Bab al-Sharqi area in the middle of Baghdad. It stood out from among the nearby buildings with its two cone shaped domes. The church bell was in one of those domes while the second one constitutes the high ceiling of the church hall. That dome rose to a height of around 40 meters. The church also included a graveyard to its side and within its gates. Behind it was small separate Christian cemeterywhere British Goodwill Ambassador and archaeologist Ms. Gertrude Bell in the 20s of last century. She was buried their according to her will[2].

It was 4:15 pm on Friday, 3 January, when Maha's car reached the Armenian Church in Bab al-Sharqi, and, of course, the cab was watching its moves and stopped at a nearby distance. The man inside the cab noticed Mahdi and Maha getting out of the car and walking towards the church's entrance, while the Black Sand tracking device was still working regularly.

The secondary small door was open for the church visitors while the main door had remained closed for years since the fall of the Iraqi regime in 2003. Mahdi and Maha crossed the single door to find themselves on a paved road. To the right of it was a graveyard where its tombstones carried the Christian cross. As they picked up the pace entering, a middle-aged man approached them. He appeared to be the church's gatekeeper.

"Hello!" Maha approached him and extended her hand to shake his.

"Hello!" she repeated. "May we enter?"

"Well, what do you have here?"

It is wrongly rumored that Ms. Bell is buried in the English Graveyard in Waziriya, but the author personally confirmed the existence of her grave in the graveyard behind the Armenian Church in Bab al-Sharqi as the author has visited most of the locations mentioned in the novel to personally confirm the information.

Maha looked to Mahdi while her brain was making up the next lie.

"Although we are Muslims, we have always longed to enter this church when we passed by it. I have never been in a church before, so I suggested it to my uncle—she pointed to Mahdi—and barely convinced him to let us come in here and he agreed on…"

"Okay, okay, you can come in whenever you like, but try to hurry up as I'm about to close the doors. The situation today is strange and tense," said the church gatekeeper while he headed to close the small door before going back in their direction.

Mahdi and Maha followed the man who turned left entering through another door leading to a space with what appeared to be a small stage and a Christian logo two meters high in the middle of it. Mahdi and Maha looked at it before the large white building of the church with its two unique domes grabbed their attention. The three passed by the small stage and took a left towards a secondary door in the building.

Another left and they were inside one of the absolutely most spectacular churches in Baghdad.

The seats were neatly organized in the church's rectangular hall whose ceiling rose as high the cone dome that appeared spectacular from the inside as its octagonal shape before the pointed dome was permeated with eight colored glass mosaic windows, and six large chandeliers hung from the ceiling.

They took a few steps forward until they were standing between the two lines of seats inside the church hall. Mahdi and Maha felt a strange spiritual spirit in the quiet place as they looked at the altar before them. It was separated from them by a classy low wood and iron fence. The altar was composed of an arc with words in a strange language. A white figure resembling the church's domes was placed under the arc, with a picture of the Virgin Mary with her Son, Christ in the middle of it. In front of that figure was a wooden piece of art with meticulous carvings, and a two meters high dome rose above it, also resembling the church's cone domes.

Mahdi and Maha gave in to the strange effect they felt standing in the middle of the church hall surrounded by paintings embodying Christ and the Virgin Mary. The light inside the entered the hall quietly through the long windows in the walls and the colorful mosaic windows in the hall's dome.

Above an altar of grapes and pomegranate cross…

Mahdi approached the altar. The ornamented wooden art piece in front of him caught his attention. Its ornamentation showed carved crosses placed between two types of fruit…

grapes and pomegranate.

Maha approached him. The sound of her high heels echoed in their ears, shattering the place's quietness.

"Above an altar of grapes and pomegranate cross," she said to him in a low voice while the gatekeeper was standing at the hall's door. They looked at what was above the altar and the breathtaking scene mesmerized them.

Above the arc with the incomprehensible words, which the altar is placed under, inside a half circular frame hung a wonderful oil painting with gorgeous colors and large size. The two looked at it admiring it. In the painting appeared people wearing old costumes like the clothes worn by the people in the Last Supper painting. They spread across the banks of a small river. Behind them was a lush green tree. At the river bank stood a man with a robe wrapped around his waist and a long mace in his left hand. His other hand was placed on the Christ's head who was standing the river with a yellow halo of light above his head.

That was John the Baptist in the scene of the baptism of Christ.

Above an altar of grapes and pomegranate cross.

An oil painting! Maha tried to find something in the painting; the three palm trees to the left of Christ, the green tree to his right, the blue river water…

But Mahdi was thinking of something different. He counted the number of people in the painting, including Christ.

"Maha, if there was any doubt that we are in the wrong place, it's gone. Look at the number of people in the painting. They are eleven."

In lightning speed, Maha reviewed with her eyes the number of people connecting that to number 11 that has appeared thrice in the Advisor's letter.

The eleventh women…

Eleven arrows…

Eleventh hour…

And eleven people in the painting above the altar of the Armenian Church.

Chapter 79

Mahdi and Maha were amazed by what they saw in the painting. Christ standing in a small river below John the Baptist's shoulder, and on both banks a number of people spread making the total number of people appearing in the painting eleven persons.

Eleven...Is this what the Advisor meant?

Maha took out her phone and took a picture of the painting.

"Okay, let's get out now!" Mahdi rushed, as many thoughts stormed his mind.

The two headed towards the small door to the left of the altar wall where the guard who let them in through it was standing.

"Have you satisfied your curiosity?" he asked, smiling.

"Yes, the place is great!" Maha gushed as she followed him with Mahdi, then she asked him, "What does the writing in the strange language on the arc above the altar say?"

The gatekeeper looked aside to remember.

"Come to me, and I will dissolve you of your sins."

Maha nodded looking to Mahdi. The two followed the man outside the church building heading back to the path towards the door. A few minutes later, after the two had thanked the man, they sped towards her car. The man in the yellow cab watched their exit. They got into the car and Mahdi looked at his watch: 5 pm. Only 15 hours remained until the demonstrations.

The countdown had begun.

"Where to now?" Maha asked, who had turned on the car's engine. Maha reviewed the text of his father's letter in his hand after he put on his glasses.

Behind a cross and a banner…

"We should go now to a Mandaeic manda close to the river," he was surprised by the idea that suddenly sparked in his brain, "and that would be none other than their General Manda!"

"Manda?" Maha asked pushing her hair back behind her ear.

"Yes, a manda is a place of worship for the Mandaneans. I know that the most important manda for them is in Karkh side. We will try to get there and ask around about the closest place of worship for them that is close to the river."

And collect from her waist the three divine jewels…

But he continued inferring after he remembered the exact location of that manda, "Or it may be the intended one itself!"

"How?" Maha asked.

He looked at her like he found what he has been looking for and said, "Maha, the largest manda for Mandaneans in Baghdad is at the riverbank. It's in Qadisiya neighborhood. We have to cross Jadriya Bridge and turn from under it on Karkh side. I remember its location well."

Maha changed gears and started driving.

"Are you sure?"

"Perfectly. Let's head to Karrada and then to Jadriya. The same path to Dr. Husam's house except we would cross the river via the bridge to get there."

Maha nodded after she remembered the route. She drove while a yellow cab moved behind them.

Chapter 80

5:30 p.m. Baghdad time.

14 hours and a half hours until the demonstrations.

The man in the elegant suit was making a call to one of his assistants from his wood-walled room. There was not much time left. He gave his orders for his assistance to carry them:

The alternative plan.

On the bridge leading to Qadisiya neighborhood coming from Jadriya, Maha was driving at 120 km/h making use of the bridge being empty from cars except police cars and military vehicles stopped on the right of the bridge not moving and leaving the remaining lanes almost empty.

Within a few minutes, they would go down to the neighborhood where the Mandaeic Manda is in according to Mahdi's description.

"It's almost sunset. Darkness will fall in minutes, Maha."

She laughed, "I'm not thinking about darkness now as much as I'm thinking about making up a lie to enter the manda."

Mahdi smiled worriedly despite his confidence in her ability to making up fabricated excuses. She slowed down preparing to turn right and get off the bridge heading towards Qadisiya.

The man in the elegant suit's assistant received his instructions. The alternative plan will be…deadly.

In his office in central Baghdad, Scott Oziling had also given his instructions to his assistants to prepare for a sudden move that could be executed under the tense security situation in the capital was living. The time to get the target had neared.

He could barely wait anymore.

On Qadisiya Street, Maha was carefully driving while Mahdi observed the buildings on his right. Suddenly, from among the buildings appeared a white high figure of a cross with a banner wrapped around it. Behind the crossing of its two sticks appeared green olive branches.

The General Manda for Mandaeans in Baghdad…and Iraq in general.

"Stop here and wait for my signal," Mahdi instructed. Maha stopped the car to the side of the road and he got out of it.

He closed the door and moved in the direction of the building's door. He spoke with two armed men at the door then turned and signaled for Maha to approach with her car and park it. She parked the car and got out of it approaching Mahdi who was still talking with the two men. They seemed to not want to let them enter as darkness has started taking over the sky and the security situation was concerning.

Maha's mind was a blur. She did not know what Mahdi talked about with the two men, so she would not be able to come up with a lie that didn't contradict what he told them. The argument between Mahdi and the two armed men went on without there seeming to be a possibility of their changing their minds. But shortly after, a man came out from inside the building and approached the door intending to leave. He was dressed in a white gown covering his whole body and put a white head covering on his head while his long beard was snow white too.

The bearded man approached the door from behind the fence separating it from the street without taking his eyes off the four standing at it. He passed the door and went to them greeting them.

He looked so dignified and calm. His white dress pleased the observers, giving them a feeling of assurance. Mahdi felt comfort upon meeting him.

"Hello, sir," the man said and reached out his hand to shake Mahdi's. His eyes expressed his question of the reason he was there and what he wanted.

"Sir, I'm Professor Mahdi, a professor of Law at the Baghdad University. This is Maha, my student. She asked for my help for her research on the role of Iraqi lawyers in showing the religious coexistence in Iraq whereas the global media obliterate it," Mahdi said.

Maha was surprised this time by the lie Mahdi came up with to enter the manda.

"And what can I help you with?" the man asked in a calm tone.

"All we need," said Maha, "is to see your temple from the inside. Only ten minutes."

The bearded man gave the two men a rebuking look as he was a religious cleric onsite and nothing would please him more than to shine light on his religion whose followers were considered a minority in Iraq.

"Follow me," he said to Mahdi and Maha.

The three entered a vast courtyard after they passed the door. There were two buildings on both sides. The one on the right seemed to be more recent than the other, while a third building was at the end of the middle path, to the right as well. It seemed to have been built in the eighties of the last century.

The man pointed to the building on the right, "Here is the management of the manda, and the newer location that has recently been built, and there—he pointed to the eighties building—the building that was recently included in this place. Originally it was poet Abdelrazzaq Abdelwahid's house and we bought it from him."

The two were surprised by what they heard. That was the house of a known poet, and it overlooked the Tigris while its back was to the other two buildings, and coincidentally, Abdelrazzaq Abdelwahid was also Mandaean.

"To the left here," the man continued, "is the place where we pray." He pointed to the other building on the left.

"Well, sir," said Mahdi, "could we enter your place of worship?"

The man looked at him smiling, "Of course."

The three approached the temple with the cross and wrapped banner on top of it. The man took out some keys and opened the temple's wooden door. He pushed it and it made a creak.

With the door open, the lighting inside the place was still on. The place was composed of a large hall with seating couches on both sides, while the wall facing the door was a square of black ceramic centered by a constructional figure surrounding a painting with prominent colorful carving. To the sides of the black ceramic in the wall, there were two enlarged photographs pasted on the wall. In front of that side of the hall's walls, a long table and four black chairs behind it were placed.

The three entered the hall and Mahdi felt the quietness of the place fill his ears. He looked at the walls of the hall while Maha looked around her, astonished. The walls had Aramaic and Arabic writings. Mahdi read some of the words that were written in Aramaic without understanding their meaning as although they were written in letters that were comprehensible for him, but as words, they were strange for him.

Akeh heyi… Akeh mari… Akeh mendad heyi…

And below them a fourth phrase:

Beshmahyoun ad heyi…

The bearded man understood Mahdi's surprise at what he read. He told him with a lasting voice, "They are our hymns. Almost similar to your Muslim hymns."

Mahdi smiled and nodded. Although curiosity filled his head with many questions, he did not have enough time to ask about them.

The gypsum drawing on the temple's roof caught his eye. The cross with the banner and above it, olive branches and the pigeon of peace. Behind it, a sun spreading its golden rays.

Behind a cross and a banner...

He returned to looking for what he came for. He has come across many figures and paintings of a cross and a banner since he entered here. Which of them is the intended one?

"Professor!" Maha whispered sharply as she approached the table with the four chairs, "come look."

Mahdi looked to the man, excusing himself, and went closer to her.

Maha was pointing to a glass box placed behind the table with a cross and a white banner wrapped around it. That place looked like the altar in the Christian churches.

Behind a cross and a banner...

The two raised their eyes to behind that glass box. What the Advisor's letter meant was the colored painting above that box...in the middle of the hall's wall.

Chapter 81

"Derfsha ad yehya."

The bearded man said, "It is the symbol of our religion. John's banner wrapped around two sticks resembling a cross. Prophet John is the one we Mandaeans follow."

Mahdi and Maha heard that while looking at the painting.

Behind a cross and a banner...

The colored painting in the wall carried the scene of a man in a white gown baptizing another sitting inside a running river and wearing a white muffler.

Like a computer, Mahdi connected the painting before him with the one he and Maha saw at the Armenian Church.

John the Baptist was baptizing in the middle of a running river.

He looked to Maha to read her eyes. She nodded. She understood what he did. The two paintings match, and the common denominator is...water. The two turned to the man and approached him. They had to talk to him to remove any suspicion about why they were there.

"The head of your righteousness, do not twist your words, and do not love lying and calumny."

Maha read that phrase from among other phrase carved in Arabic on the walls of the hall. The bearded man smiled and said, "It's from our book Ginza Rabba, or the Holy Ginza, where from we draw our teachings. Exactly like your Quran."

"There is a big similarity between those phrases and our teachings," said Mahdi reading another text: "The head of your faith, believe in the king of light, God, who exists in all his virtues."

"We are very similar to you Muslims," said the man, "we pray three times a day and we perform ablution, too."

"Ablution?" Maha asked, and the man answered, "Yes, in a way that is quite similar to your ablution except that we also wash our knees and that is not in your ablution."

Mahdi and Maha looked around the place while listening to the man, but Mahdi looked at his watch and said to her, "We have to go now, Maha."

He looked to the man apologetically and said, "I promise to come back again, but it's late."

The man nodded smiling and turned around towards the door while the two of them followed. When they left the hall, darkness had completely fallen and the weather was bitterly cold. The watch indicated it was five past six o'clock in the evening.

A few minutes later, Mahdi and Maha got into their car followed by the cab and along with the tracking device.

Chapter 82

John the Baptist baptizing Christ in the middle of running river…

And the Mandaean cleric baptizing someone in the middle of a running river…

"What is the Advisor trying to say?" Maha asked while slowly making her way with the aid of the car's front lights.

Mahdi answered, "We were focused on the eleven persons in the painting at the Armenian Church and now we are focusing on water."

"Mahdi, it's obvious. The eleventh woman is the Tigris, and the two paintings refer to water. We have to cut any remaining doubt with certitude that would confirm the correctness of what we are thinking."

"The green crescent," Mahdi said, "it would be the conclusive thing to knowing what my father's letter meant."

Maha asked, "Did you figure out the one meant by it?"

He answered, "Let's think about what we have of mosques close to the river, and there has to be something with the color green in it. We'll start with the mosques close to the Tigris on Rusafa side."

He closed his eyes and prepared his fingers to count:

"Imam Adham Mosque, Khalani Mosque, Wazir Mosque, Sayyid Sultan Ali…" he kept trying to squeeze his brain looking for a green mosque that is close to the river. All those mosques had earthy colors.

"Nothing?" Maha said driving slowly as they did not have a specific destination other than what would be the green crescent with the feet close to the eleventh woman's waist.

"Let's go back to Karkh now!" Mahdi said adamantly, trying to remember the closest mosques to the river, "I don't remember its name, but there is a mosque to the right of Bab Al-Mu'adham Bridge, but its dome is blue and it's earthy; and there is another…"

Suddenly, the sun of hope exploded in his head again.

"I found it!" Maha turned to him.

"It's the Khidr—Green One—Shrine!"

Chapter 83

6:45 p.m. Baghdad time.

13 and a half hours until the demonstrations.

An Oz of gold is for 3,250 USD.

The tan young man who was watching Mahdi and Maha at a café on Palestine Street entered Scott Oziling's room after he was called by him.

"Get our best men and provide them with clothes similar to the Iraqi security uniform. I'll be heading the force. The zero hour has come." Oziling instructed the young man who was Iraqi, but also a Black Sand operative.

The young man headed to the other rooms at the base, mobilizing the members he carefully selected from the company's operatives. In a few minutes, they would be in their vehicles dressed in the Iraqi security uniform and armed with the deadliest weapons.

Scott Oziling had received information about the gold's locations, but he is waiting to confirm it.

***

"Khidr Shrine?" Maha inquired, pressing the gas pedal.

"Yes, Maha," Mahdi said enthusiastically, "it is a small building with a green dome on the Tigris bank on Karkh side. At the feet of a green crescent. Indeed, the Tigris water is so close to it."

"What do you expect we would find there?"

"I don't know," Mahdi answered, "perhaps a symbol, or a painting, or a text, or something else. I haven't been to it in a while. We have to get to it now."

Maha recalled the route to the target. She started driving, heading for the traffic on Haifa Street where the Khidr Shrine lies at the bank of the Tigris under Bab Al-Mu'adham Bridge. To the same destination followed the yellow cab.

***

The man in the elegant suit hung up the phone. He was informed that the alternative plan was ready.

It was time to use weapons.

Although he knew that the plan of his would be costly, he believed that the end justified the means.

Chapter 84

The checkpoint at the entrance of Haifa Street delayed Mahdi and Maha by about half an hour. Despite the low number of cars on the street at that time, but the delay accumulated a number of them creating a long line.

7:30 p.m.

The distance between them and the Khidr Shrine was not much, but they had to cross the checkpoint. Another boring few minutes and they passed the checkpoint with a signal from one of the policemen who did not wish to stop them.

The heavy movement of the security forces was still ongoing, with a noticeable closure of commercial stores and markets. Baghdad seemed to be holding its breath for the unknown tomorrow.

Maha's car reached Bab Al-Mu'adham Bridge. She took a right and used the road going down under the bridge towards the riverbank. The green dome of the Khidr Shrine was clear from there.

Khidr Shrine was made up of a small room sized building with a green dome at the top. Colorful light cables hung on the building with Quranic verses ornamentation on the outer walls. The shrine sat exactly at the shore. Some Baghdadi women light up candles, fixing them on cork and leaving them to sail on the river water as a tradition for making requests and vows. The families nearby came to this place sometimes to spend time by the breathtaking river scenery. But on that cold night, the place was completely empty except for several people. That was what Mahdi and Maha noticed going down the stairs towards the shrine.

"At the feet of a green crescent," Maha recited, looking at the building. The letter was clear. The shrine's foundations were so close that they were almost touching the river's water. The building had completely green painted dome, and it carried the name "Khidr".

The two stepped to the building's door after going down the wide stairway leading to the shore. They reached it and the scent of incense pervaded from inside the building where a few men were praying. There was an old fashioned wooden bookshelf containing copies of the Quran and prayer books. The color of the walls on the inside was also green.

Mahdi's eyes checked the walls inside the shrine while Maha read the Quranic verses decorating the building on the outside:

"They found one of our slaves whom We had granted mercy from Us and whom We had taught knowledge from Ourselves."

***

"The time to execute the alternative plan has come," said the man in the elegant suit lighting another cigar. The situation has become too critical. While he was drawing the first puffs of his cigar, the safety of a gun was pulled on Haifa Street…

Very close…to Khidr Shrine.

Chapter 85

"They're on Haifa Street," the tan young man said to Scott Oziling after he took a look at the screen in the adjacent room, which was transmitting the coordinates from the tracker attached under Maha's car.

Oziling sheathed his Alberta 9mm in its sheath preparing himself for the mission for which he mobilized his best men.

"Let's get out hands dirty!" the young man shouted.

With a quick jog, the young tan man moved and called the other Black Sand operatives participating in the missions. Everyone ran towards the company's base's courtyard where the cars were waiting for them. There were ten men including Scott and that young man. They would be in two armored Chevrolet cars.

***

Mahdi turned around the corners of the Khidr Shrine building hoping to find a symbol or a clue that could tie up the puzzles the President and the Advisor have left. The building was a modest construction with no signs of flashiness.

"Mahdi," Maha quietly spoke, "what we came for cannot be here except that we confirmed that the letter's meaning is referring to the river."

Mahdi nodded his head, still checking the shrine building's front.

"The painting of the baptizing of Christ standing in a river," he said, "and the Mandaean cleric baptizing another in a river; and the Khidr Shrine overlooking the river."

"See?" Maha responded, "The letter focuses on the Tigris and it confirms it again. The eleventh woman from the Freedom Monument."

Mahdi exhaled, "I don't know what the point is of using three clues to the same destination. We are turning around the same target."

Maha answered pushing her hair behind her ear, "In my opinion, it is because the idea of the gold being in the river would not be accepted by whomever's hands the Advisor's letter falls into. Therefore, the Advisor emphasized the river in the letter like this. Indeed, now we are certain the treasure is somewhere in the river."

Mahdi nodded, looking the Tigris water upon which reflected the lights of Bab Al-Mu'adham Bridge and the City of Medicine building.

"Well, Maha. The remainder of the letter will determine the search location in the river. Let's go now."

The two headed to the stairway back to the top of the shore, while someone was watching their approaching that stairway. He fixed his posture and reached his hand in his clothes.

Mahdi and Maha got up the wide stone stairway while the man went down on it. When he was facing them, he tripped on one of the steps and grabbed Mahdi's arm strongly. Mahdi tried helping him get up. When he stood, he gave Mahdi a suspicious look and nodded his head without speaking. His eyes glowed with a strange look and he continued his way down the stairway.

Maha was surprised by what happened next to her earlier. She held Mahdi's arm and asked: "Are you alright?"

But Mahdi was pale and confused. He did not answer and only nodded his head. Maha looked behind her to the man. He had disappeared in the darkness under the bridge. She looked back to Mahdi who was looking behind him to confirm the strange man had gone.

"How could a guy like that trip like a child on a stairway like this?" she pondered critically.

Mahdi looked to her and said, "It was intentional," he opened his palm, "he left this paper *in my hand!*"

Chapter 86

8:15 p.m. Baghdad time.

The man who handed Mahdi the paper had watched the lawyer and his companion riding their nearby car. He stepped back towards the stairway making a call on his cellphone.

The lawyer was handed the letter.

He finished his call and walked a short distance where he parked the yellow cab he was using. He got in and took out his gun. He put the safety back on after having pulled it. He had prepared his gun as a precautionary measure in case he faced anything out of control.

His yellow car was the one that watched Mahdi's movement for a long time.

***

"I have watched you for long…I know what you're looking for to save the situation. It is located in an iron container inside the Tahrir Square Tunnel."

Those were the words that Mahdi read in the paper the man gave him at the stairway. He read them to Maha inside the car with the aid of its roof light and his prescription glasses. He pushed his head back and leaned on the car seat's pillow closing his eyes.

"Impossible!" Maha said, "That cannot be true. If it was, why doesn't he go find it?"

Mahdi looked in the paper again. An iron container inside the Tahrir Square Tunnel.

"It would be suicide, Maha. If I go there, it could be a trap."

"Of course, Mahdi," she answered, "I'm really worried. Why did this person watch us for long as he says? And how did he know of the information we have about the treasure's location?"

"I don't know, Maha...I don't know. Then again, Al-Mukhtar and the Advisor's letters led us to searching for the treasure in the river, and this man's letter says it is in the Tahrir Square Tunnel."

"Despite that the tunnel is close to the river, I still doubt what this person really wants." Maha said.

Mahdi contemplated the scene before him with eyes looking at the Tigris from inside the car that was still stopped. He fought for long to reach this stage of the quest. Less than 12 hours remained until the next day's demonstrations, and the economic collapse had started destroying Iraq's economy gradually. He remembered his dream of President Al-Mukhtar asking him to move.

"Everything will collapse, Mahdi."

He glanced at Baghdad City across the glimmering Tigris water. He could not be less patriotic and zealous than his father the Advisor or Al-Mukhtar himself. He would not allow himself to let his city, Baghdad, collapse under the painful strikes of the economic fall. The country had withstood enough tragedies in the past decades. Now, he was all Iraq had to survive, with a paper his father left him and an iron necklace carved with a mysterious number.

"Maha," He looked at her and continued, "I will follow this man's letter, come what may!"

"This is insane, Mahdi!" she said angrily, "They are luring you to where they want!"

He replied, "Listen, Tahrir Square is filled with security personnel now. No one could hurt me in front of them. Besides, if this person wanted to kill me, he would have done so here. The shore is almost empty of people. No one would see him if he wanted to shoot me."

"Please Mahdi, let's finish deciphering your father's letter's puzzles and let go of the Tahrir Square Tunnel thing…Please!"

Mahdi took out his father's letter from his pocket and read the remainder of the lines to himself.

Plant the necklace where the lost knight's spear was planted…

It will turn like the sun disk…

When some of eleven arrows pierce it…

At the eleventh hour…

The light of the mirror shines…

To show a buoy opening by the meeting of the four elements of existence…

Or you will find it asleep at the cover of…

He finished reading the text in front of him and with great rage, he hit the car door with his fist yelling "We won't have enough time to solve this crap!"

"Please…" Maha pleaded.

"Enough, Maha!" he put his head between his hands and said in a low voice, "I'm going there, and if that meant my death, I will leave the letter and necklace with you. If they wanted to catch me, they won't find anything with me."

He looked at her and said, "You will remain far from me while I enter the tunnel."

Maha tried to dissuade him from his idea, but she did not find the words to deter him from his determination to enter the tunnel. She turned on her car's engine while he rolled down the window and smoked a new cigarette.

The distance between them and the Tahrir Tunnel would not be long. The tunnel was under the roundabout which the Freedom Monument overlooked; the place they passed today.

Chapter 87

8:45 p.m. Baghdad time.

Maha's car crossed Bab Al-Mu'adham Bridge and turned right towards Khalani Square The streets were almost clear of cars. A few minutes after passing Khalani and they would reach Tahrir Square.

Mahdi took out his father's letter and the necklace from his pocket. He reached his hand into Maha's leather jacket and put them in her pocket.

"You will stay far away from me. Promise me that."

She looked at him living the deepest states of worry for him, "Be careful, please! I promise I will stay where you leave me, but don't take too long. I can't stay alone for long in that square."

Mahdi nodded his head and started thinking of what he would find here inside the Tahrir Square Tunnel.

***

The two Black Sand Chevrolet cars' engines were thudding waiting for Scott Oziling's orders to move. The ten operatives, including Scott, got into the cars all dressed in similar outfits to that of the Iraqi SWAT team.

Suddenly, Scott received a call from inside the base.

It has been confirmed. The target is heading to the same location.

Scott's face gleamed with happiness. Mahdi was not heading to the same location he had received information about saying that the gold is in it, which confirms that it is there. The tracker in Maha's car was extremely useful.

As an immediate reaction, Oziling gathered his orders for his men to execute the mission.

It was time to move.

The two Chevrolets left their base nearby the square and headed towards it. Scott remained in contact with his assistants at the Black Sand base to inform him of the location the lawyer and his companion's car reached.

Minutes separated them from reaching the Iraqi treasure.

***

Meanwhile, the Iraqi security personnel dispersed by the square and around it were carrying their tasks preparing for tomorrow's demonstrations to protect the square from vandals who may plant a bomb in it at night to detonate during the morning demonstrations, which could give an impression that the government was targeting its citizens demonstrating against it. That was the last thing the government needed at such a critical time.

A few minutes later, at exactly nine o'clock, Maha's car entered the Tahrir Square roundabout from the direction of Khalani Square. Mahdi observed the situation in the square and the security personnel. He was afraid the tunnel would be closed due to the current security conditions, but anyhow, he had to get out of the car and approach the tunnel's gate under the Freedom Monument.

He indicated for Maha to stop at a distance from the tunnel; precisely around the street adjacent to the monument and leading to the highway.

Maha stopped her car while her heart was throbbing intensely that she almost ripped it out of her chest. Mahdi looked to her before getting out of the car. Her eyes were holding the tears of fear and awe. She reached her hand towards him and held his. Mahdi felt her hand cold and sweaty from the fear. He felt it with his fingers as he looked to her. He gave her a half smile and nodded with eyes that say, "Don't worry!" Then he turned his face and opened the car door. He got out of it and was hit by the cold wind outside. He closed the door behind him and prepared to cross the street towards the Freedom Monument where the tunnel's entrance lay beneath.

Mahdi noticed the dispersed security personnel in the square. Some of them were wearing special clothes. Some of the armed men were standing in the Nation Garden to the back of the monument putting on black head masks that only show their eyes and wearing desert colored uniforms while carrying modern weapons. The distance between them and the tunnel's entrance was no more than 50 meters.

In those moments, two armored Chevrolet cars entered Tahrir Square. They stopped by the Turki Restaurant overlooking the Tigris. A small Iraqi flag was hung on one of the antennas of one of the cars to give the impression that they were affiliated with the Iraqi security. The two vehicles stopped and eight men got out of them; Scott Oziling was at the forefront, while the two drivers remained inside their vehicles.

Oziling and his men headed before the eyes of the security personnel, who did not find it strange because of the intensified security, to the other entrance of the Tahrir Square Tunnel in front of the Turki Restaurant at the same time that Mahdi started going down the steps leading to the first entrance of the tunnel below the Freedom Monument. That entrance faces the entrance where Oziling and his men entered. The tunnel's entrances from both sides were open.

Maha did not take her eyes off Mahdi until he disappeared going down the stairs. But in those moments, she noticed something that heavily pumped the adrenaline in her body: The armed men standing in the Nation Garden moved in Mahdi's direction.

She could not help herself. She opened the car door and ran across the street. She wanted to scream for Mahdi to be careful, but she was in sight of those armed men. She stepped up on the pavement and approached the tunnel's entrance as fast as possible. She held the handrail and started going down. The armed men hurried behind her and came to the stairs. Maha found herself in the tunnel behind Mahdi by about ten meters. He was walking slowly towards what appeared from the round tunnel's turning corner to be like a large iron container. It was about 30 meters from him. He made use of the tunnel's lights to see it. He kept walking towards it carefully but he was surprised by armed men coming down the tunnel from the other side. Everything about them pointed to their being of the Iraqi security forces, except their Caucasian skin tone.

Maha drew a breath to scream, but one of the armed men behind her put his hand on her mouth while his other arm encircled her waist. The other security personnel coming from the garden entered the tunnel. One of them took out a gun with a laser pointer and aimed it at Mahdi's back. In his spine, and before Maha's eyes, with a silenced gun, he fired.

Maha looked at Mahdi falling to the ground. His body tensed up for a second from the pain of the hit, then his muscles relaxed completely.

He became a lifeless body on the ground...

Mahdi Al-Ali has died.

Chapter 88

Quickly, one of the masked armed men went forward towards Mahdi's body and carried it back while another armed man pulled Maha out of the tunnel. By the stairs, he put a plastic bag on her head to prevent her from seeing and cuffed her hands behind her back in skillful speed.

In those moments, Black Sand operatives were standing in front of the iron container on the other side of the tunnel. One of them took out iron scissors from the toolbox he was carrying on his back. Scott looked around to ensure the tunnel was clear from others. The operative with the scissors stepped towards the locks that were placed on the large container's door. He broke the first lock and tossed it on the ground. Then, he put the second iron lock between his scissors' jaws and broke it, too. Oziling's heart rate was accelerating looking at the container that was about to be opened. His assistant broke the last lock.

Two other operatives stepped towards the container and grabbed the handle that locks it before starting to lift it.

Meanwhile, the armed men quickly led Maha towards the Nation Garden while one of them carried Mahdi's body towards it. They made use of the garden's darkness to cross from it to an armored van they had parked on the street next to the garden. They got into it with their catch, closed its door, and drove away.

The container was ready to be opened. The two operatives of Oziling's companions held the two heavy doors that close it and started to gradually open it while the other six operatives stood in front of the door waiting to see what was inside. When the two doors opened almost completely, the Black Sand operatives shone the lights from their guns inside the container, which suddenly reflected on their faces...

A golden yellow glow...

Chapter 89

Maha felt the iron bench under her shake with the movement of the vehicle she was led into. After a few seconds, despite the vehicle engine's thud, she heard a loud explosion followed by words mixed with manly laughs around her. Someone put his hand on her head and took off the plastic bag on it. Her pupils narrowed under the light in the van's roof. She looked around her. Three men armed with rifles sat on the bench across from her. Only their eyes were showing from their faces. Two other armed men were sitting on her sides. On the van's floor ay Mahdi's body on its face with its hands tied behind its back with metal cuffs and a plastic bag on its head.

The man sitting in the middle in front of her reached his hands towards the cuffs on Mahdi's hands and opened them. She was shocked by what she saw. Mahdi moved his arms!

The man helped him sit on the car's floor, then reached for the plastic bag on his head to remove it.

Mahdi was alive except that his facial expression spoke of pain. He looked around him and was shocked to see Maha sitting to his left.

"Mahdi!" Maha wept.

Mahdi held her knee feeling pain in his back. He managed to speak, "Maha...are you okay?"

She answered through her tears, "Yes, yes, fine!"

The person sitting to her right removed the cuffs from her wrists. She embraced Mahdi, crying on his shoulders, unable to believe he was still alive.

The person sitting in the middle on the bench across from her patted on Mahdi's shoulder. Mahdi looked to him. His eyes were gleaming. The person raised his hand to the cover on his face. He held it from below and lifted it from his head. Mahdi and Maha were shocked by what they saw…

That man was…

Captain Fadhel.

Chapter 90

9:45 p.m. Baghdad time.

Ambulances and fire-engines rushed to Tahrir Square after a loud bang was heard in the tunnel.

Preliminary security forces' reports indicated that eight armed men affiliated to Black Sand Security Company in a mysterious explosion inside the tunnel. The two remaining operatives who stayed behind in the cars by the Turki Restaurant were apprehended, pending investigation.

The bomb was placed in the iron container and its detonator fixed on its door. As soon as the Black Sand operatives opened the container's doors wide open, the detonator switched on and the container gleamed a golden glow in their faces as the first spark of the explosion that tore them to pieces, including Scott Oziling and the young tan Iraqi man.

***

Mahdi and Maha did not say a word while they are were the hands of Captain Fadhel, the man who assassinated President Mohammed Al-Mukhtar with a poisonous inhaler inside his cell at the 5th Division.

Fadhel reached his hand towards his gun, the one he used to shoot Mahdi. He took it out. The gun looked strange. He looked to Mahdi and said, "I'm sorry, Professor. It's bad that our second meeting had to go this way. This is a taser gun that only paralyzes. That's what I shot you with. Don't worry. The pain will go away quickly."

He said that not knowing what the Hyena had done of delivering the camera recording from cell number 12 to the lawyer before he was killed.

After a few moments of silence inside the van, the vehicle stopped announcing that it has reached its destination. One of the men inside it opened the vehicle's back doors and let Mahdi and Maha out of it. They looked around to see themselves in front of a building they had never seen before. Four of the armed men led them inside the building. Fadhel was amongst them. The building was quiet and clean on the inside with various paintings hung on its walls. After passing through several corridors, the armed men stopped in front of a door at the end of the corridor. Fadhel knocked the door and entered the room. Seconds later, he got out and indicated for Mahdi and Maha to enter while the other men remained outside.

Mahdi and Maha entered the room with Captain Fadhel. The room had wooden walls and was lit by low lights. It was filled with the smell of smoke of fancy cigars. Mahdi looked in front of him to the end of the room. There was a wooden desk sitting behind it a full-figured man smoking a cigar and wearing an elegant suit.

It took Mahdi a moment to realize he was standing before the state's fiercest man.

That was Major-General Maher Abdelfattah, General Director of Intelligence.

Chapter 91

9:45 p.m. Baghdad time.

Mahdi no longer felt the stinging pain made by the two pointed heads that launched from Fadhel's taser gun onto his back when he found himself standing before Major-General Maher Abdelfattah.

Maher put his cigar out and crossed his fingers, leaning back and looking at Mahdi without saying a word. He lifted a hand and pointed for them to approach. The distance between the three and the Major-General's desk was about 10 meters. Mahdi and Maha felt it much longer due to the awe of the situation in which they found themselves.

"Thank goodness for your safety, Professor Mahdi," the Major-General said with a full voice.

Mahdi answered, "Thank you."

The Major-General got up from behind his desk and walked in confident steps. He turned around his desk and sat on one of the side chairs in front of his desk. There were four opposing chairs. He pointed for Mahdi and Maha to sit down. Mahdi sat facing him next to Maha while Captain Fadhel remained standing.

"Anything to drink?" asked the Major-General. Mahdi and Maha exchanged looks.

"Water, please." said Maha, while Mahdi asked for coffee.

The Major-General looked to Fadhel, who understood his look and turned going out of the wood-walled room.

"Counselor," said the Major-General, "you have proved your smartness by understanding the clues we sent you. I ordered Captain Fadhel to write the number 39 on the wall of the cell where President Mohammed Al-Mukhtar—May God have mercy on his soul—died in, and to have the three recordings of the trial to re-peat in the way—I believe—you saw to clue you to the same num-ber." He turned his gaze to Maha and carried on, "We also sent you a message from the Middle Ages and placed the Missile Painting in front of you on the screen."

Mahdi nodded, his head filled with worry.

The Major-General went on, "It's good that you understood what we want, Professor Mahdi. Your many movements with the Miss have showed us that you are looking for something, something we want and must find…as soon as possible."

He said those last words extremely slowly.

Mahdi looked at his watch. Less than 10 hours remained until the demonstrations would start. He knew that the dollar lost a lot of its value now and that the economy was currently reeling, but he was not sure what the Major-General would do with the gold. He may confiscate it for his personal account or smuggle it out of the country.

"Major-General, I don't know the location of what you want. You could have asked President Al-Mukhtar about it when he was im-prisoned since he was the one who hid it."

The Major-General pursed his lips and moved his body forward. He looked into Mahdi's eyes and said, "You're worried about the gold's fate and you have a right to that. You're a good citizen, but let me assure you. Have you ever wondered why the government hasn't announced its knowledge of the existence of those tons of gold? Or why it didn't seem to look for it?" he smiled and contin-ued, "Because none other than the three of us in this room now know what we know. If the government knew that there is gold Al-Mukhtar had hidden somewhere, it would have subjected him to a harsh interrogation, perhaps even torture. It's good…and also unfortunate that Al-Mukhtar has passed without letting anyone know of what he had hidden."

Mahdi gathered his strength to answer. "How did you know about that, Major-General?"

Maher's gaze was piercing and he said, "Mr. Mahdi, remember that I was Director of the General Intelligence during President Al-Mukhtar's first years of presidency. We together, he, I, and your father the Advisor, put the plan to save the country from an anticipated global economic collapse. We—the three of us—decided to complement each other in the puzzle of finding the treasure. It cannot be found without solving all the connected puzzle pieces. Each one of us has a piece of it. Indeed, we have collected a great deal of gold together. I executed the support operations for the Somalian pirates, drawing a large quantity of gold from the bank's treasury in an intelligence operation, and many other operations. I was a believer in Al-Mukhtar's idea. But what happened is all of us collected a portion of it together and during the stage of hiding it, Al-Mukhtar removed me from my post."

Mahdi knit his brows listening. He remembered Al-Mukhtar's letter: A first did, a second carries the first's secret, and a third unveils the curtain, and the words from Nostradamus' prophecy surfaced on his mind, The Empire is enslaved and three men substituted!

"I don't understand," Mahdi said, befuddled, "Why did he remove you? How did you get back to your position after he was removed from the presidency?"

The Major-General did not answer as Captain Fadhel entered along with a young man wearing a black suit and carrying a tray with the drinks. He distributed them on the table and walked back out while the Captain remained standing in the room.

"Mr. Mahdi, it seems that Al-Mukhtar wanted to make an adjustment to his plan, so he allowed me to know half the secret, which is the existence of gold, and hid the second half from me, which is where it is hidden. As for my return to my post, it's because I raised a complaint to the new government against Al-Mukhtar after he was removed from the presidency. I said that I was dismissed for political reasons by the removed President and that I requested to be reinstated after his reign was over. The request was approved and I was back running the Intelligence until the day came when we needed the President's treasure more than ever."

Mahdi sipped his coffee and said, "You said that the plan involves a puzzle of three parts distributed on three people, and Al-Mukhtar has removed you from being the third person."

Maher nodded his head and said, "The first is Al-Mukhtar and the second is your father the Advisor."

Mahdi and Maha exchanged looks, then the Major-General asked, "Who do you think is the third person now?" Mahdi was surprised and did not respond.

Maher smiled, "It's you, Mahdi!"

Mahdi was shocked by what he has heard. He never thought about that. He immediately remembered images from his dream of the President yelling in his face, Everything will collapse...Mahdi!

He knew his father was the second man, but the third—who unveils the curtain—had not occurred to him that it would be him.

"Me? How?"

Maher took a sip of his coffee and said, "When I was removed from my post, there was no third man then. Therefore, Al-Mukhtar had to find someone to trust to hand him the head of the thread. There was no one better for Al-Mukhtar to elect for that mission other than his loyal lawyer and son of his loyal Advisor, Mahdi Al-Ali. Therefore, you alone would be fit to be the third man. I have worked with Al-Mukhtar for years and know how he thinks, but the only thing I missed was that the President had put together all of the puzzle pieces, including removing me from the third man's task and finding an alternative in time, during his first days of thinking of collecting the gold, which explains your father continuing to be involved in the puzzle although he has passed seven years ago. The President collaborated with the Advisor seven years ago in putting the puzzle pieces."

Mahdi remembered his father's will before his death about his wing in the house.

Don't sell the house and don't enter the wing unless necessary, and if you do enter, don't move a thing.

While he was collecting his thoughts before the storm of surprises that hit his mind, Maha asked the Major-General, "Major-General, are you responsible for the message Professor Mahdi received at the Khidr Shrine?"

Maher answered, "Yes, to tell you something, have you noticed something strange by your house, Mahdi, in Zayouna?"

Mahdi gathered his thoughts. There did not seem to be anything strange except…

"The Cherokee car! I saw it over and over and noticed it late."

Maher said, "Aha, they were Black Sand."

Maha was surprised by their conversation. She did not understand what they were talking about. "Who?" she asked pushing her hair behind her ear.

"Black Sand," The Major-General said slowly, "a private American security company. It entered Iraq according to a deal with members of the Council of Representatives and men in the government. I knew what they wanted to do. Foreign intelligence was somehow able to find information about a treasure the President had hidden to save Iraq from the great collapse and used Black Sand to find it. I didn't know what Black Sand was thinking of, stealing it or destroying it, but the goal is one: Make Iraq defenseless in the face of the crisis so no one would survive the game of the global bankers who took down the major countries, and so we would become—like all other peoples—under their control, too."

Mahdi asked, "How did you know what Black Sand was doing?"

Maher answered, "Black Sand's apparent job is protecting prominent Iraqi figures, but we knew of their other target here, simply because we are the Intelligence in this country. What confirmed it further for us was our observation of their patrol in your neighborhood."

"So, you have been watching me," Mahdi said bluntly.

"And protecting you too," Responded the Major-General, "Have you noticed a security camera on the house facing your house?"

Mahdi recalled in his mind the house facing his. He did not remember a security camera, "No, I haven't."

Maher said, "There wasn't just a camera. The house facing your house was a full Intelligence base. No one in the neighborhood was aware. There were cameras that we have watched you with and watched the Black Sand patrol, in addition to a SWAT team we have stationed there to intervene if the Black Sand operatives tried to raid your house. You have also been watched in your movements via Intelligence cars in various looks."

Mahdi and Maha were amazed listening to the experienced Major-General before them. They had been watched all this time.

Maha said, "Sir, you have not answered me about the message Professor Mahdi received at Khidr Shrine."

Maher replied, "Aha, yes." He sipped some of his coffee, "I couldn't eliminate Black Sand directly, as they have support from people in the government and Council of Representatives as I've told you; and because we know all your movements, we delivered the message to make you bait to draw Black Sand to where we wanted, which was the Tahrir Square tunnel. At the time, we had also delivered misguided information to them through our agents telling them that the treasure was there, and because Black Sand operatives are not stupid, we confirmed the validity of the information in an indirect way by making you go to the tunnel yourself. That confirmed to them that what we hinted for them was true, so they went there, we saved you, and sent them to hell."

Mahdi's eyes protruded, "How!"

Maher laughed, "The iron container in the tunnel had a bomb. They have been killed there. As for what remains of Black Sand in Baghdad, we will be able to kick them out of Iraq by raising a lawsuit against them on the grounds that they have been moving in the capital without authorization as evidenced by what happened in the tunnel. No one will be able to defend them in this case."

Mahdi himself was like a straw before a tornado of surprises as he listened to the Major-General. He put his elbows on his knees and his head between his palms thinking of the most important question on his mind since he saw Major-General Maher in this room.

He raised his head and said to Maher, "Sir… *Why have you killed Al-Mukhtar?*"

Chapter 92

11:00 p.m. Baghdad time.

Major-General Maher's eyes were sparking in anger looking at Captain Fadhel after he heard Mahdi's question about Al-Mukhtar's murder.

How did the lawyer know about what happened in the cell 12? It cannot be unless...

The Hyena!

He faked calmness and looked to Mahdi, "Counselor, I believe you have watched the press conference the Ministry of Justice has held during which it was confirmed that the President's death was by ..."

"Untrue!" Mahdi said feeling he had surpassed the wall of fear, "I have received information on how Al-Mukhtar has died." He turned to give Captain Fadhel a piercing look.

The Major-General said calmly, "You can help us then in exposing the truth of what has happened."

"Major-General, tell me, why have you killed Al-Mukhtar?" Mahdi responded.

Maher looked at his watch. Time was running and they still have not started talking about what Mahdi had reached in his quest for the treasure. He looked at him. "Alright, I'll tell you, but first tell me, which is more important: Al-Mukhtar's life, or the fate of more than 35 million persons?"

Mahdi was surprised by the question. Maher continued. "You are a patriotic man, Mahdi. Believe me, if the government knew what the President had hid, it would have subjected him to all kinds of interrogation, and when it extracted the information about the location of the treasure from him, it would have found it so the powerful in it would use it for their own benefit; and if they didn't, they would have wasted it before the collapse came; and when it came, we would have been defenseless in its face."

Mahdi remembered the words from the President's letter:

Don't reach your hand for it before it's time...

That it would turn into a gallows noose...

Nor too late...

That everything would be over.

"So," Maher continued, "we had no option but to protect the treasure this way, protect Al-Mukhtar from a painful interrogation, and the country from the abyss."

Maha's eyes did not blink as she looked to Major-General Maher, but tear drops fell from them on her reddened cheeks recalling the recording of Al-Mukhtar's assassination by the poisonous inhaler. The President's look as he took the inhaler, pressed it in his mouth, and collapsed on his bed fighting the suffocation and hitting the bed with his foot until he passed went through her mind.

The Major-General looked to Maha and saw her tears. He reached for the tissue box in front of him, drew a couple of tissues from them and gave them to her, while Mahdi covered his face filled with sadness for the President.

"I'm sorry for that," Maher explained, "the country is more precious than the President. If I had another solution, I would have picked it, Mr. Mahdi. I'll send you to rest a little before we talk about the location of the treasure. We have to find it tonight and announce its existence before the media so the government would cancel its recent decision of austerity and the economy goes back to its natural status in our country."

Mahdi did not know why he felt a push of confidence in Maher. He did not know why he had a feeling that Maher would do that, and would put the country's best interest before his personal interest to really save the economy. Perhaps because he preferred to be a public hero than to be a fugitive traitor.

Maher told Captain Fadhel to take Mahdi and Maha to a nearby room to get ten minutes of rest and come back later to the wood-walled room to discuss what they have reached in loosening up the treasure's joints.

The Captain left the room taking the two with him, but he was thinking of what Mahdi knew of information about Al-Mukhtar's assassination. His mind sparked in fear for his fate if the Judiciary knew of what he had done through Mahdi. Rather, Mahdi himself was a threat to him having been Al-Mukhtar's lawyer.

He tried to calm himself. He thought that the lawyer may have known what happened in cell number 12, but he did not know who exactly did it. All he could assure himself with was thinking that Major-General Maher would protect him.

Chapter 93

Captain Fadhel closed the door on Maha and Mahdi after he let them into a room close to Major-General Maher's base. The room was small and had black leather couches and a glass table in the middle.

Mahdi sat down and felt the pain of the two stings in his back. Maha sat facing him.

"Mahdi, do you trust this man?" Maha asked.

He lit a cigarette and looked at her, "Listen, we can only continue searching for the treasure with him. The collapse has hit the country. If we don't cooperate with him, the destruction would take the economy even more. But if we work with him to find it, there would be a chance to save the situation. If you ask me what I think …" he drew a breath from his cigarette, "I don't know why I feel I have confidence this man despite what he has done."

"Where does this feeling come from? This man has killed the President!"

"Maha," answered Mahdi, "In the Intelligence world, the principle of the goal to justify the means is prevalent. The Major-General did not want for the treasure to be wasted before its time, and Al-Mukhtar staying for longer would have possibly lead to his questioning by governmental authorities who have power over the Judiciary if those entities knew about the treasure."

"But what if the Major-General smuggled the treasure?" she asked.

"Don't worry. It's a very large amount. I don't think he'd do it. I told you, I feel I have confidence in this man."

Maha was hesitant to tell the Major-General the results of her quest with Mahdi, but Mahdi's words gave her a push of assurance. Only five minutes remained before their break ended and they would return to the wood-walled room.

Meanwhile, Baghdad was preparing to enter a full curfew that would take effect at midnight. The streets seemed desolate while the security forces' movements were alone prevalent at that time.

In other countries in the world, the streets of many countries had turned into stages of clashes and protests after the global collapse came into the economy of most countries. The rich started running away from their cities and countries whereas the hungry started revolting to get what would sustain them—exactly like President Al-Mukhtar had predicted.

**

A few minutes later, Captain Fadhel knocked on the door of the room he left Mahdi and Maha in earlier. He opened the door and entered. He had taken off his repertoire, his armor, and his weapon except for the gun he kept on his thigh.

"Shall we go now?" he asked and indicated for Mahdi and Maha to get up. They followed him to the Major-General's room. After a few steps in the corridors of the base, the three entered the room. Major-General Maher was smoking a cigar. He had taken off his jacket and loosened his expensive tie, showing his gun's shoulder belt. He pointed for them to come in while he was watching TV from behind his desk. Images of the demonstrations in some cities of the world were taking over the screen.

Mahdi and Maha approached the chairs in front of the desk and sat side to side when Maher pointed for them. He got up from behind his desk and sat in front of them. He drew a breath from his cigar and said, "Now, where have you reached?"

Mahdi reached his hand into his jacket's pocket to take out his father's letter and the necklace.

But they were not there.

He checked his other pocket and started searching his clothes, but was surprised with Maha extending her hand before his eyes holding them. He looked at her to see her smiling. He exhaled remembering he had left them with her when he went down into the Tahrir tunnel.

He took the letter and necklace and put them on the glass table in front of him. Maher was watching what he was doing. Mahdi opened the letter and said: "Major-General, our search has lead us to finding a clue the President had left at the Martyr's Memorial for his Advisor. When we searched my father's, the Advisor's, safe, we found this letter in addition to this necklace." He presented them for him.

Maher took the letter that was written in the Advisor's handwriting in blue ink. He put his prescription glasses on and read its text that ended with an erased word by effect of water drops falling on it. He admitted to himself the difficulty in understanding its meaning. He put it on the table and took the necklace. He looked at what was written on its ring.

1/40,000

He pursed his lips and took off his glasses, "What have you been able to understand from it?"

Maha answered, "Sir, the Advisor meant in the letter…"

She took the letter to explain to Maher what the Advisor had written about a Sumerian seal in the middle of Baghdad, and the eleventh woman of it, and about his references to the three temples which also pointed to the Tigris. She explained what she and

Mahdi could solve of those puzzles.

"The Tigris?" asked the Major-General.

"That's what we have been able to deduce," Mahdi answered.

Maher reached his hand to take the letter from Maha and read the phrase the two has reached without solving its puzzle.

Plant the necklace where the lost knight's spear was planted!

"That's what we couldn't understand," Maha said.

The lost knight's spear…Those words were not strange to Major-General Maher. They were said to him once when he asked someone about the meaning of the design of one of the monuments in Baghdad when he was placing a flower bouquet on it on the anniversary of the establishment of the army next to President Al-Mukhtar during his first years of ruling.

With a mind plunging into the depth of memory, Maher mumbled the words, "The lost knight's spear…The lost…knight…"

He glanced at Mahdi and said, "I think he means…*The Unknown Soldier Monument!*"

Chapter 94

11:30 p.m. Baghdad time.

Mahdi immediately recalled the shape of The Unknown Soldier Monument searching in it for a spear. All he could remember about the shape of the monument was that it was a huge half elliptical figure planted in the ground from one of its sides, next to a silver pole wrapped in the four colors of the Iraqi flag.

"The Unknown Monument?" Maha asked.

"Yes," replied the Major-General, "the lost knight is the unknown soldier. I remember during one of my visits to the monument with President Al-Mukhtar to put a flower bouquet on the Military Day when I asked someone what the monument design meant. As I recall, he mentioned to me that it consists of a knight's shield that has fallen from him and revolved around one center three times, which form the three steps around the monument. As for the silver pole adjacent to that huge shield, it is the unknown knight's spear that fell from him, too, after he died and was planted in the ground and wrapped with the four colors of the Iraqi flag. The knight himself however, is unknown."

Mahdi looked to Maha surprised by what he had heard. "The unknown soldier. The lost knight. Exactly! That makes sense!"

"That means," said Maha, "that the necklace should be planted there. Where is the monument from where are now, Major-General?"

Maher replied, "It is next to the Festivities Square, very close since we're in the Green Zone now."

"The Green Zone?" Mahdi asked, surprised. He and Maha did not know where the closed van has taken them to.

Maher laughed, "Yes, you are somewhere in the Green Zone now."

He reached his hand towards Maha saying, "Let me see the necklace."

Maha handed over the necklace to the Major-General. He flipped it in his hand and put his prescription glasses on. All that is on it is a ring inscribed with the number 1/40,000 and hung by a metal chain. He concentrated his gaze on it.

"Major-General," said Mahdi, "what do you expect to find there?"

Maher answered in a confident tone, "I believe we don't need to go to the monument. Our work will be on paper."

Mahdi and Maha exchanged looks of wonder. Maher handed the necklace to Maha and said, "Look at the number on it." She took the necklace and started looking at the number on its ring with Mahdi who also put on his glasses.

1/40,000

"What does that mean?" asked Mahdi.

The Major-General answered having opened the Advisor's letter in his hand and started reviewing the text again, "Plant the necklace where the lost knight's spear was planted…It will turn like the sun disk…"

He folded the paper and went on, "The number on the necklace is a map scale."

They looked to him in wonder and he said, "The fraction number is a map drawing scale where the necklace is to be put on so its center would be the spear of the Unknown Soldier, i.e. it is used to draw a circle with the lost knight's spear at its center. It would turn like the sun disk."

Maha said surprised, "Sir, I don't understand. How?"

The Major-General reached his hand towards her and took the necklace. He put it on the table and put his finger at the center of the ring hung from the chain, put his other finger at the end of the chain, and made a circle around the fixed ring.

"Imagine that the stationary finger at the center of the ring is now at the location of the Unknown Soldier's spear on a map with a drawing scale of one to forty thousand, and my other finger will turn around the center of the spear to make a circle. It will turn like the sun disk."

Maha pushed her hair back behind her ear surprised by the Major-General's words, while Mahdi was watching what Maher was making in wonder and said, "You mean the necklace will work like a caliper?"

"Precisely," answered the Major-General and looked to Captain Fadhel saying, "Fadhel, quick, I want a map of Baghdad from the Monitoring Department with a drawing scale of one to forty thousand printed on paper with The Unknown Soldier Monument at its center."

Fadhel nodded and left towards a nearby room with special computers and staff.

Mahdi took out his pack of cigarettes thinking of what the Major-General had explained. Al-Mukhtar's plan was genius.

He put a cigarette between his lips and was surprised by the Major-General lighting it up for him. He felt more at ease with him and asked him, "Sir, why did the President put all these puzzles to get to the treasure? He could have simply referred to its location and told that person he trusted about it."

Maher leaned back, "Not possible. The President complicated this task so that finding the treasure would depend on more than one person and more than one puzzle. Besides, he knew whom he would hand the head of the thread to. That person had to be someone close to him; exactly like you. That close person would know how Al-Mukhtar thought. He also put into account that if the secret was left to one person and that person was interrogated by some entity, the treasure would be found. So, he kept the head of thread of the puzzle to himself, which is a fuse that would lead to a chain of ignitions of the quest by more than one person until the treasure is found and kept in safe hands."

Mahdi smiled, "You can't imagine, Major-General, how we opened my father's safe and how complicated it was!"

Maher smiled but before he answered, someone knocked on the door. A few seconds later, he opened it and entered stomping the ground in salute. It was a young man in uniform carrying a communication device and a plastic bag containing a small black object.

"Sir, we brought the Miss' car and searched it. We found this," he held the bag in front of the Major-General.

Maher pointed for the young man to approach, took the bag from him, and looked at the black object inside it. He smiled, "It's good that you have deactivated it," he looked to Maha and presented the bag to her saying, "a tracking device. Surely by Black Sand."

Maha took the bag and looked at the device. It was not giving any activity after the Intelligence staff deactivated it. It completely stopped sending its signals.

"Well," said the Major-General, "take it and identify its internal components and make. Let it be an evidence to indict Black Sand before the government. That would prove their chase of Iraqi citizens."

Maha gave the device to the young man who took her car keys

from his pocket and looked to the Major-General. Maher gestured for him to give them to her. Maha took her car keys, happy that her small red car was back to her.

"Lieutenant," said Maher to the young man, "please send me the apprehended man."

The young man nodded and left the room with Mahdi and Maha not understanding the Major-General's point as he was waiting for a map that Fadhel was bringing. He looked to at his watch. He was not sure of the time they would spend to know the location of the treasure, but it had to be found before the morning demonstrations. Only eight hours remained until that event.

Chapter 95

Midnight, Baghdad time.

Ten minutes passed since Fadhel went to get the map that Major-General Maher asked him to bring. While the three in the wood-walled room were waiting for that map, the door was opened and a white spotted with black cat appeared. Maha looked at it. It was…

"Tara!" yelled Maha, who was shocked. Mahdi looked at the cat who seemed hesitant of entering, and before he realized the question of how it got here, Dr. Husam Mohammed Saleh entered the room as well in his home clothing.

Mahdi and Maha were astonished by what they had seen. Husam walked closer and said to Mahdi, smiling, "You're here, you trouble maker!"

Mahdi got up and gave Husam a warm hug, while Maha quickly gained Tara's trust and carried it in her hands.

The Major-General was watching the scene before him, smiling. Dr. Husam sat down to join the three.

Mahdi asked him, "What brings you here, Doctor?"

Before he answered, the Major-General said, "I'm sorry about what happened to him, but your visit to his house made us suspect he had information regarding Al-Mukhtar's treasure. Hence, we brought him in and questioned him."

Mahdi looked to Husam and said, "I'm sorry about what happened, my friend! They should have apprehended me, not you."

Maher replied again smiling, "I wish I could then, but doing that directly would have caused a major issue. The newspapers would have wide headlines the next day talking about the abduction of Al-Mukhtar's lawyer under mysterious circumstances."

Husam said in his usual humor, "Mahdi, you owe me a fancy dinner after the horror I have lived thanks to you."

Mahdi nodded in agreement while laughing.

Husam asked, "What in God's name treasure are you talking about?"

Mahdi hid his smile and looked to the Major-General who gave him an approving look before he started telling Husam the story. Captain Fadhel entered carrying a map of Baghdad on a medium sized paper in black and white. The Major-General took the map and put it on the table. Before starting to find what the necklace was indicating to look for, he said to Husam, "Doctor, you'll know everything later, but now we are in the middle of something serious."

Husam pursed his lips and looked at the map following what the three were doing.

The Major-General put the ring of the necklace on The Unknown Soldier Monument and put his pen inside it making a hole in the map's paper after he made sure it had the required drawing scale. Then, he took a pencil from his desk and put its tip in the chain's end and started drawing a circle.

It will turn like the sun disk...

His pencil carefully turned drawing a circle until it two ends connected. He lifted the pencil and necklace. The circle was perfectly drawn with The Unknown Soldier Monument at its center.

The Major-General looked to Mahdi and said, "Now, what does the next phrase in the letter say?"

Before Mahdi could answer, the cellphone on the Major-General's desk rang. Maher got up and picked up his phone. He looked at the screen and knit his brows before pressing the answer button and bringing it to his ear.

"Hello!" he answered with that word only and his features started to change.

The others watched the Major-General's facial expressions. There seemed to be something wrong.

Seconds passed during which Maher did not speak another word. He finished the call with, "Okay, understood." He hung up the line and looked to Captain Fadhel with raging eyes.

He said in a coherent voice, "Fadhel, let's all get out of here…

immediately!"

Chapter 96

Those in the room did not understand what was going on, but Fadhel rushed out of the room. The others exchanged looks of wonder and fear, while the Major-General put on his jacket and put his cellphone in its pocket. After a few seconds, Fadhel came back in wearing his full uniform and carrying his rifle.

"Alright, sir. The car is ready."

The Major-General folded the map and gave it to Mahdi, and put the letter and necklace in his pocket. He said to them, "Let's get out of here."

Mahdi, Maha, and Husam followed Major-General Maher out of the wood-walled room. After passing through several corridors, they moved out of the building where a Ford SUV was waiting for them. Maher got in the front seat and the three took the back seat, while Fadhel got into the driver seat.

The Ford's windows were completely tinted and a long antenna swaying on its roof. Fadhel drove it at a great speed on the streets of the Green Zone. From the gate that follows the gate of the Ministry of Planning that is adjacent to the presidential area, the car exited towards Salhiya Residential Complex.

Although the curfew was in effect, the security forces could not stop a government vehicle with such description. It had governmental license plates and a long antenna that is only carried by state vehicles. Fadhel crossed a checkpoint and turned towards Salhiya Complex. Before entering the complex, he made a short phone call.

Major-General Maher was extremely nervous. He was still making his calls over his private cellphone with several people. He found out through his sources that the government's hand was going to reach him, so he made an early escape from his base before it did.

The communications device inside the car was quiet after Fadhel disconnected it. During that time, terror took over the other three passengers. Maha fought with her throbbing heart, holding Tara in her hands, while Husam was feeling continuous waves of terror. As for Mahdi, many thoughts went through his head and an overwhelming fear of the unknown.

What is going on?

He went back to ask himself the most terrifying question. He was now in the hands of Fadhel, the President's killer, and Maher, the Director of Intelligence; what would happen to him...to Maha... to Husam?

He felt a sting in his conscience when he remembered them. He dragged them into this. Maha was innocent of all this, and Husam, that old man who still did not know what was going on other than what he heard of the treasure during the Intelligence's interrogation of him.

Would the night be over...or would it be a nightmare?

His train of thoughts was cut by the sudden quietness of the Ford's engine after Captain Fadhel parked it among the buildings of Salhiya Complex, next to one of the residential buildings. He quickly got out towards the building, entering its door and disappearing in the darkness of its corridors. Seconds later, he returned and opened the Major-General's door, "Get out, sir! Quick!"

Everyone got out of the car and followed Fadhel into the residential building. The hallways inside it were completely dark and quiet. Fadhel used his military flashlight to see the way. He made sure the stairway was clear of anyone and climbed up followed by the others. On the first floor, he stood in front of a wooden apartment door and opened it with a key he had.

Everyone entered the apartment and Fadhel closed the door.

The apartment seemed to be completely furnished when Fadhel switched on the lights: leather couches, a TV, wooden displays, antiques, a laptop on one of the glass tables, and garnished curtains in front of windows overlooking the main street leading to Alawi. Before they sat down, Fadhel's phone rang. He quickly pressed the answer button and put it to his ear. He nodded and said, "Okay."

Maher sat on one of the couches, took out a cigar, and started puffing on it. Mahdi, Maha, and Husam were astonished of what was going on. Suddenly, someone knocked on the door.

Mahdi held Maha's hand and took her and Dr. Husam to one of the rooms to get away from the door. They entered into the room's darkness and started watching from its door crack what was happening, while Maher got up to sit in one of the corners so the visitor could not see him. Fadhel went near the door, held its handle, and opened it.

A young man in a security uniform was standing there. Fadhel took what appeared to be car keys from his pocket and handed them to him. The young man left and Fadhel closed the door.

Maher called out Mahdi and his companions. Mahdi looked at them and they walked to the hall. The Major-General was still quietly smoking his cigar. He got up, took off his jacket, took the necklace and letter out of his pocket, and walked to sit on a couch with a table of glass in front of it.

"Come closer," said Maher, "there is no need to worry. We sent the car with that man to hide our location from the authorities."

Hide from the authorities!

"What is going on, Major-General?" asked Mahdi.

Maher raised his eyebrows, "Actually, Professor Mahdi, our fate is connected to the treasure's fate now more than ever before. We are all now wanted."

"How!" Mahdi's eyes widened.

"Yes, Mahdi. Someone caught wind of this. If we don't find the treasure, we'll all be captured and it won't be found in time."

Mahdi collapsed on the couch while Maha sat next to him putting her head between her palms. As for Fadhel, he had taken off his bulletproof vest, put his weapon on one of the chairs, and started watching the street from the window by removing the curtain a few centimeters.

"Can I go back home? I'm not a part of any problem!" said Husam angrily.

Maher smiled, "No one is getting out of here, old man, unless all of us were going to somewhere else or to the treasure." He looked at his watch and continued, "The curfew will be lifted at five o'clock in the morning. We'll be out of here anyway." Husam sat back down mumbling angry words.

Mahdi did not say a word. He lit his cigarette and leaned his head back. He closed his eyes and remembered again that night call that opened a storm of trouble on him which led him to be a wanted man, Hello, sir. This is Captain Salam from the Palace…how quickly things had happened!

Maher was looking at all of them calmly with half a smile.

We are all now wanted.

His words had deceived them.

Chapter 97

Half an hour passed during which Mahdi and Maha absorbed Major-General Maher's words. The apartment's atmosphere was charged with worry and anticipation. Maher was turning the necklace between his palms.

He looked up and said, "Mahdi, shall we finish what we've started?" Mahdi wiped his eyes and got up forward towards the Major-General. He sat on the couch facing him and took the map from his pocket placing it on the table. Maha came closer to sit next to him while Husam held his cat and remained seated on one of the couches in the hall.

Maher read the last part they had reached in the Advisor's letter.

It will turn like the sun disk...

"Indeed," said Mahdi in a worried voice, "the circle we have drawn represents the sun disk!"

Maher read on, "When some of eleven arrows pierce it."

Maha pushed her hair back behind her ear. Her face was pale. She said, "Eleven arrows. I don't think we have any monument within the circle with arrows or referencing them."

Mahdi shook his head in negation, too. "We have to go back to thinking in symbolism."

But Maher interceded. "Don't think about what's inside the circle only. He says some of eleven arrows, i.e. the remaining lies outside the circle, the sun disk."

"Right," said Maha, "what's inside the circle should complete the number 11 for something that some of it lies outside it."

"Eleven again," said Mahdi, "this number often repeats."

The Major-General said, "Don't think about the number as much as about the arrows now, Mahdi. The similar numbers in the letter is just a coincidence in my opinion."

"I suggest…" said Maha, "…that each of us thinks of something significant and try to find its number. Like I count the shrines, Mahdi counts the universities, and you sir count the hospitals. Whatever we find that its total is eleven and some of it lies inside the circle and some outside, we try to understand its connection from there."

The Major-General liked the idea, but Mahdi was still hesitant. Their memory would not help them that much. Baghdad was a large city inhabited by around seven million people. It has a lot of institutions and sites, and if they could not find the connection, they would have to find other things to count. That would take time they did not have.

"We need maps of Baghdad, on paper or the internet. We cannot remember all that," said Mahdi, "we need a lot of time."

The Major-General turned to Fadhel who was still watching the street from the window and called him. "Fadhel, bring the laptop over there."

Fadhel carried the laptop and turned it on.

"Searching on the internet would be better," said the Major-General putting the laptop on the table, "based on Maha's idea, let's count now. Anything with a total of eleven in Baghdad, we will consider seriously."

As soon as the operating system started working, they heard a strange sound. They turned to its source in the hall. That was Husam…

He was snoring having fallen into deep sleep.

Chapter 98

3:00 a.m. Baghdad time.

Fatigue and exhaustion were clearly apparent on Mahdi, Maha, and the Major-General. They spent around three hours counting what could be counted in Baghdad, hoping to reach a connection with the phrase (some of eleven arrows pierce it). They counted hospitals, colleges, universities, museums, murals, monuments, shrines, major markets, and many other places, but there was nothing that fit that line in the letter.

Mahdi felt the fatigue exhausting his joints while Maha gave in to a snooze on one of the couches. Fadhel remained seated by the window, exhausted too. As for Maher, his worry increased after he received a phone call earlier telling him that a security force had raided his base in the Green Zone and his wood-walled room. That force apprehended everyone who was there and confiscated the computers in his office.

Mahdi cracked his neck. There was not much time left and the puzzle was still insurmountable. He grabbed his father's letter from the table and started reading it again while Maher was watching him.

A Sumerian seal...In the middle of the Round City...

Look in it for the eleventh woman of it...

He remembered how the woman referred to the Tigris, and suddenly, a gleam of hope sparked in his brain.

"That could be right!" he said and Maher's eyes narrowed hearing Mahdi's words.

Mahdi held the computer and turned it towards him. The Tigris... the eleventh woman...eleven arrows! He zoomed out in Google

Earth to show Baghdad from afar. He started counting to himself while Maher was looking at the reflection of the map on the screen on Mahdi's prescription glasses.

Five...six...seven...eight...and here is nine...ten...eleven!

"I found it!" he gasped and put the laptop on the table.

"What? Tell me!" beckoned Maher.

Mahdi replied turning laptop screen towards him, "Sir, there are eleven bridges on the Tigris."

Maher looked at the screen. He recounted them himself. Indeed, there are eleven bridges since the Tigris enters Baghdad and until it leaves it. He took the map and stared at it. Some of Baghdad's bridges entered the circle on it. When some of eleven arrows pierce it...

"Indeed!" said Maher, surprised, "Shuhadaa, Ahrar, Sinek, Jumhouriya, and the Suspended Bridges all fall within the circle."

Mahdi responded, "While the other bridges remain outside, and the total is eleven."

Maher leaned on his chair, "How genius!"

Mahdi did not respond and looked at his watch. Only five hours remained until the demonstrations and two until the curfew would be lifted, and the treasure's location was still unknown.

Maher took the letter and read the remaining code:

At the eleventh hour...

The light of the mirror shines...

Maher's voice cut through the silence in the apartment as he read those two phrases. Husam had slept, and Maha snoozed, while Fadhel quieted with eyes that are fighting sleep in front of the window. The Major-General and Mahdi remained alone in front of the table solving the letter's puzzles.

Mahdi said, "Sir, tell me, why did we run to here?"

Maher looked at him and said, "You'll know everything at the right time. But I promise you that if we find the treasure before it's too late, we will survive."

Mahdi loathed knowing half stories, but he did not want to insist on Maher. All he cared about was for Maha and Husam to be well, and for the treasure to be found and fall in the right hands.

"So," he said, "the number eleven comes up again in the letter now."

Maher nodded looking at the map, and without raising his eyes from it, he said, "Mahdi, you can get some sleep now. I will try to understand this phrase."

But Mahdi was still feeling some uncertainty towards Maher. He was still hiding something—why he ran from his base with them. "I'm fine," He said resisting his urge to rest, "The eleventh hour. Let's figure out what this means."

Maher said turning the pen between his palms, "Eleven arrows; eleven bridges…The eleventh hour…"

He put out his cigar and leaned on the map.

He put the pen vertically on the map inside the circle so that its lower tip was at the center—The Unknown Soldier's spear—and its upper top up. Then he said to Mahdi, "Give me your pen."

Mahdi took his pen out from his jacket's pocket. Maher took the pen from him and put it on the map, too. He pointed its lower tip to the same center and slanted its upper tip to the left a little. The circle looked like a clock indicating eleven o'clock.

"What do you think?" Maher asked. That grabbed Mahdi's attention.

It will turn like the sun disk...

When some of eleven arrows pierce it...

At the eleventh hour...

The light of the mirror shines...

"Eleven!" He exclaimed, "Major-General, there is no other solution. The circle looks like a clock with the monument at its center. It has to point to eleven. That makes sense."

Maher replied, "It makes a lot of sense. There are two directions now. We have to keep going with the letter to know the final direction for the quest. What time is it now?"

Mahdi looked at his watch, "Half past three."

Maher smiled, "Some puzzles only take minutes and others take hours."

Mahdi replied, "I hope the remaining puzzles won't be of the second category."

Maher read the next line in the letter, "The light of the mirror shines!"

The two looked at the map. Their sitting and facing each other was liked two professional chess players moving pawns on a chessboard between them.

The light of the mirror shines...

Mahdi said, "We have to reverse something; either the map or the clock hands."

Maher replied, "Right, the mirror reverses what it sees, but you didn't think that what you said would lead to the same result."

"How?" asked Mahdi.

Maher held the pen that represents the short hand indicating the hypothetical eleven on the circle and put it in a complementary position making the clock indicate one.

"If we put the hands like this or we turn the map to a mirror image without changing the hands, the hands would indicate the same thing. So, I'll choose to move the hour hands on the same map."

Mahdi understood what he said. Indeed, both procedures would indicate the same shape.

The two focused on what the map is indicating...one o'clock. The short hand is indicating one.

Look within yourself for salvation...

Plant the necklace where the lost knight's spear was planted...

It will turn like the sun disk...

The eleventh woman...

The light of the mirror...

Those phrases from the President's letter, and his father's, the Advisor, crammed into Mahdi's head. Where is Al-Mukhtar trying to get to?

Maher held the letter and read the line before the last.

"To show a buoy opening by the meeting of the four elements of existence..."

They both looked at the map.

"A ring," said Maher, "does he mean the river?"

"How?" wondered Mahdi.

Maher replied, "The Tigris forms a ring like a buoy around Karkh side from the east."

"Opening by the meeting of the four elements of existence." said Mahdi and continued, "The elements of existence are water, fire, soil, and air."

Maher looked at him without moving his irises from him and asked, "What does that mean?"

Mahdi looked at the map again. He studied the hypothetical hour hands that Maher made. Something strange caught his attention.

"Sir, do you see what I see?" Maher looked at him and Mahdi continued, "Do you see that the long hand points exactly to Shuhadaa Bridge while the short one points exactly to Ahrar Bridge?"

Maher brought his face closer to the map looking. Indeed, the tip of the pen pointing to the hypothetical 12 was pointing to Shuhadaa Bridge while the other pen pointing to the hypothetical 1 was pointing to Ahrar Bridge.

"That means," Mahdi said, "that the search area lies between the two bridges." He remembered the three Divine jewels that all pointed to the Tigris, "and the treasure is in the Tigris there!"

"The Tigris?!" Maher said and Mahdi replied, "Sir, you haven't read Al-Mukhtar's letter in which he said Look within yourself for salvation, I have thrown you the buoy. Then he said To show a buoy opening by the meeting of the four elements of existence. What do you notice? The word 'buoy' has repeated in the two letters. According to the map, it should be between Ahrar and Shuhadaa Bridges. In the water. The buoy is the treasure."

Maher's calculations shook in his head. He looked at the map and then to the Advisor's letter reading it again.

A Sumerian seal...A buoy opening by the meeting of the four elements of existence...it has become clear now that the search area was between the two bridges in the Tigris water...Baghdad's buoy.

"What does he mean by the meeting of the four elements?" Maher asked.

"I haven't figured that out, but the only thing I understood is that water is one of those elements, which affirms the existence of the treasure in the water."

Maher held the letter and read its last line with the deformed ending, "Or you will find it asleep at the cover of…"

"Damn it! One word could solve everything!" he said that while Mahdi grabbed the laptop and started looking at satellite images of Baghdad.

"I get it," he said, "the four elements of existence."

"What does that mean?" Maher replied in a tense tone.

Mahdi hesitated about telling Maher what he understood, but he remembered his words: Our salvation lies in finding the treasure.

He knew where Al-Mukhtar's treasure is…

Exactly.

"Sir, I apologize, but I cannot tell you where it is exactly, the point it is at, before I guarantee my safety and my companions' safety and guarantee that the treasure would be in the hands of the government before the people." Mahdi said while Maher's eyes were sparking in anger hearing those words and said to him, "Mr. Mahdi. We have come a long way in the quest. You cannot leave things at this point. The treasure is in the water between the bridges, but where? Tell me!"

Mahdi got up and headed to Maha who was sleeping on the couch. He touched her hair with his fingers and whispered in her ear to wake up. She opened her eyes and looked at him. She was surprised for a moment of the place she found herself in, but within seconds she remembered what brought her there. She sat looking to Mahdi who bent his legs sitting in front of her.

"Maha, I know where the treasure is. Everything will be over soon."

Maha had not heard anything happier in a while. "Really? Where?"

"You'll soon know," answered Mahdi.

"Mr. Mahdi," said Maher, "I swear to you that you will be safe and that the treasure will go into the right hands. Tell me where it is."

Mahdi looked at his watch. It was a quarter past four in the morning. Time was going by fast. He was unsure of what to do. Should he tell the Major-General about its location when he did not guarantee the fate of the treasure in his hands? Or leave it until he found the right opportunity? But there was no opportunity before the demonstrations. He realized the frightening acceleration of the national and global economic collapse. Every passing house was enough to make the country's economic future darker, and the number of the hungry exponentially larger.

Everything will collapse…Mahdi!

"Okay, sir." said Mahdi, "let me make a private phone call and then we'll go together to the location of the treasure."

Maher was afraid of what he would say, "How long will you be?"

Mahdi responded, "Just a few minutes. Be certain that I work for the country's interest with regard to the treasure." Maher hesitated, but he eventually nodded in approval.

Mahdi took out his cellphone and headed towards the apartment's balcony. Fadhel received the Major-General's nod and unlocked it saying to Mahdi, "Try not to be seen by any of the security forces on the street." Mahdi nodded and walked into the balcony. Fadhel closed the door behind him and walked away.

The situation inside the apartment was concerning. Maha was watching what was happening. The Major-General was sitting with a mind burning with worry. Fadhel was becoming more anxious regarding Mahdi's call, while Dr. Husam was still asleep.

Despite the harsh cold weather outside, Mahdi took out his cellphone and touched its screen. The call started and a girl answered on the other end of the line, "Connect me to the director of broadcasting now, please."

Mahdi had a friend in the media working as the director of a department at one of the most significant independent satellite channels in the country. A few seconds and his friend was on the phone during his night duty. Mahdi told him about a scoop. Something important would happen at a location he specified for him. He told him to have his camera crew record it from hidden locations. The time would be at first light. The man agreed. The call ended and the channel started preparing its camera crew to secretly send them to the location where that 'scoop' was going to take place. They would film what would happen from buildings and placed where they will not be noticed.

Mahdi walked back inside the apartment. He was very calm. He put his cellphone in his pocket and sat next to Maha. He said to the Major-General, "Sir, we will need to move the minute the curfew is lifted in about half an hour."

"Where to?" asked Maher in a confident voice.

"To where the treasure is," said Mahdi. Maher felt a wave of relief. Mahdi will take them to the treasure. He turned to Fadhel and said, "call for a security car from one of our men to here. Have it here by five minutes to five."

Although he was being chased and his base in the Green Zone had been raided, Maher had a wide popularity amongst his men. Therefore, some of them still followed his orders despite the spread of the news of the raid on the hiding Major-General's base among the security and Intelligence forces.

Fadhel started making calls with someone. Everyone was listening to him. It seemed he was calling the same person who took the Ford away from Salhiya Complex. He asked him to come and to be there before the curfew is lifted by five minutes.

Everyone would go on a trip…towards Al-Mukhtar's treasure….

Chapter 99

4:45 a.m. Baghdad time.

"Sir," said Mahdi, "Would you do what I ask of you to find the treasure?"

Maher nodded in agreement.

He carried on, "I want you to have a security force that you trust to be near the area between Shuhadaa and Ahrar Bridges, close to the river, with a drilling machine and welding and iron cutting tools."

Maher was surprised by what he was saying, so were Fadhel and Maha. Was Mahdi going to drill into the Tigris?

"I don't understand. What do you mean?" asked Maher.

"Please, just do!"

The Major-General replied, "You said the treasure was in the river. Is it under water? What will we do with welding tools under water, Mahdi?" he said laughingly.

Mahdi smiled, "Just do that, Major-General."

Major-General Maher got up holding his cellphone and headed to one of the apartment's rooms closing the door behind him. He talked to one of the men who was still loyal to him. Maher had secretly established a small special force under the cover of the security forces. He relied on them during the difficult situations. Now, he needed them more than any time before.

He finished his call and got out of the room. Everyone was surprised by a knock on the apartment's door.

Fadhel got up, put on his bulletproof vest, grabbed his gun, and headed to the door. He looked through the bird's eye lens fixed on its door before opening it. The young man in security uniform was standing.

"Hello, the car is ready, sir."

Mahdi and Maha got up preparing to leave while the Major-General appeared in his jacket before the security man. He was surprised by his presence. Fadhel let him in and closed the door. The young man saluted the Major-General, "I'm at your service, sir!"

Maher nodded his head as he was folding the map. He handed it along with the letter and necklace to Mahdi saying, "You'll keep all this."

Maha awoke Dr. Husam and carried Tara in her arms. He got up still in an upset mood. "Okay, Doctor. We'll get out of here." Mahdi said to him with fear of another angry response from him.

After a few minutes, everyone left the apartment. They went down to the street and got into the Ford.

Mahdi said to the Major-General, "Sir, will everything be ready?"

Maher answered, "The force will be there within minutes. Currently, a drilling machine is being located and supplied with cutting and welding tools."

"Fine. Can we be there and stay close to the site inside this car?" Mahdi asked.

Maher replied, "We're safe here as long as we're in a governmental car with tinted windows. No one will stop us, but my men will try to get there with the tools as soon as possible."

Mahdi said, "That's terrific, sir. Let's head over there. If they're there before us, let me know so I'll be able to tell you what needs to be done."

Maher nodded in agreement and ordered the driver next to him to move to the designated area, while Mahdi, Maha, and the Doctor sat in the back. Fadhel sat in the very back seat of the car.

Darkness was still prevalent in Baghdad, but Mahdi knew that the time the drilling machine would spend digging up what Al-Mukhtar had left would last till morning. Then, the satellite channel cameras would be able to record what he finds there. His idea was clever. If Maher tried to confiscate the gold, there would be someone to expose what he had done—the channel cameras recording everything.

The curfew was lifted and the Ford took the main road crossing Sinek Bridge while Maher continued calling his assistants to ensure the near arrival of the drilling machine to the location where the treasure would be dug up as Mahdi wanted. As for his force, its presence would be normal in the place same as all the other security forces spread in the capital ready to secure it during the demonstrations that were only two hours and 45 minutes away.

The Ford crossed the bridge heading north towards the designated area. A few minutes later and it was on the street overlooking the Tigris between Shuhadaa and Ahrar Bridges.

Maher watched the situation from inside the car. The security personnel spread there were indeed his men. It seemed like they had arrived shortly before as some of them were still getting out of the vehicles with their front lights on since the sunlight has not shone yet.

Everyone in the car was watching what was happening. They were waiting for the drilling machine which would take longer to arrive than expected. Tension overshadowed everyone. As for Mahdi, he was getting more worried. The most important question on his mind, "is this really the sought place? Will there be gold in it?"

Half an hour passed but the drilling machine was still not there. Maher kept on making his calls to rush it. Despite the close distance between him and his men spread on the bank, he did not get out of the car as he knew he was a wanted man.

After a few other minutes, the roar of a huge engine could be heard from somewhere on the street. The drilling machine has arrived.

Everyone in the car looked to the back. On the same street the Ford stopped on, the drilling machine came from behind overcoming the Ford and heading forward.

"Well, Mahdi. The machine is here. Where do we dig?" asked Maher.

"Sir," answered Mahdi, "are the welding and iron cutting tools definitely available?"

"Yes, I have just confirmed that they are on the drilling machine itself."

"Okay," Mahdi said, "I'll tell you where to dig now."

Heavy silence dominated the atmosphere inside the car before Mahdi spoke about the location of the treasure. He pointed his arm towards the river and said, "Do you see that silt over there on the riverbank?"

Everyone was surprised by his question. He shocked them more when he said, "An iron container containing the gold is under it."

Dredging machines worked all year long to clean the rivers from silt and weeds. Many times, they gathered it by the river to the bank's direction and left it there for them to later become parks and entertainment locations, but this old stack of silt remained as is, since Al-Mukhtar's time. The President insisted to keep it so until his last days of ruling, which ended months ago, burying in it the greatest treasure in the country's history to save it from the terrifying global collapse.

Hesitant by what Mahdi said, Maher gave the order to his assistants over the phone to start digging the ground formed from the silt to the side of the river with the drilling machine. Minutes later, the machine started preparing to extend its shovel from the bank to the lower silt.

A glimpse of the morning light started shining from the east while the clock was indicating ten minutes past six. With that silent light, the roar of the drilling machine rose louder. It removed the dirt from the place and started digging deeper. The eyes of everyone in the Ford were anticipating what would come from under the dirt.

The shovel was working like an old clock's pendulum. A returning churned in the air as the shovel removed the silt from each other until its teeth hit something hard making a loud iron ringing.

"Be careful not to damage it. Dig carefully. There is an iron container below. Dig from the side of its door only," commanded the Major-General to one of his assistants as the morning light revealed itself more.

The machine removed the dirt from what appeared to be an iron door for a rectangular container buried there.

Mahdi's heart throbbed heavily. The camera must be filming now from their hiding locations. The treasure could not go in vain.

Chapter 100

6:30 a.m. Baghdad time.

One and a half hours until the demonstrations…only.

After several minutes of digging, everyone in the Ford saw the iron door of the large container buried in the silt revealed after the drilling machine removed the dirt from on it. The door could be opened now.

Maher could not hold himself. He looked from the car's window to make sure his men have secured the place completely. He then turned to Captain Fadhel in the back of the car and asked him, "Fadhel, do you still have the face mask?"

"Yes, sir. Here it is," Fadhel said and took his black mask from the pocket of his protective shield.

Maher took it and put it on his head. He said to Mahdi and Maha, "Follow me."

Mahdi and Maha exchanged looks. Maher got out of the car and headed to the container after he gave his order to stop digging and he wanted them to go with him. Mahdi prepared to get out while Maha handed Tara to Dr. Husam to follow them, but Mahdi held her hand and said, "You'll stay here!"

She shook her head like a stubborn child and said, "No way…with you!" Mahdi tried hard to stop her, but she insisted.

"Hurry up!" Maher yelled. The two got out of the car and followed Maher, whose eyes only were showing, towards the riverbank. The three walked down to the silt ground. Maher called the commander of the force. He spoke to him alone with strange words. Those words were like a code they used between them. The commander was sure through that code that the person standing in front of him wearing a mask was Major-General Maher Abdelfattah.

Maher went back to stand in front of the container with Mahdi and Maha while all the other personnel went up the bank under the order of their commander, who received the order Maher. The three were now facing the iron door.

"Now, Mahdi, I know why you asked for iron cutting and welding tools," said Maher.

Mahdi answered, "Opening by the meeting of the four elements of existence: water is the river; soil is silt; fire and air are the thermal torch that will melt the edges of the iron door to open it."

Maher looked to him with eyes full of words. He called the unit commander and ordered him to bring the welding tools. Two persons went down from the bank carrying the tools. They kindled the torch head and started melting the iron at the edge of the container's door.

***

At the 5th Division, a strange movement went on. Three Chevrolet security vehicles left the Division's headquarters heading somewhere in Baghdad where someone had told of a certain wanted person's location. At the head of that force was one of the most important Intelligence figures.

***

Finally, the container was ready to be opened. Maher gave his orders to the two men to get back up to the riverbank. The container's door was back facing only three persons standing before it: Maher, Mahdi, and Maha.

The three kept looking at that door waiting for it to cool down after its edges were melted by the iron cutting torch. They were waiting until it could be touched.

Look within yourself for salvation...

I have thrown you the buoy...

So hold on to it tightly...

Each one of the three was deep in thought in those moments. Mahdi was remembering the dream in which he saw the President... Everything will collapse! He remembered his meetings with him before he was assassinated. Despite Al-Mukhtar's brightness and political wits, he was a good-hearted man with a smiling facial expression. Mahdi's family has always been loyal to him. He left leaving this thing buried here, confident of the victory of his idea. He did the impossible for his people and his country.

In front of that door too, Major-General Maher was thinking of what would be behind that iron door. He planned the assassination of Al-Mukhtar to keep the treasure. Even Fadhel, he used him to implement his crime. That young officer may become a scapegoat to save the country, but Iraq was worth the risk. The tape of events passed before his eyes since he started watching Mahdi until he stood now on this spot of land mixed in with the water of one of the greatest rivers in the world, in his country's capital, which he had always loved.

As for Maha, all her concern was for Mahdi to find the treasure here, not just for the country, but because he sacrificed so much for it. He suffered through surveillance and chase and even injury. He was a truly patriotic man. He did not want to forget his President's letter. He risked his life for his promise to the President to expose what was in the letter in the right time. He spent days in horror, thinking, and exhaustion in order to keep his promise...for this moment.

The cold morning air coming from the Tigris' horizon fondled Maha's blond hair just as it fondled the large Iraqi flag on top of the Ministry of Industry's building on Nedhal Street. Baghdad was holding its breaths for the unknown. Nothing would save it other than what was behind the lid to the container.

Mahdi moved towards the container. He touched it with his fingers. The iron had cooled down during the past minutes. He held the opening lever and turned it, then grabbed the door hand with both his hands. Maher and Maha moved closer to him. He pulled it and it opened.

The sunlight coming from the east flowed into the container to reflect the most beautiful scene a person could wish to see. The container was filled with…

Gold bars!

Maha jumped from happiness for what she saw, while Mahdi collapsed to his knees crying in front of the container. Maher turned his face east to hide his tears of happiness.

Al-Mukhtar has delivered on his promise.

Mahdi raised his eyes to look at the iron door on the inside again. He fought the fogginess of his tears that made it like he was looking through a crystal ball. Al-Mukhtar had left the container's door on the inside a sign of golden tin with writings in black.

You will realize how right I was…

For doing what I did…

For us to live how we want…

At a time when everything is collapsing around us…

Relentlessly!

Sincerely yours,

Mohammed Al-Mukhtar

How this man had loved his country!

In that atmosphere of happiness, police cars' sirens invaded the air. Everyone looked from the silt ground to the bank.

A security force of three Chevrolet cars seemingly affiliated to the 5th Division has arrived accompanied by other security cars.

Everyone was surprised, and Major-General Maher was shocked when he saw the Brigadier-General, Director of the 5th Division, getting out of one of the cars. Maher's men tried to prevent him from coming closer, but he took out a paper from his pocket that appeared to be a court order and showed it to them. He went down to the bank with three security men.

He saluted Major-General Maher and raised the paper in front of him saying: "Sir, there is no point of running anymore. Allow me to bring you in. You are accused of planning the assassination of President Mohammed Al-Mukhtar."

Maher did not seem to care. He lifted the mask from his face and glanced towards the Ford on the bank. Security men have surrounded it and took Captain Fadhel down from it. It seems he was wanted, too.

Two persons approached Major-General Maher. One of them held his hands to bend them behind his back and put cuffs on his wrists.

Maher looked to Mahdi with half a smile and said: "Thanks for what you've done. I'm sorry for lying to you. I'm the one the court wants, not you."

The security personnel took Maher to the bank and got him into one of their cars. The Brigadier-General ordered Maher's force to withdraw before going back to look at the gold container…and be shocked.

Chapter 101

One month later…

Mahdi was sitting on a bed in a room at Palestine Meridian Hotel holding a remote control and watching the recording the local and international channels had broadcasted for the thousandth time since it was broadcasted by the channel that he had asked to record the events by the Tigris.

The whole world knew Iraq had found a huge amount of gold in its capital and saved itself from the major global collapse. The Iraqi government moved the gold to the fortified safes of the Central Bank and started painting new economic policies for the country according to the change in the global economy. As for the demonstrations that day, they did happen and they were massive, but they were not against the government. They were demonstrations of overwhelming joy that people came out on spontaneously after the government announced through its spokesperson that a large treasure of gold was found; hence, in effect the austerity measures would be greatly reduced.

Major-General Maher Abdelfattah and Captain Fadhel were apprehended on the charge of assassinating Al-Mukhtar after the Brigadier-General, Director of the 5th Division, and his companions found a video recording hidden on one of the computers inside the surveillance room in the Division where Captain Fadhel's face appeared inside cell 12 after killing the President with a poisonous inhaler. It seemed that the Hyena had copied it and saved it somewhere on the computer before he was killed.

As for the disappearance of Professor Salem Jerjis, the investigation could not reach a clear conclusion regarding his disappearance yet, but time would tell as it always did…it's masterful at exposing secrets.

The spontaneous smile was clear on Mahdi's face while he watched the news. Iraq has survived a certain disaster. As he was watching the TV, the bathroom door in the hotel suite he was at opened and steam pushed out of it. Maha appeared like a gorgeous crystal wrapping her hair and body with two pink towels. Her look took Mahdi's breath away. She came and sat next to him pressing a loving kiss on his cheek. She felt with her fingers to check the wedding ring on his finger. He kissed her hand with his eyes closed, diving into the sea of love that he could not express before.

"The happiness is now tripled, Hammurabi's descendant!"

She smiled, "Thank God! My mother is much better now and is at home since she came back; and Iraq is much better now after what happened; and…"

"And we're much better now alone."

Maha got up laughing. She threw her hair towel on the ground, turned off the lights in the room, threw her other towel, and the two delved into an amazing wedding night.

Epilogue

It was three o'clock after midnight of that moonlit night of February nights. Mahdi stood smoking a cigarette on the hotel room's balcony after spending hours of a lifetime with Maha who was now in deep sleep. He was looking at the Tigris with its sparkling water from the balcony. This river had always been a source of life for this country…

Even when it held Al-Mukhtar's treasure.

He took a breath from his cigarette, looking at the river, and suddenly, his thought ships threw its anchors when something sparked in his head. He threw his cigarette and rushed towards the closet. He took his father's letter from his wallet and went back to the balcony again. He read the last line of it using the moonlight; the line they could not understand.

Or you will find it asleep at the cover of…

He took off his glasses smiling. His father had intentionally spilt drops on the last word of the line to mix with the blue ink making it watery to mean…

The river!

Mahdi exploded in laughter. It seemed as the Tigris was laughing along with him.

Table Of Content

CPSIA information can be obtained
at www.ICGtesting.com
Printed in the USA
BVOW03s1807010817

490708BV00003B/237/P